750

Comet pb~/5/ou

ALSO BY DALENE MATTHEE

Circles in a Forest

This is a Borzoi Book
published in New York by
Alfred A. Knopf, Inc.

Fiela's Child

DALENE MATTHEE

Fiela's Child

ALFRED A. KNOPF　NEW YORK

19 🐎 86

Copyright © 1986 by Dalene Matthee
All rights reserved under International and Pan-American
Copyright Conventions. Published in the United States
by Alfred A. Knopf, Inc., New York.
Distributed by Random House, Inc., New York.
First published in Great Britain by
Penguin Books, London.

Library of Congress Cataloging-in-Publication Data

Matthee, Dalene.
Fiela's child.
I. Title.
PR9369.3.M376F5   1986   823   85-45672
ISBN 0-394-55231-8

Manufactured in the United States of America

To Larius, Amanda, Toni and Hilary

ACKNOWLEDGMENTS. I would not have been able to write this book without help, and would like to thank the following:

Elizabeth Grimble who knew Benjamin and told me his story
Maans McCarthy
Wilhelm Grüter
Edyss Scott
Koos du Plessis of Wolwekraal
Errol Zondagh of Avontuur
Barbara Tomlinson of the National Maritime Museum, London.

Other sources:
Arthur Nimmo, *The Knysna Story*, Cape Town, Juta, 1977
Winifred Tapson, *Timber and Tides*, 4th ed., Cape Town, Juta, 1973
Dr F. E. Calitz, for use of his MA thesis (University of Stellenbosch, 1957), 'Die Knysna-boswerkers: Hulle taalvorm en denkvorm, met spesiale verwysing na hulle bedryfsafrikaans.'
The Department of Environment Affairs, Knysna
Hartenbos Museum
Millwood House, Knysna
The Private Diary of the Village Harbour-Master, 1875-1897: John F. Sewell, edited by D. C. Storrar, Ladywood, 1983.

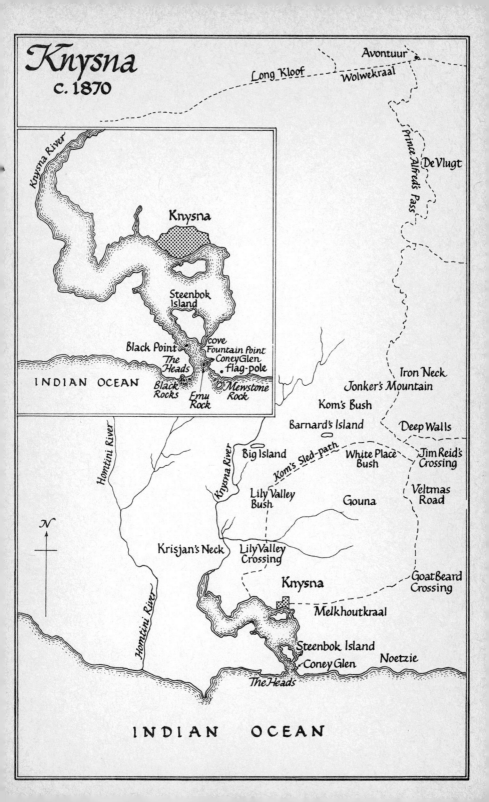

Fiela's Child

1

The day the child disappeared, the fog came up early and by midday it seemed as if the Forest was covered in a thick white cloud. Elias van Rooyen put down his axe and went to sit in the shed on the pile of yellowwood beams that had already been finished. It was no good working when the fog was that thick – the wood got damp and would not yield to the axe. And besides, he did not believe in a man working himself to death, as the woodcutters did. He believed in a good plan and a bit of luck, although luck was rare in the Forest.

'Barta!' he called towards the house, 'bring me some coffee, I'm done for!'

The fog was really thick. He could only just make out the house from the shed; just enough to see that he would have to fix the roof before the coming winter, before the whole lot collapsed on top of them. Somehow he would have to get hold of a few second-hand sheets of corrugated iron. The winter before Barta had kept on moaning about the children sniffing and coughing because of the damp in the wooden house.

Of the four families that had built houses on Barnard's Island, he was the only one who was not a woodcutter. And he was the only one that earned real money instead of having to barter for everything with the two wood buyers in the village. Not that he thought himself much better off than the woodcutters for the money he made from the beams he cut was only just enough to live on if he trapped the meat for his pot himself. But making beams was far easier than cutting wood and it also meant that you could sleep in your own bed every night instead of in a shack somewhere in the Forest.

When he heard Barta coming with the coffee, he quickly grabbed the hatchet and examined the handle so as to look busy. Barta could never understand that you sometimes had to sit down quietly in order to think properly.

'Elias, isn't Lukas with you?' she asked, standing at the open end of the shed with the coffee and looking worried.

'No. You can put the coffee down on the block there, I've got my hands full.'

She was still good-looking, he thought to himself as she walked slowly away – she would have to get some shoes.

Perhaps he should get Krisjan Small's eldest boy from Lily Valley Bush to come and help him at the beams so that he could produce more. Krisjan's boy was used to working for coffee and sugar and meal and might as well earn them from him. On the other hand it meant putting him up and the house was too small as it was. The children were getting big and before long he would have to get some planks and add a third room. Krisjan's boy could not walk from Lily Valley Bush every day – he would only get to work at sun down.

He started thinking further ahead; the only way a man could make himself a decent bit of extra in the Forest was to buy a gun and shoot elephants. Bigfeet. For the tusks. But how did you find money for a gun, powder and shot? And how did you get past the wood buyers in the village to get the tusks to the ships to sell them? The ships paid well for ivory but according to the buyers *they* were the only ones with licences to deliver anything to them. Martiens Willemse had told him it was a bloody lie, for the wood buyers had to smuggle the elephant tusks to the ships too.

'Pa . . .' Willem, the eldest of his four children, came in under the shed. 'Pa, ma says Lukas is not in the house.'

'Go and see if he's with Aunt Malie. And blow your nose!'

If you did get to the ships at night and deliver the tusks, how did you get back through the Forest afterwards in the dark without the elephants trampling you?

To the north of the clearing he heard Anna Olwage shouting

4

at her bunch of children as usual. Maybe he should get Anna and Dawid's eldest boy, Kransie, to come help him at the beams. Kransie was a lad of about fifteen and Dawid's team had too many hands as it was. They were struggling.

'Pa, Lukas isn't with Aunt Malie.'

'Did you ask at Aunt Anna's place?'

'No, Pa.'

'Why do I have to tell you what to do all the time?'

'Yes, Pa.'

A man had to struggle until his children were big enough to help him and there was still a long wait ahead for him. Willem, his eldest, was only six and Kristoffel five; Lukas was three and Nina still on the breast. Willem was old enough to help Barta in the vegetable garden but the children were of little use to him yet. He would ask Dawid about Kransie. The boy would have it easy with him; making beams was not ox labour like cutting wood, sawing it, dragging it out to load it on to the wagon and then getting it to the village.

'Elias?' Barta emerged from the fog like a ghost.

'What is it this time, woman?' Couldn't they see that he was busy?

'Have you seen the child?'

'I told you he wasn't here. I'm sure you haven't looked everywhere. Go and see if he's with Sofie.'

'I've been to Sofie's, he isn't there.'

Half an hour later all was confusion: women were searching and calling out; people were running into each other in the fog, their faces filled with anxiety; everyone was asking, 'Have you found him yet?'

He told them the child must be somewhere in one of the houses, that he must have fallen asleep somewhere. If only they would stop carrying on like this and give him a chance to look for the child properly they would soon find him. If only the fog would clear a bit so that everything did not look so misshapen

5

and if only Barta would not keep on walking up and down and calling out as she did. The child was not missing.

And then Malie had to come and make things worse:

'It happened to my aunt back in Karatara's Bush. She thought the child had gone with the others to collect firewood and by the time she discovered that he was missing, it was late afternoon. Took them more than a week to find the little body. Frozen to death. We all went to the funeral.'

Barta put her fist to her mouth and bit into her knuckles.

'How often must I tell you that the child is not missing!' he said, for the hundredth time. 'Go back to your houses, all of you, look under every bed and search everywhere!'

'We've already done that, Elias,' Sofie van Huysteen said.

'Go and look again.'

Old Aunt Gertie, Anna's mother-in-law, took Nina from Barta; Barta did not even seem to notice.

'I don't understand how you could have let the child out of your sight, Barta!' he scolded, in despair.

'I was trying to get the fire going, Elias, the wood was damp – I thought the child was with you.'

He went into the Forest at the south end of the clearing, calling out as he walked. The child is not missing, he told himself, trying to repress his fears. The child is not missing.

He went to the west side of the Island. Then east. Every time he walked a little deeper into the undergrowth. When he searched to the north, Aunt Gertie walked with him, calling the child's name.

'He can't hear us because of the fog, auntie,' he said. It was getting harder not to worry. 'The child must be playing somewhere.'

'Elias, we must turn back. Anna will have to fetch the men; they must come and help us search before it's too late.'

'But they're cutting at Draaikloof, Aunt Gertie!' he said, trying to stop her. 'It's four hours' walking from here and the child is not missing. You're imagining things!'

'The child is missing.' The way she said it, her certainty, shattered the last of his resistance. When you grew up in the Forest, you knew what awaited a child that wandered from a footpath or a sled-path when there was no one with him. When the fog closed in, you kept your children in the house.

'I can't understand how he could have just disappeared, Aunt Gertie! I can't believe it.' He was still trying to deny it.

'A child, Elias, is like a tortoise. You think he's slow, but he's gone before you know it. Anna must go and fetch the men.'

'I'll go myself.'

'No. Barta's going to need you. Anna will go. She knows the footpaths and she knows what to do when there are bigfeet along the way.'

Malie and Sofie and he searched and called out for the child until dark. Aunt Gertie stayed with Barta. They put Barta to bed and gave her some wild-bughu tea every now and again and saw to it that she stayed warm. Later it seemed as if she could no longer cry, she just made the most awful sounds, like a puppy dog whimpering. He told her to stop it – they would find the child.

But the house became like a house of death. Aunt Gertie sent someone to fetch ash-bread from her house; Sofie brought a brew of coffee and took Nina home with her; Malie brought a bowl of honey and a few cooked sweet potatoes.

Willem and Kristoffel stood bewildered in front of the hearth.

'The last I saw of little Lukas was at the corner of the house when ma gave him a sweet potato. He stood there eating it,' Willem kept saying.

'Kristoffel, where did you last see him?'

'Here in the house, Pa. He was playing with his stones.'

Malie sighed, despairing. 'Only the good Lord in heaven could know the whereabouts of a little child in this vast Forest tonight – the same thing happened to my aunt. At Karatara.'

7

'I don't understand it, Malie. I should at least have found his tracks.'

'There are many children on the Island, Elias, many tracks.'

'I still don't understand it.'

'What about Flip Lourens who disappeared that time? Same kind of fog. They still haven't found a trace of him.'

'Flip didn't get lost, Malie. Everybody reckons it must have been the bigfeet that killed him. Flip would never have got lost, he knew the Forest too well.'

'That's the other thing that's worrying me, Elias: the bigfeet. All week they've been tearing off bark and branches and eating around here. They would not even feel it if they stepped on a child in this dark night.'

'Elephants don't step on children,' Aunt Gertie said.

Anna and the men were back at midnight. Malie's husband, Martiens, took over and gave the orders while they had something to eat, standing up as they were.

'The fog's clearing,' Martiens said. 'I'll search to the south. Dawid, you go west. Koos to the north and you, Elias, you go east. Every hundred paces we'll call out and on the tenth call we'll turn back and move over fifty yards or so. Are the lanterns ready, Malie?'

'Yes,' she said, 'Sofie and I got them ready.'

'What about the bigfeet?' Aunt Gertie wanted to know.

'The nearest ones are in Gouna's Bush,' Dawid said. 'We are safe over here.'

Martiens gave the women orders too: 'Anna can go and lie down, she's had a hard walk. Aunt Gertie must watch over Barta. Malie, you and Sofie make a big fire in the middle of the Island; if the child has fallen asleep somewhere and wakes up, he'll see the glow and come back.'

By morning, the fog was gone, except for a few patches in the deepest gorges. Sofie's husband, Koos, left for Deep Walls at daybreak to tell the nearest forester about the missing child. By midday, fourteen woodcutters were taking part in the search and on the next morning the constable came from the village to help as well – the forester had sent a message to the magistrate in the village. Towards the evening they heard the constable calling for help in a gorge near Jonker's Mountain and had to go and get him out, battered and totally lost.

When they got him back to the Island, he addressed them all:

'I'm afraid you will have to accept that the child can no longer be alive.'

'How can you decide, mister,' Martiens flared up, 'whether a child is still alive or not? In this Forest a child is tougher than you think.'

On the fourth day twenty-four men were searching; all of them woodcutters except Elias and the forester, Mr Kapp. On the fifth day, there were thirty. Wherever the news had spread through the Forest, the woodcutters laid down their axes and came to help. On the sixth day there were forty.

And at the end of the eighth day it was Martiens who took it upon himself to say what had to be said:

'He can no longer be alive now.'

Malie and Sofie had to support Barta between the two of them. Barta looked old and forlorn and exhausted, and she was clothed in black, borrowed from Aunt Gertie.

Elias just hung his head and shook it slowly from side to side, as if refusing to admit it to the very end.

Seven months later, in August 1865, heavy rains fell over the Forest and shortly after that the forester came to tell him that parts of a skeleton belonging to a smallish child had been found amongst the driftwood along the Gouna River. But it could have been part of a baboon's skeleton.

2

Benjamin had always known that he was his parents' hand-child. Like the hand-lamb the ewe does not want that has to be hand-fed. He had always known it, but it never mattered because he was just like Dawid and Tollie and Kittie and Emma in the house.

They lived in the Long Kloof and the Long Kloof lay between the mountains that stretched from west to east for a hundred miles long. Wolwekraal was on the sunset-side of the Kloof and his mother always said it was the better side. The only trouble was that the stupid Laghaans also lived on that side.

3

Only in retrospect did Fiela take account of the omens – she did not recognize them at first. The puff-adder at the back door the day before had taken a dozen blows to smash its head in. It did not occur to her that it was Satan's own tidings; she took it as being summer and snake-time. On top of that, the hawk came and caught the most beautiful chicken of the whole brood. Omens that should have warned her, but her mind was on the ostrich and she did not heed the warnings.

The horse-cart came from the west down the Kloof, the children and the ostrich from the east. She was standing up at the house, trying to judge who would reach the road branching off to the house first, the cart or the children. The ostrich was going at a good pace and the children, waving their thorn-tree branches to keep her in the right direction, had to run to keep up with her. Benjamin was right in front of course.

'Just look at Benjamin, Selling! Right in the way of the ostrich after I had expressly told him he could go on condition that he stayed at the back!'

'Leave the child, Fiela, he's not one for staying at the back. That cart has been up and down the Kloof the whole week. I don't know it.'

'Pedlars. There are more of them around here these days. If it goes on like this there will be a buyer for every ostrich feather before long.'

The children and the ostrich reached the road first and Fiela's hands were fidgeting with excitement under her apron.

'She's beautiful, Selling. Perhaps a little skinny round the backside but we'll get her nice and fat, just wait and see.'

'It's too far to see what she looks like, Fiela – seems to me the cart is turning up this way.'

'If they're pedlars looking for hides and things to buy, you tell them straight out we're dealing with Rossinski.'

'There are quite a few rock-rabbit hides ready.'

'Fine, they can have them but not for under two pence a hide.'

The heat was running in waves above the hill-tops on the other side of the Kloof. Towards Diepkloof, to the east, a whirlwind spun up dust along the road and then suddenly died down again. When she looked up, the hawk was hanging almost motionless in the sky above the yard.

'Scoundrel!' she shouted to him, 'caught my best chicken when my back was turned yesterday, hey? Go and try your luck somewhere else today, I've shut them in!'

'The cart's coming this way, Fiela.'

'Not a single hide for under two pennies.'

Down in the valley the ostrich suddenly swerved to the right with the children following at a pace that made the dust fly from under their feet.

'They'll have trouble getting her here,' Fiela said with a smile, walking up the slope behind the house to the chicken-coop.

The summer was a harsh one. She looked up at the bare, rough, red-brown hills above the house and saw the mist trailing over the top and disappear again against the blue of the sky. It was as if the heat on the Kloof side of the mountains would not allow even a shred of mist to come over and give a little relief from the heat. Why it had pleased the good Lord to put a mountain between the Kloof and relief, God alone knew. On the seaward side of the mountain he had planted with a lavish hand, made it rain and sprout till a forest had sprung up, stretching for miles and miles in every direction. But by the time he made the Kloof side, God had had nothing left but stones and dust and wagon trees and rhinoceros bush and aloes.

That was sinful thinking, she said to herself; the all-good God had not left the Kloof altogether unprovided for, for he had put ostriches there. And in the years when the rain came at the right time, the Long Kloof blossomed and food for man and beast grew with abundance and made you forget about the drought, when everyone and everything had a struggle to survive. Like this year. But that was sinful thinking too, because every day a little water still trickled from the spring into the pond. The goat milked well still. The few sheep they had were still on their feet, and Selling also brought in something by dressing skins and making whips. Most of their shoes he made himself too. There was not much left of Selling, his health had been poor for years but his hands could still work even if there were days when it took her a lot of talking to get them going. Ill-health or no ill-health, Selling had to do his bit. Idleness and trouble were the best of friends, she had always said.

The ostrich made a wide turn through the veld before the children could get her back in the direction of the house and the new enclosure.

To the west of the house, in the old enclosure, the male ostrich was grazing. Pitch black, a magnificent bird; wings edged with waving white plumes and his tail feathers thick and yellow-white.

Fiela felt proud of him as she walked to his enclosure.

'I told you I was going to get you a hen!' she called out to him over the hedge. 'Look there, there she comes! Did I lie to you?'

'Fiela,' Selling called from the house, 'the cart's coming up here!'

'Let it come!'

There was a lot of room in her heart for that male ostrich. For Kicker. To get hold of him, she had had to arm herself with a whitethorn branch and sit in the aloe hills above the nest of the wild ostrich pair for days until she had finally managed to steal three chicks to bring home. Of the three, only Kicker had survived. Ostrich chicks had a way of dying for no reason at all.

In the coming month Kicker would be three years old and it was time he had a hen ostrich. To have one ostrich was good, but to have a pair of breeding birds was as good as having a trunk full of money under the bed. From Kicker's feathers alone she had made six pounds three shillings the August before, and the year before that, four pounds six shillings. According to Rossinski the price was climbing because foreigners wanted more and more ostrich feathers for shawls and hats and costumes and whatnot. If Kicker and the hen started breeding, Wolwekraal would be able to supply the world with quite a few more plumes to swank with.

Kicker would have to take a liking to the hen first, though.

Down in the valley, where the road to the house crossed the stream, the pedlar had stopped his horses to let them blow. Where the buttercups flowered on the slope, the children kept the hen ostrich going and headed straight for the house with her.

'Make a turn with her round the old enclosure!' she called out to them. 'Bring her round so that Kicker can have a look at her before you drive her into the other field!' The children came up from below with her. 'Stupid!' she shouted at Kicker. 'You don't even lift your head! You don't even bother to look and see how pretty she is!'

'Careful, Ma!' Dawid, the eldest of her sons, warned her as they came round. 'Don't let her get past you, Benjamin!'

The hen was thin and bewildered but her neck was straight and proud as she ran past with the shouting children chasing her and driving her from all sides.

'Work her gently!' Fiela called to them, looking back to where Kicker was still pecking the ground. 'Shame on you! I had to trade a lot for her and you didn't even look at her!'

She had got the hen from Koos Wehmeyer and she should have known that Koos would not give her one of his best yard birds – but she promised herself that she would get the hen fat and pretty before the mating-season.

She heard the children struggling to get the ostrich into the field on the other side of the house, and grabbed a branch to go and help them.

'The cart's coming this way, Fiela!' Selling said as she passed him.

'Two pennies a hide, nothing less!' The hen was tripping nervously along the hedge. 'Emma, you and Kittie block her way down at the bottom!' she ordered the tired, dusty children. 'Dawed, you and Benjamin guard the top, and Tollie, you come and help me!' If she could rear even six chicks from a brooad of twelve or sixteen eggs, it would mean more money in Wolwekraal's trunk than ever before. 'Careful, stop her at the bottom there!' But they had to have rain first. God knew, the drought had the Kloof on its knees again. The earth was bare. Every afternoon the thunder-clouds swelled out behind the mountains to the north, only to disappear again without leaving a drop of rain in the dust. What the stupid Laghaans, west of her boundary hedge, were living on, they alone knew. 'Careful, Benjamin!' If only the clouds would come and lie over Jan Koles's Peak so that it could rain before the ostriches had to go to pasture. When the hen tried to get past them, they directed her swiftly into the enclosure. 'Close the gap!' Fiela ordered the children, throwing down her branch.

The children were done for.

Tollie came up. 'Master Koos says ma must send him an extra whip, the one you've sent is too thin,' he said.

'You go and tell Koos Wehmeyer he'll wait a damn long time to get another whip from me. Benjamin, get away there from the hedge! If that ostrich breaks loose today, she'll kick to kick your stomach open!'

'She almost kicked Kittie, Ma. If Tollie hadn't been there with the branch, Kittie would be stone-dead now!'

'Benjamin's lying, Ma,' Kittie said. 'It was *him* she almost kicked.'

A trickle of sweat ran from under Kittie's headcloth and made a shining trail through the dust on her brown skin. Emma lay down on her stomach at the stream, lapping up the water. Next to her, Dawid knelt and splashed water over his face. The ostrich had exhausted the children.

'Go into the shade and give the hen time to settle down.'

'I want to go and see how far my boat has drifted first, Ma,' Benjamin said, and started running down along the stream in the direction of the pond.

Fiela smiled to herself as she watched him. No ostrich would keep him away from his boats. He was always busy with his boats, hollowing out pieces of wood to make new ones.

'There are people coming, Ma,' Tollie warned her as he came past on his way to the stream.

'Let them come; we're dealing with Rossinski – unless this one pays a better price for rock-rabbit hides.'

She watched the cart coming up towards the house and saw the chickens scatter before the horses' hooves. A faint shock went through her. It was not a pedlar. It was two men in black suits and black hats.

'What's this?' She went and stood by Selling at the corner of the house. She was always nervous when strangers came to the house. She had had good reason to fear strangers.

'Maybe it's preachers, Fiela,' Selling suggested.

'Who comes preaching on a day as hot as this?'

The preacher-pedlars fastened their horses under the pear tree and walked up to the house. One was tall and bespectacled and the other short and fat and had a red face as if he had high blood pressure.

'Good afternoon.' The tall one spoke first. 'Quite a handsome bird you've got in the enclosure there.'

'He's not for sale,' she said brusquely, wondering if they were not pedlars after all. The tall one had a book in his hands, and pen and ink.

The short one took off his hat and wiped the sweat from his brow. 'It gets hot here in the Kloof, doesn't it?'

'Yes,' she agreed. Selling just stood there.

'Can we have something to sit on?' the tall one asked.

'What's your business, master?' Strangers were not asked to sit down in her house.

'Census.'

'What's that?'

'The Government wants all the people in the country counted; we've just started in the Kloof.'

Fear shot through her. 'What do they want to count the people for?' she asked, hastily.

'Don't you count your chickens at night?'

She did not answer him. Years of apprehension flooded over her; she began to look for a way of escape: if only the hen ostrich would break loose from her enclosure and run away so that the children would have to follow her. If only Benjamin's boat had drifted away so that he would have to go and look for it and would stay away from the house. If only God would put his wings round the child and hide him from the two peace-breakers.

'Can we have something to sit on?' the tall one asked again.

She turned round and walked into the brown clay house; on the threshold she waited for the daylight to get out of her eyes so that she could see in the half-dark house. Only the wooden shutter in front of the kitchen window had been taken down; the shutters of the other rooms were kept shut to keep the heat out and the coolness in.

She took two low stools outside to where the strangers were waiting in the strip of shade to the south of the house. Selling was standing to one side; he looked as if his mind was barely working.

'Can any of you read and write?' the short one asked.

'Yes,' she said. 'Me. I had schooling with Mr Hood, down at Avontuur. I went through the first and the second book, in fact.'

The tall one sat down with his back to the wall; he put the book on his lap and balanced the ink on the stone ledge at his feet. The short one had difficulty finding a place level enough for his stool.

'First names and surname?' The tall one asked Selling, but she answered for him.

'Selling Komoetie.'

The man wrote it down. 'Date of birth?'

'He doesn't know.'

'Very few of you Coloured people do know,' the short one said, somewhat disgruntled, and waved the flies away. 'It's almost two weeks since we started here in the Kloof and I don't drink we have found three Coloured houses where they knew their own details – they either had to call the master or we had to guess.'

Selling looked uneasy. 'My father always said I was born when they were helping to transport the English by ox-wagon.'

'Transport them where?'

'I don't know, they were the English people that came by ship and got the farms.'

'It could be the 1820 lot,' the short one suggested. 'He looks quite old to me and damn poorly on top of it.'

'He's not strong!' She stood up for Selling. She saw Kittie peeping round the corner and shooed her away. In her heart she prayed that the hen ostrich would break loose even if it meant they would never catch her again and lost the whips they had paid for her.

'And you?' the tall one asked her. 'During which pestilence or disaster were you born?'

'I'll go and fetch the Bible, it's written down there.' She turned round and walked back into the house. Only God could help her now, she thought, as she felt along the walls with her hand to where the Bible lay on the shelf. Outside she opened it and read: 'Fiela Maria Appools. Born 19 October 1836. Married Selling Komoetie on 3 January 1859.'

'Where were you born?'

'Here. But our house was down there in the valley where we were washed out during the flood. I was about knee-high then.'

'Who does this land belong to?'

'To me.' Perhaps they didn't want to count the children, just the adults. 'My father and my grandfather worked for the Wehmeyers for many years. I suppose you could say they killed themselves working for the Wehmeyers. After the old master's death this twelve morgen of Oude Wolwekraal was put in my father's name; the papers to prove it are with Mr Cairncross in the village, at Uniondale. We're not tenants or yard hands.'

'Children?'

God, let Kicker break loose now! Let him drop stone-dead, let me sacrifice him this day, but please keep Benjamin away from the house.

'How many children do you have?'

'Five,' she said, and saw that Selling was looking even more frightened.

'Names and dates of birth?'

'Let me see . . .' She opened the Bible again – how many times had she told herself to write down Benjamin's name and she had never got round to doing it! 'Kittie, our eldest, was born on 4 January 1856,' she read. 'The year after that our Dawid was born: 2 March 1857.'

Please, God, take Kicker, let him get stomach rot this minute and take him. Please, God.

'Next?'

'Tollie. On 17 November 1858. The year after that Selling and I got married and did not have children. Emma was born on 6 February 1860, the year they were building the white people's church in the village with old Master Wehmeyer's money.'

He wrote it all down with long, scratching strokes. 'And the fifth child?'

She glanced at Selling and pretended to read it straight from the Bible: 'Benjamin. Born 13 February 1862. He's twelve now.'

Pen dipped in ink, slow scratching strokes . . . 'Anyone else with you in the house? Brothers, sisters, uncles, aunts, mothers, fathers, grandpas, grandmas, friends?'

'None.'

'That's very strange. As a rule there are more hangers-on amongst you people than there are people in the family.'

'There is no room for idlers at Wolwekraal,' she told him shortly. In her heart she was shouting to him to get up and go, and to take the other one with him! She had Benjamin registered in the book of the Government, and somewhere comfort and relief were waiting to enter her mind where there had never been ease before. But first they would have to get up and leave.

'How do you make your living?' the tall one asked, turning to a new page.

'From what we do with our hands. We're not like the Laghaans, who live on honey-beer and do nothing.'

'How, exactly, do you make a living?'

'A little wheat, a little maize, a few vegetables, a few sheep and a goat for our milk. All depends on the water. For the rest Selling dresses a few skins and so forth, and now and again we sell a few feathers.'

'Which church to you belong to?'

'Independent Church. It's our own church which we founded after the London Missionary Society left us to carry on with almost nothing. I want master to write it down in that book that the money for the church was collected here in the Kloof because the church was to have been built down at the crossroads at Avontuur. But then Mr Hood had to tag on after the Stewarts to Uniondale, not only taking the money with him, but also building the Coloured people's church there. Now we must get up at dawn if we want to be in the pew in time. Selling, with his ill-health, never sees the inside of a church any more.' It was the sound behind her that made her spin round. At the corner, beaming, and with his wooden boat still dripping wet in his hands, Benjamin stood plain for all to see. Her tongue grew thick in her mouth with shock.

'It had drifted right down into the pool, Ma! I had to take a stick and hook it out and it hadn't even capsized.' Then he seemed to notice the two men, and greeted them respectfully: 'Good afternoon, master – good afternoon, master.'

The tall one pulled off his spectacles and the short one's mouth fell open. Selling's hands started working convulsively.

God! she screamed in her heart, take everything I have! Take the whole lot, but don't take Benjamin!

She had always known the day would come when she would be exposed before the world because of that child of hers. Many a night she had lain awake preparing herself for that day and going over what she would say. In the Kloof over the years everyone, white and Coloured, had had to give way before her tongue; she had made them keep out of Wolwekraal's affairs. The Kloof had got used to the child being with her.

'Whose child is this?' the tall one asked, aghast.

'Mine.' They would never see Fiela Komoetie cowed.

'But that's a *white* child!'

'Yes, he's white.'

The short one started fanning himself vigorously with his hat. 'And a beautiful child at that. Whose child is this?'

'It's Benjamin, my hand-child.'

'Come here, sonny!' the tall one said to the child, but she stepped between them like a watchdog.

'Leave the child alone! If there's something you want to say, say it to me.'

'Listen here, woman, you know as well as I do that there's something very strange going on here. This can't be your child but you gave out that he was yours. Where did you get the child from?'

'He's my hand-child.'

'I asked you where you got him from!'

'Where do you get house-lambs from?' She had the courage of a tigress defending her young. She had long been prepared for this day. 'I found him where his mother left him, that's where.'

'Where was that?'

'Right there where master is sitting.'

'When?'

'Almost nine years ago. In the middle of the night.'

'He looks older than nine to me,' the short one said.

'He is.'

'How old is he then?'

'I don't know, I put him down at three that night.'

The tall one kept on staring at the child. 'You say you found him here at your back door? Was he standing or sitting or lying down?'

'Standing.'

'I think you're lying.'

'What would I be lying for? I woke up that night because of the child's crying and when I opened the door, he was standing there. Somebody had left him at my door.'

'Did you hear anything?'

'No. Only the child.'

'That did not give you the right to keep the child. It's a white child!'

'Should I have left him outside?'

'Don't try to be funny, woman,' the tall one warned her, 'you have a white child on your land and in your house among your own children and you know as well as I do that that is not right.'

'What about the Coloured children who live on white people's land and in their homes together with the white children?'

'That's a different matter. They're the farm-labourers' children and at night they go to their own homes. What we have here is wrong.'

'Who says so?'

'I say so.'

'If you took a lamb and reared it, who's going to tell you whose sheep it is?

'Why didn't you take the child to the farm next door? To Master Petrus Zondagh at Avontuur? He's a prominent man, he would have known what had to be done.'

'Master Petrus was at the coast.'

'Then you could have taken the child to the village, to the magistrate.'

'What magistrate? Our village only got its own magistrate recently.'

'Fiela ...' Selling said, with difficulty, 'tell the master about the sergeant.'

'What about the sergeant?' the tall one asked.

'A week after I had found the child, I went to the village to tell the sergeant but he had gone to Dugas after people who had stolen sheep. A week later, when I went to see him again, they told me he had gone to a funeral down at Haarlem.'

'You didn't go again?'

'No. By that time the child wouldn't let go of me any more, so I took him.'

'In other words, you kept the child without telling anyone.'

'I didn't steal him from anyone.'

'Ma ...'

'Go and play, Benjamin. Go and find your boat.' But the child still stood behind her as if he was trying to shelter in her shadow. She had always known the day would come when she would have to fight for him, but the danger had come from a direction she was not expecting. She had always thought it would come when Petrus Zondagh came to talk about the child for the second time and she had prepared herself for that. Not for this, though.

'Hang on – wait a moment!' The short one suddenly threw his hands in the air as if he had something to announce. 'How long ago did you say it was that you found him here at your back door?'

'Nine years ago.'

He turned towards the tall one. 'Do you remember the child that got lost back in the Forest? I was accompanying a new forester to Deep Walls that day and the other forester asked me to take a message back to Magistrate Blake at Knysna about the child that was lost. Mr Blake sent out the constable the next day to help the woodcutters in their search. Do you remember?'

'Yes. But was it as long as nine years ago?'

'Easily. And they never found that child.'

'Was it a boy?' The tall one was obviously interested in the story.

'It was. And I'm almost prepared to swear that he was three at the time too.'

She felt the blood seething in her veins. 'Look, master,' she flared up, 'you're fishing in a piss-pot now!'

'Wait – wait! The child I'm talking about disappeared in Kom's Bush. It's all coming back to me now. If you drew a straight line from here over the mountain I bet you'll come out in the Forest exactly where the child got lost.'

'Master,' she said, standing right in front of the short one, 'have you ever seen what it looks like straight over the mountain at the back here?' They had hold of quite the wrong idea and she had to stop them! 'It's not just one mountain, it's one mountain after another between here and the Forest and you know what the Forest looks like, too. Are you suggesting that a child of three could have wandered over here? You're not right in the head if that's what you're thinking.'

'It's not impossible.'

'Jesus, master, it is just as impossible as it would be for that male ostrich over there to lay an egg; even a strong man would take more than a week to get here from the Forest.'

'What about the road? Say he had got on to the road?'

'Which road? Nine years ago the road was not made. They were working on the road, yes, and if master's looking for one that knows that road ...' – she saw Selling's feet shuffle about nervously and put him at ease with her eyes before she went on – '... ask me. I know that road. But suppose the child *had* got on to the half-finished road – somebody would have found him, because hundreds of convicts were working on that road. No, master, the child I found at my back door had not walked far.

He was clean and tidy. So don't come and stick pieces together that do not belong together.'

The tall one got up. 'This is a serious matter; it's a case for higher authority, not for us.'

Please, God, see my need, *help* me! she prayed in fear and started pleading with them: 'Master, leave this thing alone, leave the child alone.'

'Can't the child remember how he got here?'

'No.'

'Sonny, come here,' the tall one said to the child.

'Leave him alone!'

'I just want to ask him something, woman.'

'I've asked everything that had to be asked, he knows nothing.'

'Maybe we should take the child with us,' the short one suggested.

'You'll have to cut my throat first!' she protested. 'It's *my* child and my child he'll remain! Everybody in the Kloof knows it and accepts it, but now you want to come and get your claws into him? You, master, *you*,' she pointed her finger at the tall one, 'you wrote down his name in the book of the Government as Benjamin Komoetie and that is how it shall remain till the end of our days!'

'You lied to me!'

'I don't know the truth any more than you do, master.'

'Did you ever try to find his mother?'

'No. A ewe that throws away her lamb does not turn back.'

The short one had waited his chance to get round her and trap the child against the wall. 'I won't harm you, sonny,' he said soothingly. 'I just want to look at your boat.'

'Leave the child alone!'

'I won't touch him – it's a nice little boat. Did you make it yourself?' The child was frightened. 'I'm just asking, I like boats. Did you make it yourself?'

'My father had helped me, master.'

25

She saw them look at one another because of the 'master'. 'He talks like us, it can't be helped.'

'Tell me, sonny, how did you get here? Think carefully now and then you tell me.'

'I don't know, master.'

'I'm sure you'll remember something if you think hard enough. Something about your house or your mother.'

The child turned his dark blue eyes pleadingly towards her as if he wanted her to free him from the man. Selling sadly shuffled nearer and pleaded with the tall one.

'You frighten the child, master. He knows no other mother. He only knows Fiela.'

The tall one slammed the book shut and picked up the ink. 'We're going back to Knysna tomorrow, we'll inquire about the other child.'

4

February. March. April. The first signs of winter.

It was as if the stone that had been weighing her down since February had got lighter by the middle of April. She no longer woke up every morning thinking, today is the day they will be coming back. She stopped seeing omens in every snake she found near the house or in the veld. Or in every hawk flying over the house or in every owl's hoot in the night.

Not that all her fear had left her; when she walked in the rocky hills she often looked up apprehensively to scan the cart-track down in the Kloof. There were times when she felt the house getting too tight round her and when she had to go outside and stand at the corner of the house watching the road.

'They won't come back, Fiela,' Selling told her one day as he came up behind her. 'Not any more.'

So the stone started getting lighter.

They named the hen ostrich Pollie. With the full moon in March the mist came over Jan Kole's Peak and on that very same night the rain came and soaked the earth half a spade deep. The veld was refreshed.

'Children, as from tomorrow the ostriches will go to pasture,' she told them the week after the rain. They were all under the pear tree dressing rock-rabbit skins for at least two new rabbit-skin blankets had to be finished before the winter. All the signs were pointing to a winter with snow. 'Petrus Zondagh says I must still keep them apart, however, and that's why I want Kittie and Tollie to take Kicker to pasture one day and look after him, and Dawid and Emma to take Pollie the next day.'

'What about me, Ma?' Benjamin wanted to know immediately.

'You stay at home because you don't listen when I tell you to stay away from the ostriches' legs. One of these days they're going to kick you open.' It was hot. She and Kittie were stitching together the skins that were finished while the others were preparing skins. 'And I don't want you to drive the birds too hard and frighten them. Just see that they don't go into the Laghaans' veld or into Master Petrus's fields. I see part of his wire fence is lying flat up near the wagon trees ... When we've got a dozen ostriches, I'll have Wolwekraal fenced in too and no idler or his accomplice will put a foot on my land again.'

'Ma, can't Benjamin go with me instead?' Tollie grumbled. 'The two of us can look after Kicker. Kittie will just lie down behind the first bush and go to sleep and then I'll have to watch the ostrich all by myself.'

'If Kittie lies down behind a bush, I will come and get her up with the strap!' she promised.

Dawid had objections too: 'I don't know about Pollie, Ma. She's never been out of the enclosure since we put her in there. What if she takes flight?'

'We'll have to wait and see.'

She was not at all easy about the hen herself. There was a wildness in her that no wheedling in the world could remove. When the dung in her enclosure had to be picked up, at least three of them had to keep her away with thorn branches. Yes, a bit of wildness always remained in an ostrich, but it seemed as if there was an extra devil in Pollie. Perhaps that was why Koos Wehmeyer never said a word about the other whip again.

When she got Kicker, people told her the only way to get the wildness out of an ostrich was to put him in an enclosure as near the house as possible while still young so that he could see people every day. The closer you made his run to the house, the better. At six months, he was so tame that only one person with a thorn branch was necessary when the dung in his enclosure had to be

picked up. At eight months, he grazed round the house as tame
as a chicken with only Selling to keep an eye on him. Not that
Selling had much of an eye left, but at least he could call one of
them if the ostrich wandered too far.

It was Pollie that worried her. There had been a cussed streak
in her since the very first day. Fiela thought a little spoiling
would get it out of her – the regular titbit from the table, the
fresh green fodder from the veld every second day, the sandpit
like Kicker's with sand from the river down at Avontuur's
Crossing and wood ashes and sulphur mixed in the sand so that
she could scratch herself clean from lice and nothing would
bother her. Apart from that, anyone who had nothing to do was
sent to the hedge to talk to the hen. When it was not too hot,
they dragged Selling's bench to the hedge so that he could talk
to her while he was working.

Sometimes it seemed to help; then Pollie came to the hedge
and pushed her long neck over the top, peering towards the
house as if she was curious. The very next day she would seem
to be too haughty to turn a feather again.

When it was Benjamin's turn to go and keep the hen company,
he quickly got tired of it.

'I don't know what else to say to that hen, Ma. I've already
told her everything I know!'

'Go and recite a psalm to her.'

'Ma!'

'Don't talk back.'

'But she doesn't even hear what you say to her!'

'She hears.'

Still, the hen got nice and fat and full round the buttocks; by
August she would give a good crop of feathers. Not that she
would ever give plumes like a male, like Kicker. Why the good
God had to leave the hens so grey and dull and give all the
beauty to the males, no one could tell.

*

'Knead that skin, Benjamin, it's not a piece of washing you're rubbing!'

The child could get so absent-minded sometimes.

The next day they took Pollie to the pasture for the first time. To get her out of the enclosure was less trouble than they had thought it would be; she ran ahead of the children with her head in the air and all the old haughtiness about her. By midday she was grazing peacefully in the valley below.

'See there, Selling,' Fiela said, resting on the yard broom for a moment, 'see how she pecks and cajoles with her body like a flirt.'

'I see her, Fiela.'

'You're lying, you're like Kicker, you don't even look up.'

The veld was beautiful. At the end of March the rains had fallen for two days, soaking the earth deeply. The first red hot pokers started blooming up in the ravine where the spring rose, and in the hills the bitter sap started swelling in the aloe leaves.

'We can start tapping aloe shortly, Selling.'

'Isn't it a bit early?'

'Not at all. It's a little late. My father always said, on the first day of April the aloe sap must flow. By the time the Laghaans realize it's aloe time this year, I want to be finished. Rossinski promised to pay more this year than last year's tickey* a pound – Selling, whose hooded cart is that coming up the road down there in the Kloof?'

'It's Master Petrus, Fiela. You must stop being frightened by every cart.'

'The fear somehow remains in me, Selling.'

'You must talk to Master Petrus about the child, Fiela, he'll tell us what to do. He's a good man.'

'No.' She gave a few wild sweeps around her. 'Petrus Zondagh does not ask my advice about his children and I don't ask his about mine.'

She swept in an ever-widening circle across the yard and kept

* Three pence.

her eyes on all of them. On Selling's hands that so often wanted to rest; on Dawid and Emma down in the valley watching Pollie so that she would not go to the road. She watched Kittie and Tollie sitting next to the house, shelling maize cobs. She kept her eyes on Benjamin at the stream.

She needed no advice about Benjamin. As long as she was alive, every Komoetie would have a place. Wolwekraal was their place and Benjamin was a Komoetie.

'Keep your hat on your head, Benjamin!' she shouted down to the stream. The child had invented a new game. Every boat had to have oarsmen and his oarsmen were tapping beetles. The boat that drifted into the pond first, with both beetles still on top, was the winner. He wore himself out running up and down the stream from boat to boat to save the beetles that fell off.

The child had a deep hold on her heart. She did not believe in loving one child more than the other, but the trouble was, you always had a feeling of pity for a hand-lamb as well.

Yes, Wolwekraal would be looked after. Petrus had said one day, the Kloof was worn out and ravaged because everybody just kept on planting and sowing and grazing the veld and the earth got no rest. The fields were tired of giving year after year; the earth had to rest in between. Since then she had seen to it that Wolwekraal's fields got a regular rest. You could see the difference when you walked west towards the Laghaans' eight-morgan land they rented from Koos Wehmeyer and saw how dust-trodden and ruined it was.

'Keep those hands working, Selling!'

'I'm very tired today, Fiela, I don't know why.'

'The sun is still far too high – you can't be tired yet, Selling. Work!'

Towards the end of April something else began to worry her. It was more than four weeks since they had started taking the ostriches to pasture and still Kicker showed no sign of being ready to take the hen.

'Just see how well he looks, Selling!' Fiela complained, disheartened. 'Strong and handsome but not a sign yet of his beak or his shins getting red. He does not even *look* at her!'

'You're in too much of a hurry, Fiela. You heard what Master Petrus said, that he might not be ready until next year.'

'I can't wait until next year – they have to start breeding this year. Wolwekraal must raise many ostriches and pluck lots of feathers; the price is going up and there must be money under the bed by the time the Laghaans have finished themselves off with drink.'

'What are you talking about now, Fiela?'

'I want to buy the land the Laghaans are on.'

'You must be dreaming. How many times has Master Koos been here to ask you to sell him back this twelve morgan of your late father's? He'll never let you have another eight; they don't want to see bits of land in Coloured hands any more.'

'They can forget about my twelve morgan. I'll put the eight of the Laghaans' in Benjamin's name. He's white.'

'Who says the Laghaans will ever move away?'

'They've already had to sell some of their goats to pay last year's rent. You'll see, they can't last much longer. The ostriches better start breeding; I think Kicker is overfed, he's too fat. Petrus reckons he might be too lazy to get interested in the hen. Perhaps I'll starve him a bit from tomorrow and see what happens.'

'Who says Pollie's ready for him yet? And who says Kicker's going to take her the day you shut them in together? I've seen a male ostrich fight a hen that didn't appeal to him.'

'I'll knot his neck for him if he doesn't take her.'

'As if you'd knot *his* neck!'

'Then he better take her. Just see how pretty she is. The day she came here she was all skinny round the back and scraggy over the stomach; see how she's filled out now. No, Selling, I can't wait till next year. They will have to start breeding this year and that's that.'

'Master John Howell's Kollie tells me they give their birds stuff to drink prepared by an old man at Oudtshoorn; it apparently brings them on.'

'What? I'll get a bucketful and make him take the lot!'

'Just keep a little for Pollie too,' Selling warned her. 'I don't think she's ready yet either.'

It was the day after that, while she and Kittie were preparing the evening meal in the kitchen, that Benjamin came running across the yard to the house shouting, 'Ma! Ma! Ma!'

The fright she got made her drop the piece of firewood she had in her hands, for the first thing that came to her mind was that the two people-counters were on their way again! At the back door the child almost knocked her down and he grabbed her apron and started pulling and pulling.

'Ma! Ma!'

'What is it?' she cried.

'It's Pollie, Ma! She's dancing!'

The relief was as great as the shock she had had. 'Pollie's dancing?'

'Yes, Ma.'

'Selling, Pollie's dancing! Dawid, Tollie! Kittie, Emma, Pollie's dancing!'

When she got to the enclosure, her heart leapt – Pollie *was* dancing. Wings spread out and plumes waving, she tripped round and round on her toes over the golden-yellow sorrel. Proud, graceful, long-necked, she was performing the strange ostrich dance of joy.

Pollie was either happy or broody.

And Benjamin was safe.

5

Yes, indeed, he liked the plan. He liked the plan more and more.

Elias van Rooyen was sitting on the log outside the back door so that he could think for a while; a man could not keep his mind on his work when his head was teeming with important things.

'Aren't you going to finish that beam first, Elias?' Barta came and asked behind him in the doorway, timidly.

'Pity you can't feel what my back feels like,' he said reproachfully, thinking to himself: How can a man think out his plans with a woman breathing down his neck all the time? The older Barta got, the more she moaned. He could swear she sometimes counted the beams to see how many he had finished. It had to end. He had two sons now bringing in food, it was no longer necessary for him to kill himself working. Willem was in Martiens Willemse's woodcutter's team and Kristoffel was with Soois Cronje of Little Skew Bush. According to both Martiens and Soois the boys were hard-working and there was no need for him to worry about them. And he did not intend to stop making beams; it's just that a man should have an easier time when he had sons to help earn a living. Certainly he no longer delivered as many beams as he used to, but you get tired of making beams. Johannes Carelse, the other side of Goat Beard Crossing, had also started making beams. Door frames too. The wagon from the Long Kloof now came and loaded Johannes's beams first and then his. This was no skin off his nose; they could not get enough beams.

Barta was still standing in the doorway.

'How about a drop of coffee, Barta?'

'The coffee's finished. Perhaps Willem or Kristoffel will come home tonight and bring us a few brews. Didn't Kristoffel say they'll be taking wood to the village today?' She sat down on the doorstep, stretched out her legs and started worrying about the beams again: 'Isn't the wagon coming next week, Elias?'

'Haven't you got work of your own to do, Barta? Weren't you supposed to dig the garden today?'

'I finished digging yesterday. Malie said she'll bring me a few pumpkin seeds to put in.'

'Well then keep your mind on the pumpkin seeds and let me keep mine on my affairs. I've got big plans.'

Dawid Olwage had come back from the Forest with the story the week before. All the Barnard's Island woodcutters had been at home as it was Sunday.

'You know,' Dawid said that night, 'I saw something on Friday which made me think my eyes were deceiving me. When we were coming back from Gouna through that particularly dense stretch of bush, I told the others to go ahead; I wanted to walk through Stinkwood Kloof to see what we can fell next week. The wood buyer is grumbling about stinkwood again; cut stinkwood and he wants yellowwood, cut yellowwood and it was kamassi he wanted. Anyway, as you know, there's a footpath down in Stinkwood Kloof and one up on the hill going over into Brown's Kloof.'

'I know that footpath at the top,' Martiens said. 'It may be a short cut into Brown's Kloof but it can be a very dangerous one when it rains.'

'That's true,' Dawid said, 'but I was taking the bottom path. And as I came to the waterhole beneath the rock cliffs, I thought I heard bigfeet but I knew in my heart it couldn't be, for no bigfoot would dare go into Stinkwood Kloof down those gorges and ravines. But then something made me look up, and as I did so, I saw six bigfeet coming up the footpath at the top. Right

35

there where the path comes round the front of the hill to the precipice before it swerves away with that very sharp bend to go down into Brown's Kloof.'

'On *that* footpath?' Koos tried to deny the possibility. 'They couldn't be.'

'I'm telling you, they were. You can go and see for yourselves, the tracks will be there still. But that's not all. I stood there, thinking that the bigfeet would be in real trouble for once: that very sharp, narrow bend on the edge of the cliffs was ahead of them and I knew no bigfoot could get round it. In my mind's eye I could already see the one in front falling down the precipice; I was hoping he would kill himself so that I could hack off the tusks for myself. There is nowhere up there where a bigfoot can turn his massive body round.'

'What happened?'

'I was waiting for the big crash when the one in front got to the bend. But sure as I'm sitting here, he did not fall, he stretched out his trunk and curled it round the candlewood tree on the bend and moved his body round, backside to the cliff's edge, shuffling round the bend while he kept holding on to the tree with his trunk!'

'You must be lying!' they all exclaimed together.

'I'm not. I've told you, the tracks will be there if you want to go and have a look for yourselves. One after the other they got round that bend and safely down the other side. When it came to his turn, each one curled his trunk round the tree and shuffled round, backside to the precipice.'

'Well,' Martiens admitted with respect, 'I've always known the buggers to be clever, but I didn't realize they were *that* clever.'

Koos laughed. 'What? I once saw a herd get through the mud up a slope where I never thought they would dare go. First they pushed the one in front up until he got a foothold and then he turned round and gave his trunk to the second one and pulled him up past the mud. Each one, as it got to the other side, turned round and helped the next one up by the trunk.'

'I once saw them pulling up underbrush,' Martiens said. 'Before putting it into their mouths they knocked off the earth against a tree. They don't eat dirt.'

When Elias went to bed that night, it was neither Martiens's nor Koos's story that stuck in his mind – it was what Dawid had seen happening above Stinkwood Kloof. Say a man could carefully saw that tree up there on the bend so as to leave just enough wood and bark to keep it up?

The longer he thought about it, the more he liked the plan. He did not see how he could ever afford a gun; if he had the chance to get a couple of tusks without one, he should grab it.

'Barta!' he called out, and was startled when she answered right behind him. He had forgotten that she was sitting in the door. 'I want you to pack me some food for about five days on Monday. I want to go and have a look at the wood in Gouna Bush.'

'Why there?'

'They say there are plenty of young yellowwoods left there.'

'Why don't you cut bigger trees, Elias?'

'Bigger trees?' He was annoyed. 'And how am I to get them dragged out here? I've only got my own two hands and the two ancient oxen!'

'But you talk as if you see your way clear to drag out young wood from Gouna Bush that's hours far from here and through heaven knows how many gorges and drifts.'*

Barta was not always stupid, he thought to himself.

'I didn't say I was going to bring out wood from there, I said I want to go and have a look at the wood.'

Nina wandered across the clearing from the woodcutters' side. In one hand she held an empty bottle by the neck and in the

* Fords.

37

other a stick with which she hit the bottle every few steps. He watched her. It seemed as if there was a game going on between her feet and the tinkling of the bottle.

'Barta, can't you cut the child's hair? See how she looks. Like a werewolf. Or plait it.'

'She will not let me.'

'Since when has a brat got a will of her own?'

'The scissors won't cut either.'

It was better if a man didn't have daughters in the Forest. They could help their mother in the house and in the garden but that was all, they could not help to earn food. For the rest they only caused worries. And only the good Lord knew what was to become of that one. Thin and wispy, just like a goat, always climbing and jumping. When she had to have a hiding, you had to stalk her with the ox rein, for if she got a chance to get away, it took you half a day to get hold of her again. And by that time you were too tired to beat her properly in any case. Barta was definitely not up to controlling the child.

'Nina!' he called out over the Island. 'Go and ask Aunt Malie for a brew of coffee till tomorrow.'

She finished the pattern of steps and tinkles before answering; 'Aunt Malie doesn't want to lend us any more, she says we don't repay her.'

'That's a bloody lie!' As far as he knew, they only owed Malie the last brew. 'Go and ask Aunt Anna then. Tell her we're expecting Kristoffel, we'll repay it when he comes.'

One, two, three, tinkle. One, two, three, tinkle – if he had had something to throw he would have thrown it at her.

There were days when he felt like knocking down the house and moving to another clearing there and then. If you were not a woodcutter in the Forest, the others looked down on you. Accused you of not giving back what you'd borrowed. There was just as little in everyone's pockets, they were all as needy as each other, but there was hardly a day when he did not get the feeling that the woodcutters were looking down on him and calculating amongst themselves how much he was making from the beams. Jealous. Afraid he would make a penny more than they did. But he would show them yet. If luck stood by him and if the story Dawid had told was true, he would soon have quite a bit of money in his pocket and they could try and work out where he had got it from. He would not tell them.

'How old is Nina now, Barta?'

Barta was no longer at the door. The child must surely be ten or eleven already, he worked it out for himself. Somebody once told him that the English in the village took in white girls to look after their children – depends on what they were prepared to pay.

On the Monday, at threequarter-day, he was in Stinkwood Kloof in the upper footpath. On his back he carried the crosscut saw, the hatchet, the ox reins and a blanket; in the knapsack was enough food for a week.

The elephant dung he came across in the footpath was a week old and he reckoned he would not have to wait for his chance for too long. The stinkwood trees in Brown's Kloof were dropping their berries and the elephants would be sure to come – they couldn't keep away from stinkwood berries.

The only trouble he foresaw was that he might have to borrow extra oxen to haul out the tusks. The woodcutters were forever borrowing oxen from one another without asking anything in return, but Elias van Rooyen would have to give up a tusk in return and he did not want to do that. Willem or Kristoffel could stay home for a while and help him haul them out one by one.

The tree was exactly where Dawid had said it would be. The old candlewood stood right on the bend like a mighty corner post; it could not have grown in a better place. At the height of an elephant's trunk, the bark was smooth from many years of use. The excitement of expectation suddenly stirred in Elias. No elephant, falling down there, would get to the bottom alive. Rascals! Probably thought no one would ever discover their trick.

He had to work carefully and take care that no hand or shoulder touched the tree to leave behind a trace of human scent. An elephant had a fine sense of smell. After a day or two all human scent would be gone, but just in case his luck was closer than he thought, he kept his body away from the tree.

And he did the sawing skilfully: from the back and about calf-high from the ground till there was just enough core wood left at the front to keep the tree upright and put an elephant at ease. When the one in front had his trunk round the tree and started shuffling his backside round the precipice, his weight would do the rest. There was only one other thing Elias van Rooyen could hope for, and that was that the second elephant would rush forward to help the first, and that both would tumble down.

He was down in Stinkwood Kloof at sunset. He found himself a place further along the brook from which he would be able to watch the footpath at the top and he built himself a shelter of branches there.

He slept badly that night. He was not used to lying on the ground as the woodcutters were; the longer he lay, the more lumps seemed to be sticking into him.

On the Tuesday he heard elephants ripping off branches in the direction of Draai Kloof. Wednesday passed without a sign of them; the only thing that came within a stone's throw of his shelter was a very fine bush-buck ram on his way to the water but he had nothing to make a proper snare with.

On Thursday, at about half-day, he got in under his shelter for a snooze to while away the time and woke up thinking he heard people talking. He hoped he was dreaming, but as he was getting up, he saw Fred Botha's team going past right in front of his shelter. He felt all his hopes give way under the shock. If they had come to cut in Stinkwood Kloof, all his trouble would have been for nothing. He tried to duck so that they would not see him, but Fred had already seen him and stopped short in his tracks, surprised.

'My goodness, Elias, what on earth are *you* doing here?'

'Having a look at the yellowwood,' he lied, trying to keep cool as he crawled out from under the shelter.

Fred let his heavily laden team stop to have a rest and a smoke. While they were sitting around it came out, mercifully, that they were on their way to Michiel's Crossing to work there and had only taken a short cut through Stinkwood Kloof.

'By the look of your fireplace it seems as if you've been here for quite a while, Elias?'

'Yes. Did you come across any bigfeet on your way?'

'We passed a herd at sunrise, this side of Rooihout, but you're safe down here, they can't get down here easily.'

'I was just asking. I might be going in that direction myself this afternoon.'

'How is it going with the beams, uncle?' one of Fred's sons-in-law asked.

'It's going well.'

'I saw one of uncle's boys in Martiens Willemse's team.'

'Yes.'

There were eight men in Fred's team and Elias got the feeling they were looking at him as if they were suspicious about something.

'But isn't there plenty of yellowwood up in Kom's Bush where you are, Elias?' Fred continued, puzzled.

'Old trees, yes, I'm looking for young wood.'

'I would have thought bigger trees to be better, give you at least four beams to a log. Why would you drag out wood from here for just one beam?'

'Don't talk of things you know nothing about, Fred.' He was getting irritated.

'I see your second son is with Soois's team.'

'That's right.'

'Why don't you take in your sons yourself to help you make beams instead?'

'It's no use all of us cooking in the same pot.'

'The day I get out of debt at the wood buyers, I'll start making beams and things myself, but I don't want to be worse off than I am now. It's bad enough as it is.'

He felt relieved when they got up and started cleaning their pipes. As they were getting ready to go, he saw them looking surreptitiously in under his shelter for who knows what. But it was better that they should think he was hiding something there.

On the Friday he was beginning to get tired of waiting. He could easily have gone home and come back after a day or two, but suppose his big chance came falling down the cliffs while he was gone? In the Forest findings was keepings, and who would believe that it had been his plan to saw the tree and that the elephants were his? No woodcutter would let go of a tusk once he had his hands on it.

A slight movement in the direction of the hill caught his eye. When he looked up, his heart missed a beat! Where the footpath came round the hill were three elephants coming up the path. Slowly, as large as life, they were approaching – it was like watching a wish come true before his very eyes. When they came out into the sun, he knew that luck could never have picked him three better elephants. Enormous creatures with yellow-white tusks curved away from the sides of their heads and all with the tips unbroken.

He crawled carefully out from under the shelter and stood up ... There was no hurry in the elephants as they came up the increasingly steep path. After a while his jaws became stiff from clenching his teeth and his breath was catching in his throat but he dared not cough; no sound must go up from below to disturb them. Nothing. It was his big chance. His alone. The one in front was the biggest of the three; if only he would fall, all the trouble and all the waiting would be rewarded. He could hack off the tusks before dark and hide them. If two were to fall, he would finish the hacking off the next morning and then go home to fetch the sled and the oxen.

Slowly, step by step, they moved along. He felt like bursting with impatience and wished he could urge them on from below. The steeper and narrower the footpath got, the slower and closer together they walked: head against backside, head against backside.

What a pity, he thought to himself, that he could not put a new tree up there every week; if he could do that, he would never have to make another beam in his life . . .

Say one of them was not killed when he fell down? Say the elephant only broke his legs or his back? There was a safe distance between him and the spot they had to fall but a half-dead elephant was the most dangerous thing on earth, even for a man with a heavy gun.

He took another look at the distance the elephant had to come down and knew that he was only scaring himself; no elephant would fall down there without getting himself killed for sure.

About a hundred yards from the tree, where the footpath was at its narrowest and most dangerous, it seemed as if they were pushing one another forward. Thirty yards from the tree. Twenty. His breath rattled faster and faster in his chest. He stooped down to pick up the hatchet, as if picking up a weapon to give him courage. Ten yards. They took the last few steps like old people. When the trunk of the one in front started to feel for its grip round the tree, the two at the back came to a standstill. Elias felt his chest tightening when the trunk started curling round the tree. Then the elephant suddenly lowered its trunk and just stood there. As if in thought. Or like a creature praying.

'Go on! Take hold of it!' he shouted inside himself. 'Go on.'

But they just stood up there. Frozen. Trunks drooping. Once it seemed as if the one in front made to lift his trunk and then stopped.

'Are you waiting for the bloody tree to grow again?' he felt like shouting to them. No human scent could be on the tree; they could not have caught his scent down in the kloof for the wind was in his face. Not a single lourie bird gurgled or hissed anywhere near to warn them. He could not understand why the elephant did not put his trunk round the tree and hold on! The bugger could not have known that the tree had been tampered with – it had been done with the greatest care!

They stood there on the footpath for almost an hour before they very carefully started stepping backwards. A man with a gun could have shot them down, taking his time, but Elias van Rooyen was not lucky enough to have a gun; he had to stand down there powerless and watch how everything went wrong. All he could do was strike the hatchet deep into the trunk of the wild elder beside him. Bastards!

It took them till dark to find a place where they could turn their heavy bodies round. It was too late to walk back to Barnard's Island and it meant he had to spend another night under the shelter with his stiff, painful body and the taste of bitter defeat in his mouth.

The next morning, as he was climbing the last slope at the upper end of Stinkwood Kloof to take the sled-path home, he would have been a dead man but for the grace of God. Quiet as cats, they had taken cover in the thicket ahead of him, the elephants, and the first he noticed was the ears flapping among the foliage. All he could do was throw everything down and run for his life. He could not tell how many there were and he did not care – he just had to keep running to get back down into Stinkwood Kloof where they could not reach him. Whether they were the same elephants, he could not say; he only knew that the undergrowth kept breaking right behind him and that death was breathing down his neck.

It took him a day's walk to get home by a roundabout way.

When he pushed open the back door, Barta cried out. 'Elias, what happened? Did the bigfeet chase you?'

'You still asking questions? I was within a hair's breadth of being trampled by them, woman!' He was a broken man. Bitter. It had all been in vain. 'But I'll get them, I'm telling you, I'll get them for it!'

Willem was at home. 'Did pa have to throw down pa's things?' he asked in awe.

'Everything. The hatchet, the saw, the ox rein, everything. You must go and see if you can't find them tomorrow. I'll tell you where the bastards stood waiting for me.'

'What about the blanket, Elias?' Barta asked, anxiously.

'When the bigfeet are on you, you can't choose what you let go of and what you want to keep, woman!'

'It's just that we are so short of blankets, Elias.'

Nina came in like a shadow from the dark. 'Why are you making such a noise?' she wailed. 'There is the most beautiful owl sitting on the shed, hooting.'

'Chase him away!' Barta said, frightened. 'He'll bring us bad luck!'

The next day he moved round the house with the sun to give his body a chance to recover while he tried to understand how his plans could have been messed up so! How could the bloody elephants have known?

'Van Rooyen?'

When he looked up, the forester from Deep Walls stood right next to him and it startled him. The day the forester came and called you by the name it could only mean trouble. But his wood licence was paid for, he had no traps set – true, the yellow wood on the stack did not carry the forester's mark but who in the Forest could afford to cut where the keepers said they could? They had never been able to enforce the regulations.

'Mister, if you've come to bring trouble, you've come to the wrong man,' he said, straight out. 'I'm a ruined man. I was nearly trampled by the bigfeet yesterday. Look at me.'

'I'm not here to bring you trouble. I'm bringing you a message from the magistrate at Knysna.'

Magistrate? That could only mean bigger trouble than usual.

'A message from the magistrate?'

'Yes. There's a strong possibility that your son, the one that got lost, has been found. Found alive, that is.'

No.

No, it could not be true. The man was mad. Elias tried to get up but he was overcome by shock.

'What did you say, mister?'

'They found him on the other side of the mountain, in the Long Kloof.'

'Mister, I can't take in what you're saying. My mind's gone blank.'

'You better calm down first, Van Rooyen. It's taken some time to sort out because it was Mr Blake that worked on the case at the time of your son's disappearance. The new magistrate, Mr Goldsbury, had to read up on it first. But many things point to the likelihood that it's your son, although it's not settled yet. And that's why the magistrate wants you and your wife in the courtroom at the village on Friday.'

'You say they found the child in the Long Kloof?'

'Yes. With Coloured people. I believe he's been there for the past nine years.'

'You say they've found our Lukas?'

'The possibility seems quite high.'

He could not believe it. 'Where is he now, mister?'

'Still in the Long Kloof. They will be sending for him tomorrow.'

6

When Fiela opened the back door that morning, she knew the aloe would not flow that day for a north-west wind was blowing. Even if you cut the fattest leaves and packed them upside-down – even if you stood on your own head – they would not yield you a spoonful of sap, for when the north-west wind comes the aloe keeps its bitter sap.

Behind her, in the half-dark kitchen, Kittie was breaking dry twigs to get the fire going. In the small paddock above the house, Dawid was milking the goat.

'Blow out the candle, Kittie,' she said over her shoulder as she walked outside.

The last veil of the night still lingered over the earth; on the other side of the Kloof, at the foot of the hills and the cliffs, it was still quite dark. The moon was in the west, shining-white, shrunk almost to nothing. At the pigsty the red rooster crowed as if he had to break the day himself.

Walking in the fresh morning air, she planned the day ahead. Tollie would have to stay in the house. Pollie had kicked him the day before. By God's grace, it was only a blood-scratch down the thigh to the knee, but it could have been ugly. Children pay no heed when you warn them. They have to get hurt before they will listen. When she had finished scolding and bandaging Tollie's leg she had walked up to the pigsty and thanked God right there on her knees by the earth wall. The child could have been killed.

It was because they did not know what it was like when an ostrich kicked hard. She knew. When she was young a wild ostrich had kicked open Nicolaas Dannhauser at Diepkloof. The

Dannhausers were strangers, white folks, who had moved into the Kloof, and the stupid man had to go walking through the valley where the wild birds were breeding. They had to go pick him up there with the horse-cart and rush him to the village. Someone had to sit next to him and hold his bowels together. Old Dr Avis managed to sew him up and pull him through but Dannhauser was never healthy after that. And children think you're talking just for the sake of it.

She walked over to Pollie's enclosure. 'The devil's in you, isn't he?' she scolded across the hedge. 'Had you kicked open my child yesterday, I would have wrung your neck for you!' The bird kept on pecking along the ground, unconcerned. Behind the hills the sun came out and spread its warmth over the Kloof.

As she turned round, a thought came to her, tentatively at first and then more forcibly until she had to stop herself. What if she were to make a mistake? What if she were to bungle everything?

But the idea would not let go. This was the day that Pollie would be put in the enclosure with Kicker and that was that. When she walked round the house to his enclosure she was not without serious doubt, however.

'Kicker, I want you to listen carefully to what I'm about to say,' she said to him. He stretched his neck and looked at her as if he knew she had come to talk about something serious. 'I'm going to put Pollie in with you today and I'm warning you of two things: she's a devil and you must be careful of her; on the other hand, I want you to have a proper look at her so that you can get to like her and mount her. Don't bring disgrace upon yourself. Don't let it be said of Wolwekraal's male ostrich that he was incapable. The most handsome male bird in the Kloof, with a limp cock, how would that sound?' He *was* handsome. His body feathers were soot black and shiny against the snow-white plumes of his wings. 'Pollie is fat and beautiful, and you'd better take her because I don't have another hen for you. And don't drive her out of here, either.'

The house smelled of the morning when she got back to the kitchen. The rhinoceros-wood fire was glowing cheerfully under the water for the coffee while Kittie was putting freshly roasted coffee into the pot.

Everyone was out of bed except Selling.

'We will not be going to the veld today, the aloe will not flow,' she told them.

'I thought so too,' Dawid agreed. 'The wind is from the northwest.'

'Stop looking so glad, Benjamin, you'll sweep the yard and help to clean the hen-coop before you can go and play at the stream.'

'Yes, Ma.'

She cut the bread herself and spread the lard on it before giving each his share. She said nothing about the ostriches at first.

'Make the coffee and pour it out for us, Kittie. Emma, I want you to walk down to the crossroads later in the day and take Miss Baby and Auntie Maria each a bar of soap. Tell them the soap didn't come out as well as Miss Baby's did last time, but ma will make up next time.'

'Tell them to blame Benjamin,' Kittie snapped. She and Benjamin had been quarrelling in the aloe hills the whole week. 'Tell them he was playing with his boats instead of stirring the soap pot!'

'That's a lie! You didn't come stir when it was your turn!'

'Stop it, children! Pour out the coffee, Kittie. Drop in at the shop on your way, Emma, and bring us a measure of meal. Benjamin, go and tell your father to get up. We must get finished, Pollie's going in with Kicker today.' She knew that would surprise them. 'Yes, you heard me.'

'Ma must be joking,' Dawid said.

'I'm not. Today's the day. Tollie will stay in the house and keep his leg still. The others will help me drive her into his enclosure.'

'My leg's fine, Ma!'

'Fine doesn't look like that – go and tell your father to get up, Benjamin!'

'What if Kicker doesn't want her, Ma?' Kittie asked, concerned.

'Then I don't know myself.'

Benjamin came back from the bedroom and asked for some more bread. 'Master Koos said at the shop the other day, I must tell ma he'll swop ma two male birds for Kicker.'

'If he thinks I'll swop Kicker for two of his moth-eaten birds, he can think again. I'm not stupid.'

'I told him ma's not stupid.'

'Benjamin!' She swiped at him with the dishcloth. 'You're not to talk to grown-ups as if they're your equals.'

'Master Koos didn't hear me, Ma, one has to shout to make him hear you these days.'

'Eat decently, don't stuff your mouth like that.'

'It's because the bread is so nice, Ma.'

When Selling came into the kitchen, she gave him one look and knew that it was not only the aloes that were affected by the wind.

'Pour your father his coffee, Kittie.'

'Give me some of the buck-bush brew first, Fiela – I feel dizzy this morning.'

'You can't feel dizzy today, Selling; Rossinski's coming next week; the whips and the skins must be ready.' She poured him a full mug of the brew and stirred in two spoonfuls of sugar. 'My late mother always said, when the world starts spinning, it's a sign that your stomach's standing still. I'll send the children to pick you gansies this afternoon and brew them for you, but I can't do it this morning; I need everyone to help because I'm going to put Pollie in with Kicker.'

'Fiela?'

'Today.'

'You're making a mistake, Fiela, wait another week or two.'

'No. I've kept them apart long enough, I had them out at pasture for weeks, I've put paraffin into their ears so that there wouldn't be a single tick to worry them, I've let Kicker starve – I'm not waiting any longer.'

The dew was still lying when she handed out the thorn-tree branches. Tollie would not listen to her; he insisted on helping.

'Please, Ma.'

'All right then, you can see to it that Kicker doesn't come out; stand inside the opening and hide yourself when we bring her round. Don't let her see you.'

At Pollie's enclosure she ordered Kittie and Emma to block the way at the bottom end while she and Benjamin blocked it at the top. When they had her out of the enclosure, they would take her round the back of the house and then down to the other enclosure.

Selling was standing at the corner of the house still trying to talk her out of it. 'Fiela, you're over-hasty, there's no sign yet of Kicker's shins colouring. Nor his beak.'

'Maybe they will if she's with him in the enclosure.' She shouted to the children to get ready. 'If she breaks away, let her run, we can always round her up again, but don't frighten her!' She went into the enclosure alone to bring her out. 'I want you to stop being so stand-offish now,' she said to the bird, soothingly, keeping the branch between them. 'He's the most handsome male ostrich in the Kloof and he won't like a silly hen.' In her heart she said: Please, God, if I'm making a mistake today, just don't let them ruin each other fighting. Feather time is coming and if they wreck the plumes, I'll get nothing for them. To Pollie she added provokingly: 'If he does not appeal to you, I'll get him another hen.' Then she gently urged her towards the opening; with the second try she got her out neatly and waved to the children to come closer and help her.

'Fiela!' It was Selling calling from the house, but Selling had to wait, the hen had her neck pulled up straight and was moving like a horse wanting to bolt.

'Slowly . . .' She kept the children back. 'Lower your branches a little and watch the sides.'

'Fiela!'

The confounded ostrich would not go round the house and they had to follow her up the slope to go round the pigsty at the top.

She knows very well she's not going to pasture, Fiela thought. The hen's head kept on turning from side to side as if the large black eyes wanted to see everything and everywhere. She was like a chicken being singled out for slaughter and getting suspicious.

'Pollie!' Benjamin shouted to the ostrich, 'if you marry Kicker, ma will bake you a sugar-cake!'

'Higher with your branch, Benjamin! If she jumps round today she'll kick to kick home! She's looking for trouble.'

When they came round the pigsty with her and started going down towards Kicker's camp, the horse-cart was coming up towards the house. The shock that tore through her left her numb but she kept on running with the ostrich. Oh God, don't let it be true, not after all these weeks!

They had almost reached Kicker's enclosure when Pollie suddenly veered off to the right and made them follow her round the pigsty again. When they came down a second time, Kittie jumped quickly after her and got her into the enclosure.

It was the same two men. The tall one and the short one.

Her mind started working in two directions at the same time.

'Come out of the enclosure there, Tollie! Close the entrance!' Pollie started running up and down inside the hedge. At the bottom she turned round, stones flying up from under her toes, and ran to the top again. Down. Up. She was trapped and was looking for a place to break loose.

The two peace-breakers had fastened their horses and were walking up to Selling. Benjamin stood a short distance away from her with his thorn-tree branch held out before him and she knew he knew that this was the day she had warned him of.

The hen started to run faster and faster, up and down along

the hedge. Kicker stood in the middle of the enclosure as if he could not decide whether he should start running too or chase her out.

Suddenly she did not care any more what he did. She felt like shouting to Benjamin to run for the hills and hide but her mouth would not open and her heart was thumping.

Benjamin had questioned her in the aloe hills one day. They were tapping aloes and he had been helping her to cut the leaves and stack them in a circle with the cut ends down so that the sticky, bitter, yellow sap could drain into the concave iron sheet.

'Ma?'

'Pack another layer, Benjamin.'

'Ma, ma always says I am ma's hand-child.'

'That's right. Now don't let the thorns scratch you like that! Grasp the leaves like you would a puff-adder; stay away from the sides where the thorns are.' She knew where he was heading and was trying to distract him. 'We must hurry. Kittie and Emma already have two stacks draining. Tomorrow we'll have to boil them again.' Benjamin liked the tapping, but when they had to boil the gathered sap till it was thick and black and glossy, he always made excuses to get away.

'Everything tastes bitter, Ma, even the air! The smoke makes my clothes and face and everything bitter. I'd rather do something else for ma.'

She always allowed him to get away – he was so willing when they had to tap.

But she could not get away from his questions that day.

'Why was ma so afraid when those two men came to count the people?'

'I was not afraid.'

'Ma was. I saw it.'

'When you find yourself up against an adder it does not mean you're afraid just because you get stones ready to kill him.'

He helped her to pack the oozing leaves round and round on the stack. 'Ma, why is a person white or brown?'

'Are you asking me about the good Lord's work now? Why is a starling black and a weaver bird yellow?'

'Why are you all brown and I'm white?'

'Because you're the hand-child. Shift that leaf forward a little, it's not dripping on to the sheet.'

'Why did ma say they would have to cut ma's throat first before they could take me that day? Were they going to take me then?'

'That was just talk. You can't just come and take somebody's child away.'

She got up but Benjamin stayed where he was.

'Ma?'

He sounded anxious. She looked away into the distance where the pale blue mountain peaks closed in the Kloof and she knew the child was going to ask her something she would not be able to lie about.

'What is it, Benjamin?'

'Are they going to come back and take me, Ma?'

He had a way of looking at you as if he was looking right into your heart. 'Ma will not let them take you away, Benjamin, but sometime a day is coming when only God will be able to help us.'

'Are they coming back?'

'I don't know. If they don't come back, some other adder will come some other day. We'll have to wait and see. But ma won't let them take you.'

She saw Benjamin lower the thorn-tree branch and turn round and look at her. Oh God, she said within herself, why do I suddenly feel so strange?

'Fiela!' Selling called, anxiously.

The hen kept on running and Kicker kept on trampling about in the middle of the enclosure. Dawid and Tollie and the two girls were closing up the opening in the hedge but their eyes kept turning towards the house.

'Fiela, come here!'

She threw her branch down by the hedge and started walking across the yard. At every step, she felt as if her blood was draining away.

'Good morning!' the tall one said, cheerfully. 'I see you're still busy with the ostriches. Are you going to let them mate?' She did not answer him. 'I believe the price of feathers is going down.'

When the short one came nearer he spoke nervously: 'I see you have had some rain ... We stayed at De Vlugt last night, with the Standers; we left Knysna a bit late yesterday.'

Pollie was still pacing the ground; at the pigsty one of the hens started cackling.

'Mr Goldsbury, the new magistrate at Knysna, has sent us,' the tall one said, without looking her in the face. 'He wants to see the child.'

She did not raise her voice. 'That's all right. He can come and see him.'

'He wants to see the child at Knysna.'

'He can come here and see him.'

The tall one got annoyed. 'Look, we're tired; don't make things difficult. We've come a long way. A magistrate is not someone you fool around with; he wants to see the child and that's all there is to it.'

'The day after tomorrow,' the short one added. 'Friday. Mr Goldsbury just wants to clear up the case of the child that disappeared in the Forest about nine years ago. That's all. Settle the matter. The mother of the missing child will also be in court at Knysna on Friday to see if it could be hers or not.'

'He's not her child.'

'All the more reason to let her and Mr Goldsbury see it for themselves,' the tall one said. 'The case would be settled then.'

They were driving her into a corner. She knew it. 'Why can't the forest woman come here if she wants to see the child?'

'Because this is no ordinary matter; these are things that must be said and done before a magistrate. If she comes here, you can both say whatever you want to say, but at the magistrate's you'll be under oath and will have to watch your words. Apart from that, the forest people are very withdrawn. The forester himself said he doesn't know how they're going to get the woman to the village, let alone into court.'

They have you cornered already, Fiela Komoetie, she told herself. What they are doing now is closing in on you. She felt Selling's weakness seep through her own limbs. No struggle or outburst could help her, but she would not give in easily.

'I'll take him to Knysna myself.'

'That's impossible!' the tall one said, his impatience coming through strongly. 'The magistrate wants to see him in court on Friday, the day after tomorrow! Not next week. It would take you at least two days to get there on foot and even longer with the child! It's too far for him to walk.'

'I don't follow you at all, master. According to you, he got over the mountains on his own when he was much smaller. Now you say it's too far for him to walk?'

'I did not say that this *is* the child; I said the magistrate wants to see the child so that the case can be cleared up.'

'And I'm saying, you're wasting your time, master; it's not the same child.'

'Perhaps you're hiding something from us – you seem so sure of it?' the tall one asked suspiciously.

'I have nothing to hide, all I'm saying is, it's not the child. He didn't come all the way from the Forest, somebody left him at my back door in the middle of the night when no one would see. But I'll get the child to Knysna by Monday and show him to the magistrate and the forest woman and that will put an end to it.'

Then the short one's patience gave out. 'You can't tell a magistrate what to do. If he said Friday, Friday it will be, or he'll write you down on the wrong side of the law and you'll have to stand in court on Monday yourself, for contempt of court!'

'Then I'll go with you on the horse-cart.'

'We can't take you on the cart,' the tall one broke in. 'You know yourself how terrible the road over the mountain is. Only last month the post-cart had an accident again, in the place where Mr MacPherson was killed.'

'Now you want to get my child killed?'

'That is why I said we can't take you on the cart! We have to keep the cart as light as possible.' The tall one was annoyed. 'We'll come and fetch the child early tomorrow morning. Tomorrow night he'll sleep at my house in Knysna, and on Friday morning I'll take him to Mr Goldsbury at the courthouse for the forest woman to see if he's her child.'

'It's not her child!'

'If he's not her child, we'll bring him back on Saturday.'

She knew then what the mother hen felt like when the hawk hovered above her and there was no shelter to run to. She tried pleading with him.

'Master, please, I've promised the child I won't let anybody take him away. He's so attached to me, he's only a child, master, he can't take decisions for himself. We must decide for him and God looks down on us and writes down every tear a child sheds if we harm him. Have you no heart, master? All I'm asking is that I should go with the child. Take me with you. We'll walk back.'

'We can't,' the short one said. 'But we'll look after him well, you need not worry.'

She *was* worried. She could no longer fight them. They had the law on their side and the law was above all. If it was true that the magistrate only wanted to show the child to the forest woman, she had nothing to fear. But what if there was something else? There were so many other things that could be hiding under their skulls of which she could not know, and that was what made her desperate and made the rage flare up within her.

'Why did you go and report the child? If you had kept quiet, this would not have happened!'

'You could not have hidden the child for ever!' the tall one argued.

'I was not hiding him!' she insisted.

'People say the child never goes to church, he's becoming a heathen.'

His words frightened her even more. 'So you discussed the child with others? You went gossiping behind my back?'

'They say the child has not been to school like your other children.'

'I teach him about God. Tollie and Dawid taught him as they were taught in school. Every afternoon. Miss Baby Stewart, down at the crossroads at Avontuur, next to the shop, took him for sums twice a week because Tollie and Dawid did not always understand the sums themselves. In the end Benjamin explained the sums to them. No, master, I did not hide him, I just kept him where I could because he's white. I just kept him away from adders like you!'

'Fiela!' Selling knew her when she got furious. 'The master said they'll bring him back on Saturday.'

'How do I know they're not lying?' she shouted.

'Master,' Selling asked the tall one, bewildered but straight to the face, 'are you lying to us or not?'

'We're telling the truth, but if the magistrate hears of your wife's attitude, things will look bad for you. All the magistrate wants to do is show the child to the forest woman. And I have had to listen to a Coloured woman insulting me and I've had enough of it! Tomorrow, at daybreak, I'll be here to pick up the child and if he's not outside and ready, I'll go back without him and the magistrate can send the constable to fetch him. He won't come and reason with you as I have tried to do, he'll just take the child.'

When they drove away, Wolwekraal came to a dismal standstill. Except Pollie.

Fiela's mind started exploring every direction to find a way out: she could take the child up the spring-kloof and hide there with him. No, she must go to the crossroads and hide him with Miss Baby. Or with Auntie Maria. Auntie Maria was cook at Petrus Zondagh's homestead, working during the day. She must go to Petrus, he would know what to do. No, the hills would be best.

Selling sat hunched on his bench by the house; Kittie and Emma were crying under the pear tree and Dawid and Tollie walked away into the veld.

Benjamin took his boats to the stream.

O God that looks down upon man, what am I to do?

'Ma?'

'Quiet, Benjamin, ma's thinking.'

'What are you thinking about, Ma?'

'Everything.'

By the afternoon the storm in her had abated and she was left with two choices: either the child had to go into the hills alone and hide and they must all swear he had disappeared as he had come – walked off. Or she had to prepare herself and let him go to Knysna. And stay on her knees till Saturday and pray that they would bring him back. He was not the forest woman's child, she would swear to that on the Bible without ever having seen the woman.

'Ma, Pollie has calmed down, she's grazing now. Kicker too.' It was as if Benjamin wanted to comfort her with the news.

'Go and play, Benjamin, Ma still has a lot of thinking to do.'

The child was not stupid; he knew they were trapped, she could see it in his eyes. And he did not go back to the stream, he went to sit with Selling against the wall.

No, the child could not go to the hills alone. It would be a fool's way out. Besides, the tiger that had killed one of the Laghaans' skin-and-bones sheep the month before would still be around somewhere.

Dawid and Tollie had come back from the veld and were

sitting on the outcrop of rock behind the house. Kittie and Emma were standing at the corner of the house. She knew they were waiting for her panic to subside so that she could come to a decision and tell them which way they had to take.

There was only one way left.

'Dawid!' She went and stood where they could all see and hear her. 'Get on your feet, you must go to the village. Tollie, get the wood ready and make a fire outside for hot water. Emma, make a fire in the kitchen and get food on for us. Kittie, fetch the tin with the sewing.' They just sat staring at her and she saw she would have to tell them straight out. 'Benjamin's going to Knysna. We have no choice.' She saw Selling's hand reaching out to rest on Benjamin's head. 'I've thought out all the possibilities and found no other way. But I'm telling you one thing, they'll be bringing him back on Saturday. Do you hear me, Benjamin? On Saturday they'll bring you back and God help them if they ever set foot on this land again! Ma is sending you with them so that the magistrate and the forest woman can have a look at you and get it over and done with. But you won't have to hang your head because you have been entered into the Government's book as Benjamin Komoetie. Dawid is going to take the short cut over Jan Kole's Peak to the village with three sheepskins and two whips and he's going to get you a nice new shirt and a pair of readymade shoes – Selling, trace the child's foot there on a piece of hide. Tollie, get the fire going. Kittie, bring the sewing, there's a seam split in Benjamin's best pair of trousers.' They were still fearful and they just stared at her. 'Get moving! We must get the child ready. We don't want him to be ashamed of us.'

The sun was going down when Dawid came back from the village. The shirt was a bit big but better too big than too small. A nice shirt. Blue. The shoes were just right.

And the children were no longer so scared. It was almost like getting ready on the last day of the year to go down to Auntie Rosie's at Haarlem.

'Bring us something nice from Knysna, Benjamin.'

'They say there are elephants in the Forest, perhaps you'll see one.'

'Just think how nice it's going to be, riding on a horse-cart!'

'Don't cry, Benjamin. Perhaps you could catch us a nice big fish!'

She let them carry on. It made Benjamin feel better, even a little important, and it helped them not to notice how worried she was. Only Selling kept watching her, anxiously.

She herself had much to do. The white rooster had to be slaughtered, she had to knead and bake pan-bread, for the child had to take enough food with him to last till the Saturday. She cut his hair, his nails, she rubbed his feet with paraffin and candle-grease so that not a trace of roughness would be left on them. She did not want to be ashamed, no one would point a finger at a Komoetie.

She let the children tease and talk. She would have a chance to talk to him when she had him in the bath for a good scrub.

They ate shortly after Dawid came back. She was not hungry but she kept on eating because Benjamin was watching her as if to make sure that she was not upset.

While Kittie and Emma washed the dishes, she went outside and found Dawid at the fire.

'That water's ready, Ma.'

'I'm waiting for the girls to finish in the kitchen.' Dawid was fast becoming a man. The agony on his face, in the glow of the fire, was that of an adult. 'I'm going to the ostriches for a while, Dawid.'

'Ma,' he stopped her, 'what if he *is* the child that disappeared in the Forest?'

'He's not. Wait until you've seen what it looks like behind those mountains and you'll know that it can't be him. You only

know the short cut through Broom Reed Ravine and down to
De Vlugt. I know the other route. And De Vlugt is only behind
the first of the mountains – no, Dawid, he's not the forest woman's
child – that's our only comfort tonight. On Friday she will know
it too, for a ewe knows her lamb.'

She turned away and walked into the darkness. The stars
hung bright over the Kloof, peaceful, as if there were no cares
above the earth.

Please God, go with Benjamin, she prayed as she walked, stay
with him, he's softer than us because he's white, be with him
when he has to appear before the magistrate, see that he stands
there neat and clean and see that his shoes are fastened.

At the ostriches' camp she peered over the hedge till she found
Pollie sitting there in the dark.

'I thought you would be worn out,' she said to her, and walked
to the bottom corner where Kicker was standing. 'What are you
standing like this for? Are you making up your mind whether to
take her or drive her out? I'm warning you, don't try anything
tomorrow or the day after or on Saturday, there's enough trouble
on Wolwekraal as it is.'

The nightjar gave its sorrowful call somewhere in the hills.
When Benjamin was small and the nightjar had come looking
for beetles round the house giving its eerie cry, the child used to
get into the bed between her and Selling.

'What's that, Pa?'

'Nightjar.' Selling never slept well, he liked company in the
night. 'It's a kind of owl.'

'But it doesn't sound like an owl.'

'It doesn't look like one either. You can walk in the rocky hills
and walk right over him without seeing him. He looks like the
stones and stays flat on the ground when he sees you coming.'

'Tollie says it's a ghost.'

'Tollie's lying.'

Selling's stories about the veld and the creatures of the veld –
many of them a bit steep and far-fetched – often kept Benjamin

holding the thongs for hours when Selling had to plait a long whip. There were times when it seemed as if Benjamin had more patience with his father's weakness than the other children had.

She went back to the house.

'Bring in the water, Dawid.'

They had to fill up the tin bath for her. She took out a new wash-cloth, clean flannel to dry him with and the best piece of soap. When the child stood naked a new fear came weighing down on her: wasn't he too thin? Wasn't he too pale? What about the scratches on his arms and legs? When it was aloe time they were all covered with scratches; it was just that his skin was so white and the scratches showed more on him.

'Ma . . .'

'Get in, Benjamin!'

'Ma!'

'Get in!'

'Ma, the water is too hot.'

'It's not too hot, I felt it.'

'I told ma I'd go and wash at the stream. I'm not a baby.'

'You cannot go and stand before the magistrate with only a stream wash. Sit down!'

'Ma, I'm scared.'

'Be brave. And remember not to call the magistrate *master*. You call him, "my lord".'

'Is he the Lord?'

'Don't pretend you're stupid, Benjamin! He's the magistrate, the big man of the law. Anyone who lies to him, gets thrown into jail backside first!'

'Ma must come with me.'

'There's not enough room on the cart.'

'Ouch! You're washing my ears off my head!'

'Sit still! Tell me what I told you to say when the magistrate asks you your name?'

'Benjamin Komoetie.'

'Who's your mother?'

'Fiela Komoetie.'

'Who's your father?'

'Selling Komoetie.'

'Where do you live?'

'Wolwekraal in the Long Kloof. Our own property.'

'How come you're ma's child?'

'What did you say I must say?'

'The good God gave you to ma.'

'The good God gave me to ma.'

'Again.'

'The good God gave me to ma.'

'If he asks you to write, do your best writing. If he asks you to read, read your best as you always do when you read to ma from the Bible. Ma's not worried about the sums.'

'I don't know how to multiply by nine any more, Ma.'

'He won't ask you multiplication tables.'

'How can ma tell?'

'He won't.'

'I'm scared, Ma.'

'Be brave.' Please God, she said in her heart, take away my own fear.

'What if they don't bring me back again, Ma?'

'The magistrate will see to it that they do. Saturday. As they said. The magistrate's word is law – give me your foot.'

Selling came to sit on the bed and peered into the candle as if his mind was far away.

'Ma ...'

'Keep your foot still, Benjamin! I've packed your things in the small box; your nightshirt at the bottom, then your other things; on top I've put your best trousers and the new shirt. Put the new shirt on on Friday but take it off again after the magistrate has seen you. Put it back neatly in the trunk. Don't crumple it up.'

'I won't.'

'And Dawid's lending you his best coat. Don't put it on on

Friday, though; put your old shirt on underneath the new one if it's cold, your flannel shirt too if you want to.'

'Yes, Ma.'

'I'm tying five shillings in the cloth for you, leave it in the trunk. Just in case.'

'In case of what?'

'In case the magistrate asks you whether you have money. He must see the Komoeties aren't penniless.'

'And what if ma needs it?'

'I won't need it till Saturday. But don't you go and spend it, you bring it back as it is. You'll have enough food.'

'What if I lose the money?'

'Then I'll wallop you.'

'What if they take it?'

'Better not make trouble. Don't bother about it.'

In the room next door she heard Kittie sniffing. She knew the others were listening to every word that was said. Selling's hands kept fiddling nervously.

'Fiela . . .'

'What is it, Selling?'

'I wonder if it wouldn't be better if he called the magistrate "your worshipful lord"?'

Your worshipful lord. It sounded very good and respectful.

'Has pa been before a magistrate?' Benjamin asked. She saw Selling panic and almost did so herself. 'Tollie says pa have been in jail.'

She thought her heart was going to stop beating. 'If you say your father has been in jail when you stand before the magistrate, there will be trouble!'

'I didn't say I'd say, Ma.'

'Jesus!'

'I won't tell, Ma.'

She got up at daybreak, made the fire, put the water on for coffee, buttered the bread, made sure the child's things were ready. Her head felt light, she had not slept. She had told God, if he saw her child safely back again, she would take half of Kicker's plumes in August and give it to the church at the village. And when the ostriches had mated, she would take the three strongest chicks, sell them and take that money to the church as well. God knew her, He would know she would not make promises just because she was so worried.

The others got up one after the other and came into the kitchen. They did not talk much. Benjamin ate his bread and drank his coffee and his eyes were full of tears. He looked frightened. When Selling started to cry, she went outside and waited till the light of the horse-cart lantern could be seen down the road in the Kloof. Then she went to wait inside.

The tall one was curt, he did not greet any of them. Tollie and Dawid had to lift Benjamin on to the cart; he would not get on by himself.

7

Where the narrow, winding road went over the top of Avontuur Mountain, they stopped to let the horses blow for the first time. The short one got down to put out the lantern.

'Don't you want to get down too, sonny?'

He put the box down beside him on the back seat, stepped carefully over the front one and got off.

He was shivering because it was very cold.

Far behind them, to the north, the hills were bluish-black in the dawn; where the sun was coming up, the sky was coloured red.

Sometimes, on a Sunday, and when it was a very clear day, they took a short cut along the hills from Wolwekraal to the top of Avontuur Mountain to go and look at the sea in the distance. If it was at all hazy, you could not see the sea. But if it was very quiet and the breeze came from the east, you could even hear the sea as well. Tollie always said it was the wind in the broom bushes they heard, but his mother said it was the sea. The place where the ships came in through the Heads up the Knysna River lay to the south. It was hard to believe, for to the south was nothing but mountains. To the west as well.

'Where does the Forest start then?' Dawid always wanted to know.

'Behind those mountains.'

They started going again. As long as the two men did not speak to him, it was not altogether bad.

'Are you warm enough, sonny?' the short one asked.

'Yes, master.' It was cold. They had a thick blanket over their legs and he had folded Dawid's coat round his.

'You will have to stop saying *master*, you're among white people now.'

'Yes, master.'

They looked at each other and laughed. His mother had said he was not to call the magistrate master, but she had said nothing about the others.

He was worried about Pollie. If she did not stop her nonsense, Kicker would never take her and then they would not have chicks. His mother had said, when the ostriches had chicks, many things that were crooked would get straightened out.

The road kept on along the mountain ridge for quite a long time and the horses trotted easily with the cart. When Tollie and Dawid had had to lift him on to the cart he had kicked and screamed but when his mother had started crying, he had stopped.

The tall one was still cross; perhaps it was because his mother had told him it would be straight to hell with him if Benjamin were not back in the house on Saturday.

He could not see around him very well; the hood of the cart was still raised and the two men on the front seat filled up most of his view of the road.

As long as the magistrate did not ask him the nine times table. One times nine is nine. Two times nine is eighteen. The fear of the magistrate came over him like nausea; no matter how hard you swallowed, it came back again. Three times nine is ... He started counting off the answer on his fingers: nineteen, twenty, twenty-one. But he got no further. Beyond the horses' heads the world suddenly tumbled forward and down the mountain side, with the road zigzagging down to the bottom. He grabbed hold of the seat on both sides of him and cried:

'Must we go down there, master?' It was surely the place where the post-cart had overturned and killed one of the passengers.

They looked at each other again and laughed, and the short one turned round.

'How else did you think we would get down?'

Did the cart have a brake? He had not seen a brake. The pedlar's wagon had a brake.

'Master, has this cart got a brake?'

'Where have you heard of a horse-cart with a brake?' the short one asked. He pointed at the horses. '*There* are the brakes.'

It seemed as if the horses were holding back the cart with their backsides, as if they were pulling back in the harness to keep the cart and themselves from tumbling down the mountain.

'Master, I want to get off!'

'Sit down!' the tall one scolded.

He held on to the seat with one hand and opened the trunk with the other one; the best would be to get the five shillings in his pocket and at least save that should everything else be wrecked.

'I want to get off, master!'

The short one turned round again. 'Don't shout like that, lad, you're scaring the horses.'

He clenched his teeth but the fear kept on making noises in his throat. He should have listened to Dawid, Dawid had told him to run away. But then his mother said the best would be if the magistrate and the forest woman had a look at him so that he could come back home again.

One times nine is nine. Two times nine is eighteen. Three times nine is – nineteen, twenty, twenty-one, twenty-two; he counted down nine fingers. Three times nine is twenty-seven. How far was it to the magistrate's? His father had said it would take them till dark to get there by cart.

The road gradually got whiter. Later on the dust was like dry, white lime; the wind blew the dust against the bushes and it lay like ash over everything. Three times nine is twenty-seven.

On the next bend it seemed as if the horses' feet were treading the air, so near to the precipice did they tread as they went round with the cart.

'Please, master, I want to get down! I want to go home!' They did not take notice of him, they just laughed. 'Please, master!'

The tall one turned round sharply. 'Stop it now!' he said. 'We don't want trouble with you all the way, we've had enough difficulty in fetching you. If the constable had come to fetch you, you would have had a few good slaps by now. Keep quiet now and stop shifting about in your seat!'

'I want to go home, master. Please, master.'

'Stop your whining!'

He should have run away as Dawid had said.

Down at the foot of the mountain they came to a narrow, wooded ravine where the horses rested again. The short one got down to see whether the harness was still secure. When he lowered the hood, the world was lying open around them and the road along which they had come down the mountain was held up by stone walls all along the side of the mountain. Giant stone walls which only God could have built up there like that.

The road along the ravine was level and not so bad. But after about an hour, they were heading straight for another mountain – perhaps there would be a big hole through the mountain for the road and the cart. Three times nine is eighteen. No. The nearer they came to the mountain, the barer and rougher it looked.

'Is the road coming to an end out front there, master?'

'No. Sit still!' The tall one was still cross.

The road started to turn. Gradually. The more it turned, the wider the mountain split apart. The nearer they came to the split, the more it seemed as if it were two mountains, standing so close together that there would hardly be room for the horse-cart between them.

When the road turned in between the mountains it tumbled down a slope with the most frightening, soaring cliffs on either side. He knew they could never get down there without brakes, they would definitely be killed.

'Master, I want to get down!'

They did not look round or laugh. As the horses were taking the first bend, the short one threw himself to the middle and lay like that until they had rounded the bend.

'Master, I want to get down!'

Round the next bend the tall one threw *his* body to the middle of the seat. It was not two mountains; it was one mountain that had been rent in two, and the deeper they went down into the chasm, the higher the cliffs became on each side. A stream of water rushed along beside the road over boulders and waterfalls; at times they were high above the stream, then down below it and then alongside it again. Enormous stone walls held the road to the sides of the mountain. Every so often, the road crossed the water on a narrow wooden bridge over which the horses' hooves and the cart's wheels made a different, rumbling sound. Deeper and deeper they drove into the mountain's belly. The road was a red-brown snake twisting and searching for a way out.

'Master, if a cart comes the other way we're dead!'

On some of the bends the road was so narrow that he was sure the cart had gone round with one wheel in the air. White, foamy sweat broke out on the horses' backs. Everything around them became the same red-brown colour: the road, the rocks, the stone walls, the dust. Upright and upside-down became the same feeling – only the streak of sky above the gash was blue.

When the road found its way out of the mountain, his head was giddy. They came to a ford where the horses pulled and tugged them through and on the other side they unharnessed.

They were in a ravine once more. In front of them was yet another mountain. A higher one.

'Whichever way I look, it's just mountains, master!' he said to the short one.

'This is De Vlugt and the mountain you see ahead of us, is De Vlugt Mountain. It's a tough one.'

The two men ate. He was not hungry. He wanted to cry and he wanted to go home. Before they had come to pick him up, Emma had said he must lie down on the floor and pretend to be dead, but he was afraid they would tickle him and see he was lying. He should have done what Dawid had said. But it was too late.

When they were on their way again, the road gradually became steeper. As the road climbed higher, so did the stone walls. The horses strained in the harness, they pulled more and more slowly. It was not long before the tall one had to stop them and let them rest again.

'Sonny,' the short one said, 'this is De Vlugt Mountain that I told you about. Before we get to the top, the horses will have to climb many a steep slope; they'll be having a hard time. You will have to get down and walk because the lighter the cart is, the better. The moment we start going down, you can get on again.'

He took his box and started to climb down but the tall one immediately started scolding. 'Where the hell are you taking the box?'

'I thought the other master said you wanted the cart lighter.'

'Put the damn thing down!'

He fell in behind the cart and kept up quite easily. It was better to walk. The only difficulty he had, was that his throat and eyes were burning with the tears he had to keep back all the time. Dawid had told him not to cry. Not in front of white people. One times nine is nine. Two times nine is eighteen.

The road was covered with small round ironstones with sharp ones in between. How long still was it to Saturday? Two nights' sleeping. When they came back, every uphill would be downhill and every downhill uphill. He would have to walk a lot. But they could just bring him as far as De Vlugt, he would get home on his own from there.

The magistrate only wanted to see whose child he was, whether he was the forest woman's child. He was Fiela Komoetie's child;

all he had to do was to go and tell it to the magistrate. Kittie had said Master Petrus or Miss Baby could have written a letter to the magistrate to say that he was Fiela Komoetie's child but his father said the letter would take too long to get there. The post-cart only came every second week.

His feet started to burn like fire inside the shoes, the shoes no longer fitted him, they had shrunk or something. And then he could no longer keep back the tears.

Every time one of the men on the cart looked round, he hung his head so that they would not see he was crying. He did not want to cry, but he could not help it. And he started falling behind because his feet were burning more and more in the shoes and he was sure they were bleeding. Tollie had said he wanted to borrow the shoes when he got back; he wanted to go dancing at Avontuur with Siena Jakoos. If his mother found out about it, there would be trouble for Tollie. She always said the Komoeties don't mix with all sorts and they did not mix with Uncle Jakoos and his family. Tollie could have the shoes, though.

'Don't get too far behind, sonny!'

Go to hell, he shouted back in his heart.

When the tall one stopped the horses to let them blow again, he sat down and took off the shoes. Fortunately, his feet were not bleeding yet, they were just very red. His mother had told him to keep the shoes on so that the people could see the Komoeties were decent people and wore shop shoes. His father only made their yard shoes.

'Seems to me you've been crying?' the short one said.

'I haven't – how far is it still, master?'

'To where?'

'To Knysna, master.'

'We're not even half-way yet, lad!'

'What time is it then, master?'

'Twelve o'clock.'

When he fell in behind the cart again, the tears came in torrents and he had to wipe his face on Dawid's coat to see where he was going. His feet, without the shoes, were as bad as when he still had them on. Worse. His mother had scrubbed off all the tough skin and the stones were sharp. And Dawid was going to be cross because of the snot on his coat, he would have to wash Dawid's coat.

And they were not even half-way yet. How would he ever make it? One times nine is nine.

He climbed up on the sides of his feet when they told him to get on again.

'I thought those shoes would pinch you,' the tall one said, laughing.

On the other side of the next mountain, the horses were unharnessed again. He was not hungry yet.

'Are we half-way now, master?'

'Yes. A little over half-way; we should be in the Forest in about three hours' time – can you remember anything about the Forest?'

'No, master, I don't know the Forest.'

Before they got to the Forest, he had to get down twice to make the cart lighter. But there were not so many ironstones now and the road got whiter again, the stones in the walls too. If he stepped carefully and kept to the thick white dust at the side of the road, it was better for his feet.

By four o'clock the worst of the mountains was behind them, the peaks behind them were higher than the ones ahead.

'Why are you sniffing so?' the tall one asked after he got back in the cart.

'I don't know, master.'

'And *I* don't know how they are ever going to get you white again. You must learn to say *uncle*! You're white, not coloured!'

He did not like the tall one at all. The short one was not so bad. And his mother had said, God help both of them if they ever put a foot on Wolwekraal again after Saturday.

The sun was low down in the sky by the time the road turned into a green tunnel of trees and bushes.

'Is this the Forest?' His backside was sore from sitting.

'It's the beginning of the Forest,' the short one said, sounding worried.

Everything was suddenly different. The air smelled like the mud where the spring rose in the hills above Wolwekraal. Only more so, more damp. The breath in his nose was colder.

'Is this the Forest?' he asked again to make sure.

'Yes.'

It was beautiful. The most wonderful ferns were growing everywhere amongst the trees. His poor mother had a lot of trouble to keep the fern growing in the tin at the back door, and here they were growing under the trees. Not even in tins.

'Are there people living here, master?'

'Mostly woodcutters.'

'And elephants?'

'They're here somewhere.'

Everything sounded softer: the horses' hooves, the cart's wheels. There was no dust any longer, it was as if the dust was damp and stayed down.

They kept on driving through the Forest for a long time. The trees grew thicker and taller and closer together. If an ostrich got lost in those thickets, he thought to himself, he would not like to be the one that had to go and get it out. There were places where an ostrich would not even get through; his legs and his neck would get caught and he would be strangled – what the feathers would look like, he would not know. Rossinski would give them nothing for them.

Every time they stopped to let the horses rest, he could hear birds, although he could not see them. And he could only see bits of the sky through the treetops that came together high above the road. He wished that he could pull up a tree to plant next to the house for his father to sit under. And one for his mother's fern to grow under.

'Where are the elephants, master?' They did not answer him. There were no houses, there was no room for houses amongst the trees and the bushes that grew under the trees. 'Where do the people live then, master?' Again they did not answer him. They sat stiff as rods and as if they were on the lookout for something that might come out of the thickets.

Only when they stopped to light the lantern did the short one speak to him again.

'Sonny, from here on you've got to keep both your eyes open and help us watch out for the elephants.'

'Yes, master.'

But he must have fallen asleep after that, for when he woke up, the horses' hooves sounded different again. They were in a street between houses. The short one got off at one of the houses, and the tall one and he drove on alone to another house where a woman stood waiting under a verandah with a lantern in her hand.

She came up to the cart. 'I thought you had had an accident,' she said, lifting the lantern higher. 'Is this the child?' She stared at him as if she had never seen a human being before.

'Yes,' the tall one said, 'it's him.'

Fear welled up in him and made him feel sick again.

The walls inside the house were white. The woman kept staring at him.

'Put down your box, sonny. Are you hungry?'

'I've got food.'

'Would you like some coffee?'

'No, missus.'

When the tall one came back from outside she gossiped about him: 'He called me *missus*, Ebenezer, it's too terrible. Like a Coloured.'

Someone was walking the horses up and down past the window. The woman took him outside and showed him the water tank where he could wash himself and the place where he could pee. She left the lantern with him and went back into the house. The man walking the horses came past the tank and said, 'Good evening, young master.' It sounded funny. He knew he was white, but nobody had ever called him master. If Dawid and Tollie had been there, they would have killed themselves laughing.

Then the woman showed him where to sleep and gave him a candle. He ate some of the food in the trunk and tied the five-shilling coin back in the cloth. The Komoeties were not penniless.

The next morning his whole body was full of fear, but at least one night's sleep was behind him and only one more night lay ahead. He got up and put on his new shirt as his mother had said. Not the shoes, however. His feet were too sore. And the shirt's sleeves were too long, they kept on falling over his hands when his arms hung at his sides.

The woman gave him bread and coffee in the kitchen and he had to stand at the table while he ate. There were chairs. She came to stand in the door and kept looking at him again; the tall one came and stood behind her and they spoke English to each other.

'The lash marks on your legs, sonny,' the woman asked. 'Did they beat you?'

'No, missus.' She must be stupid. 'We're tapping aloe. We'll be tapping till next month, it's the thorns that scrape your legs like this. Missus should see what my brothers and sisters look like.'

The woman turned away and shook her head.

He went outside to wash his hands and stayed outside. It was better there. Then the man came and called him. It was time to go to the magistrate, he said.

One times nine is nine. Two times nine is eighteen. Three times nine is – he had forgotten what it was.

The houses of the village had thatched roofs and tin roofs like Uniondale's houses, the streets were just as full of holes too. When they reached the street at the top, a wagon drawn by weary oxen came down the street. It was loaded with huge blocks of wood. There were funny-looking people with the wagon, white people, but they looked very poor.

At the foot of the village lay the biggest pool he had ever seen. It was not the sea.

'Where's the sea?' he asked, remembering to leave out the *master*.

'If you look through those hills beyond the lagoon, you might see it.' The tall one was no longer cross. 'But stop looking back now. I want you to know that your life might change today and I want you to behave well. When the magistrate asks you a question, answer him respectfully and don't be difficult.'

'Am I going home tomorrow?'

'It depends on what happens in court today. Your ... er ... the people back in the Long Kloof must have told you about the child that disappeared here in the Forest years ago and that the mother of that child is coming to see whether you might be that child.'

'I'm not her child.'

'It's not for you to decide!' The tall one got cross again and started walking faster.

The magistrate's place was like a big school. With many windows and classrooms. A man came from one of the classrooms and spoke English to the tall one. A constable was standing in the passage, his buttons were much shinier than those of the constable in the Kloof. When the constable came up the road on his horse, he always had to hide under his mother and father's bed. Then the constable drank coffee in the kitchen, not knowing that he was under the bed. Just in case, his mother always said.

He kept his eyes on the man in the passage in case it was the magistrate. The constable came up to them and stood looking at him until the other man told them to go and wait in one of the classrooms.

His teeth were chattering from fear and the tears were choking him again. It was a large room with many wooden benches like a church and there was a pulpit too.

'Is this a church?' he asked the tall one.

'No. It's the courtroom. Sit there on the bench and sit still.'

'Was it the magistrate standing in the passage?' The tears kept on rising.

'No, it was his clerk. The magistrate is busy with other things. They're still waiting for the forest people to come – you can't cry now! You can't cry in front of the magistrate!'

'Will you take me home tomorrow?'

'Not if you cry.'

That stopped the tears and he went to sit down on the edge of the front bench.

'Is the magistrate very strict?'

'No. He's a good man and a clever man. Sit still now. Stay here – I'm going outside for a while.'

It was cold in the room. The cold crept up his legs and he wished he had Dawid's coat for he had forgotten to put on his old shirt or his flannel shirt underneath the new one.

One times nine is nine. Two times nine is eighteen.

Miss Baby had been very strict when it came to knowing your multiplication tables. She once made him neatly write into his sum book: 'Let not the learning of the tables sadden you, my lord. Be diligent, and sweet will be your just reward.'

8

'Good gracious, Barta, can't you walk a bit faster?'

'I'm coming, Elias, I'm coming.'

By the time they got to Jim Reid's Crossing the sun was already coming out and they had to be with the magistrate at ten. Really, he thought to himself, since the day the forester had come with the news that they had found the child, Barta had completely lost her wits. Lord knew, the news *had* been a shock, but you came round again and your mind started working again. But apparently not Barta's.

He had told the forester that it would be better if he went to the magistrate alone, as Barta never really went to the village. For Barta, to appear before the magistrate was much the same as being called upon to appear before the Throne. But the forester insisted that it was Barta the magistrate wanted in court. Him too, but particularly Barta.

He had wanted them to set out the day before and sleep at Knysna; from Barnard's Island to the village was half a day's stiff walk and the days were short. For them to be at the magistrate's by ten, they had to start out at four o'clock in the morning and for all you knew you might walk straight into an elephant at that time of the night. But Barta would rather be trampled by an elephant than sleep in the village.

'No, Elias, I don't sleep on a stranger's bed. The village is not my place, I don't know the people.'

'But I told you that my cousin Stefaans, the one that left the Forest years ago, works in the village. At the place where some of the wood is dipped into the creosote before they ship it. I'll just ask around a bit, I'll find him and he'll have a place for us to sleep.'

But she would not. And it had been a nuisance getting up at that time of the night and starting out in the cold. By the footpath as far as the sled-path, by the sled-path to Deep Walls where the gravel road started; had it not been for the lantern they would not have been able to see their hands before them, it was so dark. And he did not dare to take the short cut through the Forest to Goat Beard Crossing; if you met an elephant there in the dark it was as good as your own death standing there before you. In a sled-path you at least had the chance to run or to get up a tree. He told Barta not to throw down the lantern, should anything happen – it would start a forest fire.

He was far from being at ease about what had happened back in Stinkwood Kloof. Who says the bastards were not still waiting somewhere for him? It was said that if an elephant had his eye on you, he kept it on you. Not that they could have an eye on *him*, they could not have seen who had sawn the tree.

Barta was falling behind again. 'You must hurry, woman!' The nearer they got to the village, the more slowly she walked. 'I can't tell the magistrate we're late because you didn't want to sleep in the village!'

'Elias, suppose it's not Lukas?'

It was the hundredth time she had asked.

'But that is why we're on our way to the village, Barta, to go and *see* if it's him!'

'Will I still know him?'

'The first thing you do, is to stand stock-still and just look him over carefully. I'll have a look with you. The magistrate will allow us enough time.'

To hear, after nine years, that they had found a child that might be yours, was not news that you could take lightly.

And if it was the child they had found, only the Lord in Heaven could know how he had got over the mountain to the

Long Kloof. He himself had been there only once in his life when he went with Jeremiah Eye to deliver a wagonload of stinkwood to a man called Zondagh. And he nearly got into trouble with Jeremiah as well. For the wood buyer at Knysna, where Jeremiah always delivered his wood, came to hear of it and sent for Jeremiah. He asked Jeremiah to show him his trader's licence and Jeremiah took out his woodcutter's licence. The wood buyer said, that's for *cutting*, not for trading! Jeremiah was well aware of it, but playing stupid was his only chance, otherwise he could have been dragged before the magistrate, losing his cutter's licence as well.

Afterwards Elias used to say that people talked of the Long Kloof as being on the other side of the mountain, but it would be nearer the truth to say that it was on the other side of a wilderness of mountain peaks. That's why he had told Barta to stay calm and wait until they had seen the child.

But if it turned out that it was their child, it would be quite a thing to have three sons again suddenly. Barta had not got pregnant again after Lukas had disappeared; old Aunt Gertie reckoned it was the shock that did it.

Martiens said, if it was Lukas they had found, he would take him into his team – they were short of a young hand to do the odd jobs for the woodcutters. He told Martiens they would have to wait and see first. If it was Lukas, he did not want to put him in a woodcutter's team straight away. Willem and Kristoffel were woodcutters already; perhaps he should take Lukas in with him making the beams.

'You must hurry up, Barta!' he called over his shoulder.

'Elias, won't you go ahead and tell the magistrate I can't make it? I think I'm going to faint.'

She was jittery because the village was getting nearer, he thought to himself. He said, 'It's because your stomach's empty, Barta; we can have something to eat before we enter the village. The magistrate will be very upset if I turn up alone and he's the one man on earth you mustn't anger.'

'That's why I feel so terrible, Elias, it's knowing that I must appear before him. It's not our way of doing things.'

'I know, Barta, but this is not like appearing before a magistrate because you're in trouble.'

'You can go by yourself, you'll be able to recognize the child without me. I'll hide somewhere here and wait for you.'

'It's no use talking, Barta, you will just have to go through with it.'

One thing about the woodcutters, even if he still sometimes got the feeling that they looked down on him, he had to admit that they stood by you when darkness descended on your house. Koos had come with his whole team and finished the beams for him, hauling them out to Deep Walls as well. Martiens had come and lifted the sweet potatoes and Dawid had carried them into the shed. You couldn't work when something like that happened. Anna had offered to keep an eye on Nina and Malie had lent Barta a pair of shoes.

'Come on, Barta!'

It could not be ten o'clock by a watch yet, he reckoned; the sun showed it was about nine o'clock.

'Elias . . .' Barta caught up with him. She carried the lantern in her one hand and the shoes in the other. 'Do you think I'll recognize him, Elias?'

'You will.'

'And if it's not him?'

'Then you tell his honour and we go home and bear it as we bore it at the time that he disappeared.'

'How could a child, that small, have made it to the Long Kloof?'

'Nothing is impossible in the hands of the Lord, Barta.'

'How did he get through the ravines and the creeks?'

'The Forest was dry that year, Barta, the water was low.'

'They could have brought the child to the Forest. I could have looked him over there.'

'Stop grumbling, Barta, that was not how the magistrate

willed it. And anyway, you know how scared the village people
are of coming into the Forest. They don't like coming further
than the edge. Today we do as the magistrate wants because his
will is the law. And don't be timid when you stand before the
man, Barta. You have a way of mumbling when you're scared
or bashful; speak up when he asks you something. I want him to
get a good impression of us, one never knows when you will have
to appear before him again.'

'What do you mean?' she asked, stopping dead.

'Don't let yourself be frightened out of your wits by everything,
Barta! Come on! I only said that because one never knows
whether the forester's watching when you're setting traps. Everybody sets traps, for who can live without meat? But there are
times I get the idea that only Elias van Rooyen is being watched.'

'That's not true, Elias. They've never caught you yet, and it's
really only the little blue bucks they don't want the people to
catch; I don't think they bother much about the bush-bucks.'

'I just want you to make a good impression, Barta. One never
knows.'

He guessed it to be nearly ten o'clock when they came to the
crossroads east of the village where the gravel track turned
towards the village and the track from the hills to the sea and
Noetzie. He let Barta sit down to rest and they had some of the
sweet potatoes and ash-bread in the knapsack. When they were
finished, he hid the sack and the lantern under a camphor bush
because it would not look right to stand in the presence of the
magistrate with it. He would get it out when they came back
again.

'Put the shoes on now, Barta, we must go.'

'Elias?'

'Don't look so alarmed! If it's not the child, it's not the child,
and if it's him, then it is!'

'His eyes were blue, like Nina's. Not dark like yours and
Willem's and Kristoffel's.'

'You'll know him if it's him. Come.'

Malie's shoes were too big for Barta. With every step she gave, they flapped on her feet and after a while he could not take it any longer. Barta could not go walking up to the magistrate sounding like that. He would have to do something about it.

'Really, Barta, you sound like an ox! Take them off!'

'What will it look like if I go and stand barefoot before the magistrate, Elias?'

'You will not be barefoot and you won't sound like that either. Take them off! I've got an idea.'

He pulled up some grass from beside the road and stuffed it into the toe of each shoe until they fitted tightly on her feet and then it was better.

9

He waited and waited and waited.

When the tears started to well up and his nose pricked, the multiplication tables helped. Or he opened his eyes as wide as he could and counted the planks in the ceiling: twenty-seven. There were twenty-one benches.

People walked past in the passage but nobody came into the room. The tall one did not come back either. There was a man with big, slow steps and one of his shoes squeaked. Perhaps it was the constable. Perhaps they had forgotten about him. If he could find the road leading from the village to the Forest, he could find his way home. Perhaps Pollie had laid an egg already. Twenty-four hen's eggs to one ostrich egg. He always wanted to know who had stuffed the hen's eggs into the ostrich egg and counted them. If you wanted to bake a real nice sugar-cake, you had to have an ostrich egg, his mother believed. One day he and Dawid had had to watch the wild ostriches from the rock-rabbit cliffs in the aloe hills to see where they were laying. His mother had wanted an ostrich egg. On the fourth day, down below them in the valley and right there on the bare earth between the stones, the stupid ostrich sat down, scrabbled herself a hollow with her body and started laying. When she got up, they could see the big white egg from where they were sitting. She shook her feathers, sat down again and when she got up, there were two eggs.

'We can go home now,' Dawid said, 'we know where her nest is.'

'Why don't we take ma an egg?'

'You heard what ma had said, we must just watch out for the nest, she'll come and get the egg herself.'

He tried to talk Dawid round. 'Maybe there won't be as good a chance tomorrow, look where the other birds are grazing, they're not even near the nest.'

'It's obvious that you've never seen how fast an ostrich can run.'

That was before they had had Kicker and before he knew much about ostriches. People sometimes came and shot the wild birds to get the feathers because you could not drive a wild ostrich between poles and pull a sack over its head to cut its feathers, they were too dangerous for that.

He tried to persuade Dawid. 'What if somebody comes and shoots the ostriches or one of the Laghaans comes and steals the eggs?'

'It will be quite some time before that hen's finished, she won't stop laying until she has at least twelve eggs under her.'

'Does she count them?'

'Yes.'

Dawid had wanted to go home but Benjamin wanted to take an egg to his mother. 'Come on, Dawid. I'll take the thorn branch and drive her from the nest and while I keep her away, you grab the egg and run.'

'Oh yes?' Dawid asked, annoyed. 'And then the ostrich chases the one with the egg, and that's me?'

'Very well then, you take the branch and get her off the nest and I'll grab the egg,' he volunteered. 'Or we can each take a branch.'

'The one that grabs the egg will need both his hands, it's too slippery and heavy for one hand only.'

'I'll grab the egg. Just think how pleased ma will be.'

'Fine then. But take a branch in case and don't throw it down before the last moment. If something happens and the ostriches go for you, fall down flat on your stomach and hold your head with your arms, let them tread on you, but don't let them kick you open with their toes. Don't try to run away.'

His father always said, as long as there was a whitethorn branch between you and an ostrich, you were safe. They took two of the branches they had brought with them from the house and started creeping down the hill, hiding behind the branches.

'The ostriches will think we're walking trees,' he whispered to Dawid.

The one with the squeaky shoe came down the passage and stopped right in front of the door. Two times nine is eighteen. Three times nine is twenty-seven – cold, together with fear, kept going through his body – the squeaky shoe went away again.

He and Dawid had been about five aloes' lengths away from the bird when she suddenly stretched out her long neck.

'Run, Dawid! Get her off!' he shouted, throwing away his branch. 'Frighten her and drive her off!' When Dawid rushed at her, the bird got up from the nest and stood over the eggs with her wings spread out. 'Get her off!' Dawid rushed at her, yelling and waving his branch; she took a few steps on the spot and then went to stand on the far side of the nearest aloes. 'Keep your eye on her, Dawid!' He ran forward and grabbed the first egg, but he had hardly got the egg in his hands when Dawid shouted:

'Run, Benjamin! The male bird's coming!'

The egg was warm and slippery but he held it tight to his body and ran for the hills. There was no time for picking up his branch or looking back to see how far behind him Dawid and the ostrich were. And no time to care how his clothes got caught and torn, or the skin on his legs. He would not stop and fall down on his stomach for then what would happen to the egg?

Nobody could ever beat Tollie at running, but that day he would have easily outrun Tollie; he did not stop before he was safely up at the first rocks.

When he looked back, Dawid was standing down below, roaring with laughter. The hen ostrich was back on the nest and the other ostriches were grazing peacefully in the valley. Dawid had lied to him.

'Bloody stupid!' he screamed at Dawid. His arms and his legs were on fire from the scratches and his clothes were ruined. He put down the egg, and threw stones at Dawid until he hit him and he stopped laughing.

It was late when they got home. His mother took one look at the egg, took down the strap from behind the door and beat their backsides well for them.

The next day she baked a sugar-cake with the egg.

'Ma can't deny it, ma was pleased about the egg,' he said as he licked out the bowl.

'You could both have been dead.'

'Ma gave me more lashes than ma gave Dawid. It's not fair.'

'You grabbed the egg, your death was closest.'

'Kittie says ma's baking the cake for me. Is it true?'

'Yes.'

'Why are you baking me a cake?'

'Because it's going to be your birthday tomorrow.'

'How do you know?'

'The black crow came and told me.'

Always, when his mother did not know or did not want to tell, she said the black crow came and told her.

He was sure that they had forgotten about him. He got up carefully and went to sit on the bench in the second row. After a while he moved back another row. In the end he was right up at the wall at the back and that was much better. He would tell his mother that he had been in a place just like a church. The day Dawid and Tollie had been confirmed in the church at Uniondale, he went with them but his mother never took him again after that. She said it was because he had kept on looking round. Emma said that was not true, it was because he was white and the people had kept looking at him. Then Emma had to clean the chicken-coop by herself as punishment.

If they had forgotten about him and locked the doors, he would climb through a window. The trouble was the box. He could not go home without the box – Dawid's coat and all the other things were in it. Fortunately he had put the five shillings in his pocket again.

There were more people outside in the passage suddenly, more doors opened and closed. Then it was quiet again. For a long time. Then the door of the room he was in opened and he jumped. A man in a black suit and a shirt with a very stiff front came in.

'Why so far back, lad?' the man asked and went to stand in front of the pulpit. 'Come up here.'

It felt as if fear was in his legs and he could not move. He knew it must be the magistrate.

'Come to the front and tell me what your name is.' The man peered over his spectacles; he did not look strict, but he didn't look friendly either.

'Benjamin Komoetie,' he said as he stopped half-way down the aisle.

'Come closer, I cannot hear you.'

He walked to the front, coughed, and said it again. 'Benjamin Komoetie.'

The constable came in as well and went to stand at the front bench, looking at the ceiling.

'Are you cold, lad?' the magistrate asked.

'No.' He wondered when he had to say your worshipful lord.

'Very well then, Benjamin, I am now going to ask you a few very simple questions – I want you to answer them clearly for me.'

The cold moved up to his knees, his legs started trembling and he could not keep them still. On top of that, the magistrate had looked down at his bare feet and he knew his mother would be cross when she heard that he had stood there without his shop shoes on.

'Are you sure you're not cold?'

'It's nothing, your worshipful lord.'

The magistrate's cheeks sucked in and bulged out again. 'Can you remember a time when you had another name? When you were still very small.'

'My name has always been Benjamin Komoetie.'

'Fine. Can you remember anything *before* you arrived in the Long Kloof? Anything at all?'

His knees felt as if they were giving way. 'No, your worshipful lord.' He kept his eyes on the man's face as his mother had said he must do.

'Maybe you can remember a cat or a dog you had. When you were very small. Perhaps you can remember your dog's name or what he looked like?'

'We had a dog once, but the tiger killed him. The tiger killed our goat and then Master Petrus Zondagh brought his spring-trap and set it, and when the tiger was trapped, he was not quite dead and bit our dog's throat.' The magistrate sighed and looked up at the ceiling. Perhaps he had not answered correctly. 'Now my mother doesn't want to get another dog for Wolwekraal – she's afraid he'll chase the ostriches.'

'Let's forget the dog. I want you to think back as far as you can and tell me everything you remember.'

'I can't think so well when I'm scared, master.' The words just came out. And the magistrate's cheeks bulged in and out again, like the tapping beetle's back when you pressed it in a little. He did not understand what it was the magistrate wanted him to remember. He did not want to keep on standing there any more, he wanted to go home. Perhaps the magistrate was cross because he had forgotten to say your worshipful lord.

'You need not be scared, lad, I just wanted to make sure whether you remembered anything. It does not matter if you don't remember things – come, stand a little farther forward and stay there.'

The constable opened the door and called something down the passage. The magistrate got on to the pulpit, sat down and folded his hands in front of him. Then four boys came into the room, pushing one another and laughing. They came and stood on both sides of him. They all had shoes on and they were all as big as he was. He suddenly wished his shirt's sleeves were not so long and that they did not hang over his hands – the children might think he did not have hands. And he could not understand what was going on. His mother had said that the forest woman would come and look at him, that he must keep still so that she could do so and get it over with and then he could go back home. Nobody had said anything about other children.

'Silence, please!' The magistrate looked at them crossly. 'You know why you're here and I don't have to remind you that this is a serious matter. You will behave yourselves and stay where you are until I dismiss you.'

The magistrate motioned to the constable and the constable left the room. Down the passage a door opened, someone came down the passage very slowly and then a funny-looking woman came into the room, together with the constable. It was a white woman. Her dress was greyish-black and most of her hair was pushed in under a headcloth. She was very scared. He could see it. At first she just stayed standing at the door without looking up.

Then the magistrate spoke very kindly to her. 'Come closer, Mrs van Rooyen, come close to them and take your time. Look as long as you want to.'

When she looked up, she just glanced at the other children before she came forward and pointed her finger straight at him; then she turned round and started crying.

Many other people came crowding in the door and whispered amongst themselves. A poorly dressed man pushed his way through them and came and stood next to the woman. She pointed at him again and the man stared at him as if he had had a shock. The tall one came into the room too, and went up to the magistrate and said something to him. The magistrate called the constable and said something to him, and then the constable told all the people to leave the room. Then he and the magistrate were alone again.

'Lad ...' The magistrate took off his spectacles and leaned forward. 'Do you understand what has just happened here?'

'Can I go home now, your worshipful lord?' He was suddenly very scared. 'Is the forest woman finished now?'

The cheeks bulged in and out. 'I don't think you really understand. Many years ago a child disappeared in the Forest, the child of the woman who was here a moment ago. The possibility that you could be that child was very great, but I had to make sure first. I sent for the woman, and I sent for you as well. Then I put you between four other boys so that it would be difficult for her to pick out her own child. But she came in and recognized you without a hint of doubt. Do you understand now what that means?'

'I'm Fiela Komoetie's child,' he cried. Something was very wrong.

'Wait, lad, this has not been an easy task for me. At the beginning you will find it strange to be back amongst your own people but you will soon get used to it. I am very disappointed, though, that no one reported that you were there with the Coloured people in the Long Kloof.'

'I'm Fiela Komoetie's hand-child.'

'I beg your pardon?'

'I'm her hand-child. The good Lord gave me to her.' He was suddenly as afraid as on the day his boat had drifted too deep out into the pool. When he tried to reach it, there was suddenly only water around him. His feet could not touch the ground and every time his head came above the water, he was pulled down again. Then Tollie was there and Tollie helped him to where he could stand again. 'I'm Fiela Komoetie's child, your worshipful lord. I swear to it, master. The forest woman's lying if she says I'm her child.'

The magistrate came down from the pulpit and came and stood right in front of him. 'You are not Fiela Komoetie's child. I think you are big enough to realize it yourself and that is why I don't want you to be unnecessarily difficult. You are going home with your parents now and I will be inquiring regularly how things are going. One day, when you've grown up, you will come back and thank me for this day.'

'I'm Fiela Komoetie's child, master, we're not penniless people, I swear. I have five shillings to prove it.' He was saying everything round the wrong way because he had to hurry for the magistrate was already on his way to the door. 'Please, master!'

'I never want to hear you use the word *master* again! You're a white child and you will learn to speak like a white child.'

'Please, your worshipful lord, I'm Fiela Komoetie's child and Selling Komoetie is my father!'

But the magistrate did not believe him.

10

Friday.

The north-west wind had died down, and the aloe sap was flowing like water. Fiela's hands worked but her heart was on the other side of the mountain with Benjamin. As long as they did not frighten him, she kept on hoping. Not that he was a child that could be frightened easily, it's just that he was not used to strangers. She had always said to Miss Baby, should anything happen to her, Miss Baby must take him and bring him up. Miss Baby had promised her she would. Auntie Maria would also take him, but Miss Baby would be better.

They started tapping early that morning. Before long the yellow sap flowed into the receptacles and the bitter fumes rose into her nostrils. Like the bitterness rising in her body.

There was no way she could have stopped them, she kept telling herself. The short one came and started it, and then the tall one followed and took it back over the mountain with him to be scratched over and opened up. And *her* child was to be inspected like a lamb for the slaughter.

But the worst was to pass the time until Saturday – and to keep a check on the anger growing inside her.

'They've been grazing peacefully in the enclosure the whole day, Fiela,' Selling said when she and the children got back from the aloe hills that night. He had been watching the ostriches; had they started fighting there was not much he could do, but at least the birds knew that someone was keeping an eye on them.

Selling had done little during the day. She let it pass. Selling could no longer take suffering that made demands on his strength.

The house felt empty. They had an early meal and went to bed. She slept a little during the early hours of the morning and when she woke up, she felt a little easier, because it was Saturday.

And she would not be silly and stand at the corner of the house the whole day to watch the road, she decided. That way all your blood went to your feet and your head became empty and stupid. They would work to get through the day; Knysna was a long way off and they would not be back with him before dark.

The children were slow and Selling was full of pains.

'We can't stop now, we must keep going!'

'The aloe finished us yesterday, Ma,' Tollie said.

'Me too. Dawid, take down the shutters, Tollie, you and Emma can start carrying out all the stuff – everything in this house is to go out in the sun and be cleaned today. Fodder must be fetched for the ostriches, we must kill a chicken and we must treat the fowls' legs with paraffin.' Selling sat with drooping shoulders at the table. When he looked like that, she knew she had to get him to his feet. 'You can go outside now, Selling, the sun's out and the whips must be made today.'

'I can't even hold my head up this morning, Fiela, let alone work.'

'Your head will come right when it gets a bit of sun. Your hands too. This is a day when we must not lie down!'

The will to work and to keep all the others working was part of the fight going on inside her. At times she even went up to the ostriches to scold on them.

'Good-for-nothings! All you can do is eat! Why don't you do something to earn your fodder at least!' Kicker was more handsome than ever. 'I want at least twelve eggs from you and I'll wring your necks if you break even one of them. Twelve chicks I want to see running round the house. During the day Pollie will sit on the nest and during the night, Kicker – in case you don't know how you are supposed to do it.'

She had things planned far ahead. The Laghaans could not last much longer. Drinking shortened your span bottle by bottle. They would have to give notice. And on that day there had to be enough money in Wolwekraal's chest for her to be able to go to Koos Wehmeyer for the title-deed. And the land would be put in Benjamin's name.

But then the ostriches had to start breeding. Petrus had paid twelve pounds for two young chicks at Oudtshoorn. Twelve pounds. It was enough to make you more impatient than ever. And Petrus had told Selling he would buy every chick Kicker sired and which they did not want to keep for themselves. The first three chicks were God's, after that she would select her own and Petrus could have the rest. Five pounds a chick.

Later in the day she had a fire made in the clay oven outside and baked a sugar-cake. When she looked round, Selling was standing beside her.

'Have you finished the whip you were working on?'

'Almost. I'm just stretching my legs a bit.'

'The work must get done, Selling.'

'Yes, Fiela – Fiela, I've worked it out, if they started out at daybreak, they could be here with him just after dark.'

'I've worked it out like that too.'

'That's if they keep their word.'

'Don't be a Job's comforter, Selling! We must have faith.'

'Yes, Fiela.'

She did not like the way he stood there, his arms dangling at his sides. 'What are you standing there like that for, Selling? Get back to your work and stop imagining things.'

'It's just that there is so much uncertainty in me, Fiela.'

'Do you think it isn't in me too? Don't you think the Devil chose this day specially to come and tempt us? He always waits for the day you only have your faith to cling to to do his work. The more idle he finds you, the easier it is for him to strangle you. Go and finish the whip and kick the Devil in the arse.'

'You always say you get a feeling about things, Fiela. I came

97

to ask you what your feelings are saying about Benjamin today.

'I dare not listen to my feelings today, Selling, the confounded Devil keeps barging in on me!'

When the sugar-cake was turned out on the kitchen table, the sun went down in the west and for the first time that day she could no longer repress her dread.

Dear God, she prayed as she walked to the hills above the house, I'm in a bad way now. One moment I see the horse-cart coming through De Vlugt poort* and the next moment I see nothing. Not even a puff of dust. Then the Devil tells me they're not even on their way. Please God, this is not the first time you and I have had to go through deep affliction here at Wolwekraal; the trouble is, this time I'm not a young woman any more and this time it's Benjamin. Wolwekraal is bare without him, God.

The crickets started chirring, and down at the pool the first frog croaked. How many times had the child tried to get hold of a frog to put on his boat as an oarsman!

'Then ma will see how we row the shit out of the beetles!'

'Benjamin! Don't you come talking like a Laghaan!'

The first stars came out. Down at the house one of the children had lit a candle and the yellow glow was like warmth in the open door.

Please God, if they're on their way with him in this dark night, stay with them over the mountain, especially over De Vlugt Mountain and through the poort. In desperation she added: Better be with the two peace-breakers too.

'Are we going to eat or are we going to wait, Ma?' Kittie asked her when she got back to the house.

'We'll wait.'

They sat like chickens gone to roost and getting more and more quiet. Later on they just sat there at the table, and Selling's head slowly dropped lower. The nightjar came and called close

* Gorge.

to the house; down at the ostriches' camp the plovers flew screeching into the night.

'We will eat now,' she said when it had got very late. 'We'll eat and keep his food warm.'

Midnight. The others went to bed one by one but she stayed sitting at the table. It was as if she wanted to punish her body and make herself so tired that there would be no strength left in her for fear to get a hold on. As the hours passed, she stopped putting wood on the fire. When the candle wick drowned in the last bit of grease, she did not get up to light another candle, she just sat there in the dark until the red cock crowed.

Then she knew that they had lied.

'Perhaps they slept at De Vlugt again,' Selling said when he got up.

'Perhaps, yes.'

'Then they'll be here any time now, Fiela.' He went to stand at the corner of the house and watched the road, waiting and hoping.

But the Saturday went by and so did Sunday.

On Monday, at dawn, she got up and started getting ready.

'Ma?' Emma was the first to come and stand in the doorway. 'What are you doing?'

'I'm buttering the bread. Go and wake the others, there's a lot that has to be said.'

'Ma?' Kittie lingered at the door, anxiously.

'Go and get them out of bed!' Inside her, it was like a summer day when the earth became still under the scorching sun and the clouds soared above Potberg Peak carrying the storm that would follow.

They gathered round the candle, frightened, Selling at the back.

'I'm going to Knysna,' she announced.

'Ma?'

'Fiela?'

'How will ma get there?' Dawid asked.

'I have feet.'

'But ma can't go alone,' Tollie said, 'I'll go with ma.'

'Nobody's going with me, I'm going alone. Tollie and Emma must keep on tapping the aloes; Dawid, you and Kittie must start digging the field for the corn. The ostriches' enclosure must be cleaned and see that they get fresh fodder every second day. As from tomorrow, you can throw it in one place only so that they learn to eat from the same heap.'

'Fiela . . .' Selling seemed short of breath. 'Fiela, I've thought about the whole thing again, they'll bring him back today. I'm sure they just could not manage it over the weekend.'

'Then I'll meet them on the way and turn back, Selling. But I'm not going to sit around here till dark again just to find out that they haven't brought him.'

'Wait until tomorrow, Fiela.'

'No. Before the sun is out, I'll be on my way.' She knew they knew they could not argue with her. 'Don't milk the goat too early at night, Dawid. Selling, you must get ready for Rossinski. Kittie, see that Mr Rossinski gets something to eat before he leaves. I'll take the two shillings that are in the tin, you'll manage until Rossinski comes.'

Emma started to cry. 'When will ma be coming back?'

'I want to sleep at Knoetskraal tonight, or a little further on perhaps. By tomorrow evening I want to be in Knysna.'

'What can ma do?' Tollie asked.

'Do? I'm going to fetch Benjamin, that's what I'm going to do!'

'What if . . .'

'What if my foot!'

'But ma, what if Benjamin is the child that disappeared there?'

'Then I'll eat this table, legs and all.'

Selling kept fiddling with his hands. 'Fiela, if only I had the strength to go with you.'

'Don't worry, Selling, I'll manage.'

*

The man carried the box on his shoulder. The woman carried the shoes. A little way from the village they took a lantern and a knapsack from under a bush and the woman carried that as well.

At first they did not speak to him, they just kept looking at him as if they were afraid of him. He did not speak to them either, nor did he cry; he just walked.

When the constable had come to fetch him from the room, the tall man was standing in the passage with his box. The man and the woman and the magistrate came from another room and the tall one gave the box to the man. When they wanted to go, he stayed with his back to the wall but the magistrate got cross and told him not to be difficult.

Then they started walking.

His mother had said expressly that he was not the forest woman's child, that it was a lie. Now they came and said the woman was his mother and the man his father. They said his name was Lukas. His name was not Lukas. His name was Benjamin Komoetie. He had told the magistrate, he had shouted it at him when they all stood in the passage but nobody listened to him. Nobody would believe him.

They walked and walked along a road that crept deeper and deeper into the Forest. He wanted to ask where the elephants were, but he did not want to talk to them.

'Elias . . .' The woman still looked frightened. 'Don't you think he's tired?'

'Are you tired, Lukas?'

He just kept looking ahead of his feet. He was not Lukas. His mother had told the tall one he would go straight to hell if he did not bring back her child on Saturday. How was he to get home?

'Were the people in the Long Kloof good to you, Lukas?' the man asked.

He did not answer him, he just walked faster. But the man caught up with him.

'I see you have a nice shirt on. What's in the trunk?'

'My things.' Fortunately the five shillings was in his pocket.

The woman fell behind and the man had to hurry her on every now and again. Bits of her mole-brown hair came out from under her headcloth and hung like strings round her face.

He got tired, for the road was endless, but he would not tell them that he was tired. The man shifted the box from the one shoulder to the other.

'I think he's tired, Elias.'

'We can take a rest at Goat Beard Crossing.'

His mother had told him the day would come when only God could help them. He knew that this was that day, although he did not know where God was, but his mother would know. He knew he was white and his mother and father and Dawid and Tollie and Kittie and Emma, brown. He was white because he was the hand-child.

'Why is the child so speechless, Elias?'

'He's still feeling a bit strange, he'll come round.'

They talked as if they thought he could not hear them.

'He's a beautiful child, Elias.'

'Yes.'

'Is he not a bit thin though?'

'He's like Nina.'

The magistrate had said that from now on he was white again. He had always been white. And they were not to think that he was going to stay in that Forest, he was not an elephant. He would find out which road they had come along from the Long Kloof and he would walk back home even if it took him a week to get there.

'Ask him if he's tired, Elias?'

'Are you tired, Lukas?'

His name was not Lukas.

'We'll have to stick to the road again, Barta, we won't make it home before dark.'

'You must let the child rest, he's tired. I can see it.'

They walked until they came to a clearing along the road. The man put the box on a log and sat down with the woman.

'Come, Lukas, come and sit with us,' the man called.

He did not want to sit with them, he squatted down beside the road with his back to them and wondered if it could be the road to the Long Kloof.

'Come and sit over here, Lukas!'

'Leave him alone, Elias, he's still shy.'

The man came and stood behind him. 'You must come and eat something,' he said.

He shook his head to make the man go away. He would never eat again. Not before he was home. He peeped through under his arms and saw the man's feet walk away. They opened the box and ate some of the food his mother had packed.

The house was made of wood. The table was four tree-stumps with smooth planks on top. There was a chair and he sat down on it because he was too tired to stand. They were somewhere deep within the Forest, it was dark and he was very scared for he did not know how he would ever get out of there again. It was like when you crawled into the crevices after rock rabbits to get at them with a stick and it got so narrow around you that you started sweating with fear.

Other people came, people looking like the man and the woman. The room was full of faces with eyes that gleamed in the light of the candle. Children gawked at him with mouths hanging open. One of the women kept on crying and saying that she had always known that he wasn't dead. An old woman without teeth and a poke-bonnet on stood in the corner at the hearth and she looked at him as if she was sorry for him. He would ask her to show him the way out of the Forest.

Some of the children came and touched him and he kicked them away.

'Leave him!' the old woman with the bonnet shouted at them. 'Can't you see he's done for and that he's scared!'

The old woman would show him where the road to the Long Kloof was, he just wanted to sleep first.

'Lukas,' the man said and stooped over him, 'look up and greet your brother Willem and your sister Nina.'

He would not look up.

'Leave him, Elias,' somebody said.

But the man lost patience. He had been getting more and more impatient on the way there. 'Greet your brother and sister, Lukas!'

'Leave the child alone, Elias!' the old woman scolded. 'He's bewildered as he is. He must first get used to being home again.'

It was like a door slamming shut. The old woman also believed he was Lukas, she would not show him the road. And the tears started running from his eyes and his nose and he could not stop them.

11

As Fiela began walking, the anger welled up in her. She would keep to the road in case they were on their way back with Benjamin.

Whenever she walked too fast, she slowed up; two days' walking lay ahead. Goliath Petro had walked to Knysna in little more than a day but Goliath Petro could outrun a mule. She would have to spare herself at the beginning. Not that she was afraid of the walk ahead, not Fiela Komoetie. And it was not the first time that she had crossed those mountains and ravines. There had been a time when she could find every short cut in the dark and knew every rock on the way ahead. But that was from another part of her life. A part she had shut off inside her ... Just shows you, she thought to herself, you could not say, I shall never come back here. For she had once sworn never to set a foot on that road again.

The walking was better than the waiting. The waiting would have driven her out of her mind.

Selling had been worried and restless while she was getting ready; he had stayed near her.

'Fiela,' he had said, 'listen to me! Don't go looking for trouble at Knysna, you know what you're like when you get angry. When you want something from a white man, you must stoop low. Slither through the dust like a snake and you make it easier for yourself. You can always dust yourself down again afterwards. But once you become obstreperous and they have to shove you into the dust, your case is lost.'

Selling was right. She would ask God to help her.

No. She was angry with God. It was no use telling herself what a sin it was to think like that, she was angry with God just the same. Mortal beings could not bargain with God and yet she wondered how God could have refused the three ostrich chicks, plus half of Kicker's feather crop, that she had promised him for Benjamin's safe return, when the church at Uniondale was always on the brink of bankruptcy!

Sorry, God.

Selling was right. She would start with the magistrate and if it was necessary she would lie down so that he could tread on her. Where else could she start? The child had appeared before him.

If only the devil did not keep on pestering her so! He knew very well she was angry with God and now he was grabbing his chance. One moment he told her the child had been killed in an accident on the way there. Then again that the child had jumped off the cart and had run away. Or the child had fallen ill. But the thing he plagued her with most of all was that someone had told them about Selling. Perhaps they had not really fetched the child to show him to the forest woman. Where had the two peace-breakers heard of the child not having been to school? That he did not go to church? Who else but the Laghaans would have told them? What else had they told them? For how many years had she stood between the world and Wolwekraal with the aid of the tongue God had given her? For how many years had she had to hold up her head when she felt like hiding it in the ground? And why? Because Fiela Komoetie had sworn that no one would see her and her children brought low. As time went by, she got more confident; she thought people would forget and bury the past, but they had not forgotten. When the two strangers came counting the people of the Kloof, they had been told of the child that had not been to school or to church. Would they have left out the other thing? No. And that was what was eating her inside. She did not fear the magistrate, nor the forest woman, it was Selling's past that stood against them.

For Selling had committed murder.

She had been pregnant with Emma at the time. Selling had murdered in December 1859 and Emma was born in February 1860.

She had been young and pretty when Selling Komoetie moved into the Kloof from far away in the Swartberg Mountains, to work for Petrus Zondagh as a harness-maker. There was not a Coloured man in the Kloof that could even match his shadow; he had had his own horse, his own saddle, and beautiful manners and ways. Every young girl lingered at the shop down at the crossroads from Avontuur hoping he would notice them when he came past from the old Zondagh homestead to his own rooms. But it was her, Fiela Apools, that Selling had chosen.

First Kittie had been born, then Dawid. People talked, and her mother went to see Petrus in his house and promised to smash Selling Komoetie's skull for him if Petrus did not do something about him. But Selling would not stay away from her. He was saving to set up house but times were bad; for three years running it had hardly rained in the Kloof. There was no money for getting married. When Tollie was born, Petrus came himself to talk to them and the following January she and Selling were married. Petrus drove the wedding-cart himself and gave them five pounds as a start. It was a lot of money. But on the other hand, Petrus had been afraid that he would lose Selling for Selling had heard from a man by the name of Barrington near the Knysna River who was looking for a good harness-maker. Not that Selling would have left his idol, Petrus Zondagh, but he wanted Petrus to know that others wanted him as well. That way you could make a white man realize how much he needed you. Especially a good white man.

It went well with her and Selling. Her mother had still been alive then and Selling moved in with them at Wolwekraal. In his free time he helped them till the land. Later on Selling became key-bearer for Petrus Zondagh and foreman when the Zondaghs went to the village for Communion or to the sea at Plettenberg Bay for a holiday at the end of the year. Selling was right-hand man to Petrus Zondagh and she was proud of him.

It was the day before Christmas; Petrus and his family were at the coast. Selling locked up early down at the homestead for he still had to come and slaughter the sheep for her. The sheep had been grazing with the goats in the valley below the house that morning but when Selling got home, he said he could only see the goats, where was the sheep?

How was she to know? The sheep had been there that morning. It was a lamb Petrus had given Selling the June before to fatten for Christmas; little did she know that it would turn into a trap set by the devil. Selling took the knife and went back into the blazing heat to look for the sheep.

He stayed away a long time and when he came back, it was without the sheep; she asked him where the knife was. It never occurred to her that something was wrong. Selling went and washed his hands at the stream, and she went up to him and asked if the sheep could perhaps have got in with Petrus's sheep. When Selling looked up, his face was strained and then it came out that he had seen something moving in Broom Reed Ravine and thought that it might be the sheep. When he got there, he found two of the Laghaans skinning the sheep.

Her father had always claimed that when a family of people are born bad, it was not long before they were rotten.

She caught a goose and killed it for their Christmas dinner. She told Selling to go to the village and report the theft of the sheep to the constable, for they could not just leave it at that. But Selling was acting as if he was trapped: he kept wandering through the house and seemed to want to kick the walls down. She thought it was because of the sheep.

The next day, on Christmas morning, two constables on horses came riding up to the house; it came out that Selling had stabbed Kies Laghaan with the knife when Kies tried to pretend that it was a Laghaan sheep they were skinning. And Kies had died during the night.

The world went black before her eyes.

If Selling had murdered a white man, if he had knifed Petrus Zondagh himself or burnt down the Avontuur homestead to the ground ... but it was on account of a good-for-nothing Laghaan that he was handcuffed and driven out before the horses like a beast that morning.

And Petrus was at the sea. There was no one that could go and plead for Selling. In the Kloof everyone had been dumbfounded that Selling Komoetie had committed a murder. The news was like a bone being passed from dog to dog to be gnawed a little barer each time.

The next day the funeral was like New Year's Day – they said only the preacher was sober.

And she went to the village on foot by the path over Jan Kole's Peak to speak for Selling, but it was in vain. It was murder. Selling had to appear before the hanging judge at Oudtshoorn.

It was as if the rope had been put round *her* neck and was getting a little tighter each day. She got so taut with fear that sleep and waking became the same thing; when awake her eyes were just open, when asleep they were barely closed.

Shortly after the beginning of the new year they took Selling away to Oudtshoorn. She was eight months pregnant with Emma. A week later Petrus and his family came back from the sea and heard about the murder for the first time. Petrus got on to his horse that very same afternoon and rode through the night to get to Oudtshoorn. What he said and did there, he alone knew, but Selling did not get the rope, he got a life sentence.

That was at the end of January. At the beginning of February Emma was born, the only time they had to call Dr Avis from the village for a birth. She had simply not had enough strength to get the child out on her own. And not until the end of March was she able to get up again. Petrus's wife Margaretha came every second day to see how she was getting on. Miss Baby too. At the beginning of April, Petrus himself came one morning.

'I've brought you news from Selling, Fiela,' he said when he sat down at the kitchen table.

She had to hold on to the table to stay on her feet. There was not a day or a night that Selling's face was not with her, that she did not wonder where he was, what was to become of her and the children.

'News of Selling?'

'Yes. He's behind the mountain where they're working on the pass. According to what I've heard, he is in one of the gangs working in the poort.'

Petrus might just as well have said Selling was home! For the first time since Emma's birth the milk shot into her breasts and filled them.

'Where they're making the road, you say?'

'Yes.'

Everybody knew about the road they were making from Knysna to the Long Kloof. It was said the road would result in the Kloof and the whole land to the north prospering as it never had before because it would be a short cut to the ships that came in to the Knysna River. But the road had not been finished, and people began to think that it would never be finished. The only road over the mountains was over Devil's Kop, miles away to the west, and the devil himself could not have chosen a better place to give his name to.

Then Petrus came and said Selling was making the new road over the mountains.

'I must go to him, Master Petrus.'

'You can't, Fiela. I will try and find out how he is from time to time.'

'I must go to him!'

'Feila, it is hard to accept, but Selling is a convict. There are many convict gangs with their guards beyond the mountain – it's no place for a woman.'

'I must see Selling.'

'Had I known you would be so foolish, I would not have told you.'

She poured Petrus some coffee and talked about other things. She told him about the corn they wanted to sow, she and her mother. Her mouth spoke the words but in her mind she was already heading for the mountain.

After Petrus had left, her mother came to stand between her and the mountain.

'You can't do it, Fiela!'

She kneaded the dough and baked the bread. She killed a hen. She packed coffee and sugar and lard, and let her mother talk on.

'What about the child? You must feed the child.'

'The child's going with me, Selling will want to see her.'

'What about the tigers in the mountain?'

'Tigers are afraid of people. You just have to see that you don't get between a tigresss and her young.'

'What about the convicts that escaped there last year? What if they're still hiding in the ravines?'

'They won't be there any more.' Nothing would stop her.

With the child tied on her back and Selling's food in the knapsack, she left early the next morning.

The first convict gang she came across was just behind Avontuur Mountain and she passed them by a roundabout route. Selling was not amongst them.

The veld was beautiful and the heather was still blooming. Brilliant patches of pink reed flowers covered the mountain slopes and sugar birds, wings whirling, hung suspended in the air, getting the sweet sap inside. When she came back, she would pick an armful for the house, she decided. There had been no flowers in the house for a long time.

Years ago, before she had married Selling, Mr Andrew Bain had surveyed and marked off the route through the Forest and over the mountains from Knysna to the Kloof. It had been a big event for the people of the Long Kloof. When he got to Avontuur, they had arranged a party for him such as they had never held before. Her mother had had to go and help down at the homestead with the preparation of the food. Her father had still been alive then. The night after the party, when her mother got home with lots of goodies that had been left over, she had a lot to tell. About all the people that had been there, about the speeches in which Mr Bain had been praised for the miracle he had achieved in finding a route from Knysna to the Kloof.

'What's so miraculous about that?' her father had asked. 'I would have done it for them just as well.'

'How can you say that?' her mother asked. 'Old Master Kerneels says it looks like hell itself on the other side of the mountain. He says he doesn't know how Mr Bain ever managed to find a route through the Forest without getting lost. And he won't be bringing the road from De Vlugt to Avontuur through Broom Reed Ravine – no wagon could get through there in any case – he's bringing the road through the poort where they say the mountain is split in two.'

'I would have done exactly the same,' her father insisted. 'The only difference is, they would not have held a party for me.'

'And how would *you* have done it?' her mother challenged her father, still siding with Mr Bain.

'Exactly like the clever Mr Bain did it. He did not find that route, the elephants found it hundreds of years ago.'

'What do you mean?'

'Andrew Bain may have driven in the pegs and got himself a party on top of it, but he did not find that route on his own. How do you think all Jakobus Wehmeyer's fruit trees and vines and rose trees got to the Kloof? They didn't fly here. My brother Apie and I carried them in wet sacks on our backs from the ships at Knysna and we did not go over Devil's Kop, we went straight over here at the back, following the old elephants' track. Jakobus, God rest his soul, took us to the top of Avontuur Mountain and showed us the path, and said we wouldn't get lost as long as we kept to it. It took a day and a half and we were half-dead, but we got there, to Knysna, and I saw a ship for the first time in my life. Huge white sails they had, like wings.'

'I don't understand this at all now,' her mother said. 'If there is a road, why would they want to make another one?'

'I never said it was a *road*, leave alone a wagon road. And I did not say Mr Bain was not a very clever road builder, I said it was an elephant track. How Mr Bain is going to make a wagon road out of it, I don't know. Especially through the split in the mountain you talked about. But I tell you those elephants were clever when they made that track; not a bend too sharp or a ravine too deep. Ages ago, they say, when the Kloof was still wild and the Forest had had too much rain in winter, the elephants brought their calves to the Kloof to get some sunshine for them. And I myself have walked the track they made then.'

Not long after that they heard that they had started making the road. The years went by, but nobody ever said anything about the road being finished.

She had kept to the old elephant track until the sun was right above her head. Then she sat down to rest and fed the child while she looked round her carefully. She could not be far from the split in the mountain, from the poort where Petrus had said Selling would most probably be. Her common sense told her that she would not be able just to walk up the poort and start looking for him. What about the guards and the rest of the convicts? She would have to make her own route up the mountain ahead of her; at the top she would turn east and follow the ridge to the split where she would be able to look down from above and see where he was.

She took the child away from her breast, secured her on her back again and started climbing.

Before she was half-way up the mountain, she realized that

she had taken on a rough and difficult climb and that it was steeper than it had seemed from the bottom. But she did not want to turn back, for how else could she get there? At places it was too dangerous to go straight ahead and then she was forced to find another way round; she hurried on and stumbled often because the sun was already past its highest. How far west of the split was she? A mile? Two? Three? Before she got to the top, she gradually started veering east in the direction where the split should be and tried to gain time and distance that way. It was thickly overgrown and the bushes caught at her; ticks kept landing on her, which forced her to stop every so often and get them off her dress before they could get to the child.

It was when she stopped to get the ticks off again that she heard the sound of pickaxes in the distance, to the south of her. Not to the east where she had been expecting it. And it meant that she had to climb higher still.

When she came to the top of the mountain, she kept going south and the further she walked, the more clearly the split opened up ahead of her: the mountain had not cracked open like an over-ripe watermelon, it had somehow been torn apart.

The nearer she came to the gash, the deeper down into the earth the noise of pickaxes and sledge-hammers seemed to be. For the last few paces she went down on her knees and hands and crawled to the edge of the abyss that gaped in front of her, afraid that someone might look up and see her up there.

When she came to the edge, she found she was looking down on a picture that had hung in Mr Hood's classroom at Avontuur years ago: the picture of Daniel in the lions' den. Terrible rocks rose on both sides of the gash – no one trying to escape would have been able to climb them; the bottom was strewn with stones and rocks, some of them as big as houses. Only the convicts themselves and the dark, shining stream of water that ran along the foot of the rockface on the other side were not in the picture of Daniel.

Her eyes were searching for Selling while her hands took the whining child from her back and put it to her breast. Amidst the confusion she could see parts of neatly packed stone foundations carrying the road along the rockfaces, made of enormous stones. Everywhere straining bodies were breaking loose more rocks, rolling them along, trimming them. Others were smashing stones with sledge-hammers. The deafening sound rose up and hammered at her ears until it seemed to be crashing around inside her head.

The guards wore a green uniform. They were only keeping watch at the top and bottom ends of the gorge for no one could escape unseen up the sides.

A convict would have had a chance against a lion, but not against that abyss down there.

She picked him out. Selling. Chained to the man next to him and working with his feet in the water. He was breaking loose rocks with a crowbar. He was a convict. Something in her gave way as she realized for the first time what that really meant. Her beautiful Selling. Life for one miserable bloody sheep – one miserable bloody Laghaan. A lifetime. God in heaven, how long was a lifetime? He would never be free. She felt like tearing the bushes out of the earth around her! Would death not have been better? Her beautiful Selling, the man of her heart, the man of her flesh. It was a life-sentence for her too.

How was she to get to him? Please God, she had to get to him! She pulled the child away from her breast, took the knapsack and set out along the ridge, looking for a place where she could climb down.

Find my feet a way to get down to him, she prayed, make me a way to him.

Past the lions' den and past the guards, she found a ravine where she could get down, but not with the child. The child would have to stay at the top.

She worked fast, tearing off branches to put underneath the tiny body. She wrapped the baby in the blanket, laid her down gently and stroked the little back until her eyes closed.

As she climbed down the crack, she tried not to think – that would have driven her back and she had to get to Selling. If she could manage to get into the thickets growing alongside the stream, she could get past the guards to Selling. Nobody would hear her above the din and if she crawled on her stomach nobody would see her.

It did not take her long to crawl past the guards. Then it went more slowly, for she had to pull herself forward through the thickets by her elbows and the knapsack kept sliding off her back. At times she had to crawl through the water and over boulders; her knees and elbows were grazed and her dress was torn, but nothing mattered as long as Selling stayed where she had last seen him. The deeper she crawled up the gorge, the more violent the noise became. Every pickaxe and crowbar and hammer blow echoed from side to side between the rockfaces before it died away at the top.

Fear became her strength. What if they saw the bushes moving? What if the child woke up? How far had she crawled already? When would she dare to look? What if she looked up in the face of a guard?

The next moment someone blew hard and fiercely on a bugle and she stopped dead. Had they seen her? Had it been some kind of warning? She dropped her head on her arms and just lay there, waiting for whatever was going to happen. But nothing happened. It was just strangely quiet ... Then she suddenly realized that the bugle had been the sign that they were finished for the day. She was too late. All the convicts were taken to De Vlugt at night where they were locked up and fed. She carefully pushed away the twigs in front of her and saw Selling standing less than twenty paces away, but between him and his chain-mate and her were two other convicts and a guard, and the guard was ordering them all together.

She had been too late.

And all the convicts that had been chained in pairs were chained together in a row and led away first. Selling passed within a few paces of her and he did not know it. Her heart cried to him, but her mind checked her tongue. Selling was still strong then. Still a man. The only thing that was different was that the chains had eaten into the flesh of his ankles.

She lay there in the bush and prayed that the child would not wake up and start crying, that the ants would not get to the child and that the vultures would not peck out her little eyes. Please God.

When the last convicts and their guard had gone, she got up and walked to where she had to climb to the top again. The child was safe, the big red ants had only got on to the blanket. And only when she had the child on her back and she was walking home did the tears come and she wept until she could weep no more. She was back on the elephants' track by dusk.

A week later she succeeded in crawling right up to him. And for four years she managed to smuggle food to him that way. Four years in which she learned to stalk better than an animal stalking its prey. She got to know every short cut across the mountain. She saw the road with its dry-stone walls grow and she saw Selling break under the stone. The food alone could not save him and he had to share every crumb with whoever was in the chains with him. During the second year her mother had died and she was left behind alone with the children at Wolwek-raal. Her mother died in November and in February of the next year, she woke up one night and heard a child crying.

When she took food to Selling again, she put a note between two slices of bread telling him about the child, hoping that the man with him in the chains would be able to read. She did not say that it was a white child.

In the last few months before the road was finished, the work had ruined Selling's health and they no longer regarded him as worth a day's work. Fresh gangs of convicts were brought in from elsewhere because the road had to be finished so that the land beyond the awesome mountains would no longer have to struggle as it did.

Old Mr Bain's son Thomas built and finished the road in the end, and although he himself was good to the convicts, the same could not be said of his guards. How many convicts had died there, nobody could say. Nor what had happened to some of them. Especially those that had died in the poort. You couldn't dig a grave there, so a convict that dropped dead had to be propped up in a crevice and covered with stones.

When the news came that the road was finished and that the first wagons with wood from the Forest were on their way, another feast was prepared at Avontuur. Koos Wehmeyer's wife sent a message to her, Fiela, to come and help with the preparations. She sent back a message, telling them all to go to hell and take the road with them.

The following day Petrus came and said he had been to the place where they locked up the convicts at night and that Selling was still alive.

'You mean, he's still breathing, Master Petrus,' she said bitterly.

'They will shortly be sending the convicts away. I will try and see him before they take him away.'

She did not answer Petrus Zondagh. In her heart she had already buried Selling. As long as she lived, she would never set foot on that road again and she would hate the Laghaans as long as they lived. For the rest she would build a wall round Wolwekraal with her tongue to protect herself and her children. Especially Benjamin.

One day not long after that, she was trampling clay to build the pigsty when she looked up and saw Selling coming down the slope above the house. He was walking with difficulty and he was in convict's clothes.

She was frightened. Was she out of her mind? Was it Selling's ghost? Had he died? She stumbled off the clay and started running. When she got to him, she knew he was not dead. There was only one other possibility: he had escaped. She would have to hide him. Where? Not in the house. In the hills.

'Fiela.'

'My God, Selling, how did you get here?' There was nothing left of her beautiful Selling but a skeleton with Selling's eyes.

'I got a remission, Fiela.'

Selling had not escaped. The truth came out little by little. He had been one of the lucky ones that had received a pardon from the Prince. Prince Alfred, Queen Victoria's son who had come to shoot an elephant in the Forest. As the road through the mountain had just been finished and the people wished to honour the Prince, they named the road after him: Prince Alfred's Pass. The Prince declared the road open himself; to mark the event, some of the convicts who had made the road were pardoned. Selling's name was right at the bottom of the list. Petrus had been there too.

Selling was shocked when he saw the child was white.

12

Benjamin sat by the house: he did not cry any more for it did not help. He no longer kicked and screamed when they came near him – something warned him that the man's patience would not hold out much longer.

Five days had passed since they had come for him that morning at Wolwekraal. Three since they had brought him to the Forest. Every morning he woke up and said to himself, today my mother will come and fetch me and cause big trouble. The Willem-boy had gone woodcutting somewhere with Dawid's coat on, the box was now a kitchen cupboard and a seat and his nightshirt had been given to the girl, who wore it like a dress. What they had done with his shoes, he did not know. But they could not lay their hands on the five shillings. He had pushed it through a hole in the mattress stuffed with dried leaves on the bed he had to sleep on in the kitchen.

The girl came from the house. 'Do you want a sweet potato, Lukas?'

'No.'

It did not help not to answer when they called him Lukas. It just made the man more angry and the woman more scared. He was no longer sure whether the woman was scared or just simple-minded. It was one or the other.

The girl came and sat down beside him and ate a sweet potato. 'Can you keep a secret?' she asked.

'What secret?' She was definitely simple-minded. And if she had been Fiela Komoetie's child her hair would have been cut long ago.

'If you come with me, I'll show you the secret.'

'I'm not going anywhere.'

'You'll get monkey-buttocks from just sitting here all day.'

'I'm waiting for my mother.'

'Pa said he'd give you one more day to sort yourself out and from tomorrow on he'd stand no further nonsense from you.'

'I don't belong to you people.'

'You do.'

'My mother will come and fetch me, you'll see.'

'You're Lukas that was lost!'

'I'm Benjamin Komoetie.'

'Hush!' She held her head to one side as if she was listening to something. 'Do you hear that?'

'What?'

'Are you deaf? It's a woodpigeon and a bush lourie singing together.'

There was something he wanted to ask her. 'Listen, do you know how far we are from the road going to the Long Kloof?'

'The gravel road?'

'I don't know. The road that goes through the Forest. They brought me by it from Knysna.'

'That's the road going past Deep Walls; the other roads in the Forest are only sled-paths for hauling out the wood, and footpaths.'

'How far are we from this gravel road?'

'A long walk.'

'Do you know how to get there?'

'Yes.'

'Will you show me how to get there?'

'The secret I want to show you is on the way there,' she said, slyly. 'Perhaps we could run as far as the sled-path in Kom's Bush; it's easy to get to the gravel road at Deep Walls from there without getting lost.'

She threw the sweet-potato skin on the roof of the shed and got up. When she stood up and walked away, he jumped up and followed her – she was his only hope and he had to stay with her.

If he could get to the road, he would walk home; maybe he would meet his mother along the way as well.

The girl went into the Forest along a footpath at the southern end of the Island. The thick undergrowth at the foot of the trees was full of dark shadows and it scared him a little.

'Where are the elephants?' he asked.

'I don't know – come on!'

'Won't they chase us?'

'Just see that you choose a thick tree to climb when they do.'

He did not trust her. The nightshirt was far too big for her, and was hanging below her knees; one sleeve was rolled up high and the other one hardly at all. Her feet were as swift as the little red-brown buck's that lived in the rocky hills above Wolwekraal. Where the footpath was muddy, she stepped from tree root to stepping-stone as if she knew every inch. She walked faster and faster and then finally she started running. Where the footpath was about to go down a steep hill, she stopped and said:

'Keep to the side of the path, it's slippery down here to the bottom.'

'Where are we going?'

'Down to the creek.'

'How far are we from the road that goes to the Long Kloof?'

'A long way. Come on!'

The Forest smelled of mud and rotten leaves. The footpath was a narrow tunnel through the undergrowth with quivering rays of sunlight all around. In places the trees were so close together that a man could hardly pass between them. Some of the trunks were as thick as giants.

She was the first to slip and land on her side in the mud.

'Just look at my nightshirt!' he cried. 'When my mother sees that, she'll wring your neck!' But the stupid thing just laughed and wiped her hands on his nightshirt as well. 'How do you think my mother's going to get that clean again?'

'Ma will have no trouble getting it clean.'

'I'm talking about my mother!'

'You're Lukas that was lost,' she retorted, impatiently. 'My ma is your ma and my pa is your pa.'

'That's not true. I'm Fiela Komoetie's child.'

'They say she's brown. How can a brown person have a white child? You're our Lukas that disappeared.'

'That's a lie!'

'Pa says ma recognized you immediately.'

'Your pa can say what he likes, *I'm* telling you I'm not that child.'

'Whose child are you then?' she snapped.

'I don't know.' He was suddenly scared, as if trapped. What if his mother came to look for him while he was in the Forest with the girl? 'We must go back,' he said, 'take me back to your house!'

She would not. She just started running down the slope like a wild animal without looking back.

'Girl, stop!' he called after her. 'Girl – Nina!' He saw his nightshirt disappear round a bend way down the footpath and then he was all alone up there on the path between the never-ending thickets. 'Nina!' A bird answered high up above his head in a tree; somewhere a tree creaked as if a very big hand was slowly rocking it. Like a tooth. 'Nina, wait for me!'

He ran down after her. Along the side of the footpath the forest floor felt spongy under his feet and he was afraid the earth would give way. Along the middle it was so muddy, he had to keep his body taut all the time so as not to slip. Where he had seen his nightshirt disappear, the path swerved to the left into the undergrowth and on the next bend it spilled over a fearful rocky ledge.

'Nina?'

She wasn't anywhere. There was a patch of tiny blue flowers beside the path at the foot of a tree; a forest bird called from close by in the bushes – stopped – called again. High up above the forest roof the sun must have gone behind a cloud for all around him the shadows suddenly grew darker still.

'Nina!' he called. He called her again and again until his throat hurt, but she was not there. Perhaps she was hiding from him, she was foolish enough. Or perhaps she was down at the creek already. He started going down the slope as fast as he could; around him the ferns got as high as a man – anything could be hiding in them and jump out at him! Behind him, way up the slope, the forest bird kept repeating its long-drawn-out call as if it were saying, 'Come back! come back!' But turning back scared him more than going on. He had to find the girl. Where the path got too steep, someone had put logs to serve as footholds and just below the logs the footpath swerved away to the right again.

That was when he realized that she could not have gone that far ahead, that he must have passed her somewhere along the way. He turned round and clambered back up the hill as fast he could, his heart beating faster and louder in his chest. What if something had grabbed her and dragged her into the under-growth? They say a tiger once grabbed a woman's baby when it was lying right beside her in the hills where Wolwekraal spring rises. The tiger dragged away the baby and ate it. Tollie said, only the baby's hand was left. Master Koos's father came with his dogs and followed the tiger's trail for two days and when they shot him, they found that all his teeth were worn down with age. The tiger could no longer eat tough meat.

What if something had bitten off the girl's head? He didn't want to see a person without a head. At Avontuur's Crossing, where the shop is, there was the ghost of a man without a head; he never wanted to go and see Auntie Maria after dark.

Everything around him looked the same. He could no longer remember where he had last seen her, whether he had passed the place or not. She could not have flown away in the air! Perhaps he had turned back too soon ... They said he had got lost in that Forest in the wink of an eye when he was small. *No. It was not him!*

In his haste and fear, he misjudged a step and landed in the mud on his hands and knees. When he got up, the tiny blue flowers were right beside him; the forest bird gave a long-drawn-out call and then suddenly stopped, as if someone had strangled it.

'Nina?' he cried out in fear. He started to tremble and could not stop. He was sure something was watching him from the undergrowth, probably the thing had strangled the bird. He had to get away from the place but his feet slipped from under him again; the bird called clearly and close by again but the bird sounded funny, as if it was laughing.

'Nina?'

When she burst out from the undergrowth, he realized that she had been the bird. She laughed and laughed.

'You bloody fool!' he snapped at her in fury.

'You were scared stiff, stiff, stiff!'

'Idiot!'

'You couldn't find me, find me!'

'Stupid thing!' He wished that he could call her the ugliest name he knew but the word would not come and anyway she had started running down the path and all he could do was to follow her down the creek. She walked up and down over the fallen branches to make them crack before she started digging behind an old uprooted tree covered with dry, rough moss.

'Remember, Lukas, you promised not to tell.'

He had not promised her anything and he didn't care. All he wanted was to know the way out of the Forest. Nothing else.

'How far are we from the gravel road?'

She dug up four empty bottles behind the tree and took them to the water without a word and washed them one by one. There were two thin, dark blue bottles of the castor-oil type, a greenish one and then a pot-bellied water-bottle with little patterns on it of the kind Miss Baby kept her drinking-water in on the dining-room table.

'What's all this,' he asked, curtly.

'You'll see.'

She lined them up on a big, flat rock, dried her hands on his nightshirt and sat down.

'Whose bottles are these?'

'Mine.'

'Why are you hiding them here?'

'Because I want to.'

'Where did you get them?'

'The olive-oil bottle and the two blue ones I picked up and the water-bottle I stole from Aunt Gertie,' she admitted quite openly.

'What did you do that for?'

'Because the water-bottle makes the best sound.'

She picked each bottle up in turn and blew lightly across their tops, making a different sound with each. She left the water-bottle for last; its sound was softer and more hollow than the other's.

'What's so good about bottle-blowing?' he asked.

'It's music,' she bragged. 'I can whistle like a red-chested cuckoo, and mimic a mouse bird, a big lourie and a bush lourie; I can coo like a woodpigeon and whistle like many others. It's just the chorister robin that I can't do properly.'

'You're simple-minded. You're all simple-minded!'

'Uncle Koos has a guitar without strings but as soon as he has money, he's going to buy strings and then I'm going to steal the guitar as well. You can get many sounds from a guitar. Sounds that go together. Have you heard a bush shrike and its mate singing together?'

'You said you'd show me how to get out of this Forest.'

'I said I'd show you how to get to Kom's sled-path; from there it's still quite a way before you get out of the Forest.'

'Show me how to get to Kom's path then. Please.'

'Why?'

'I want to go home.'

'You must stop your nonsense; if pa gets angry and takes down the ox rein, he'll beat you to a jelly.'

'I've got five shillings.'

She was about to blow on one of the bottles again but stopped. 'Where did you get it from?' she asked, suspiciously.

'My mother gave it to me in case.'

'You're lying. Pa shook out all the stuff in your box to see if there was any money.'

'It was not in the box.'

'Where was it then?'

'Sometimes in my pocket, sometimes in my mouth.'

'Where's it now?'

'Where I've hidden it. If you show me how to get out of this Forest, I'll tell you where.'

'Say.'

'Not before you've shown me the way.'

'What if I show you and you run away because you've lied about the money?'

'I swear.'

She sat twisting her finger in the neck of the stolen bottle, considering. 'How much is half a crown?'

'Half of five shillings.'

'At Peuter Island a man bought a mouth-organ for half a crown in the village.'

Hope flared up in him. 'You can buy yourself *two*!' he said.

'What do I want to buy two for? I've only got one mouth – maybe I'll buy myself a blanket. The bigfeet messed up my blanket when pa had to throw down all his things and run away from them.'

'What are bigfeet?'

'Don't you know?' she asked, quite shocked. 'The animals with the trunks, *elephants*,' she whispered. 'You're not supposed to say the name out loud, they'll hear you and think you've called them and come and trample you. If you give me the five shillings I'll buy myself a mouth-organ and a blanket and I'll show you how to get to the gravel road.'

'Perhaps you should buy yourself a comb.' Her face was not too bad, just dirty and hidden under all the hair. 'Then you can comb your hair.'

'We used to have a comb, but its teeth fell out.' She picked up one of the blue bottles and held it out to him. 'You blow on this one and I'll blow on the water-bottle.'

'But you said you'll take me to the road!'

'I'll take you tomorrow.'

'Why not now?'

'It's a long walk to get to the gravel road. You can't start out in the middle of the day, you'd have to walk until dark and then you'd get lost again.'

'Swear that you'll take me tomorrow.'

'Swear that you'll give me the five shillings.'

'I swear.'

'If you're lying to me, I'll show you the wrong way and the bigfeet can trample you nicely flat for all I care.'

'Swear you'll show me the way.'

'I swear. How I'm going to get to the village to buy the mouth-organ, I don't know, but I swear.'

It felt as if the Forest opened up above him and the sun was suddenly shining down on him. He would run all the way to get to the gravel road first and from there he would walk until he was home.

He let the girl have her way and blew on the bottle till his lips were sore; at first he did it wrong but quickly learned to blow into the bottle softly and at an angle and to let the sound roll to the bottom of the bottle. She blew on the water-bottle.

'Now you blow one note, then I blow one, and then we blow one together.' He kept on forgetting when it was his turn to blow because in his mind he was already on his way home to Wolwekraal. She got angry and said he was stupid and that it would be better if he disappeared again anyway, for then they could have the other bed in the kitchen for Willem again, and they would not have to sleep three in one bed when Willem and Kristoffel were both at home.

No, Elias said to himself as he sat down to think over the whole situation again, it was all well and good, but something must be done before things really got out of hand. The child was as stubborn as a mule and a mule could cause you a lot of trouble.

Barta stood in the back door, staring in front of her as if she could see nothing and her mind had stopped working altogether.

'Isn't it time you took the sweet potatoes out of the ash, Barta? You know I don't like a sweet potato that's baked too dry – Barta!'

'I heard you, Elias. I looked at the sweet potatoes just now, they're not soft yet.' Her eyes did not move.

'Stop worrying, Barta. As from tomorrow I'm going to put him on the beams and teach him to hold an axe so that he can sweat out his nonsense.'

'Don't beat him, Elias.'

'I will not beat him if he listens to me.'

'The magistrate said he would inquire after him regularly.'

Since they had gone and fetched the child, Barta had had the magistrate on her brain. As if she were afraid. 'He can inquire if he likes, but the thorn is in *my* bed. If Lukas starts kicking and screaming again, or goes and sits apart, I'm going to wallop him. I will not be made a fool of by a child.'

'Aunt Gertie says he'll get used to things.'

'I'm telling you, he's been amongst those Coloureds too long. That's what it is. Hearing your own flesh and blood call another man "master" . . .'

'He hasn't done it again since you've told him not to, Elias.'

'Pour me some coffee.'

The thing that bothered him most was that the child would

not say a word unless you forced it out of him. And when he did, it was without saying *pa* or *ma*, as if the words stuck in his throat. The magistrate had warned them that it might take a little time before the child fitted in in the Forest. But *he* said: To the devil with fitting in. The Forest did not ask you whether you fitted in or not, it was bend or break and that was that. It was not the Kloof, where you had the whole day to sit in the sun. He had made up his mind, Lukas was going to work on the beams. When *he* was twelve years' old, he had already been helping his father cut wood for a long time. If he taught Lukas and all went well, they might have some money to spare for a change.

Lord knew, the child was unexpected and now Barta would not stop nagging him about an extra bed and blankets and he would have to get them from somewhere. He had said they could push the two beds in the kitchen against each other and all four children could lie head to tail when Willem and Kristoffel were both at home. But when Lukas found out he was to share a bed, he carried on so much that Malie came over from the other side of the Island to see what was going on. You could not keep anything private any more. In the end Barta pleaded for the child until he had to give in. But Elias van Rooyen had had enough. He was not afraid of the child as Barta was. All right, the child had been on the other side of the mountain for nine years and was like a stranger in the house, but things could not go on like that. Lukas would have to start working.

Barta brought his coffee, and went and stood in the doorway again. 'I see he's gone into the Forest with Nina this morning.'

'Yes, I noticed. As long as he does not think he can go loafing around with her every day. I've told you so often to keep her occupied; she just goes about making mischief all the time.'

'She did hoe the whole of last week, Elias.'

'You mean, she danced about with the hoe!'

'She hoed as well.'

He wasn't worried about Willem and Kristoffel. Up to the

day the forester had come to tell them about Lukas, he thought
he had only Nina to worry about. When he went to the village
again, he would ask if anyone was looking for a servant. He
would not let her go into service for nothing, he would set his
price for her.

'Elias, perhaps you should not set him to work yet. The
magistrate said we must give him time to get used to things.'

'But we have given him a chance, haven't we? And it's not
Lukas I'm worried about, it's Nina. You must see that she stays
away from the Forest; it's not a place for a girl all by herself.'

'You can't keep her out of the Forest.'

'I'll tie her up as you do a runaway ox. I'm telling you, there's
something wrong with that child, she's too much like your sister
Nonnie, who ran away to the Cape, for my liking.'

'Nina's a child still, she'll be all right.'

'Why doesn't she play with Malie's Bet or Gertrude? Or with
Sofie's Liesbet?'

'They don't want to play with her.'

'And why not, I'm asking you; there's something wrong with
her. Has she got worms?'

'I don't know.'

No, Barta would not know, he sighed to himself. He had to
see to everything himself, take things into his own hands. But as
soon as he had Lukas working at the beams and Nina in service,
and perhaps had a little luck with an elephant, things might look
a bit brighter for a change.

And Lukas seemed better when he and Nina came back from
the Forest. As usual, he hardly said a word, but at least the worst
sullenness was gone.

That night he waited until Barta had gone to bed before he
called him to the table to speak to him.

'Both your brothers are earning their own keep now. Uncle
Martiens offered to give you a place in his woodcutting team but

I want you here with me at the beams.' The child sat looking at him but he got the feeling that he was not taking in a word of what he said. 'I'm going to teach you to make beams, I said. When I was your age, I had already been swinging an axe for a long time. Do you hear me, Lukas?'

'Yes.'

The child was definitely not as bewildered any more. Nina sat on the bed, whistling and at the same time making a racket with a spoon on the coffee-tin.

'Didn't I tell you to stop that noise!' He would have to find some pomegranate roots and make a brew to give her. There was nothing better for worms.

'When will pa be going to the village again?' she asked, as she put away the tin and the spoon.

'When I have reason to.'

'Will you take me with you?'

'I took you with me once and I said I would never take you again. Go to bed now.'

'I promise I won't run away this time, Pa. I'll stay with pa.'

'Go to bed, I said!'

'Just this once, Pa. Just this once.'

'Nina, I will not tell you to go to bed again!' From the corner of his eye he saw Lukas backing away from the table. 'And I'm not finished with you yet!' he said. The child stopped short and glanced in Nina's direction, half pleadingly. 'I get the feeling that you two have been up to mischief.' He was suddenly suspicious.

'We haven't done anything, Pa.'

'Nina, you're too good at making up lies. What's going on between the two of you?'

'Nothing, Pa. But I badly want to go to the village.'

'She wants to go to the village,' Lukas confirmed, frightened.

'What for?' It was not at all to his liking.

'I just want to go to the village for a change, Pa.'

'You may go to the village sooner than you think, and for a different reason from whatever you're planning.'

'I'm not planning anything, Pa.'

'I'm just warning you.'

Tuesday was not a day too soon to start Lukas working. From the moment he got out of bed he was making trouble again, wanting to know where his shoes were.

'You don't need shoes for working on the beams! Come on!' Outside, at the scaffold behind the shed, he first of all tried to teach Lukas the difference between a side axe and felling axe. 'The felling axe is the axe for cutting down a tree when you need one and for dressing your log roughly – *and* you can hack off your toes with it if you are looking the other way!' The child kept turning his eyes towards the house as if he was restless about something. 'You must listen to what I'm saying, Lukas! The other axe here is the side axe for making a round log square and as smooth as a table-top. Do you get that?'

'Yes.'

'When I was your age, there was not a tool in this Forest that I did not know how to use. Use properly, that is. You have a lot to catch up with. You'll have to learn fast. The wagons come here for beams because the people are building more and more houses and where are they going to get wood if not from the Forest? Before long we'll have to fell bigger trees so that we can get more beams from a log but in the meantime we cut younger trees and make one beam from each log. I'll show you how – You must pay attention to what I'm saying, Lukas! I'm not going to repeat it a hundred times. I'm going to roll a log on to the scaffold and teach you to cut straight with a side axe even if it takes you until dark and again from daybreak tomorrow.'

Nina came sauntering along from the house and sat down on the log behind the scaffold.

'Go and help your ma!'

'I've helped her already. Ma said I could go and play.'

'There's no time for playing. Hand me that pole behind you, I want to roll a log on to the scaffold.'

She got up and started dragging the pole with the sharp end towards him. 'The thing's heavy, Pa!'

'Rubbish, it's not heavy. Bring it here and fetch another one.' When she came past Lukas she whispered something to him and dropped the pole. 'Bend down, Lukas!' he said. 'Drag it over here so that your hands can feel what wood feels like. Nina, bring the other pole.' Very well then – the plan suddenly dawned on him – if her ma could not keep her out of mischief, he would. Why shouldn't she help at the beams until such time as he could hire her out? Even if she just did the rough work.

As she was bringing the second pole, she again said something to Lukas from the side of her mouth.

'What are you two scheming?'

'Nothing, Pa. I just asked Lukas to help me.'

'I think it's time that I gave both of you work to do. Take the poles and fetch that log over there and get it on to the scaffold.' She looked at him as if he had told her to go and cut down the whole forest. 'Get moving! The log over there at the ash heap.' He squatted down and slowly began breaking a twig between his fingers.

After a while he had to admit they were not doing badly. Making allowances for Lukas's newness to the work and Nina's thinness, they were managing the log quite well.

'Get it along the length of the scaffold, between the cross-bars.' The log kept on coming round at the wrong end but he let them struggle with it. There was nothing as good as struggling to teach you. When the log was in the right position to be rolled on to the scaffold, he gave them time to rest and spit on their hands for a while.

'Pa, we'll never get this thing up there!'

'What's a little slope like that? Wait until you've had to roll a log as thick as three oxen up a saw-pit, *then* you'll have something to complain about.' He should have put Nina on the beams long ago, he realized. Barta could easily manage the house and the garden on her own; she had far too little control over the child anyway.

'Pa, we're not going to get this thing up there!'

'It's not that heavy. Put the poles in underneath it, like levers, and lift it with your shoulders. When the log starts climbing, you start climbing too but keep the poles working along the ground until you've got the log at the top.'

'And if it rolls back?'

'Then it's your own fault and it can knock you down for it, for all I care.'

'Why can't pa come and do it?'

'You talk too much!' Lukas just stood there without a word and picked up his pole. 'Take up the other one, Nina, and make a start!' He liked the idea of her on the beams as well more and more. Two extra hands at the beams could change many things. He would have to go and cut more forked branches and poles and make another scaffold.

Again the two children did quite well. The log rolled back only once, giving them a bad fright, but with the second try they got it up on to the scaffold.

'Look for wedges now and stick them in on both sides so that it lies firmly!'

On the far side of the island, at the woodcutters' houses, the chimneys smoked lazily; Sofie and her daughters were digging in the garden and it looked as if Malie and old Aunt Gertie were sewing up mattress covers or something outside, their eyes on Elias van Rooyen's place every now and again of course. Inquisitive.

'The log's on the scaffold, Pa. Can we go and play now?' Nina asked.

'Play? You won't be playing for a long time.' He got up and climbed on to the scaffold with the felling axe in his hand. 'I'm going to show you how to trim the bark away roughly; when

I've finished, you'll take turns to do it yourselves and show me whether you've paid attention.'

Nina looked trapped. 'It's easy for pa to do it,' she said.

'Not with my sore back that creaks every time I bend down!' he told her, hacking into the log and making the first splinters fly. 'Remember, this is part of a tree; it's round and it has to be cut square. First one side, then the other; then you turn it over and do the other two sides. Before you start with the side axe, I'll show you how to make a line with a string drawn through the ashes, so that you can cut straight.'

When he climbed down from the scaffold, Malie was standing at the shed.

'Good morning, Malie,' he said bluntly. 'Barta's inside.'

'Good morning, Elias. I see you've put Nina at the beams as well.'

'Yes. Keeps her out of mischief.'

'It will take more than that to keep her out of mischief,' Malie replied, sharply. 'How is it going with Lukas?'

'Better since yesterday. A bit clumsy still at the wood but that will come right in time. Barta is in the house.' Malie and he did not eat from the same plate; she was always out to pick a quarrel with him and he had never liked her. Real old gossip she was. And he did not have time to sit and talk to her either, he had to sharpen the side axes. Pity he only had the one felling axe but at least he had two side axes. 'Don't cut too deep, Lukas, just trim off the bark!' he shouted towards the scaffold. 'It's not firewood you're making. And see that you give Nina a turn as well now!'

'He still looks surly to me, Elias,' Malie remarked. 'Nine years is a long time – does he say anything about the people in the Long Kloof?'

'Not really.' He walked past her and into the shed to get to the whetstone, but she followed him.

'It must be difficult to have grown up amongst Coloureds and then suddenly be white again.'

Malie was doing her best to get him angry. 'Could I help it? Was it my doing?'

'Are you going to make him work at the beams with you?'

'Yes.'

'Then I suppose you'll be delivering more beams again for a change.'

'You're counting to see how many beams I get finished.'

'It's not necessary to count. Anybody can see you're taking less to Deep Walls every time.'

He started preparing the axe-head and restrained himself from saying something he would regret. Willem was in her husband's team and an argument with Malie could mean trouble. The boy earned little more than coffee and sugar and meal as it was, but it was better than nothing.

'Once I've taught Lukas, things will be better. My back isn't up to it any more.'

Malie came in to the shed and sat down on the finished beams. She made no move to go home. 'One would never have thought that he'd turn out to be such a handsome boy.'

'Who?'

'Lukas. Apart from the fact that he has Barta's blue eyes and something of your nose, he does not look a bit like your Willem or Kristoffel. Martiens says, if this had happened anywhere else, somebody would have written about it in a newspaper. That Lukas was found after nine years. But nothing that happens in the Forest ever gets to the world outside. There are days that I feel we might just as well not exist.'

'The wood buyers in the village would miss us. And the wagon that comes for the beams.' He was not really listening to Malie much. All the time that she was speaking, he had the feeling that something was not as it should be but he could not make out what.

'I'm almost forty, Elias, and I've been outside this Forest only twice in my life, and that was just as far as the village. And Sofie over there – she's just been as far as Deep Walls, when the preacher came to baptize the children. Aunt Gertie is old wood; she does not even want to leave the Island any more – I say again, if we should all die from a plague this very day, few would notice. Perhaps the foresters would.'

'Perhaps, yes.' His mind was running ahead. If he could deliver forty beams every three months at four and a sixpence a beam, the amount the man from the Long Kloof was paying, then things would start looking up for him.

But Malie was not finished yet. 'People don't even know about us, Elias. When strangers come here to shoot bigfeet or something, and come across one of us, they look at you as if you're something odd. They question you as if to find out whether it's a pumpkin or a head you carry on your shoulders. And they like to come and play clever here in the Forest, like that time the stranger came and pitched his tent right next to our house. That was years ago, before I was married and we were living at Platbos Peak. This bighead with his fancy clothes and books and pencils arrived, and only pa could make out a word or two of what he was saying. Victorin his name was. I remember his face as if he were standing in front of me now. He filled his books writing down and drawing pictures of everything around, from the tiniest weed to the tallest kalander and if a bird squeaked, we had to tell him its name and help him look for it. If pa was not there, we often lied to him for fun. When a flock of louries came down anywhere near, he started clucking and drawing as if he had hatched them. He seemed to think they were the most wonderful things with wings on earth. Then pa came home one Friday night with a couple of louries he had shot and Mr Victorin almost had a fit. He told pa we were savages because we ate those beautiful green birds with their magnificent red wings. Pa told him we did not eat the feathers, only the meat. But Mr Victorin had had enough of us, and when we woke the next morning, he was gone. Two months later pa came across him and his tent in Pear Bush and what do you think was hanging under the tree, ready for the pot? Four louries and two mouse birds. Pa asked him, "What's this?" Then it came out that he had found it impossible to live on bread and honey alone. Clever wasn't so clever any more.'

He had heard Malie tell that story before. And somewhere something was still wrong, but he still could not make it out. Like when a piece of meat gets stuck in your tooth and your tongue cannot find it.

'Take that tin and fetch me some water for the whetstone, Malie, this axe is ready now.'

'Fetch your own water.'

He wanted to call Barta from the house to fetch him the water but he knew Malie would have something to say about that as well. So he got up himself. And when he came round the shed he suddenly realized what was wrong: there was no sound of the axe coming from the scaffold. Worse still, there was not a sign of the two blasted children.

'Nina! Lukas!' The axe was lying under the scaffold and hardly a splinter had been hacked off the log. 'Lukas! Nina!'

Malie came round the shed and burst out laughing: 'I thought you were a bit premature when you said the beams would keep Nina out of mischief.'

'It's because of your chattering that I did not notice it getting quiet!' Barta came from the house, alarmed, and wanting to know what had happened. 'The brats just left their work and went off! If I knew which way they had gone, I'd fetch them and take every bit of bark off their backsides for them!'

'Perhaps they went to play, Elias.'

'Then it will be their last play for a very long time. I'll be waiting for them and I'm not going to play with them!'

'Elias . . .'

'Keep quiet, Barta!'

He got on to the scaffold to wait for them, and as he waited the anger built up in him. The sun moved slowly over the Island, shortening the shadows. Rascals, he cursed them in his mind, so you'd put down my axe and run off! Scoundrels!

When the sun burnt down on the back of his neck too fiercely, he got off the scaffold and went to sit under the shed. It was an old habit of Nina's to go off into the Forest and come back when it suited her. Now she wanted to teach Lukas her tricks as well, he decided. She should have been taken away from her mother's care long ago.

At half-day Barta brought his food to the shed and stayed standing around restlessly as if she wanted to say something but was a bit nervous about it.

'Elias . . .'

'Please don't come nagging, woman. My blood's up as it is!'

'You can give Nina a hiding, Elias, I'll help you to catch her, but don't hit Lukas. The magistrate can send the forester any day to come and see how he's getting on and there might be marks on him.'

'Barta,' he warned her, 'don't pester me now. Are you suggesting that I should walk to the village to get the magistrate's approval every time I want to perform my duty?'

'I didn't mean it like that.'

'Now stop dragging in the magistrate every time I want to lift a finger to the boy. When those two brats come back from the Forest, they'll have me to reckon with. They'll take up that axe and work until they fall down. And then they can get up again and keep at it until they can hack a beam from a log to my satisfaction.'

'Sofie's children have been to fetch firewood. I'll go and ask them if they saw Nina and Lukas.'

'Borrow a brew of coffee from Sofie; tell her we're expecting Willem or Kristoffel tomorrow and we'll give it back.'

'But didn't Willem say they'll be cutting wagon wood for at least three weeks, and aren't Kristoffel and the others cutting stinkwood in Lourie's Bush? How can we be expecting them back tomorrow?'

'Don't be stupid, Barta! Just borrow a brew of coffee!'

Barta was not half-way across the Island when he saw Nina

sneak round the house like a thief and slip in at the back door.

'Rascal, come here!' he shouted and made for her. She was in the kitchen on Lukas's bed, digging into the mattress; he caught her by the leg and pulled her off. 'You little devil! You thought you could throw down the axe and just disappear, didn't you? Thought my eyes were shut! Thought I was asleep! But for this the two of you will pay until I say enough, do you hear?'

'You're hurting me, Pa!'

He was dragging her around by the hair. 'Blighter! You thought you could mess around with me, didn't you?'

'No, Pa.'

'Where's Lukas?'

'I don't know, Pa. I went looking for him, Pa.'

'What did you say?' She could lie as smoothly as a wood buyer.

'I went looking for him, Pa. You're hurting me, Pa!'

And she could scream like a pig being slaughtered when you had her trapped.

'Where's Lukas, I asked!'

'He ran away, Pa. I begged him to turn back, but he wouldn't.'

Her words knocked the wits out of him for a moment. If Lukas had run away, it meant trouble; if it reached the magistrate's ears he would have some explaining to do and if the child got lost again, it would be a right mess. He seized Nina by the shoulders and shook her till her teeth chattered.

'Which way did he go?'

'To Deep Walls, Pa.'

Barta and Sofie and Malie came and crowded together in the doorway, frightened.

'Where did you last see him?'

'In Kom's Bush, Pa.'

'How did he know how to get there?'

'He ... He ...' She stood there searching for words. 'He said he knew the way, that's the way you came here with him.'

'It was dark then!'

'Elias ...'

'Keep out of this, Barta! Nina, if you are lying to me now, I'll brain you!'

'He's going to walk to the Long Kloof, Pa. I swear.'

There was only one thing to do and he had to do it fast. When he tore the ox rein from the hook, Barta grabbed him by the arm.

'Elias, what are you doing now?'

'I've got to catch up with him, Barta. What else? Get the lantern ready and fetch my coat, I want to catch up with the little idiot before he sets foot on the gravel road and it might take me until after dark!'

13

She reached Knysna at sundown. There was still some strength left in her head and body, but her legs and feet were burning like fire with the two days' walking. The last two, three hours she had had to ignore them in order to keep going, so that she could be out of the Forest before dark. Not that she had been afraid, it was just that the jungle had seemed to be endless. There had not been much level ground for her feet; where the road had not been pitted by the forest wagons, the rain and the creeks had washed it away.

And the street leading into the village was little better than the wagon road through the Forest. The village was smaller than she had thought it would be; for a place where ships came and anchored, the houses were very sparsely situated. Everywhere along the street lamps or candles were glowing in the windows and it made her feel homeless.

At a two-storey house, right on the street, a servant was closing the shutters for the night.

'Good evening!' she said to the woman.

'Evening.'

'Could you tell me where the magistrate's place is? Where they hold court.'

'It won't be open, it's too late.'

'I know. I just wanted to know how far it is.'

'Quite some way down the street.'

The woman was not exactly forthcoming. She had intended to ask her if there was not a room somewhere at the back where a tired body could lie down, but she decided not to. A Komoetie would rather lie down behind a bush with his head on a stone than have to ask for help.

The previous night, she had found shelter in an open cave on the other side of Buffel's Neck. Before she lay down, she had made peace with God. She told him she was sorry she had thought he would be mindful of a bunch of feathers and a few feeble ostrich chicks. You couldn't live at odds with God. With the Laghaans it was a different matter. And who but God could watch over Selling and the children and the ostriches on one side of the mountain and over her and Benjamin on the other?

At daybreak she had crawled out from the cave and after eating a little of the food, had taken to the road again. When the Forest began to close in around her, she prayed hard as she walked, asking God to see that she kept to the path and the elephants stayed in the thickets, for where would a mortal flee in that impossible place?

She did not rest or eat before midday. And when she did it was only for a short while because it was like the middle of the night there; if you heard one thing, you heard another, and kept on hearing things till you were aware of every squeak and tinkle. As long as she kept on walking, at least the sound of her feet came between her and the forest sounds.

And the magistrate's place was on the upper side of the street. Grey and grim. Like the law. She had a feeling that the lifeless windows were leering at her because she dared to linger before them. The anger she had so carefully kept at bay since she had left home suddenly stirred within her. Somewhere behind those windows they had made her Benjamin stand like a goat for slaughter to be inspected because of others' foolishness. She wanted to turn round and shout at the houses: Where is he? Where's the child? Where are the two peace-breakers? Where are they staying?

'Is auntie looking for someone?'

She looked round and saw a crafty-looking creature with no

front teeth leaning against the fence. Her father had always said, when a man's skin is that yellow, he's an Outeniqua, a honey-bearer. People of the wilderness which had only just been tamed.

'I might be an aunt but I'm not *your* aunt!' she told him, putting him in his place.

'Auntie's in a bad mood.' He was sitting on the fence, rocking from his heels to his backside. 'Did auntie come from far?'

'Yes. Do you know this place?'

'If auntie means the magistrate's court, yes. I know it. The last time I was here his honour gave me four lashes for being drunk and a bit rowdy. I didn't mind, but it was New Year, you know.'

'I meant the village.'

'I was born here, auntie. Pure Outeniqua.' He sounded proud of it.

'I'm looking for two white men; one is tall and the other short and thickset. They have a horse-cart.'

'Here are many tall ones and short ones and most of them have a horse-cart or something.'

'They had two dapple horses.'

'Many dapple horses around here. They say there was a time when there were mostly greys here; George Rex's horses they were. He was the big man. He had an eye for greys.'

On the other side of the street a window flew open and a man called out to the Outeniqua to stop riding the fence or he would call the constable.

'That was old Master Jones,' the fellow said when the window had closed again. 'He is thick in the body and he owns two dappled horses.'

'It's not him.'

'Then I don't know who it is auntie's looking for. And I'd better go home now; it's getting dark, we're not allowed on the streets after dark. Auntie better get off too.'

'I still have to find somewhere to sleep.'

'Walk a bit further up the street and auntie will get to the school. My uncle, who lives in the Forest, always sleeps behind the school when he has to sleep in the village. It's safe there.'

'Is there water there?'

'Yes. I can't offer auntie a place to sleep; I'm a stable-boy at Master Stewart's and we are not allowed to bring others on the premises.'

'That's how it should be.'

When she walked away, she was still hoping to meet with one of her own kind and find an honest bed for the night. But it was getting too late; by the time she found the school, the first stars were out and she had no choice, she would have to sleep there like a thief. At first, however, she had to walk past it because two smartly dressed women in long velvet clothes came down the street accompanied by two equally smart gentlemen. A servant walked ahead of them, carrying a lantern. They were English people.

It was not pleasant to have to steal a place to sleep. She did not sleep much under the verandah behind the little school, the world around her was too unfamiliar. When she dozed off for a while, she was still somehow on her guard; when she woke up she just lay there, thinking. Her anxiety for the child was more than flesh could bear and she had to keep on repressing the bitterness in her so that it would not well up and overcome her. Selling had said she must slither like a snake. If she had to, she would strike like a snake whose spine has been crushed. But what was she to do if the magistrate had been told about Selling? How much fighting lay ahead of her then?

What had they done with the child? Where was he? He would know she would come, but how would he bear up while he was waiting?

After midnight the wind changed and brought the smell of the sea in over the village. She folded her overcoat tighter round her and found hope in the knowledge that the magistrate was a man of the law and that the law was just. You could not just kick aside the law as it pleased you. No matter who you were.

When Pace, the shopkeeper at Uniondale, wanted to take the church to court, to the Supreme Court at the Cape, because of his plots, the people laughed at him, saying the judge would cut him up – you could never argue with the church, for the church would not lie. But Pace insisted that the block of plots the church wanted to sell by auction were the plots he had bought from the Gombert Jews. The church came up with a village plan, showing that the plots were church property – Pace had better be careful of what he was saying. Pace said the village plan was as wrong as the church. Surveyor Melvill must have been in a daze when he had marked that block T. It should have been J. The description of the boundary lines and the situation of the plots corresponded with J. And J was his block of plots. The church said Pace was a liar and started auctioning the plots. Petrus went to the auction himself and was one of the men who had stopped Pace and the minister coming to blows. The whole congregation gathered round like flies, most of them on the side of the church of course. So Pace decided to go to court for his rights. The church had to follow and defend. And it was a case for the Supreme Court at the Cape. When Petrus had told Selling about the affair, she herself had said Pace was going to the Cape to get his come-uppance, for the law would be on the side of the church.

Pace and his witnesses left for the Cape on horseback. The minister and the witnesses for the church took a sailing ship from Knysna. And the ship had hardly got to the open sea when a storm came up as if it had been waiting for them. The nearest shelter was at Mossel Bay, which they reached towards the evening, crippled and just in time. But the storm had roused the conscience of the chief witness of the church and when they anchored, he got off the ship and walked all the way back home.

Pace won the case. The judge openly stated that the church had acted shamefully. Law was law. Even for the church.

She would not go home without the child, even if she had to go to the Cape on foot to fight for him.

She got up at dawn, washed herself, put on a clean dress and a clean headcloth over her hair. She was convinced that every sinew in her legs had shrunk – and how she was to get to the magistrate without limping, she did not know.

The village was still quiet and cold when she walked down the street. Here and there a servant was opening a shutter or sweeping a verandah – with care, as if they were afraid to disturb those still sleeping. A thin streak of mist was lying like smoke over the lagoon.

She had almost reached the magistrate's place when the crack of a whip suddenly broke the silence and she looked up. Sixteen straining oxen came up the street with a heavily loaded, creaking wagon, like creatures on a journey with no beginning or end. These were woodcutters, she thought to herself, and stopped to look. The oxen were old, the wagon was old. You could not tell whether the four men round the wagon were young or old; they walked in the same slow manner as the oxen – the only difference was that they did not have yokes on their shoulders. Their clothes were thickly patched, the shoes on their feet creased with age. Only the wood on the wagon was neatly worked, neatly loaded and securely fastened. Not one of them looked up as the wagon came past her. She checked the feeling of pity that welled up inside her.

It was still quiet at the magistrate's place. A dog ran up and down, sniffing, and lifted his leg against the front door.

'Shoo!' she drove him away. 'You can't come and lift your leg against the law.'

Children dressed in warm clothes came past, going towards the school. Six girls in long riding-habits galloped past on horseback, sitting side-saddle with the greatest of ease. Rich people's children, she could see. Rich people's horses. Well groomed and well trained, like Petrus Zondagh's horses.

She ran her eyes over every horse-cart that came past, hoping that it might be the two peace-breakers. Another wagon loaded with wood came down the street.

Then the man with the keys came and unlocked the door. Shortly after him three more men and a constable came and she could not decide which of the men was the magistrate. She had to restrain herself from going up to them and asking where the child was. You could not just walk up to a magistrate, she told herself, you had to wait your turn.

The sun cleared the fog on the lagoon and she saw a ship with sails coming over the water towards the village.

Then she could wait no longer. Her legs could scarcely support her body up the stone steps to the door; the door was open but she knocked and stepped back respectfully to wait. After a while she went and knocked again. From where she was standing she could see down a broad passage with doors on each side.

Please, God, she prayed, stand by my side and don't leave me.

A man, the one who had unlocked the door, came through one of the doors and looked at her.

'Yes?' he asked in English.

She could not speak English. 'I'm looking for the magistrate, my master,' she said in her own Dutch dialect. 'I've walked for two days to get here to see him. Please, my master.'

'Go to the side door.' English again.

Side door. Side door? Perhaps it was the other door, the one on the side. She had to go to the side door. All right. She went down the steps, round the corner and knocked on the side door. The same man came to the door and looked at her as if he had never seen her before.

'Yes?'

'I must speak to the magistrate, master. It's urgent. It took me two days to get there, on foot.'

'Could you say it again in English?'

Every drop of hope rushed out of her. If she had to ask for the child in English, she was in trouble.

'Jesus, master, please get somebody that can speak Dutch,' she said, frightened. 'I must see the magistrate.'

He muttered something and walked away. She did not know

whether he had said she was to wait there or follow him. She decided to wait.

The room she was in was small and bare, with only a church-bench against the wall. She could hear people talking but she could not make out what they were saying. Doors opened and closed but nobody came to tell her about the magistrate. And the longer she had to stand there like that, the more difficult it became to keep the anger in her down. *Slither like a snake, Fiela! When you want something from a white man, stoop low!* She would crawl down the passage on her knees to the magistrate as long as they did not just leave her there without knowing what was going on.

When the outer door opened behind her, she swung round and saw that an old Coloured man had come in. He had a broom and bucket – he would be the one that cleaned the place.

'I feel like shaking your hand, old man!' she said, relieved. 'Where's the magistrate?'

'On the bench, auntie.'

'Go and tell him Fiela Komoetie from the Long Kloof has come on foot to see him.' He didn't budge. 'Go and tell him I want to see him!'

'Does Mr Goldsbury know that auntie is here?'

'How is he to know if nobody goes and tell him? Does he speak Dutch?'

'Yes.'

That was a mercy. 'Go and tell I'm here.'

'What did auntie want to see him about?'

'It's none of your business!' she told him sharply.

'The magistrate's a busy man, auntie.'

'He will stop being busy once he's heard that I have a serious complaint to lodge,' she said with a sudden inspiration. 'He'll drop everything he's busy with when he hears what the complaint is about.'

'I'll go and see what I can do, but I'm not so sure auntie's right.'

When he was gone, she sat down on the bench to get the weight off her feet and give the dizziness in her head a chance to go away. She felt better about one thing, at least: the magistrate could speak Dutch. They would understand one another. Only God knew how frightened she was of what was lying ahead of her, but she was not without hope and faith altogether. And she would wait patiently.

Somebody with squeaky shoes came down the passage; when she looked up, the constable was standing in the door and the cleaner stood behind him.

'Is this the woman?' the constable asked over his shoulder.

'Yes. She wants to lodge a complaint against the magistrate, she said.'

She got up from the bench with indignation. 'He's got it wrong, master!' she cried. 'I've never said that. I want to lodge a complaint about a matter that only the magistrate knows about.'

'What matter?'

'Two white men came and took away my child in the Long Kloof and said the magistrate had sent them. They said they would bring him back on Saturday – and I'm still waiting.' Slither, Fiela, slither, she reminded herself. 'That's why I'm on my knees before you, master, and why I'm asking you to please go and tell the magistrate that Fiela Komoetie is here from the Long Kloof to see him and lodge a complaint against the two men.'

'Are you talking about the white child that was fetched from the other side of the mountain?'

'You know, master, the moment I saw your face, I knew you would know what was going on. Yes, that child is the reason I'm standing here. Benjamin Komoetie, his name is, the hand-child I reared as if he were my own.' *Slither, Fiela, slither!* 'If master will be so good as to get me to the magistrate, I'll manage on my own from there.'

'Just wait here a moment,' he said and walked away. The

cleaner stayed in the door and looked at her with renewed interest.

'You,' she snapped, 'have you been employed to stand bending that broom under your weight?'

'I'm just having a good look at the world, auntie; seems to me he's going to turn the wrong way round today.'

'Take care that I don't turn *you* the wrong way round! I'll tell the magistrate you've been prying into other people's business!'

He started sweeping down the passage with a snort. The sun came in through the window and made a broad streak on the floor at her feet. There was dust in the cracks between the floorboards.

The thing she had come to do, was weighing on her. She told herself to stay calm; she would talk as she had never talked before in her life, she would slither as she had never slithered . . .

When the constable returned, he looked as if his neck had gone rigid and he couldn't look her in the eye.

'Master, why are you standing there looking jittery?' Why did she suddenly feel so queer?

'Listen . . .' Even his voice was different. Bossy. 'The magistrate says the case is closed, the child has been returned to his parents.'

Her blood rushed to her head; the man's body toppled before her eyes and came up right again. 'What did you say?'

'I was present when the forest woman came to see if it was her child or not. She recognized him immediately. It was him all right.'

No, she had not heard right. He had not said it.

'There must be a mistake, master.'

'It's true. I was there.'

Had he come and told her that they had taken away the child because Selling had murdered a man, because the child was white and they were not, because she did not take him to church, she would have had a wall against which she could batter until her fists bled and the wall came down, but if he was the forest woman's child, there was nothing to fight against.

'Master, I stand here before you and you have condemned me – but I can't believe it's true.'

'The magistrate had him standing between four other boys of the same age and the woman recognized him without a moment's doubt. I was there.'

'It can't be, it just can't be,' she kept saying hopelessly. 'Please let me talk to the magistrate myself, master.'

'The magistrate is busy, you can't see him. The case is closed.' Just like that. Closed. Like dying without saying goodbye.

She walked till it was dark and until she could walk no more. Not for a moment, ever, had she feared the forest woman. Not for a moment had she thought she would lose Benjamin that way, that her hands would be empty when she went home. Never.

She did not look for shelter. She put the sack with her things under her head, folded her overcoat round her body and lay down in the soft driftsand along the forest road.

Deep within the thickets a branch cracked. And another. Elephants? Her mind was too weary to find room for fear as well. Somewhere in that vast Forest Benjamin would also be lying down to sleep. Where? What was going through his mind? How was he to understand? You tied an umbilical cord, you did not rip it off! Benjamin had always been the one standing at the roadside if she had stayed away a little too long visiting Miss Baby or Auntie Maria. He had never joined the other children when they talked and dreamed about where they wanted to go and work or live one day. He was the one that had always said, 'I just want to stay with ma.'

Sheer hatred came up in her against the woman without a face that had taken him after nine years. Woodcutter's woman, forest woman, white woman. Had *she* watched over him when the fever of the measles would not subside? Had she comforted him when his boat drifted away or when the mongoose stole his broody hen's eggs? Had she seen him laugh, seen him cry, seen him grow out of his clothes?

God, how could this happen?

She fell asleep from exhaustion. When she woke up at dawn, she felt death stirring in her; she knew she would have difficulty reaching home and that she would have to take every short cut to get there.

She came through the hills above the house shortly before midday on the next day, limping for the last part of the way. They were expecting her from the other direction. Selling was sitting beside the house with the whip thongs slack in his hands and his eyes on the road in the Kloof. Kittie was standing behind him. Emma was doing the mending. Tollie was standing guard with the thorn branch in the ostrich enclosure while Dawid gathered the dung in the tin bucket. There was not a sign of redness on Kicker's beak or shins. Pollie was pecking along the ground behind him.

Selling was the first to look round. Then they were all there with her. Selling's hands kept fidgeting and the words seemed to stick in his throat.

'Ma, what's happened?' Dawid asked, aghast. Someone took the sack from her, someone brought her something to sit on, someone put the beaker of water in her hands, someone took off her headcloth.

And Selling asked: 'Where's Benjamin, Fiela?'

She did not look at them, she looked away to the ground. 'He's the forest woman's child.' When she looked up, tears were running over Selling's face and the children were just standing there, defeated. Behind them, at the hedge, Kicker stood there, looking straight at her.

14

By Friday things started looking better. It was three days since Elias had gone to fetch the little rascal and bring him back, and things were already making progress. The second scaffold was finished; Lukas was on one and Nina on the other. Not that *she* was worth much. The log he had given her to practise on looked as if it had been gnawed on all sides, but Lukas's log was beginning to get smooth and square. The boy had brains. Once he had grown out of his nonsense he would be a useful son. Perhaps even more than Willem and Kristoffel. As soon as Nina had learned to do the rough dressing, he wanted to make a third scaffold; she could hack off bark while Lukas and he concentrated on squaring and finishing off. A few more weeks and he would haul out so many beams to Deep Walls they would hardly fit on one wagon.

'Stop splintering that log like that, Nina!' He was sitting on a stump and keeping an eye on them. 'Just cut off the bark and square the beam!'

'The axe is blunt, Pa.'

'That's a lie!'

'How long must I stay on this scaffold, Pa?'

'Until you cut as I have shown you.' She muttered something he could not make out. 'What did you say?'

'Aunt Gertie says it's a disgrace before the Lord that pa puts me on the scaffold like a boy.'

'You go and tell Aunt Gertie to keep her big mouth in her own backyard! If I want to put you on the scaffold it's my affair and to keep you out of mischief.' He stooped down to pick up a

twig and when he came up again, she was getting off the scaffold.
'Where do you think you're going?'

'To tell Aunt Gertie pa had said she must keep her big mouth in her own backyard.'

'Get back on that scaffold before I lose my temper!' She would try a man's patience to the utmost.

'Pa did say I was to go and tell her.'

'That's enough!'

Lukas has had his hiding, he thought, she's asking for one too. And if that did not help, he would take her to the village and hire her out, but something had to be done about her. He didn't intend to sit like a prison guard for the rest of his life to keep her on the scaffold. The whole time she was up there it seemed as if she had one eye on the axe and the other on a chance to get away.

'Nina, I'm not going to tell you again to cut square! Just hack off the bark!'

'I told pa, this axe is blunt.'

'It's not blunt, I sharpened it this morning. It's *you* that's blunt!' He turned to Lukas. 'Careful, don't cut away too much. Head to the line; keep one eye on it all the time.'

Lukas did not look up. The nonsense was not out of him yet but at least he would not try to run away again, of that Elias van Rooyen was sure. The little brat would realize that it would not pay him to play tricks, that he would be made white again and learn to be obedient. He was no longer in the Long Kloof.

How the little fool had made him walk to catch up with him! Fortunately he had used his head and taken the short cut through Lourie Bush so as to come out on Kom's path at the other side of the honey cliffs – he must have gained at least an hour that way. Not long after that he had found the boy's tracks. And once he had found a track, whether blue buck or bush-buck or bush pig, he could tell whether the buck was grazing or fleeing, fat or lean, male or female.

He had not been on Lukas's track for long before he realized that the wretch was scared, for he had kept right to the middle of the sled-path and every hundred paces or so, the tracks clearly showed that he had stopped and looked round as if he was hearing things and having the jitters. Angry as he had been, he could not help but to laugh to himself; the Forest had many sounds – it would scare anyone who was not used to the forest ways.

Then he saw that the boy had been running for quite a long way – and then walked again. Not far from Gouna Drift, he had jumped round right in his tracks and run back the way he had come. Something must have frightened him. A bush pig or something. Perhaps an elephant. When the buggers were not in the mood for chasing you, they had a way of simply standing in the thickets and watching you; it was sheer chance whether you spotted them or not.

How far the boy had doubled on his tracks was no concern of his – he had no time to waste because it was getting late. He found the track that was going on and stayed on that.

When he came to the drift, he knew he had started catching up with the boy; the footprints in the mud on the other side were as fresh as if he had just gone through. But then the devil had come and intervened – not far from the drift he got a fright himself, for the boy's tracks suddenly turned north along the sled-path leading to the Cross. It was the right direction for the Long Kloof but it was the wrong path and a most dangerous one at that. Few woodcutters would risk bringing wood along there.

And he could find no return track because it was now too dark in the Forest. Perhaps there was no track coming back. He would have to stay on the one he had. Luckily he was not far from a clearing where the light was better and he managed to find the track coming back. And then he had to run to catch up again

And sure as sure, on Kom's path, not five hundred paces from the gravel road, he saw the blue shirt ahead of him in the twilight, going at an easy pace.

And just like the elephants, who can move incredibly quietly through the Forest when they wanted to, Elias van Rooyen could move soundlessly when necessary. He caught up without a twig breaking under his feet and when the boy looked round, he was right behind him.

'You little rascal!' he cried. 'Where the hell do you think you're going?' First the child had been startled, and then he turned round and started running. It left him no choice, he had to go after the little fool. But as he was running, he took the ox rein from his shoulder, unrolled it and took one end in each hand so that there was a long piece of slack in the middle. When the scoundrel looked round the third time, he was on him and he threw the loop neatly round his body and his arms and pulled him down like a calf.

'You rotten little sod!' he shouted, out of breath. 'Just try running away now!'

'Please, master! Please, master!'

'*What?*' It was more than a man could take. Your own flesh and blood calling you *master* like a Coloured! Lord knew, he had not been that angry in years. He took the one end of the ox rein and wound it round the wriggling body while he hit him with the other end. 'What did you say?'

'Please! Please! It hurts!'

'Please *who?*' With every lash the wretch screamed and struggled harder. 'Please *who?*'

'Please, uncle!'

'*Uncle?*' A man could not take that either. He would beat it out of him if it was the last thing he did for him. 'Please who?' The end of the rein he was holding him with cut into his hand but still the boy would not give in. 'I'll beat you dead!'

'Please! Please!'

'Who am I?'

'I don't know.'

'You don't know?'

'I don't know.' But his giving in was near, he had started to cry.

'I'm your pa! That's who I am! Say it! Say who I am!' He was as tough as a piece of ironwood. 'Say who I am!'

'Pa.'

'Who's your ma?'

'Ma.'

'Who are your brothers?'

'Willem and Kristoffel.'

'Who's your sister?'

'The girl.'

'What's her name?'

'Nina.'

For every answer he gave him a lash. 'And who are you?'

'Benja— Lukas.'

'Lukas who?'

'I don't know.'

'Lukas van Rooyen. Say it!'

'Lukas van Rooyen.'

'Will you stop your nonsense now?'

'Yes.'

'Yes who?'

'Yes, Pa.'

The child had worn him out. He could not let go of him, for how could he catch him again in the dark? So he tied him up with the ox rein and left just enough slack round his legs to allow him to take a small step at a time. Then he lit the lantern and made the rascal walk home in front of him.

Barta was horrified of course.

'There was no time to look where I was hitting, woman! The blighter was as stubborn as a devil!'

'But the weal across his face, Elias?' she asked, frightened. 'If the forester sees it and tells the magistrate, you'll be in trouble.'

'Should I have left him to get lost again? Was I to go and tell the magistrate *that*?'

'No, Elias, I did not say that.'

Lord only knew where a woman's brains were.

And the devil was still in Lukas when they got home. Nina was sitting quietly on the bed behind the door when they came in and did not even look up, but Lukas went straight up to her, stood staring at her until she looked up and then he spat right in her face. If Barta had not stopped him, the scoundrel would have had his second beating right there and then. Barta wanted him to untie the boy, but who would guard him through the night? You could not trust him. He left him to sleep tied up as he was.

For every day that went by, Benjamin made a notch in one of the cross-poles of the scaffold. The day of the sixteenth notch Nina had to help him roll the second log on to the scaffold. The man was standing giving the orders.

It was better out on the scaffold than in the house. As long as he kept on hacking, the man left him alone in a way. The girl too. But in any case he would never speak to her again, for it was she who had betrayed him. How else did the man know where to find him? And he had lost his five shillings as well. His mother had always said, someone who lies will also steal and someone who steals will also lie. That was exactly what the girl had done. And she was still working on her first log – not that he cared, she could drop dead working at that log for all he cared.

If only he could know why his mother didn't come. He knew she would come, it was just that the waiting was so long. Every night he was filled with tears but he did not cry. And how his mother was going to find her way to him he did not know, but she would get to him somehow. She said a drunkard and a corpse lie down when the going gets too hard, but not a Komoetie.

'Lukas, I want to sell the log you're starting on now, do you hear?'

He pretended not to hear. Perhaps his mother was waiting to
see if they would bring him back.

'Did you hear me, Lukas?'

'Yes.'

'Yes who?'

'Yes, Pa.'

'Don't let me have to ask you again.'

On the days of the eighteenth, nineteenth, twentieth and
twenty-first notches it rained and they could not work on the
beams. Kristoffel came home first. Then Willem. Like wet fowls.
They could not cut wood either. It was crowded in the house.
All they did was sit. The woman sighed a lot and the man kept
on pulling strips of bark from the firewood and breaking it into
small pieces. Some he chewed and spat out again. Kristoffel had
his missing shoes on and Willem was still wearing Dawid's coat.
Both Willem and Kristoffel had beards.

The girl kept on making trouble because she could not sit still.
Up and down like a monkey on a rope. A hundred times a day
the man told her to stop fidgeting about.

'I want to go outside.'

'Stay on your backside and keep quiet!'

The woman made the food. The food was not nice. Willem
and Kristoffel had brought meal and sugar and coffee and
Kristoffel also brought a chunk of bush-buck meat. The smoke
from the fire made the air hazy and their eyes smarted.

The days seemed to go by more and more slowly. He began
wondering whether his mother had come looking for him and
got lost on the way. The more he thought about it, the surer he
became that that was the reason why she did not turn up. After
the second day in the house he became restless and kept asking
to go outside like Nina did. Every time he had to go outside to
pee, either Willem or Kristoffel went with him as if they had to
see that he did not run away again. He would not run away
again, not from the Forest, because you never got out of it. If his
mother was lying dead somewhere in the Forest he would have

to stay there for the rest of his life unless his father sent Dawid or Tollie to fetch him.

'Nina, stop fidgeting!'

'Pa, I want to go and pee.'

'Then let your mother go with you.'

Every time Nina had to go, the woman went with her. But that time the woman apparently did not hear because Nina went outside alone. And then she did not come back again. After a while the man got cross and took the ox rein off the hook behind the door, laid it over his knees and started pulling off bark again. The woman sighed and said:

'She's been on the scaffold too long, Elias, she was used to playing in the Forest every day.'

'And I told you it would have to come to an end. The Forest is not a place for a girl on her own.'

'I'll go and look for her.' He did not know what had made him say it; the grey plank walls had got too close round him and were driving him outside. They all looked up together when he had said it.

'What?' the man said. 'You go after her and I go after you again?'

Then they all stared at the floor again.

It was almost dark when they heard her whistling outside in the rain. The man got up, folded the ox rein in his hand and went to stand behind the door. When she pushed open the door she was still whistling and did not see the man standing behind the door. Her hair was dripping wet, the nightshirt was clinging to her body and legs and her eyes were shining as if the rain had fallen into them.

The man waited until she was well into the house before he kicked the door shut. Before the first stroke hit her, she started screaming and kept on screaming while she tried to get away round the chairs and round the table and over the beds and under the beds. Willem guarded the door and Kristoffel guarded the window so that she could not escape. The woman guarded the candle and the dish on the table. Soon it seemed as if the girl's screams could no longer get out through the wooden walls and the whole house was shaking with them, Benjamin pressed his hands over his ears and shut his eyes but it kept on and on. Like the blows.

Then the man stopped.

He opened his eyes and saw her sitting on the floor by the table; underneath her a damp stain was growing bigger and bigger. She was no longer screaming, just crying.

'Bring the scissors!' the man ordered. He was out of breath and very angry. 'I'm not going to stand any more nonsense from her.'

'The scissors won't cut any more, Elias,' the woman said.

'Give me a knife then!'

Kristoffel passed him the knife. The man grasped bundles of her hair and cut it as you cut corn with a sickle, some bunches closer than the others.

15

'Keep on looking, Kittie!'

'I've looked through the whole Bible already, Ma; I can't find it.'

Whenever one of the children had an idle moment, they had to take the Bible and search for the story about the two women who had fought over one child. Fiela knew it was somewhere in the Bible.

'What are you going to do with it, Fiela?' Selling asked.

'I don't know yet – how much did Rossinski give you for the hides?'

'Two pennies a hide.'

'That's good.'

Her mind and her body did what had to be done but her heart was behind the mountain. She could not grieve and resign herself as Selling and the children did. Day by day the bitterness grew greater and would not let go of her. At night she lay awake, missing the child more and more.

She had come home on the Friday, and the next two days had been days of sorrow for Wolwekraal. She could not lift her head from the pillow and Selling and the children lay down as she did.

On the Monday she got up and put them all to work even though she did not feel like working herself. But the Komoeties would not stay lying down; if you did you became blind and could not see a way out.

Selling looked bad that morning and it took her a lot of talking to get him outside in the sun. 'Sit up straight, Selling!' She had to hide her own sorrow behind the harshness of her words. 'Take that skin and start preparing it, you can't just sit here breathing for the rest of your life!'

'If I could only understand it, Fiela!'

'Get your hands to work, Selling, none of us can understand it.'

'The child will die over there in the Forest.'

'Don't talk like that!'

'Forest people are different, it's not open around you like here; the child does not know the ways of the Forest, he'll get sick there.'

'Give my legs time to recover, give me time to think which way to go and in the meantime pray that the child can withstand what has happened to him.' She turned away and walked to the ostriches. Please, God, she asked, keep down the rebellion in me because it's going to finish me off; the forest woman has recognized him as hers and nothing can change it.

Kicker stood pecking at the pile of fodder at the top end of the enclosure; Pollie was down in the corner.

'There's nothing I can do for you, Pollie,' she said over the hedge, dejected. 'He does not even notice you.'

She sent Dawid and Tollie down to the crossroads to cut reeds for a shelter over the ostriches' nest.

'But they're not even planning to mate yet, Ma,' Tollie objected.

'That does not mean that we won't start making a plan. As from tomorrow I want you to throw the fodder under the shelter so that they can get used to it.'

The children worked without zest and Selling looked half asleep as he worked on the hides. But as long as they kept going, she was satisfied.

The shelter was finished late that afternoon: ten feet long, ten feet wide and high enough to be comfortable for the one sitting on the nest. The two open sides faced north and south. Her hands had helped with the building, her eyes had done the measuring, her mouth had given orders and the whole time rebellion had kept on welling up in her.

When the shelter was finished, she went up to Selling.

'Selling,' she said, 'I'm going to ask you a question and I want a complete answer from you. Not half an answer.'

'What do you want to ask, Fiela?'

'Do you believe that a child of three could have wandered here from the Forest? Do you believe it before God?'

Selling dropped the rock-rabbit skin on his lap and looked away to the valley below for a long time. When he turned his eyes back to her, they were filled with tears that slowly started trickling down his cheeks. 'No, Fiela, I don't believe it. But . . .'

'I told you I want a complete answer, not one with a *but* coming up behind!'

'Then my answer is no. Not a child of three. Unless . . .'

'Selling!'

'No, Fiela, not a child of three.'

She walked back to the enclosure, telling the children to fetch thorn branches; the ostriches had to be driven into the pen so that they could cover their heads with sacks. Then she would be able to put paraffin in their ears against the ticks. The winter was dry, the pests had not settled yet. The two birds must have sensed that her patience was running low for they got them in the pen with little difficulty.

That night, by the light of the candle, she took the Bible and tried to find the place where it told about the two women with one child. In the next few days she made the children look for it and at length, on the Friday, she asked Petrus, who had come to show Selling his new stallion, and he knew where to find it.

'If I remember correctly, it's somewhere in Kings. Solomon told them to divide the living child in two with a sword and give each woman half.'

'That's horrible!' Emma cried.

Petrus laughed. 'Don't worry, Emma, they did not really cut

the child in two; the real mother begged them to spare his life and give him to the other woman rather than cut him in two – are you having a Bible quiz or something?'

Selling was going to reply but she forestalled him. 'No, Master Petrus,' she said, 'I just wanted to know. Emma, put the Bible away now and see that Master Petrus gets a nice cup of coffee. Put some of the fresh bread with it.' She avoided the questioning eyes of Selling and the children. Later, when Petrus asked where Benjamin was, she again avoided the truth. 'He's playing somewhere – how is Miss Margaretha?'

'You haven't been to Maria or to Miss Baby lately, Fiela?'

He was suspicious, she knew. 'Things are not going so well with us at the moment. I was hoping the ostriches would have mated by this time, but all that so-called dashing male ostrich can do is eat.'

'Pollie's got on beautifully. You would not think it was the same bird that you got from Koos.'

'That's true, yes.'

'Why did you say things were not going well here with you?'

'It's just my way of talking. We can do with a bit of rain. I want to sow corn at the new moon.'

When Petrus was leaving, she walked with him to his horse.

'Fiela, are you sure there's nothing wrong? Selling looks much worse to me.'

'I've sent one of the children down to the shop for some elixir to give to him.'

'You did not attend the prayer-meeting at Avontuur yesterday. Or last week neither.'

Petrus was fishing. 'Do *you* go to church every Sunday, then, Master Petrus?' she asked. She would leave the Kloof guessing about Benjamin until she had no choice. Petrus too. For years they had been talking behind her back about the white child in her house, and now they could burst with curiosity if they wanted to.

Selling was displeased when she got back to the house. 'You

should have told Petrus the truth, Feila, he could help find out where the child is.'

'Years ago Petrus wanted me to give the child to him and his wife to bring up. Bring up to what, I ask you? To be a white slave like Jan Barnard's sister's child?'

'Petrus did not mean to do that, he meant well.'

'He came here and suggested it after the child had been with us for more than a year. A child is not something you pass on from one to the other like a dog you no longer want. A child must know one home.'

'Petrus could find out where the child is.'

'It won't be necessary, I'll go and find out myself.'

'How?'

'God will show the way. I suddenly remembered something as I worked with the ostriches today; I want to go back to ask the magistrate at Knysna about it.'

'What was it you remembered, Fiela?'

'Don't ask me now, Selling, give me the chance and I'll bring you the answer and, for all you know, I might bring back Benjamin as well. Because this time I'm going to see the magistrate face to face even if I have to smoke him out like a swarm of bees!'

'Fiela!'

'Don't look so worried, Selling; tomorrow I shall take to the road again and this time they won't take me by surprise. They told Pace that he could not win either, remember?'

She was back at Knysna early on the Monday morning. Her legs and feet were as bad as they had been the last time but at least everything was familiar the second time and she knocked unhesitatingly on the side door. Decently. She would not slither like a snake again; she had made up her mind about that on the way there. She would stand with her head up and she would speak out.

She knocked again.

She had not slept behind the school like a thief again either, she slept just outside the village in a little dip and she had her words ready for the magistrate. If he had a heart in him, she would cross the first bridge without difficulty.

She knocked the skin off her knuckles and felt the devil stirring in her. Either they could not hear her or they did not want to hear her! She put out her hand and carefully felt the big, brass doorknob. The door was locked. Funny, the front door was wide open. Was the side door locked against her? Were they afraid of something?

She knocked once more and then turned and walked to the front. They did not know Fiela Komoetie when she was standing up for her rights. She walked right in through the front door. Whether he had seen her coming past the window or heard her coming down the passage she did not know, but before she had gone far one of the doors opened and a man with close-set eyes came out and looked at her as if he wanted to scare her off.

'Who are you and what do you want?' he asked.

'I'm Fiela Komoetie from the Long Kloof. I battered at the side door but nobody heard me.' Her rage was a source of strength. 'I've come to see Solomon.'

'I beg your pardon?'

'Solomon. The one from the Bible, I've heard that you keep him here somewhere.'

'What!'

'I just wanted to find out from him why only one woman was sent for when the child had to be divided.'

His eyes were as cold as an adder's and his lips thin and dry. He was struggling to keep his dignity. 'I don't think you realize where you are. Or that I can have you arrested immediately.'

'Arrest me for what? Because I've come on foot from the Long Kloof for the second time to find out what's happened to my child?'

'It was explained to you the last time what had happened; you were fully informed.'

'Then master knows that I came here the week before last as well.' Lower down in the passage a door creaked.

'I have been told so, yes.'

'Then I suppose master has also been told that I had to go home without setting eyes on the magistrate. That I had to swallow the constable's brew of lies about the child having been returned to his real mother.'

'Do you know who you are talking to?'

'No, master, but the man I want to talk to is the one that tried to play Solomon over my hand-child, the magistrate.' His lips seemed to grow thinner and his neck longer. Suddenly she knew what he was about to say.

'You're standing before the magistrate. I am the magistrate.'

It was as if she had jumped over a cliff; she could no longer stop herself, all she could do was to reach out and try to break her fall so that she would land as unscathed as possible.

'Then I am at last standing before the right man, your worshipful lord,' she said, with as much dignity as she could. 'Now your worshipful lord and I can at last talk this thing out.'

'The child was given back to his rightful parents; the case is closed.'

'That is not the whole case, your worshipful lord.' Another door creaked open, more ears came to listen. 'First you have to explain how a small child of three got over the mountains to the Long Kloof.'

'I gave you a final warning; the case is closed.'

'Has your worshipful lord ever been through the Forest and over the mountains?'

'The mother of the child immediately identified him amongst four others!' His temper was roused now. 'The fact that the child had been in your home for nine years, unlawfully, is a serious offence; we shall have to consider bringing a case against you.'

'I found the child at my back door and brought him up like one of my own for nine years! Then the two men came to count the people and suddenly I had no more say. Who says the forest woman did not point out the right child by accident?'

'She did not. There was a witness to it.'

'Listen, master, I've come far, I'm sick with worry for the child. I'm not concerned about myself today, I'm concerned about a child. God forgives many things, but God never forgives us the wrong we do to a child. I'm in your worshipful lord's power today; how can master be sure it was not just the forest woman's luck?'

'I've had enough of you.'

'Don't get hasty with me, master.' The key question she was saving like a piece of gold under her headcloth felt like solid ground underneath her; it gave her the strength to stand there almost without fear. 'I'll believe your worshipful lord, I'll believe everything, I'll rest by your worshipful lord's judgement even if it sticks in my throat like a bitter pill for the rest of my life...'

'Say what you want to say, you're wasting my time.'

'Send for the forest woman and let her tell your worshipful lord what her child had on the day he had disappeared. What clothes. I will tell master what the one I found at my door was wearing and then master can decide for the peace of your own soul, who's lying and who's telling the truth.' His eyelid started twitching fiercely; she knew she had to talk fast. 'I'm asking this for the child's sake, master. He knows no other mother than Fiela Komoetie. As soon as the ostriches start breeding, I'm going to buy the Laghaans' hired land and have it put in Benjamin's name. I'll bring master two ostrich chicks as well.' The eyelid kept on twitching.

'The child is back with his rightful parents,' he said and it seemed as if his jaw had grown stiff. 'What he had on the day he got lost can make no difference. You can put anything on him now and swear by it in the hope that I will believe you – you might even tell me you've kept the clothes and...'

'We had a plague of crickets in the Long Kloof that year, and the crickets ate the clothes, master. But I would not lie to you, master. I'll swear on the Bible. I'm asking only this one act of goodness. Send for the forest woman. Let her come and say what her child was wearing.'

'That's enough. You can decide whether you are going to leave on your own, or whether I have to call the constable.'

'Please, master, you can't just send me away like this!'

'Constable!'

The constable came out into the passage as if he had been waiting all the time. Fear shot through her like madness; if they locked her up, they might just as well cut off her hands! *Get down and slither, Fiela!* she told herself, groping for a way out. 'Please, your worshipful lord, I'll go, I did not come here to cause trouble!' When she started walking backwards, the magistrate made a sign to the constable with his eyes to stop him from coming nearer. Help me, God, she begged, hoping to the end that the magistrate would take pity on her. But his face stayed as hard as a rock and beside him the constable stood waiting for the next command. 'I'll go, master – I'm going,' she said, keeping them back. When her back touched the door at the end of the passage, she turned to the magistrate in desperation for a last time. 'Just tell me then where the child is, master, tell me who he is with.'

But she had humbled herself too late. The magistrate had won. He gave her a last warning: 'I forbid you to go near the child! I'll be writing to the magistrate at Uniondale today to have you watched *and* to take steps against you if you cause any further trouble!'

The words hit her first, then what they meant and then the desperateness of her situation. Her powerlessness.

She went home.

Petrus came again on the Friday and asked her straight out and in front of Selling what was wrong on Wolwekraal.

'What do you mean, Master Petrus?' she asked. Her body had not yet recovered from the walk, her heart was in shreds and she did not know how she would ever recover.

'There's something wrong here and you're covering it up. Have you got into trouble with the Laghaans again?' Selling's head started drooping. She did not answer. 'Is it money, Fiela? Forget your pride and tell me.' She just looked at him. 'Is one of the children in trouble?' Selling's head rolled over his chest like a drunk and she wanted to shout to him, lift your head! Don't let them see we have been beaten! 'Fiela,' Petrus was losing his patience, 'don't push away my hand when I'm trying to help. I'm asking you again, is one of the children in trouble?'

Selling's head came up. 'Tell Master Petrus, Fiela, tell him,' he pleaded, ignoring her restraint and pride.

'Then I'm right, there is something wrong.'

She could no longer hide it. If you poke about in an ant-hill, you do not stop before everything is exposed. She shrugged her shoulders and said, with undisguised bitterness, 'Yes, Petrus Zondagh, there *is* something wrong. The Komoeties have been crushed!'

'Fiela!'

'Quiet, Selling!' The world seemed unsteady around her. 'Go and tell the Kloof they can talk now and be damned to them. They came and took Benjamin away from us.'

She saw Petrus stiffen, she saw him sitting there, dumbfounded and trying to find words to say. Then she started telling him. Everything. From the day the two peace-breakers had come, the whole story poured out of her until she was hoarse and the shadows were creeping up the wall.

'Why didn't you tell me sooner, Fiela?' Petrus reproached her. 'What could you expect to gain by hiding it?'

'They said they would bring him back that Saturday. I, fool that I was, believed it because that was all I could do!'

Selling's head was back on his chest again, his whole body was limp. Down in the valley the plovers were screaming and at the pigsty the goat was asking to be milked.

'Fiela,' – there was pity in Petrus' voice – 'this is very hard. I would have done everything in my power to prevent it from happening the way it did. But one thing cannot be denied – it would have happened sooner or later.'

'Why?' she challenged him.

'Benjamin was a foundling.'

'No, Master Petrus, that's nonsense! Say what you mean – say, because Benjamin is a *white* foundling. If he had been like us, no one would have said a word about it!'

'Would you have agreed to the Laghaans keeping a white foundling?' Petrus tried to drive her into a corner. 'They're Coloured too.'

'There are Coloureds and Coloureds, just as there are whites and whites, Petrus Zondagh! Don't forget that!' She was in despair. Her mind was so tired that the words would not come. 'But I'm telling you all, Fiela Komoetie will not lie down, she'll go looking for him behind every tree in that Forest! The forest woman will have to look me in the face and tell me what her child had on that day. I'll go to the Forest and get her to tell me!'

'Fiela,' Petrus warned her, 'stay away from the Forest, you don't know the risks; don't go in there blindly – it's too dangerous. And the forest woman can't be expected to remember what her child had on on one particular day nine years ago.'

'It was not *just any* day! It was the day on which her child disappeared, and she will know. Of course she will! The moment my body has recovered, I'm going to look for him and I'm going to find him.'

'You're too angry to think properly, Fiela. The more you meddle with this, the worse it will be for you. Trust me, give me a chance to see what's happening behind that mountain.'

'What do you mean?'

'I was planning to send two horses down to Barrington at the Knysna River next week anyway. I'll go myself and talk to the magistrate.'

Selling sat up as if life had returned to him. 'If only Master Petrus can find out where he is so that we can know.'

'I'll do that, Selling.'

Petrus Zondagh had never been a white god to her as he had to Selling, but he was a man of his word and was greatly respected; he was the big man in the Long Kloof and he would find a short cut to Benjamin. She could not deny it, she needed Petrus's help. And it would not be the first time he had helped her. She was ashamed of herself for having blazed out at him to try and make him feel guilty as well, but he and Selling were so close that she felt left out; they were a house locked against her.

When Petrus rode away, her troubles seemed lighter. She was tired of fighting and sick of worrying. Petrus Zondagh meant new hope because they would not dare shut the door in his face as they had done to her.

The next day Miss Baby came. In the afternoon Auntie Maria and Petrus's wife, Margaretha, came. The Kloof had a new bone to chew. Not that they came to chew, they came to stand by her. And Miss Baby promised her that if Petrus had to go to court about Benjamin and things went wrong for them, she would offer to take Benjamin and keep him with her until the hullabaloo was over.

That night Fiela had a good night's sleep for the first time since they had come to fetch Benjamin. At dawn, something – a sound – woke her. At first she thought she must have dreamt it. But then it came again, outside, like a gift she was no longer expecting. It was the deep roar of a male ostrich getting ready to take his mate. It was Kicker.

16

A snare-pit. That was what he had to have, he sat thinking that Sunday. The sheer prospect of it brought a funny feeling to Elias's stomach for if it worked once, it would work again if you were clever enough. Elephants made themselves paths through the Forest. The old folks said they were paths along which they could escape in case of fire or some other danger. Not that Elias van Rooyen cared about reasons, the only thing that mattered was that the elephants always followed the same paths.

Some of their paths were well trampled and open for all to see; others were furtively used as if they were secret. And if you made a shelter or a house on one of their paths or stacked your wood there, it would be trampled to bits if they found it. Like the time Frans van Huyssteen had a quarrel with his mother-in-law at Big Island and moved his house to Lily Valley Crossing. The day they had to move, he, Elias, went and helped them carry their belongings. Frans had caught a nice fat bush-buck and they had a good party that night. Frans's mother-in-law had been there as well because by that time they had made peace again.

And Frans and his wife had been staying peacefully at their new place for almost a month when the elephants came one night and neatly took off one corner of the house as they walked past. The corner of the bedroom it was. When Frans and his wife came to their senses, they found they were lying with their feet out in the dew. It took Frans the whole of the next day to saw new planks and close up the corner for it looked as if it were going to rain. That very night the elephants came back and took off the corner again. Five times Frans had to knock together that corner until it looked like a sore with five plasters on, and every time the elephants came back and tore it down. Marais came and shot two of the buggers but that did not help either. Then Joram Barnard came past one day and pointed out to Frans that that particular corner of his house was overstepping an elephant path, one of those carefully made secret ones; if Frans had not moved back to Big Island he would still have been lying with his feet in the dew every morning.

He was going to keep a lookout for one of those unobtrusive paths. Pity he dared not ask one of the old folks if they knew whether anyone had dug a trap for elephants in the Forest before. The trouble was, the moment they heard of his plan, everybody might start digging traps. Common sense told him he just had to take care that the pit was deep enough. And deep enough for an elephant was not all that deep, for elephants, with their heavy bodies, could not get up any high step. He had better take great care with the covering, though; thin poles covered with branches and leaves should do it, and a prayer for a good night's rain to get rid of the human scent. Then Mr Elephant comes down the path and one moment his feet are on the ground and the next moment there is nothing underneath him. Once Mr Bigfoot was lying in the pit no amount of struggling would get him out. Not even if the others came and tried to help him out. For all he knew, it might even be the big bull of the Forest, Old Foot, that fell in first and he would get a mint of money for the tusks! It would take a while of course for an elephant to die in the pit and you would not dare to go there every day to see how near death he was; the best would be to stay away as far as possible. Every few days you could go and stand down wind from it and smell whether it was rotting yet.

He sat beside the house in the sun and saw the whole thing happen in his mind's eye. While one was dying in the first pit, you dug the next pit and you could go on like that until you had

a gun and then you would be able to shoot them as they landed
in the pits – all you would have to do would be to walk from pit
to pit...

Behind him in the house he heard Barta pottering about. He
had ordered her to see that the house was clean and tidy. He did
not want to be ashamed. Kristoffel had come home on Friday
night with a message from the forester at Deep Walls to say that
he would be coming to Barnard's Island on the Sunday to see
him.

The forester was welcome to come. It would be about Lukas
of course. The forester was free to come and inspect whatever he
wanted. Lukas had gone who knows where in the Forest with
Nina. Since Nina had been working on the beams as well, she
was like a tethered animal breaking loose on Sundays; if you did
not stop her, she would be out there long before daybreak. He
had got Lukas out of bed early that morning and told him to go
with Nina. It would be best if the forester did not find the boy
at home. The rascal had been far too full of his whims again in
the past few days. He did not want to talk and just nibbled at
his food. The work was going quite well, though. Even Nina was
getting on well hacking off bark. She had seen that disobedience
did not work, that wilfulness at work got her nowhere. But he
would not drop his plan to find out how much he would get if
she went to work in the village. Money was not to be sniffed at.

The forester turned up just before midday.

'The magistrate sent me to see how the boy is getting on.'

'Sit down, Mr Kapp, my wife will bring us some coffee. The
boy went to play in the Forest with his sister. Sit down. As a rule
they get back fairly early.' He would have to choose his words
well: he did not want to sound too anxious to get rid of the man
and he did not want to keep him there too long either. 'To tell
you the truth, Mr Kapp, I would like you to see for yourself how
he's getting on. As a matter of fact, I was expecting you earlier.'

'I could not come before now, Van Rooyen, two of the other

foresters have gone to George and it's impossible to patrol this Forest as it is. The magistrate wants to know if the boy is contented here with you and whether he is adjusting to his new life.'

Barta came from the house with two beakers of coffee.

'Contented, Mr Kapp? How would the child not be contented?' He deliberately talked with a loud voice so that Barta could hear every word. She had been very nervous recently and he had told her beforehand to be careful of what she said in front of the forester. 'Barta, Mr Kapp wants to know if Lukas is contented.'

'He's in good health and contented, Mr Kapp,' Barta said timidly, looking away.

'Bring us each a sweet potato too, Barta! Mr Kapp has come a long way.' When she walked into the house, he said to the forester: 'My wife is still overcome by the boy's return; I get the impression that she's afraid it may not be true.' The man would not chat and he only had a sip or two of his coffee. 'We only discovered last week that Lukas can read and write. Barta wants him to teach our daughter too. She's a clever child. No blockhead.'

'The magistrate wants to know if the boy is adjusting.'

'Adjusting? Mr Kapp, I wish you could see how well he's learning to work. My late father had always said, a man just has to pick up an axe and he'll tell you whether there's wood in his blood or not. I've got him helping me at the beams now and you can go and see for yourself over there what he's been doing. I don't want to brag, but I never have any trouble getting him out of bed and down to work – Barta! bring the sweet potatoes – I'll be glad if mister stays until the children get back so that you can see for yourself.' In his heart he hoped the children would stay away until dark. He had nothing to hide really, but if Lukas was in one of his moods, he could give the wrong impression. He had not been too keen to go with Nina that morning; he wanted to go off by himself.

Barta brought the sweet potatoes and stood a little apart from them.

'Van Rooyen, the magistrate said I must find out if the boy often speaks about the people he stayed with in the Long Kloof.'

'Not a word, Mr Kapp,' he assured the man. But then Barta chipped in, almost messing up everything.

'At the beginning he did keep saying he wanted to go home, Elias. Especially at night.'

He had to control himself to keep his voice level: 'That was only for a day or two, when things were still strange to him. Since he's got used to things here, he's never said another word about them.' He quickly started to talk about other things and prayed that Barta would keep her mouth shut about the boy having run away. He talked about the weather and the price of wood and said how good it was of the magistrate to inquire about the child.

'There has been trouble with the Coloured woman he was taken away from,' the forester said.

'What kind of trouble?' Barta asked, anxiously.

'I don't know, I only heard that the magistrate had forbidden her to try and find the child.'

'Find him?' Barta was scared out of her wits again.

'Go and have a drink of water, Barta,' Elias said, as he turned to the forester. 'Mr Kapp, you may go and tell the magistrate, that if that woman comes here to cause trouble, I'll be causing trouble myself. My wife will not be able to stand it.'

'The magistrate asked me to tell you that, if she comes here and worries you, you are to report it immediately.'

'I will most definitely do that, mister.'

When the sun was beginning to sink into the Forest, the man became tired of waiting.

'When are you expecting them back, Van Rooyen?'

'That's a bit difficult to say, mister. Depends. This daughter of mine is as fond of the wilderness as a buck. There's not a footpath or a sled-path here in Kom's Bush that she does not know. Just like a boy she is. I've said to my wife, it's not fair that a girl should be like that, we must make plans for her. I mean, you tell me, Mr Kapp, what future has she got in the Forest? A boy is a different matter. You often go to the village. Perhaps you could ask around to see if there are any English people looking for a servant or something. She's a hard-working girl. I don't want to hire her out for nothing, but if they give her some clothes and so on, we'll agree to a price.'

'I'll inquire.'

He could not think of anything else to say. The man was sitting there like a sapling in the way of your axe! Over at the woodcutters' houses it was all quiet, a hen or a child here and there and Malie that kept on peeping round a corner. Curious to know what the forester was doing there on a Sunday, of course. She should be keeping her eyes on her own children, rather.

He was worried about Gertrude, her oldest daughter; there was something between Willem and Gertrude – Malie herself had hinted in that direction a few times. He pretended not to hear. Willem and Kristoffel still had to work for him for many years. It was no good having sons if they went and got married, and worked for a wife and in-laws.

'Van Rooyen, it's getting late, perhaps I'd better go.'

'They shouldn't be too late.' He saw to it that quite a bit of doubt crept into his voice. It was time the forester stopped talking of going and went. You never knew when Nina would get it into her head to come home early and then everything could be messed up.

'You say it's going well with the boy, Van Rooyen?'

'Couldn't be going better. Ask Barta how the boy has grown. Just shot up and his shoulders are starting to bulge like a man's. Isn't that so, Barta?'

'Yes. He's grown. He's not a child any longer.'

Why did Barta have to stand there sounding so dreary? He was doing everything, covering up, and all she could do was

stand around and sigh! What if Kapp went back to the magistrate
with the wrong idea? He had to waste still more time, changing
the subject yet again:

'I believe they're shooting quite heavily amongst the bigfeet,
mister? Apparently a whole gang is shooting back in Gouna
Bush.'

'Yes.'

'I heard the Government is very strict about the trapping of
blue bucks now. What's going on?'

'You're killing them off.'

'Don't count me in, mister, I don't bother with blue bucks,
they have far too little meat on them for me.'

'It's getting late, I'm afraid I can't wait any longer.'

'When is it that mister has to report back to the magistrate
about Lukas?'

'Tomorrow.'

'Mister can tell the magistrate with a clear conscience that
it's going well with him. I mean, he's with his own kind now,
isn't he?'

'That's true, yes.'

'And please tell the magistrate both Barta and I send him
respectful greetings and our thanks for what he's done; we were
so happy and so overcome the day we left, I did not even thank
him.'

'I'll tell him.'

When the forester had gone, at last, Elias turned to his wife:

'Barta, I want you to pack me food for a week. Get the meat
out from under the bed and get it cooking. The forester's gone.'
He had had a bit of luck with a bush-buck the day before.

'Where do you want to go, Elias?'

'To see if I can find better wood for the beams.'

'What if the forester turns back and smells the meat?'

Barta was being stupid again. 'He won't turn back, it's getting
late and he's even more scared of a bigfoot in the dark than we
are.'

'Elias, if Lukas had been at home today, you would have been in trouble. The marks of the hiding you gave him have not gone yet.'

'Go and start cooking the meat as I told you!'

17

The first rains of winter came and fell over the Kloof. For three days without stopping. On the fourth day the sun came through and with it a lushness that seemed to spread over the whole veld.

There was a lot to be done at Wolwekraal. Kicker was looking handsome and his beak and shins were becoming red. He looked as proud as a peacock. Pollie attended to her own affairs, but even she seemed different, more secretive.

Fiela laid down new rules for Wolwekraal: first of all, Selling's bench was shifted to the west of the house. Ostriches did not like to be watched at such times; they were not like dogs and other animals that had no pride. As soon as Kicker started chasing Pollie, she told the children no one was to go near the enclosure unnecessarily. When the dung was to be picked up, three of them would have to keep guard with the thorn branches and the one that was doing the picking up was to hurry. An ostrich on heat was a very dangerous thing, even Kicker. And all the eggshells and bones from the kitchen were to be added to their food for Pollie's sake, so that she could lay eggs with good hard shells. And if she should lay an egg before Kicker had taken her, the egg was to be rolled in under the shelter so that she would know she was to lay the rest there as well.

'Ma, do you think they'll have mated by the time Benjamin comes back?' Kittie asked her that morning. Fiela knew Kittie was only asking in order to find out how much hope Fiela herself had that Petrus would bring Benjamin back with him.

'It depends on whether Master Petrus has to go to court or not.'

The rain had kept Petrus from getting away on the Monday,

and he had not left until the Thursday. By the Sunday, the days were as long as years. Selling worked out when Petrus could be back:

'First he'll take the horses to Barrington at Portland. That is quite a way. He'll stay there overnight and leave the next day. If he got to Knysna on Friday too late to see the magistrate and had to wait until yesterday, Saturday, he might not be on his way back yet. He might be waiting for them to fetch Benjamin from the Forest. I don't think we could expect them before Tuesday.'

In fact Petrus did not come riding up the Kloof until late on Thursday. Alone. A sugar-cake was waiting on the kitchen table.

'I told you he would have to go to court first!' she said, trying to keep their spirits up. Where Selling had been discouraged by the two extra days, she had seen hope. They had had to send for the child, she conjectured, and then again for his things. Delay meant hope. Selling's certainty, at the beginning, that Petrus would bring the child back with him, had convinced her as well.

And they waited like guards at the corner of the house. Away from the ostriches, because at sunset the day before Pollie had started to dance again and that morning Kicker had started chasing her.

'I've always known he's a respectable ostrich,' she had told Selling. 'He's not running her down as I've seen ostriches do, he's courting her like a gentleman.'

In her mind's eye she already saw Pollie walking about with at least twelve chicks round her feet like little long-legged plovers. Six she would sell, at say five pounds apiece, and six she would rear for Wolwekraal. In a year's time they could pluck at least eight birds, in two years' time, twenty. By that time the Laghaans' land would be in Benjamin's name.

Then Petrus came up the road without him and when he stood

before them, he seemed to be posing, as if he had been practising how he would stand: straight, steady, the driving-whip flicking against his thigh.

'Good evening, Selling. Fiela. Children.'

He spoke abruptly. She felt her heart beating faster and her mouth go dry.

'Did you see him, Master Petrus?' she asked.

'I've seen the magistrate.'

'Why are you beating about the bush?'

'I was with the magistrate for some time, Fiela, and I want you all to listen very carefully to what I have to say. Mr Goldsbury and myself talked the whole thing over very carefully and I can assure you that he is a very sensible man.'

'What sensible man would send a horse-cart over the mountain to just come and pick up a child!'

'Steady now, Fiela. The most important thing I have to tell you is that all is going well with Benjamin. The most difficult thing I have to say is that you will have to accept that he has just been lent to you for nine years, and he will not be coming back.'

She felt as if she would swoon; she had difficulty in holding her body together.

'Fiela, you must face it calmly. There is no doubt in my mind that the forest couple are his rightful parents. If I had any doubt about it, I would not have let the matter lie, but there is no doubt. I'm sorry. I wish it were different. No matter how difficult it is for you, you will have to accept that he is back with his own people and that it is for the best.'

'Did you *see* him, Master Petrus?' she asked in fury. 'Did you lay your *eyes* on him?'

'Getting angry won't help, Fiela. You will have to learn to accept it. The magistrate sent one of the foresters into the Forest on Sunday to go and see how Benjamin was getting on. He said it's going well; he has adjusted to his new circumstances completely and it would be cruel to upset him again now. He must be left alone. A child is wonderfully adaptable. He adjusts quite easily.'

'That's nonsense, Petrus Zondagh!'

'Fiela!'

'Keep out of this, Selling!' She was torn by worry and anger. 'Benjamin is no longer a child, he'll know what's happened to him! He'll understand. I have to go to him to explain to him how the minds of mad people work! I have to go and tell him!'

'It will not be fair to him to go and mess things up, Fiela; it will not help to meddle. Let him keep his happy memories of Wolwekraal.'

'You and your magistrate will have to answer to God for this, Petrus Zondagh!'

'Stay calm, Fiela. Look after Selling, he's looking bad.'

Kittie and Emma were holding Selling upright. For once she hardly cared whether his weakness overcame him or not.

'If you had seen Benjamin with your own two eyes, Master Petrus, you could have convinced me that all was well with him. But you have not seen him!'

'Don't shout the house down, Fiela!' Petrus was getting worked up himself. 'The child is back with his people and you'll be on the wrong side of the law if you try and upset things again. You would not have been able to have kept him much longer in any case.'

'Why not?'

'You know why not, Fiela. He's white. What do you think would have happened when Benjamin came to choose a wife? No one in the Kloof would have allowed him to court his daughter.'

'There is not a single white girl in the Kloof good enough for him, Petrus Zondagh! Go and tell that to the Kloof!'

'Fiela, please, we're all worked up and upset.' Petrus's voice was sympathetic. 'No one could have brought Benjamin up better than you did, Fiela. He could not have had a better home. One day he'll realize this and he'll come back and show his children where he was brought up. Wait for that day, Fiela, and you will get your reward. But don't try and divide the child – you won't get half.'

On the following Monday, the horse-constable came to say that the magistrate at Uniondale had had a message from the magistrate at Knysna: If she made any more trouble about the child, she would be in trouble herself.

18

The morning he cut the forty-first notch in the pole, Benjamin knew his mother was not coming for him. No matter how hard he tried, he no longer believed she would come. He was in the Forest for ever. It frightened him. They had once buried an old man, Uncle Peetjie, at Avontuur and, hearing something as they were lowering the coffin, they had opened the coffin and found that the old man was not dead after all. Some of the people collapsed with shock. Kittie did too. He did not, but his ears had started buzzing, and for a long time after that, when Dawid blew out the candle at night, he felt as if he was lying squeezed into a coffin and nobody could hear him knocking. That same fear was suddenly back with him. The only difference was that he could no longer cry as he did then. Somewhere in the last forty-one days the tears had dried up and his body felt strange and hollow. Powerless.

Forty-one notches. How could you pray when your mother was no longer there to tell you what to say? How did you pray by yourself? He squatted down beside the scaffold and stared at the chippings on the ground. Our Father which art in heaven forgive us our trespasses and lead us not into temptation and give us this day our daily bread. Be with Kicker, please let him get to like Pollie. Be with my father, make him strong. Be with Dawid and Tollie and Kittie and Emma. Be with my mother. Be with my mother. Be with my mother.

'Lukas, why are you sitting there like that? Is your stomach sore?'

Nina was sitting on the middle trestle astride the log so you

could see her dirty bloomers; she was trying to mimic a bird
singing somewhere in the Forest. Elias had been gone for days.
Nina was going to get a good hiding the moment he came back,
that was for sure. Every morning she got on to the trestle, picked
up the axe and made a few perfunctory cuts, and then she was
off into the Forest. One thing he would say for her, she was not
afraid. She knew what would happen when her father got back
because he had given them very clear orders about what had to
be finished while he was away.

How long was for ever? How many beams? How many trees
to be cut down? Why did the man not put him in a woodcutter's
team like Willem and Kristoffel? Once you got to know the
Forest you would know how to get out of it. Our Father which
art in heaven, hallowed be Thy name. Forty-one days. An
ostrich egg takes forty-two days to hatch. If he pushed his
lower lip over his upper lip, he could feel hair that had not
been there forty-one days ago. Dawid had lied then; he
always said white people got beard behind their ears first
and then on their faces. There was nothing behind his
ears.

He was white. They were Coloured.

Was that why his mother did not come? Because he was white?
No, he could not believe that.

'Lukas?'

'Shut up.'

'Are you saying your prayers? Your eyes are closed, I see.'

'Shut your bloody mouth!'

There were days when he didn't mind her. Stupid as she was,
she was the only one in the house that was alive at least. Willem
and Kristoffel were always tired when they were at home because
they worked hard cutting wood. The man was like a guard-dog,
always ready to growl and bite. The woman was always sad. He
noticed that she sometimes looked at him long and fixedly, and
when he looked up, she turned away. The day after the man had

left, she had come from the house and stood by him as he worked. Nina had gone off into the Forest.

'Do you want some coffee, Lukas?' the woman had asked, tentatively.

'No.' When the man was not there, he would not call her Ma.

'I've baked some nice sweet potatoes too.'

He just kept on cutting. The beam was almost finished and he did not want trouble when the man got back. She kept on standing there, however.

'Put down the axe, Lukas, I want to talk to you.' She never really spoke to him. 'Get down, I want to talk to you.' He put down the axe and climbed down. She stood rubbing her arm as if she was nervous about something. 'I just wanted to ask you ...' She had difficulty in saying whatever it was she wanted to say. 'I just wanted to ask you whether you're happy here. I mean, your father can be a bit short-tempered. It's best to obey him. I know you do, I'm just saying.' She rubbed her arm faster. 'Life in the Forest is not easy for anyone. We're used to it though ... really what I wanted to know was whether you are contented here with us. Whether you have adjusted.' He did not know what to say so he said he would have the coffee. And when she brought it, the beaker was filled to the brim. Not half full as it usually was.

'Lukas, I'm going to the Forest, are you coming?'

'No.'

'Please.'

'No. When your pa comes back, he's going to give you a hiding.'

'Then I'll run away.'

She got down and walked away to the nearest footpath, whistling as she went. He got up and climbed on to the scaffold.

*

The man came back on the forty-fourth notch. He hardly
looked at the beams that were finished and apparently did not
even notice the girl's bungling. He didn't ask where she was and
when she came home at dusk he hardly looked at her. He seemed
to have some secret. All day Saturday and Sunday he was restless
and on the Monday the woman packed two knapsacks. Bread
she had baked in the hot ashes and sweet potatoes. When
Benjamin went to start work the man stopped him.

'We won't be working on the beams today, we're going to the
Forest. You too, Nina.'

They went into the Forest at the east side of the Island; they
had to carry two spades, a pick-axe, the hatchet and a saw. After
about an hour's walk, Nina got fed up.

'Where are we going, Pa?'

'Klaas's Kloof. And keep your eyes open – the two of you will
have to come on your own sometimes. I'm not coming to look
for lost brats.'

'What are we going to do in Klaas's Kloof?'

'You'll see.'

They walked for about another hour. How the man knew
where he was going was a puzzle; at times they were not even in
a footpath or a sled-path. How Nina would ever get them along
there on her own, he did not know; and she kept on falling
behind because she lingered to mimic the birds and the man
frequently had to stop and scold her.

Then the man started walking more slowly and more carefully;
he seemed to be getting uneasy and he was more impatient with
Nina when she fell behind. With him too.

'Are you sulking again, Lukas?'

'No . . . Pa.'

They got to a place where a wide, thickly overgrown kind of
passage seemed to wind through the trees. Above the passage
the treetops intertwined from both sides and down below the
ferns grew close together and as high as men.

The man made a sign that meant they had to put down the

things and keep quiet; then he just stood there, listening for a while.

'What are you listening for, Pa?' Nina asked.

'Nothing.' The man seemed afraid of something. 'Lukas,' he said, 'do you see that stinkwood tree over there on the other side?' He pointed to a dark brown tree a little way off. It was actually a giant trunk covered with moss from which three smaller trees had sprouted – as if the tree had been felled long ago and then started growing again. 'Do you see it?'

'Yes.'

'Yes who?'

'Yes, Pa.'

'Go and climb the tree.'

He wanted to ask why. But the man was in a touchy mood, so he didn't. Anyway, it did not seem as if it would be difficult to climb the tree for its roots were as thick as legs. But apparently he did not climb to the man's liking because he called him back when he was half-way.

'You're too slow! Nina, show him how to climb a tree.'

She went up there like a cat. Where the three trunks forked from the old trunk, she turned back and climbed down again just as quickly.

'Now *you* try, Lukas!'

It was easier the second time. When he got to where Nina had climbed, the man called out to him to stay where he was and sent her up after him. There was just enough room for the two of them in the crotch if Nina squeezed her thin body in between two of the branches.

'Why did we have to climb up here?' he asked her.

'I don't know, but it's better than making beams. Perhaps pa's going to set blue-buck traps and wants us to watch out for the forester.'

'Why so far from the house?'

'I don't know.'

But that was not the reason.

'If you hear a branch crack,' the man said when they were down again, 'don't look round to see if it's bigfeet or not, just throw everything down and climb up there.'

'Throw what down?' Nina asked, suspiciously.

'You'll see.'

'But the white alder over there is a much better tree to climb to get away from bigfeet, Pa!'

'What do you think I'm going to climb to?' the man snorted.

'How long are we going to stay here then?'

'Until the pit is finished.'

'What pit?'

'The pit that we're going to dig.'

How long they had worked on the pit, he did not know in the end. There was no opportunity to cut notches in the pole for every day that went by now. Sometimes Willem and Kristoffel came and helped, sometimes the man grabbed the hatchet and hacked away roots or took a spade and helped them dig until his uneasiness drove him up the white alder again.

When the heaps of earth around the pit grew too big, they had to load it on the ox-hide and drag it away. It had to be a neat pit. Every morning they had to get up at dawn to be at the pit by the time the sun came out and it was, as Nina had said, better than making beams. Especially on the days when the man stayed at home. After a while he no longer needed to wait for Nina when they had to go to the pit alone, and she started loitering and whistling and making a row as they walked. He had learnt to find his own way to the pit. When her father was not there, she was lazy; when her father came with them and sat watching them or helping them, she too dug until she could hardly get her back straight again.

'Lukas, what do you think pa wants to do with this bloody hole?'

'Don't ask me, ask your pa.'

'Perhaps he wants to plant something,' she suggested.

'What does a man plant in a hole this big?'

'Uncle Martiens once dug a hole next to his house and planted a fig tree.'

'A hole for a fig tree is a mole-hole beside this one.'

'You're growing a beard, Lukas.'

'Leave me alone!'

'I know something you don't know . . .'

Nina had been up to mischief again that day. Her father had stayed at home and she was making believe her spade was a guitar, climbing every tree around the pit to see how high she could get or just disappearing into the thickets.

'Take that spade and help me dig, Nina!'

'I said, I know something you don't know.'

'Yes, I know. You know where my five shillings is.'

'Aren't you ever going to stop going on about that bloody five shillings?'

'Not before you tell me where you've hidden it.'

'I *did* show you the way.'

'But then you went and told your pa.'

'It's not true.'

'How else did he know where to find me?'

'How should I know? Pa knows this Forest as well as any woodcutter, he just knew where to go and look for you.' Surprisingly, she climbed into the pit after a while and helped him digging without making too much fuss. For the first few days after her father had cut off her hair, she had worn one of her mother's headcloths round her head and avoided the others on the Island. But neither the cloth nor the shyness had lasted very long. And when her hair started to grow, it formed little curls round her head and she looked better than when her hair had been wild and bushy. Bet had said Nina's hair looked better, too. But she was still wearing his nightshirt like a dress and it was unrecognizably dirty and torn in two places.

'Lukas, I say, I know something that you don't know. Not even pa or Uncle Martiens or Uncle Koos or Willem or Kristoffel or anybody on the Island knows about it.'

'Dig, Nina!' He did not want to show any interest. 'It's deep enough on that side. Dig over there and measure the depth with the pole your pa gave you.'

'I know where little elephants come from.'

'What's so funny about that?'

She thrust the spade angrily into the ground and left it. 'Stupid!' she cried. 'I told you not even pa or the others know it. Only me. *No one* knows where elephants die and *no one* knows where the little elephants come from. Go and ask pa if you think I'm lying.'

'Dig, Nina! I'll get the blame again tomorrow if we don't do enough for your father's liking.' He wanted to get her away from the little elephants. If she didn't even know that it was the female cats and ewes and women that bore the young, he was not going to tell her.

'I swear to you, Lukas, no one knows.'

'Your word means as much as a tortoise feather.'

'If I'm lying to you, may I drop dead right here in the pit this very moment and all the trees fall on me. Remember that morning ma gave me a hiding because I had peed in the bed? It was shortly after you came back from the Long Kloof.' He remembered it well but did not say so. 'I'm not afraid of ma, I'm too quick for her, she misses most of the time. She thought she still had me in the corner that morning when I slipped past her and ran off into the Forest. I chose the densest part I knew of and I did not even keep to a footpath because I wanted to get lost as you did when you were small so that they could come looking for me and not find me. I'm telling you, I ran a long way that day. Then I walked. I think I must have gone as far as Oudebrand. Or almost. Then I came to a creek where the water was quite deep in places and I decided to drown myself so that they could find my body one day when they came to cut wood.

But my head would not stay under the water so I started walking again.' She was talking faster and faster as if she was afraid he would stop listening. 'Then I came to a very big tree, a kalander. You know no one can climb a very big kalander – I don't know if baboons can climb them even – Willem says only clever bees make their nests in a kalander. Then I saw I would be able to climb up a yellowwood tree which had been blown over by the wind and was leaning against the kalander. You see that kalander over there next to the quar?'*

'Yes.'

'You see how big it is?'

'Yes.'

'It's a candle compared to the one I climbed that day. Truly. And I climbed right into its crown. The insides of my thighs were chafed raw, and when I sat up I could see all round me. I'm not afraid of heights, but I was scared that day. When I looked up, heaven was right above my head; when I looked down, the forest floor was way below my feet. So I just sat there because I was too scared to climb down again. I sat and sat. My hair and clothes got dry after a while but I was still too scared to get down. The sun came over my head at midday but I just sat there. I had already started thinking how they would find my bones up there one day when they felled the tree – they would not find me in the Long Kloof as they found you. Then I suddenly heard the undergrowth crackling down below; at first I thought it was woodcutters coming but when I looked down, I just saw humps. Elephants. A whole herd. At least ten of them. And a little way off three more were standing in a little clearing and they kept trampling the bracken under their feet until it was as smooth as grass. I thought it was some kind of dance they did. Then the other elephants came and stood in a circle round the flattened clearing, backsides inwards, and one went and stood in the middle of the circle and started swaying to and fro. Then he sort of lay down and I thought he was going to die, but then

* Type of tree.

he got up again and something came out of him at the back. I swear it. At first I could not make out what it was because the branches of a wild alder, down below, were in the way. I thought it was a piece of his stomach falling out or something, but then I saw the elephant fidget with his head at the thing and I saw it was a little elephant. It was a cow that had got a baby. How it got up her backside, I can't tell you, but may I drop dead if I'm lying to you. And when I looked again, the baby elephant was standing on his little feet between his mother's legs. It was sweet. But then a flock of louries came and made a lot of noise, squawking and hissing above my head as if it was *their* tree, and that spoiled everything for then all the other elephants went and crowded round the mother elephant and they slowly walked away with the little one between them where I could not see him. And you're the first person I've told it to. I swear.'

He realized that he had stopped digging. Something in her eyes pleaded with him to believe her.

It was almost dark when they got home that night. The man stood waiting outside and asked why they were so late? Whether they had seen elephants? Bush-bucks? Woodcutters? Foresters? Strangers? He seemed to be angry and distrustful although he had been normal when they had left that morning. When they went into the house, he followed them but stayed in the doorway. Even Nina looked round carefully – something was wrong. The woman was standing at the hearth and did not look up. A small stub of candle was burning on the table, but its flame looked feeble in the evening light.

'They've brought your things today, Lukas,' the man said bluntly from the doorway.

It was suddenly cold in the room. His eyes turned to the bed against the wall – the rock-rabbit blanket lay folded at the lower end; on it was his coat with the sleeves which had been lengthened, his other flannel shirt, the veldshoes his father had made him, the trousers Tollie had outgrown and which had been passed down to him, the other pair of trousers with a patched seat, another shirt. And on top of it all, lay an ostrich egg.

'Who brought it?' he asked. '*Who brought my things?*' The walls seemed to be dancing in the candle flame.

'She said her name was Fiela Komoetie,' the man said. 'If I had had a dog, I would have set him on her and she would still be running!'

He felt his heart would burst with joy, but he was afraid, too. He wanted to break past the man and run outside but the man stopped him.

'Where is she?' he cried. 'Where's my mother?'

'There's your ma, at the fire!' the man shouted. 'The Coloured woman has gone and I told her, and the person with her, that if they ever set foot here again, I'd go straight to the magistrate and have them arrested! No Coloured will mess about with Elias van Rooyen!'

'Who was with her?'

'A youth, Coloured, as bold as she is!'

It must have been Dawid, he thought. He had to get outside, he had to go after them and catch up with them and never come back.

'Let me out!'

'You stay where you are! I'm not coming after you again, I'm telling you!'

'Let me past!'

'Don't you shout at me! And don't you start your bloody nonsense again! I'll take the ox rein to you and I won't stop till the last trace of the brown bastards has been beaten out of you! You are just beginning to behave like a white again and white you'll stay!'

The woman stirred the pot and said over her shoulder: 'Leave him, Elias. The children are tired, they must eat.'

He did not want to eat. 'What did Fiela Komoetie say?' he pleaded to know. 'What did she *say*?'

'She's got no say around here. She brought your things and that's that. And if you try to run away again I'll get the magistrate to send the constable to bring you back. I've had enough. The magistrate told me himself, the day we went to fetch you, that the Coloureds who took you could get into trouble for it, but that we were to leave it alone for the sake of peace. But I'm warning you, if this bloody nonsense does not come to an end, I'll go to the magistrate myself and he can come and take over.'

Nina picked up the rock-rabbit blanket and put it round her as if she was enjoying it.

'Leave my things!' he screamed and pulled it off her. 'You don't touch my things with your dirty hands!'

The man slammed the door shut and grabbed the ox rein from the hook but the woman stopped him and said they had to eat.

The man and the woman and Nina ate. He lay down on top of his things and stayed there until it was morning again. You did not give someone's things to him if he was coming back. It was like saying goodbye.

From the next day on the man went with them every day to Klaas's Kloof until the pit was finished. After that Nina and he had to go back to the beams and the man went into the Forest alone for a few days. Then he came and sat at the scaffold again to watch them and most of the time there was a funny smile on his face. Every third or fourth day he went into the Forest for a while.

They loaded the beams that were finished on to the sled and dragged them with the oxen to Deep Walls where they had to wait a long time for the wagon to come and fetch them. The people on the wagon were from way down in the Long Kloof and he did not know them. The next day the man went to the village with money to buy food. Nina pleaded to go with him but he would not take her.

The man brought coffee and sugar and meal. That same evening Willem came home and he also brought coffee and sugar and meal.

'You'll see,' the man bragged at the table that night, 'one of these days Elias van Rooyen is going to be a rich man! Things are changing. They're changing. You just keep your mouths shut about the pit like I've told you to.'

'What is the pit for, Pa?' Nina wanted to know.

'It's a pit.'

Willem had his coat on and the shoes too. The man and the woman slept under the rock-rabbit blanket at night, and some of his clothes had been given to Kristoffel too.

Early on Monday morning Willem left again. He said they would be away for three or four weeks because the wood buyer at the village urgently wanted a lot of stinkwood.

But before sundown Willem was back.

'The bigfeet have gone mad, Pa,' he said as he slumped at the table, weary and exhausted. 'They tried to kill us. We were putting up the shelter when they came and trampled our food and boxes and everything. They're carrying on as if they were in a frenzy, Pa. Uncle Martiens says something must have happened up there somewhere.'

'Where?' the man asked hurriedly.

'In the direction of Klaas's Kloof, Pa. We were almost killed. One old cow had Uncle Martiens stuck up in a tree till late this afternoon and she kept on trying to shake him down. He says he's never seen bigfeet that crazy – Pa, could it have something to do with the pit? I mean . . .'

'Quiet! You keep your mouth shut about the pit! This has nothing to do with it!'

'Uncle Martiens says he won't dare go near Klaas's Kloof again for a while.'

'That would be the best,' the man said and looked away, but he was smiling.

The rest of that week dragged by like all the others; from sunrise to sunset on the scaffold, from sunset to dawn, eat and sleep. Fortunately there were no rainy days to be spent sitting in the house . . . Outside, at the beams, his mind flew to Wolwekraal much more easily. Was it one of Pollie's eggs that had been with his things? He did not want them to break the egg and cook it, but they did. He would not eat any of it. Had Kicker taken Pollie? Was the goat still milking well? Had it rained yet? Was the veld beautiful? Were the blue irises flowering already? What was his father working on? The most difficult thing was thinking about his mother. Why had she brought his clothes? Fine, they were not his father and mother and brothers and sisters for he was white and they were Coloured but that did not matter!

'You're cutting half-heartedly again today, Lukas!' The man was watching them like a hawk that day. Since Willem had come back because of the elephants, the man had been restless all week. And Nina had been wilful. If she did not get on to the scaffold with a tin on which she made 'music', she made up 'songs' that she sang over and over, louder and louder all the time, till Aunt Malie shouted from the other side of the Island that she should shut up for a change! But Nina did not stop before the man had pulled her from the scaffold and shaken her a bit.

On the Friday the man felled two trees close to the Island and dragged them home with the oxen. The next day Kristoffel came home and the man put them to sawing the logs to the right lengths for beams with the two-handed saw.

'Seems to me you are pa's right hand at the beams now, Lukas,' Kristoffel said. For a wonder he tried to make conversation; Kristoffel was not at all bad, just very quiet. 'You should be glad you're working on the beams – as a woodcutter you work yourself to death for nothing. The only ones that are getting rich are the wood buyers in the village.'

'I just wish I knew the Forest as well as you do,' he said to Kristoffel, suddenly realizing that he should get Kristoffel on his side. 'I've been here now for ages and I still know almost nothing of the Forest.'

'One gets to know the Forest as time goes by.'

'I suppose you know all the paths through the Forest?'

'Only the ones on this side of the Forest and from here to the village. The Forest is big, there are parts I've never been to.'

'Deep Walls, the place we take the beams to, there is a gravel road there ... Is that the road going over the mountain?' Kristoffel did not answer him. 'Is that the road to the Long Kloof?'

Kristoffel stopped sawing and straightened up. 'Lukas,' he said, and there was reproach in his tone, 'seems to me you're still trying to find the way back to the Long Kloof, right? You just don't want to accept us. Maybe it's true what pa had said, that you're not really white again yet.' The way Kristoffel said it, the accusation in his voice, was like a blow which knocked him backwards. 'Don't make us sorry that you did not die when you got lost that time.'

They finished the logs without another word being spoken.

Sunday was the day for Nina to go off again, her forest day, and she left the house at dawn.

Just after midday he went and sat behind the scaffolds to while away the day when she returned unexpectedly, dragging her feet. She looked straight at him but she did not seem to see him. The sleeve of her nightshirt was almost torn off, her face was full of scratches and it was clear that she had been crying. He was frightened. Something or someone must have hurt her.

'Nina?'

She walked to the shed, stood with her back to the corrugated iron wall for a moment and then slowly slid down until she was sitting on her haunches. All the whistling and singing seemed to have left her.

'Nina, what's the matter?' he asked.

'Pa is a dirty swine.' Just that.

'Why do you say that?'

'It was a trap. An elephant trap.'
'How do you know?'
'I went there. There's a dead elephant calf lying in the pit.'

19

By the end of October the winter's rain began to let up and they spent less time sitting around in the house. He was like a snake slowly shaking off its old skin and growing a new one as the months went by. He had to creep out of Benjamin Komoetie's skin and become Lukas van Rooyen. The days of revolt, when he eased his despair hacking at the yellowwood log on the scaffold grew further apart and the periods he could stay in Lukas's skin longer.

He got used to thinking of Willem and Kristoffel as his brothers. Of Nina as his sister. The most difficult part was to call the man Pa and the woman Ma, but even that became easier as time went by.

The year moved slowly. Christmas came. New Year. And as he grew out of Benjamin Komoetie, he also grew out of his clothes and had to wear Willem's old trousers and a shirt of his pa's.

But still there were days when resistance crept up on him and he had to struggle to overcome it.

'Did the devil get into you again today, Lukas?'

'No, Pa.'

'Why are you hacking into that beam as if you're not on speaking terms with it, then?'

It was rather that the devil had got into Elias van Rooyen. The day after Nina had come across the calf in the pit, he had left early for the Forest in the morning and came back late in the afternoon, weary and upset. He threw himself down at the back door.

'The bastards were waiting for me!' he cried. 'My life is no longer safe in this Forest, not even for a day. Give me some water, Barta. What are you staring at me for? I'm telling you, the bigfeet have got it in for me, they've marked me, they're going to trample me!'

His ma was frightened and sent Nina to get the water. 'What are you talking about, Elias? See how your clothes are torn!'

'That happens when six bloody bigfeet cows chase you so that you can feel the trunk of the one in front blowing between your shoulderblades! There was no time to find a tree to climb!'

'Pity they did not trample pa to death!' Nina shouted from the house. Apparently she still had not had enough hidings; the night before, she had carried on so about the calf that her pa had taken the ox rein to her. 'Pa got us to dig that pit on purpose!' she said as she came with the water. 'Pa knew what it was for, and pa went and covered it on the sly! How were the bigfeet to know that there was a trap in their way?'

'If I take the rein to you again today, you'll see a bigger weal than you did yesterday! Lukas, come and help me into the house.'

The week after that, when the beams had to be hauled out to Deep Walls, his pa helped until they were loaded on the sled and the oxen yoked, and then he called him aside.

'Lukas,' he said, looking at his feet, 'I'm not feeling well at all, you and Nina will have to take the beams to the gravel road by yourselves today. Unyoke the oxen when you get there and let them graze. But stay with the beams until the wagon comes and count the money to see that it's right. Don't let them cheat me because I'm not there.'

The oxen were old and docile. Nina led them and he did the driving. They reached Deep Walls shortly after midday and unloaded the beams. Nina had been unusually quiet all the time, she had never even tried to be funny on the way, or to mimic the birds or whistle or sing.

'Are you feeling sick too, Nina?'

'No. But I'm glad pa's not well. Perhaps he'll die.'

'You mustn't say that, he's your pa.'

'He's your pa too.' She made it sound like an insult.

He sat down on the beams in the shade and she started walking through the dry leaves that the wind had blown into heaps along the road. First up one side of the road, then down the other. Then she came and squatted down beside him and listlessly scribbled in the dust with her fingers.

'I wish I could write,' she said. 'Write my name for me, Lukas, I want to see what it looks like.'

He stooped down and wrote her name in the dust.

'Is that my full name?' she asked.

'It's *Nina*.'

'My full name is Christina.'

He wiped out Nina and wrote Christina. But she was not satisfied with that either.

'I like the shorter one better, wipe that one out.'

'You're a nuisance.'

She practised writing her name until the whole road in front of them was full of it. Then she looked bored again.

'Lukas ... Guess where this road goes to.'

'How should I know?' He pretended not to know.

'If you walk south, it takes you to the village, if you walk towards the mountain, it takes you to the Long Kloof.' It was as if she deliberately placed the words between them in the road and waited for him to pick them up. 'It's the road they brought you by.'

'What about it?' He was not stupid, he knew it was the road to the Long Kloof; the wagon that came for the beams, came from the Long Kloof. He had worked it out for himself.

She got up to go and sit in the shade a little way off and started pestering him again: 'If you get up and set out now, you could be far away by the time pa finds out. He won't be able to catch up with you this time.'

She was meddling with something he wanted to leave alone and he knew she was doing it on purpose.

'I'm not stupid, Nina.'

'You *are*! This is your chance to get away at last and you're just sitting there.'

'You just want to get me into trouble again, but you won't succeed.'

'I'll say the man with the wagon asked you to go and work for him and so you went with him.'

'You're talking rubbish,' he said to her. 'You know as well as I do that pa will put the magistrate on me this time – why don't you go and see to the oxen over there. Look where Crophead's grazing!'

She got up and wandered over in the direction of the oxen. When she came back, she came and stood in front of him and looked at him spitefully. 'I only wanted to find out whether you would do it or not. Silly!'

'The day I decide to go, I won't wait for you to show me the way. I'll find it for myself.'

'Willem says you're white now, you won't bolt again.'

He looked away because he did not want her to see that she had hurt him. He knew he was Lukas van Rooyen but somehow he did not want them to know it.

The wagon came. They loaded up the beams and he counted the money. When he and Nina started walking home, he did not speak to her.

His pa usually went to the village to buy food the day after the beams had been sold; this time, however, he said they would have to wait for Willem or Kristoffel to come home. His legs would never make it to the village, they were too sore.

'Pa was lying,' Nina said afterwards. 'There's nothing wrong with his legs – he's afraid of the elephants, they know it's him that had the pit made.'

'How can they know?' he argued. 'We did most of the digging, why aren't they trying to get us too then?'

'They know it was pa's doing, not ours. Elephants are clever.

Aunt Gertie says they know everything that goes on in this Forest.'

When Kristoffel came home a week later, he was told to walk to the village and Nina started nagging to go with him. She still had the five shillings, and he knew why she wanted to go.

They left at dawn on Friday and they were back just before dark. She and Kristoffel. She had nothing with her but he could tell that she was hiding something.

All Saturday she spent trying to get away from the beams and from under her pa's eyes, but could not. Early Sunday morning she came and woke him up.

'Come, I want to show you something.'

He had already found out by then that it was far better to go with her to the Forest on Sundays than to sit around the house. Especially with Aunt Malie's Bet hanging around as she did.

'She's taken a fancy to you, Lukas.' Nina explained it to him one day. 'You are going to marry her, Willem is going to marry Gertrude and I'm going to marry the forester's son. You'll see. The forester's son goes to school in the village and I saw him once at Deep Walls. He kept looking at me; he must have taken a fancy to me.'

He had let her talk. In the first place he would never marry a forest girl and in the second place he would not marry at all for where was he to get the two pounds for the marriage fee? When people in the Long Kloof wanted to get married and did not have the marriage fee, Master Petrus – Petrus Zondagh – gave them the money. When Anna Petro married, the Zondaghs were by the sea, so his mother – Fiela Komoetie – gave Anna the two pounds.

The mouth-organ was hidden in the undergrowth along the footpath not far from the Island. How she remembered where she had put it in those endless bushes, he could not tell. After more than a year in the Forest the world around him was still only a wilderness of trees and undergrowth where he dared not step from a footpath when he was alone.

He was still angry about his money. When she crawled from under the bush and stood there quite proudly with the mouth-organ in her hand, he felt like knocking it out of her hand.

'It's as if you had stolen it!' he told her.

'I did,' she said and laughed. When she opened her other hand, his five shillings lay intact on her palm. 'The man at the shop took out the drawer with the mouth-organs and pipes and things and put it on the counter. When he looked away, I grabbed one and stuck it up my bloomers and then I told him I did not want to look at the things any more.'

He could not decide whether he should be glad about his money or shocked about the mouth-organ.

'Nina van Rooyen, you will land up on your arse in jail!' He took the money and went on. 'The day the constable comes to fetch you, I'll tell him I don't know you, you're not *my* sister! How could you do such a thing!'

'The drawer was so untidy, the shop-man will never even notice that it's gone.' She sounded a bit uncertain, however, when she added: 'If you keep quiet about it, no one will know. Besides, you have got your money back now, haven't you? I could have lied to you and kept it.'

That was true. 'Does Kristoffel know you've stolen the mouth-organ?'

'No. He saw nothing, he didn't see me hiding it here either – Lukas, if you let this out, pa will brain me.'

There was no doubt about that. And he realized that it gave him a weapon against her that he had been wanting for a long time. 'Right, I'll keep quiet about it, but if you ever say Bet has her eye on me again, I'll tell pa.'

'I won't ever say that again. Bet's too ugly in any case; I don't think you should take a fancy to her any more. If Willem takes Gertrude, it's enough.'

'And if you ever get the other children on the Island to help

you roll *my* half-finished beam on to *your* scaffold again when I
turn my back, I'll go straight to pa and tell him about the mouth-
organ.'

'I'll never do it again, Lukas, I swear.'

'And I won't blow those stupid bottles with you again. I'm not
cracked.'

'Lukas ...'

'You needn't plead. Play on your stolen mouth-organ by
yourself.'

When the beams had to be taken to Deep Walls a month later,
his pa stayed at home. And Willem had to go to the village to buy
food.

'Lukas,' Nina asked him the following Sunday, 'have you
noticed that pa never leaves the Island any more?'

'Yes.' They were sitting on the boulders at the creek where she
kept her bottles and the mouth-organ. 'I suppose he's just lazy.'

'Pa has never been *that* lazy. I think he's afraid that the
elephants might really have put a mark on him. I heard him tell
Willem that he and Kristoffel will have to teach you to fell the
wood for the beams.'

'Pa has told me that too.'

She shook the spit out of the mouth-organ and started playing
a sad little tune. Somehow she had been able to play the thing
from the start: blew when she had to blow, sucked when she had
to suck. Within half an hour she had a tune she could play over
and over again.

He stood up and walked up the creek. Good had come from
the stolen mouth-organ, too. Nina no longer nagged him on
Sundays to help her make 'music' or to roam the Forest with her.
He could come and go as he pleased and he learned to scout the
Forest on his own. During the week, Nina seemed less wilful
towards her pa and stayed on the scaffold longer without moaning about it. And the beams she had to rough-hew were starting
to look better.

It was a beautiful day. Where the creek flowed wider, the forest roof opened and the sun came through to the water. Of all the places in the Forest he loved the creeks most of all and liked to go there on his own on Sundays. A single forest creek had enough water to keep Wolwekraal's pool full the whole year round, and they could have watered everything with it. Even the veld.

On Sundays he longed for the openness of the Kloof, or anywhere where he could have looked into the distance; the Forest was so dense, the forest people never saw far; apparently they did not miss the open country for the Forest was their home.

Often, when Willem or Kristoffel had to go to the village, they asked him to go with them. He wanted to go with them to get out in the open again but he did not want to go to Knysna. Knysna was a dog that had bitten him. You did not walk past a fierce dog twice.

He walked a long way along the creek that day and turned back with reluctance. Nina lay on her back, playing the mouth-organ.

'Put away your things, we must go home.'

'It's early still.'

'I promised Aunt Gertie I'd read her the Bible before it gets dark.'

'Since when have you been a preacher?'

'She said she'd make me a pair of trousers if I came and read to her regularly.'

'You've got trousers, haven't you?'

It was always a hassle to get Nina home on Sundays. If no one had stopped her, she would have slept out in the Forest.

'She promised to make me a decent pair of trousers.'

'Where will she get the cloth?'

'She says she's still got trousers of her late husband's that she can unpick.'

'Fine. When you've finished reading for a pair of trousers, start reading to her for a dress for me, will you?'

'Yes. But you must get up so that we can go.'

She sat up but started playing one of her tunes again, and she had nearly finished it when she suddenly stopped to listen.

'Listen,' she whispered to him, 'it's a chorister robin. Can you hear him?'

'Yes.'

She had made him wait a whole day, once, till one of the coy little robins had started singing somewhere in the Forest. One seldom saw them, only heard them. And according to Nina, they had stolen the most beautiful notes from all the other birds in the Forest and woven them together with their own. That was why they sang more beautifully than any other bird.

'Do you hear that, Lukas? He's trying to mimic the mouth-organ, he thinks I'm a strange bird!'

'It's your imagination. Come on!'

'No.'

She started a game with the bird: for every note he sang, she tried to find a note of the same kind on the mouth-organ, and after a while he could have sworn that the bird really was joining in the game.

When they got home, a tall man with a stern face was sitting with their father by the house.

'Come on, children, come on! We've been waiting for you!' Elias van Rooyen jumped up with a swagger. 'Come and say good-day, Nina! You too, Lukas. Shake hands. This is the forester from Deep Walls, Mr Kapp.' Something was wrong again. Nina just stood there, rigid with fear, and their father showed no sign of his bad back or his aching legs. Every word he said was dipped in honey. 'Lukas, Aunt Gertie is asking when you'll be coming to read to her.' He turned to the forester and remarked solemnly: 'I ask you, Mr Kapp, where would you find a young lad today to go and read the Bible to an old woman on Sundays because she cannot read herself?'

'Is pa drunk?' Nina asked from the corner of her mouth.

'I don't know.'

'Do you think it's because of the mouth-organ the man's here?'

'Lukas, go and read to Aunt Gertie now, don't keep her waiting – Mr Kapp wants to talk to Nina.'

It was suddenly clear that his pa wanted him out of the way. And Nina was scared; she stood twisting her fingers as if she wanted to break them off. He himself began to wonder whether it was about the mouth-organ – but then his pa would not have been making such an effort to be friendly.

'Go on now, Lukas, Aunt Gertie's waiting.'

When he got over to Aunt Gertie's place, she had only just woken from her afternoon nap. He hoped she would say he could come back later, but she took out the old tattered Bible, put a clean bonnet on, shooed the chickens from the house and sat down at the table with reverence. As if at church.

They were reading the Psalms that day. The old woman only wanted to hear Psalms and Proverbs and parts of St Matthew. He chose the shortest psalms and hoped she would get tired quickly.

'Why are you reading so fast today? Read more slowly!'

'I'm in a bit of a hurry, Aunt Gertie.'

'What for?'

'I'm just in a hurry, that's all.'

He skipped words, he skipped verses, whole pieces, but the old woman would not let him off. Aunt Malie came in later and asked what the forester was doing over at their place on a Sunday.

'I don't know, Aunt Malie.'

'If it's about the bush-buck traps, your pa had better be careful what he says; Martiens can't always lay his traps. Why can't your pa do it himself any more?'

'I don't know, Aunt Malie.'

She came to the table and sat down. 'Read. Let me hear God's word for a change too; I suppose we'll be dead and gone by the time a preacher comes this way again.'

He kept on reading until it started getting dark in the kitchen.

Bet came in and sat down, open-mouthed, and the chickens came back one by one.

'It's getting dark, Aunt Gertie, I can't see to read any more.'

'Light the candle, Bet.'

'I must really go home now. Ma said I had to see that there's enough kindling in. It's going to rain.'

'What?'

'The rainbird was calling.'

'I haven't heard a rainbird. Read.'

He was not half-way through the next psalm, when Aunt Sofie came from outside, saying there was a commotion at the Van Rooyens' place again; Nina was carrying on as if she was being murdered. He shut the Bible and started running. It was about the mouth-organ, he suddenly realized. When he came to the middle of the Island, he could hear the row himself and got scared.

Somebody was pushing against the door from the inside. 'It's me, Lukas!' he shouted, hammering on the door. His ma was behind the door and it opened just wide enough for him to slip inside. A chair had been knocked over. One of the beds had been pushed out of its place. Nina was carrying on like a mad thing while her pa kept on driving her into the corners and hitting her with his fist.

'Not on her arms, Elias! Not on her arms, it will leave bruises.'

He wanted to turn around and flee outside again but Nina grabbed him round the middle from the back and held him in front of her as a shield against the blows, and all the time she was yelling, 'I won't go! I won't go!'

His pa was getting tired, he was gasping for breath and nothing he did or said stopped her screaming. When it got too dark, he lit the candle, took the ox rein off the hook and tied her arms and legs together.

But she kept on yelling and wormed her way over the floor regardless of the rein; he felt like screaming too.

'Nina, please, stop it! Pa's done with you, he's not hitting you any more!' He squatted down beside her and tried to hold her to the floor by her shoulders.

Her dirty face rubbed against the rough planks and her eyes were filled with fear when she turned them to him. 'Lukas, help me. Talk to pa.'

'What must I tell him?'

'Tell him . . .'

Her pa forestalled her: 'She's an ungrateful brat, that's what she is, Lukas! The forester found her a job in the village, four shillings a week plus food and a room and clothes, and instead of being grateful, she carries on like a pig being slaughtered!'

And he, Lukas, had to walk with her to the gravel road at Deep Walls where the forester would come and get her that Monday morning.

'Take the rein with you and tie her up if she tries to run away,' her father said. 'I've had enough of her, my heart can't take it any more; I couldn't even make it to the road.'

But Nina was subdued. She walked ahead of him without any trouble; at times he had to run to keep up with her. The dress she had on had been borrowed from Gertrude and hung in a long point at the back. Her hair had been cut again but at least with a pair of scissors which he had had to go and borrow from Aunt Gertie.

'Nina, walk a bit slower!'

'Don't talk to me.'

She was subdued but far from being beaten.

'You'll see, it's nice in the village.' He tried to comfort her, and remembered how Dawid and Tollie and Kittie and Emma had tried to comfort him when he had to go to Knysna against his will. 'Just think about it, four shillings a week. Think what you can buy with it. You're going to have lots of money!'

'Shut up.'

'I don't know why you're angry with me, I didn't do anything to you.'

'You can all go to hell.'

'You're acting silly now. I'd much rather live outside this Forest and have a blue sky and sunshine above my head. You'll see how much you'll like living in the village.'

'I'm not a servant for looking after other people's children!'

'It's better than making beams.'

'And the money's not mine, it's pa's.'

He had not realized that.

A branch suddenly cracked to the right of them. Close by. The next one cracked like a gunshot. Elephants! He knew it instinctively and saw Nina's body tense ahead of him. She worked out the direction of the wind in the treetops and then turned to him, indicating that he should keep very still. High up above their heads a lourie started to kok-kok-kok, stopped, started again – another branch snapped, strips of bark were being ripped off; there was clearly more than one elephant.

Nina stepped closer to him, carefully, and whispered with her mouth right at his ear: 'If they come this way, climb the white alder over there and hang on. I'll run.' She must have heard his heart beating for she added, reassuringly: 'Don't worry, the wind's blowing towards us.'

They stayed standing there for nearly an hour. Every time he wanted to shift his feet, she stopped him with a quick warning gesture. Then the sound of branches breaking came from deeper into the Forest and the louries stopped calling. The shrill, monotonous churring of a sun beetle started up again and so did the croaking of the frogs. All around them in the dark green shades the dry leaves tumbled downwards and disappeared into the undergrowth.

'Lukas ...' The danger was over, she was no longer whispering. 'You can turn back now. The bigfeet are grazing in the direction of the river. It's safe; I'll go on by myself.'

'Pa said I was to stay with you until the forester turns up.'

'You can tell pa the forester had been there already; you can turn back right away. Please, Lukas.'

He did not like the way she looked at him: pleading and bewildered. His hand holding the ox rein was sweating; if she were to run away, he would have to catch her but he knew he would not have the heart to tie her up.

'If I turn back here, you will not really go to Deep Walls, Nina, I know you. You'll hide somewhere and tomorrow or the next day the bigfeet will trample you or you will die of hunger or you will break your legs or something, and pa will brain me for it.'

'I don't want to work in the village, Lukas. I'm scared.' It was a frank confession and he felt sorry for her.

'Don't worry. When they took me to Knysna that time, I was just as scared. It was terrible. But I promise you, it's not a bad place. You'll like living there.'

'I want to stay in the Forest!' She was very obstinate.

'Nina, if you start making trouble now, I won't know what to do,' he told her straight out. 'If you run away, I will not go after you and tie you up, and then the next time pa will send Willem or Kristoffel with you, and they won't hesitate to tie you up.' It looked as if she wanted to cry but was too stubborn. 'Come on now.' He took her by the arm and started dragging her along with him. 'For all you know, the forester's son may be at the road too and then you won't even look round to wave at *me*!'

'Go to hell!'

'You will have to learn to speak like a lady now, you know. You'll be a village girl. You heard yourself what Willem and Kristoffel said about the village girls, how pretty and fine they are.'

'The village people scorn us forest people.'

'Take no notice. Just hold up your head. The woman that brought me up, always said, as long as your head stays up, your spirits do too.'

Where the footpath joined the sled-path he let go of her arm and she did not rebel again. She only spoke when they were almost at the gravel road.

'When Willem or Kristoffel comes to the village, get my mouth-organ and send it with them.'

'I'll see what I can do.'

'And don't tell Bet, or any of the other children, about the owl's nest in the cliff.'

'I won't.'

'And if I run away from the village, you must help me when pa beats me for it.'

'I will – I mean, you must not run away, you must stay in the village.'

The forester was already standing in the road when they got there. He was irritable and in a hurry, and wanted to know why they were so late and why the girl did not have anything with her. Surely they could at least have given her a change of clothes. Nina seemed ready to turn and run, but the look the man gave her frightened her. When they walked away, she looked back once, her eyes pleading; then she followed the forester, hanging her head.

He stood there and watched them go along the road until they disappeared into the Forest. Then he was alone and a feeling of desolation came over him. It would be far better for Nina if she lived in the village, for her unruliness caused a lot of trouble on the Island and around the house. She had been forbidden to visit any of the woodcutters' houses; every child on the Island had been warned a hundred times to stay away from her. She showed no respect for the grown-ups and no chicken was safe when she was throwing stones. No, he did not wish her back. But he knew he would miss her.

Ahead of him the road went downhill to the village, behind him, uphill into the Forest towards the mountains and the Long Kloof. There was nothing in the village for him. West, where the Island was, little more. Was the road to the Long Kloof still open to him? A year and a half was a long time. In the Forest it seemed even longer. Had they forgotten him already? How long did one remember a hand-child? How could he find out? Who or what was there to stop him from taking the road to the Long Kloof? If he kept on walking without stopping, he could be there at dawn the next day. By the time they found out where he was and fetched him again, he would have had a nice long visit and found out how they all were. How it was with Kicker and Pollie and Master Petrus and Miss Baby and Auntie Maria.

The crack of a whip, higher up in the Forest, jerked him out of his dream. He turned quickly and took the sled-path home, to the Island.

2 0

No, things certainly could not go on like that. Life was passing Elias van Rooyen by and life was getting shorter. He had been trapped on Barnard's Island for more than two years now. Worse than prison, it was. At least in prison you could move about without a bloody elephant waiting to trample you.

'Lukas, leave that and help me get this beam off the scaffold.'

'I'm coming, Pa.'

It was six months since he had got back on to the scaffold himself. There was no other way. He would have to buy a gun and learn to shoot. He could not spend his life sitting in a clearing. When Nina's first wages had to be fetched from the village, he had risked going into the Forest for the first time for many months and had got as far as the second gorge – then he had had to throw down his coat and run for his life down a deeper gorge. How the bloody cow had known he would be coming along there that day, he had no idea. But something told him it had been no accident. The place she stood waiting for him had been cleverly chosen; he was just about under her feet before he realized she was there. If he had had a gun, he would have blown her brains out, but he had nothing.

'You must go and help your ma in the garden later on, Lukas.'

'Yes, Pa.'

If ever two children had been easy to deal with, it was Lukas and Kristoffel. Lukas had had his problems in the beginning but after that he had known his place. Quiet kind of boy. And Kristoffel always worked hard. If Kristoffel had had a wagon and oxen of his own, he would have been his own boss with his own woodcutter's team before long. They were an example to

others, Lukas and Kristoffel. Shortly before Christmas they had
added another room to the house, sawing the planks themselves
and everything, and at the same time they had mended the roof.
When Soois Cronje, for whom Kristoffel had been working for
many years, was lying sick to death with the summer-flu in
January, Kristoffel did not come home to sit on his backside as
Willem did when Martiens was down with the stomach trouble,
Kristoffel went and helped Fred Terblans haul ivory to the
village and came home with almost a month's provisions, and a
bed for himself to go in the back room as well. And as for Lukas,
there would soon be no one in the Forest who could compete with
him in making a beam from a yellowwood log. A clever boy. And
Lukas wanted to make floorboards too – well, he would let him
have his way with that one day.

'Looks to me we'll have a full load to deliver again next
Thursday, Lukas. No wonder they have to come with two
wagons nowadays.'

'Willem says there are no fewer than four wagons coming from
as far as Graaf-Reinet every third month now. There are woodcutters supplying them on the sly in the gravel road at Iron
Neck.'

'Yes. Till someone reports them. You can't be in debt to the
wood buyers in the village and then sell to the wood pedlars. The
wood buyers have spies everywhere. When they catch them
there'll be trouble. They could lose not only their woodcutter's
licences but half their oxen as well to pay the outstanding debt,
and what would they have gained?'

Elias van Rooyen had at least been spared that: he was not in
debt to any of the wood buyers. He was a free man – except for
the bloody elephants. Everybody could shoot elephants: Fred
Terblans, Marais, strangers, foresters, Government, everyone
that wanted to. Someone told him that you did not even have to
pay for a licence as he had thought, all you had to do was get
permission on paper from the Government and anyone that
could write could get it. But Elias van Rooyen could not read or

write and did not possess a gun, and he was the one under a death sentence. He was trapped on the Island. Bloody rogues. Pity it had to be a calf that had fallen into the pit. All the trouble and hope had been for nothing and it had backfired too because the elephants had put the blame on him. The children had done most of the digging, why did they not chase the children too then? The trouble was, they say an elephant never forgets. Especially about a calf. Years ago a man at Karatara had borrowed a gun and shot a calf for the meat and they say the cow looked for him for three years and found him up in Stripe Bush on a Sunday and trampled him to death. Perhaps it was just a story. Perhaps it had been an accident and not even the same cow. The only way out he could see was to get a gun. *Shoot* Elias van Rooyen's image from their minds if it's true that they never forget. Bastards.

He started on a new beam and let his thoughts wander as far as Willem. He would rather not think about Nina. Only the good Lord above knew what would become of that brat of his. At least he still had some say with Willem even if it was becoming more and more difficult. Willem had started to itch for getting married. He had wormed himself into Martiens's and Malie's favour over Gertrude. What good did it do for a man to bring up children so that he could have it easier if they went off and got married and worked for a father-in-law? Willem could take himself a wife when he had done his duty by his own family. But not to that girl of Malie's, she was far too much like her mother.

'Go and help your ma with the hoeing now, Lukas.'

'Yes, Pa.'

And Barta would have to do something about Malie's Bet, too, who kept coming over to where Lukas was working. She would have to go and talk to Malie about it. He no longer talked to Malie. Lukas must not be kept from his work; every beam that was finished counted. A gun was expensive, and then you had to buy bullets too. Since Nina had also started earning, things were better, but it did not mean that Elias van Rooyen was rich yet!

If only he dared to go into the Forest again. His excuses for not helping to get the beams to Deep Walls and for not going to the village to fetch Nina's wages were getting a bit thin – either his back being too sore or the rheumatism in his legs being too bad.

Bloody Nina. A man should have twelve sons before he had a daughter. The forester had gone to all the trouble of finding her a job in the village – four shillings a week for looking after children and helping in the house – with rich English people, but before the first week was out, she was back home. Rain-soaked, looking dreadful. Barta and Lukas stood up for her when he wanted to get at her with the ox rein. The next day he had to send Lukas to Spruit's Bush to fetch Willem, so that he could take her back. Lukas was too soft, took pity too easily, and anyway he always flinched away from going to the village.

Only when Willem got back from the village did they hear that she had not run away, but had been given the sack. Apparently she had hit one of the children and stolen some things. She had brought that disgrace upon them too. Willem said he nearly died of shame, and got hold of her by the hair right there in front of the woman to shake her so that the woman could see she came from a home where that sort of thing was not tolerated. The woman agreed to give her a second chance but at three shillings a week.

Less than three months after that, Lukas came home from the Forest one Sunday, saying he had found Nina at a creek where they used to play. But Lukas did not tell Elias, he went to his ma first so that she could prepare him with all kinds of soft talk. He sent Lukas to fetch her, but the moment she set foot in the house, he went blind with rage and neither Barta nor the Sabbath stopped him from getting the truth out of her with the ox rein that day. She had been in the Forest like a thief for almost a week; she had been sacked again for hitting the children and stealing things. Willem refused outright to take her back and be shamed again.

She sat at home for more than three months before the forester managed to get her back into service again. But she had thrown away her name: half a crown a week with food and clothing was all the people were prepared to pay. What could he do? Nothing. He had to accept it. But as soon as he could get to the village himself again, he would go and see if he could not get her price raised to three shillings.

21

On the second day of April 1881 they buried Dawid. At Wolwekraal, at the feet of Fiela's mother and father and next to her
brother that had died as a child.

It was a big funeral. The Reverend Schuman came from
Uniondale to read the burial service and Petrus Zondagh made a
speech afterwards. White and Coloured together cried round
Dawid's grave and in the back row the Laghaans stood sober and
wary. Dawid had had no enemies.

Two of Petrus's men carried Selling on a chair to the grave; she
stood on the one side of him and Petrus on the other.

And only God knew how smitten she was. Her beautiful
Dawid. He had milked her the cow on the Wednesday morning,
as cheerful as ever, but that night he was a corpse. Button spider.
Must have been in the sheaves he had been stacking. She lifted
him on to the donkey-cart herself and drove him to the village as
fast as the donkeys could go, but it was too late. The poison had
been too strong for him.

Seven years ago, when she had had to give up Benjamin,
Dawid had been the one that comforted her for many a day and
helped her carry on. He never told her to accept what had
happened like the others did, he always said, 'Ma, ma must wait.
Benjamin will come home one day, ma will see.'

She had had to give up Benjamin to the forest people, Dawid
to the grave. There was little difference in the bitterness within
her. The question she put to God was the same: Why, God, why?

What had everything profited her? When you had to lose your
children, everything else was nothing. Six ostrich enclosures.
Twelve birds for brooding: six males, six hens. The best and

strongest chicks were still Kicker's and Pollie's. Sixteen pounds a chick the man from Oudtshoorn had paid her for sixty six-month-old chicks the last time. Almost a thousand pounds. Four years ago, she had purchased the land the Laghaans rented and allowed the rotten lot to stay on in the house. But only in the house. The land she had fenced in with Wolwekraal and tilled herself. And she had warned the Laghaans: the day she saw even a puff of smoke coming from the chimney that was not to her liking, it was off with them. Had it not been for Koos Wehmeyer falling out with everyone about church affairs she would never have been able to buy it.

Tollie was his father's child. Horses were in his blood. Shortly after Benjamin had left, Tollie had started helping Petrus at the stables over weekends. She tried to stop it, she said everything she could against it, but Selling stuck up for him and so did Petrus; according to him, Tollie worked with a horse as no one had done since Selling. But she did not want to think about Tollie, there was enough sorrow on Wolwekraal.

Dawid had been her child. He had loved the land. He had loved the ostriches. Proud.

Kitty was married to the lay preacher down at Haarlem. She had little liking for her son-in-law. He knew everything about hell – they were all going there according to him. The people had more need to hear about heaven. When he offered to come and bury Dawid, she was glad she could tell him the Reverend Schuman had already sent a message to say that he would come to bury Dawid himself.

Emma was still at home. She and little Fiela, the child Emma had had with John Howell's yard-hand. John Howell of course wanted them to get married so that he could be rid of the good-for-nothing but she drove both John Howell and his yard-hand off her property. The whole Kloof was already full of his offspring. Wolwekraal itself would care for Emma and the child.

She had told Petrus they must get news of Dawid's death to Benjamin. She realized he would not be able to get to the funeral in time but he could always come later to see the grave.

Dawid had always believed that Benjamin would come back one day. There had been times when it seemed as if Dawid and Benjamin were closer brothers than Dawid and Tollie. Now Dawid would not be there when Benjamin came back. If he came back. Doubt had got hold of her so much through the years that she no longer knew what to believe. And how the news of Dawid's death was to get to him, she did not know either. Petrus had sent Latjie over the mountain with a message and all she could pray for was that Latjie would reach home again. When she and Dawid had gone to the Forest taking Benjamin's things as a pretext, but really in the hope of bringing him back, they almost did not return alive. Only woodcutters and elephants could live there. Not people. It took them a week to find someone that could tell them where to leave the gravel road and start their search. Mercifully the man knew who they were looking for and took them on his wagon to where the forest path they had to take turned off. He had explained to them how many creeks they had to cross and which footpath they had to take to get to a place called Barnard's Island. He might just as well have explained to them how to find a fish in the middle of the ocean. You had to be born in that wilderness to be able to tell the difference between one turn and another. For two days she and Dawid had looked for that footpath. After a while they no longer knew how far they had gone or where they had gone wrong. And to top it all they had come across an enormous elephant dropping, still steaming and fresh. Dawid got such a fright that he wanted to give up there and then. But she told him they could not just give up. They had to go on. A Komoetie did not give up. About an hour after that a whole gang of woodcutters had come from another direction and one of them had offered to go with them to the place.

But once again everything had been in vain. Benjamin was not there. It was as if God had kept on putting up one wall after another between her and the child. The man had quite a shock when she had told him who she was. And when she asked him how he thought a child of three could have walked to the Long Kloof, he had turned white-arsed and sheltered behind the magistrate and asked Dawid who had given him the right to sit on the log. When the woman came from the house it looked as if she was going to faint. Every time she had tried to speak to the woman, the man had stopped her and shouted her down, threatening her with the law and with prison too.

That day Dawid had cried with her when they walked away. And the most difficult thing to swallow, was that the man had sworn to her that the child had taken to them immediately and was happy with them. She could not believe it. Not Benjamin. Not with those people in that dense, dense Forest. He had always been a child for the open. When he was small and it was a moonless night he sometimes took it into his head that the sun would not come back again and then Selling had to make up long stories about where the sun had gone to rest and how it would come back again in the morning.

Would Dawid's death bring Benjamin back after seven years? No. It did not seem likely. By that time Benjamin would be almost twenty. A man. A woodcutter. Was he ashamed of the fact that a brown woman had brought him up? Why had God taken him away from her, but left his image in her heart? Why had he taken Dawid as well? Selling said it was not God's work, it was the button spider's.

And what about Benjamin?

22

There was rebellion in him as he stood listening to his pa's last orders in the half-dark kitchen that morning.

'Lukas, I'm telling you, you don't come back home without her.'

'And I still say we must wait till Willem or Kristoffel gets home so that one of them can go to the village.'

'I'm not waiting another day.'

His ma was busy tying food in a cloth for him for the journey. 'Go and ask at the place where she worked,' she suggested. 'Willem said it was with the schoolmaster, grand people it was.'

'Yes, Ma.' He took the food and lingered, hoping to find a way out at the last moment. He had no wish to go to the village.

His pa started getting impatient. 'Get on with you now, Lukas, it's getting light outside already! You know the way as far as Deep Walls, from there you just keep to the gravel road as I explained. Ask where the schoolmaster lives and find out if they know what's happened to her.'

'I'll do that, Pa.'

'And keep your eyes open all the time for the bloody bigfeet. You can't feel sure in this Forest any more.'

'Yes, Pa.'

It was daybreak when he got outside but in the Forest you could still hear the crickets and it was still night.

He was to go and look for Nina. His pa's moaning had grown so unbearable that he had agreed in a weak moment to go and then he could not refuse.

How many times had he not told them to leave Nina alone!

She was no longer a child. Every month there was trouble when her wages had to be fetched from the village. Willem did not want to get the money any more, now that he was married to Gertrude and was living with the woodcutters on the other side of the Island. When Kristoffel could not go, it was argument and bickering until Willem took to the road, sulking, and came back sulking. And every month there were arguments about the money, which was always short because Nina had always borrowed ahead.

The Forest was dripping with dew. A little blue buck, startled, ran ahead of him on the footpath: a little black shadow that hardly left a track, so light-footed did it live in the thickets. Nina had always said that if she could be an animal in the Forest for a day, she wanted to be a little blue buck. He always chose to be an elephant just to stop her pestering him about it. Not that you could stop her that easily.

'And if you could be a tree for a day, Lukas?'

'You say first.'

'I don't want to be a tree, I want to be a blue-buck vine, and twine and twine through the Forest and be food for all the blue bucks.'

'I would like to be a rock alder.'

'Are you stupid?' she had asked, disappointed. 'Why don't you be a decent kalander or a wild alder or a white pear? Why a rock alder?'

'It's different. It's the only one that sheds its leaves during winter and gets the sun.'

It would not surprise him if Nina was hiding somewhere in the Forest again. The longest she had ever stayed in the village without running away had been round about six months, and every time it was more and more difficult to get her back to the village again.

The previous week, Kristoffel, who had gone to the village to fetch her wages, came back without the money and with the news that she had left the people who she had last been working for more than a month ago. They were under the impression that she had gone back to the Forest.

His ma cried for a whole day. His pa walked around for a whole day, promising Nina what would happen to her if he got his hands on her. The day after that the complaints had started:

'Lukas, this time you will have to go to the village to look for your sister. You can't refuse.'

'I don't go to the village and pa knows it. Pa has known it for years!'

'You can't say no to me this time.'

His ma pleaded too. 'Something could have happened to her, Lukas. You've got to go and find out for us.'

The next day his pa started clutching his side. 'I tell you, that girl will be the end of me. She will bring disgrace upon my house!'

In the end he had agreed to go and look for her.

The sun came up and lured the larger birds to the top of the trees where they got noisier and noisier.

He put his hand in his pocket and absent-mindedly closed it round the five shillings. Strange, he thought, it was the second time he and the five-shilling piece had had to go to Knysna unwillingly. To him it had ceased to be money long ago, it was his last tie with Wolwekraal – that, and his memories. But memories got left behind while you kept walking on; every time you had to retrace your steps further to return to your memories, and sometimes it was better not to turn back at all.

He had grown used to the Forest; he had learned to understand and accept things. He was a beam-maker. One day he wanted to get his own tools and work for himself because you could earn a good living making beams and floorboards and doors and frames. He had often told his pa that he should bring Kristoffel in as well so that they could make floorboards too, but his pa's reason had gone long ago.

Everybody knew it. Elias van Rooyen solemnly believed that a certain elephant cow had been waiting to kill him for years. Sometimes he got it into his head that it was a whole *herd* of cows. Half of all the money that came in was put towards a gun and every gun he had bought had been useless. If the barrel was not cracked, it was warped, or the thing was good only to be thrown away. No fewer than five guns were rusting away under the shed already. The woodcutters now laughed at him to his face. One of them even suggested he should try and get a cannon next time – maybe that would work.

The previous month, Kristoffel had come home with the story that the forester at Gouna had a gun he wanted to sell, a proper elephant gun that would blow a hole as big as a fist through an elephant. Kristoffel should have kept his mouth shut. The forester wanted five pounds for the gun and since then they had saved every penny they could; his ma's shoes had to wait again and Nina had had to be fetched so that her wages could be added to the rest.

And he had to go and find her. What would he do with her if he did find her? They should leave her alone, he said. You could not keep picking on a person, year after year, and she didn't listen anyway. And anyway Nina was a girl and a girl should not be scolded and beaten as she was whenever she returned home. Why she still kept on coming home, he could not understand. Or perhaps it was her love for the Forest he did not understand. No one understood that. When she was small, he had often got the feeling that she played, not *in* the Forest but *with* the Forest. She had even called the mouth-organ tunes she made up by the names of the trees.

He would go and see if he could find Nina, but he refused to bring her back home with him. If nothing had happened to her and she was working somewhere, she should stay where she was. He would get more beams finished – he would light the lantern and work after dark – so that the gun could be bought and his pa could learn to shoot and get the elephants out of his system. He couldn't stay trapped on one spot in the Forest for the rest of his life. Who had to set his traps? Who had to choose and fell his wood for him?

These were days when he could not help feeling sorry for his pa though. Wrong as he was, it must be terrible to live in a trap – yes, everyone in the Forest was trapped in fact, but at least not in a single clearing, and they could get out if they wanted to.

He stopped at Deep Walls to eat something and rested there for quite a while. Not so much because he was tired but because he wanted to put off his arrival at the village. Deep Walls had become a sort of boundary line to him through the years. You brought the beams to Deep Walls. You walked with Nina as far as Deep Walls when she had to go back after she had run away again. The safety of Kom's Bush stretched as far as Deep Walls. When he was a child, the way to the Long Kloof started at the gravel road at Deep Walls.

That was a long time ago.

You did not keep on kicking a stone, especially when that stone turned out to be a mountain you could not move. There were things you could change and others you could not change. After he had come to realize that he *was* Lukas van Rooyen and accepted it, things had been better. He grew to love the Forest too in his own way. The Forest had its own way of life; it was a place where you could be alone on Sundays and let your body rest and straighten up again after a week on the scaffold. He came to know the Forest: its paths, its moods, its dangers. In the Forest he learned that unhappiness was something you got used to or something that passed.

When the shadows of the trees were stretching across the road, the Forest became thinner around him and he knew he could not be far from the place where his pa had said he would meet the road that came from the village. If he got to the village before dark, he might as well inquire about Nina at a few houses.

But soon he realized that something unusual must have happened, for everywhere along the road people were coming and going like ants. Some came from the direction of the village; others, on their way back, were dusty, as if they had come a long way. A few were on horseback, pushing past those on foot.

He sat down and watched for some time. They were different from the forest people; their clothes were beautiful, especially the women's. Most of them held little lace parasols over their heads as if they were afraid of the sun.

He asked some boys what was happening.

'There's a ghost ship at Noetzie.'

'Where is Noetzie?' he asked.

'Just follow the track to the south.'

What difference would it make if he turned south? What difference would it make if he started looking for Nina the next day? A ghost ship was impossible, but he had to go and see for himself, and that meant putting off going to the village. Perhaps he could find somewhere to sleep at Noetzie.

Just follow the track to the south.

Sometimes the track went through a little valley, sometimes it climbed high up over the next hill, giving a view of the sea on the horizon. Wide and blue. It was the nearest he had ever been to the sea. Most of the people were already coming back, and some of them looked at him as if *he* was an apparition. Where the track went through a bad patch of sand, he stood aside to let a bunch of girls pass and as they did, they kept giggling and looking at him.

It did not bother him. Since he had got on to the track and was no longer on his way to the village, he felt better.

It was further than he had thought it would be, though. Each time the track came to the top of a hill, the sea seemed as far as ever, and when he at last came to the very steep hill down to the sea, the sun was gone. About half-way down was a place where the bushes had been cut back to make a clearing where horses could be tethered and carts could be left. On the other side of the clearing the track became a footpath that descended almost vertically through milkwood trees and shrubs.

The milkwoods formed a tunnel over the path, getting denser and denser. Only once could he see through the trees and shrubs to the hills on the other side of the dark river far below. When the footpath forked, he chose the fork that looked the less used and went down on his heels to stop himself from going too fast. From the other side of the trees he could hear the sound of the sea calling to him, urging him on.

One moment he was in the tunnel of milkwoods and the next moment he stood at the foot of the hills on the edge of a bay. It felt as if the earth had given way beneath him. Where the first breakers foamed, a three-masted ship lay firmly wedged between the rocks with sails hanging from the masts like dirty, tattered rags; there was something horribly dead and desolate about the ship. He wanted to put out his hands and push the ship back into deeper water where it could float again and breathe and come alive.

When, as a child, he had pushed his wooden boats out on to the stream, a strange feeling of joy had gone through his body, and the same forgotten feeling welled up in him now as he stood there, but more powerfully. There was something about that dead ship that touched his whole being – he was like a stranger to himself, standing on the sand of an unknown bay where a ship lay wrecked that did not belong there either. The ship was trapped between the rocks and he stood rooted to his tracks. Was he dreaming?

He stayed at the foot of the hills until the darkness had driven everyone else away, except for one man at the water's edge.

'Good evening, uncle.' The man jumped. 'I'm sorry, I did not mean to startle you.'

'Then why did you creep up on me? I thought everyone had gone.'

'I'm sorry, uncle.'

'I'm not your uncle,' the man said with dignity. 'I'm Sergeant Armstrong. You'd better get up that hill before it's too dark to find the footpath. I have enough trouble as it is; I can't go after

people who are lost up there.' The man was ill at ease and kept
glancing in the direction of the ship as if he was afraid it might
suddenly sail away.

'What ship is that, sergeant? How did it get there?'

'Everybody else is asking that, young man.'

'What do you mean?'

'Nobody knows how it got there. When the sun came up this
morning, there she was. Somebody who was fishing here till late
yesterday said there was nothing there when he left.'

'Were there people on the ship?'

'Corpses perhaps. Mr Benn reckons, judging by the state of
the sails and the rigging, she must have been drifting about
for months. The tide's coming in, she'll start breaking up
soon.'

Where did she come from? Where had she been heading? Who
had set her sails and then left her to drift in the wind?

'Can't they do something to get it afloat again?'

'Not from where she's lying.'

'It's a pity that she must break up.'

'The sooner the better, young man. I said to Mr Benn – do you
know Mr Benn?'

'No.'

'He's the pilot at the Heads where the ships come through up
the Knysna River. I said to him, I'll keep watch until tomorrow
morning, it's my work, but from then on the customs people must
take over. They will have to try and find out whose ship it is. As
far as we could see, there is no name on her. It's getting dark –
you must go.'

'I was on my way to the village, I can just as well stay here for
the night.' The sergeant seemed pleased. 'Perhaps I could help
you keep watch.'

The sergeant laughed, nervously, 'I might just take you up on
that! There will be no moon tonight and the beachcombers will
be ready to close in. Especially Kaliel September. I know him.'
He sounded scared.

They gathered driftwood and made a fire. Then each ate his own food; they did not talk much.

'What do you keep on looking up at the sky for?' he asked.

'I haven't seen so many stars for a very long time.'

'Are you from the Forest then?'

'Yes.'

'Funny. You people seldom speak to strangers. I thought you were a fisherman from Plettenberg Bay.'

'I come from Barnard's Island in Kom's Bush. Where's Plettenberg Bay?'

'About four hours on horseback from here. Up the coast.'

The waves broke fiercely over the ship and over the rocks around the bay. When he closed one eye and got a star in line with a mast, he could see the ship rolling against the onslaught of the water. It would be a miracle if the wooden hull held out till daybreak.

But it was a peaceful night. Later on, when the sergeant dozed off, he got up to take a walk.

'Where are you going?'

'I'm just taking a walk.'

'Are you coming back?'

'Yes.'

'If you see anything, call me.'

'I will. Sleep a while.'

'I dare not.'

The sea and the sky seemed immense around him. To the west the hills were huge dark humps against the starlit sky; behind him the fire threw a yellow circle of light across the sand; between the rocks lay the ghostly shape of the ship. He walked along the shore, following the curve of the bay. Sand sifted into his shoes and his feet grew heavier. Was it his imagination or did the ship list more to the one side? As if it wanted to lie down like a tired beast.

He walked to the river mouth and then turned back and sat down to shake the sand out of his shoes. He did not want to think, not about the past, not about the future or the village or Nina. He just wanted to sit there and give way to the strange feeling of unreality and relief that was growing in him. Like wine. He wanted to sit there and see the sun come out. He wanted to sit there and see the sun go down again. Perhaps he had been in the Forest too long. Perhaps it was the immensity of space around him that made his mind reel.

A shooting star drew a bright streak of light across the sky and vanished.

'When you see a shooting star and wish as fast as you can, your wish will come true,' Nina had always said. You seldom saw a shooting star above Barnard's Island.

If he had to wish, what would he wish for, he asked himself. What was there to wish for? That they should deliver more beams? That they should start to deliver planks as well? Those were not the sort of thing you wished for, a wish asked for the unattainable. The impossible. No, there was nothing he wanted to wish for. Perhaps he would wish the ship would come alive.

There were days when the Forest scared him. When every beam that he finished was just one beam nearer to the time when he would make his last beam and he would look back and see nothing but beams stretching out behind him. On those days he threw down his axe and walked off into the Forest until he felt better again.

At daybreak the ship was still intact.

'I will have to leave now, sergeant.'

'Why do you want to go now? John Benn and his men will be here shortly; they're going to try and get to the ship this morning. If you go now, you'll miss everything.'

'As I said last night, I was on my way to the village.' He wanted to get away. He never liked skinning a buck.

'A pity. I want to see if they can't salvage one of the boats, the longboat perhaps.' Now that it was light, the sergeant was confident and talkative again. 'As the sea does not want to do its work, we'll have to do it for him!'

'I'll say goodbye then.'

The village was quiet. Two forest wagons, one heavily loaded and the other already emptied, came down the street. People from Karatara that he did not know well.

In front of a two-storeyed house an old Coloured man was sweeping the street, the dust flying up in clouds.

'Good morning, uncle! I'm looking for the schoolmaster's house.'

The old man looked at him askance, probably because he had called him uncle.

'There's no one at home, they've gone to Noetzie. A ghost ship has been washed up there.'

'Where is the house?'

'It's there.'

He was about to cross the street when the old man stopped him.

'Are you from the Forest?'

'Yes.'

'What do forest people want with the schoolmaster?' he asked, adding, 'Perhaps you want to learn to read and write?'

'No. I'm looking for my sister, she used to work there.'

'The skinny one?' the old man quickly asked.

'Yes. Nina. Nina van Rooyen. I'm looking for her.'

He laughed snortingly. 'That was a contrary one.'

'Who?'

'Your sister. I think the children were sorry when she walked off, but the schoolmaster was glad.'

'You don't know where she's working now?'

'No. But I sometimes see her with old Miss Weatherbury in the village. Perhaps she's working there now. She's worked all over the place already.'

'Who's Miss Weatherbury?'

'The English lady out on the old farm. At Melkhoutkraal.'

'Where's that?'

'It's obvious that you come from the Bush,' the old man said, airing his knowledge. 'My father was a slave at Melkhoutkraal when Melkhoutkraal still spread its roots right round the lagoon. When the big man, George Rex, was still alive. Now it's all in the hands of strangers. Divided up and fenced off. I believe old Miss Weatherbury has the right to stay in the little cottage below the graveyard for life. She doesn't teach any more, she's too old now.'

'How do I get there?' he asked, before the old man could start gossiping again.

'Take the first track leading south when you're out of the village. To the Heads. Towards the lagoon. But don't go as far as the lagoon. Go to the big milkwood standing almost in the path and then turn left and keep on past the first homestead and the stables and the orchard on your left. A little further on, you'll find the cottage. Thatched. Small. That's old Miss Weatherbury's place. I don't know if your sister will be there, but you could go and ask.'

'Thank you.'

As he walked away he could not decide whether luck had been on his side or against him. In his heart he had hoped not to find her, for what was he to do if he did?

The feeling of relief was no longer in him. In its place was rebellion against having to go and knock on a stranger's door because of Nina. He did not want to do it.

The milkwood was where the old man had said it would be. Perhaps he should eat a little and rest a while, he thought to himself, it was not midday yet. He ate and stretched out on the sparse grass under the tree, knowing that he would fall asleep... A short postponement would make no difference.

When he woke it was dark. He found himself a better place to lie down and slept deep into the night. At daybreak he went to look for the cottage but came back to the tree to wait until it was a decent time to go knocking at someone's door.

At the homestead, beyond the orchard, cattle lowed, sheep bleated and cocks crowed – sounds that had become almost strange to him in the Forest. Except for the crowing. Some of the woodcutters kept fowls.

The sun was high when he walked up to the cottage at last.

An old lady with her hair in a straggling bun opened the door and looked him up and down and up again from behind a pair of small round spectacles.

'Was there something you wanted?' she asked in English.

'Do you speak Dutch?'

'Yes.'

'I'm sorry to trouble you, but I was told in the village that my sister might be working here. Nina. Nina van Rooyen.' For a moment it seemed as if she was going to shut the door in his face. But she did not.

'Your *sister*, you said?'

'Yes. My sister.'

'There is a Nina van Rooyen working for me, but she has no family.'

He would have liked to turn round and walk away. Perhaps it would be best to accept the lie. He was tired of the never-ending trouble she made.

But he had to say something, he could not just stand there. 'Nina's imagination runs away with her at times, auntie.'

'I'm not your aunt, I'm *Miss* Weatherbury.'

She had said it in a decent sort of way and he liked the look of her. If Nina had found a place with her, it would be a miracle and his pa should be more than thankful for it.

'I *am* Nina's brother, Miss Weatherbury, truly. I suppose she said that because – because ... It's difficult to say why.'

'Young man ... You say you are Nina's brother; could there be more than one Nina van Rooyen?'

'No, Miss Weatherbury, I don't think there could be more than one Nina. I'm Lukas van Rooyen, Nina's youngest brother. We were worried about her for we heard that she had left the schoolmaster and we didn't know where she had gone. My pa sent me to look for her. Believe it or not, that's the truth.'

'I'll decide that for myself. Nina came here looking for work and I took her in for two reasons: in the first place I needed help around the house and in the second place I thought I would be able to help her – teach her good behaviour, see that she improved her appearance. But I am afraid that she is very disobedient. I am very worried about her.'

It was the old story. 'I'm sorry to hear that, Miss Weatherbury.'

'She is not lazy. She helps me around the house, but the moment she has done her work, instead of starting on her embroidery, she goes off to the hills. And it would be my responsibility if something happened to her.'

'She's always been like that. At home too.' He liked Miss Weatherbury – she was a lady. But he could not picture Nina with needle and thread.

'John Benn, the pilot at the Heads, has already spoken to me about her wandering around in the hills. We get a lot of foreign seamen coming here; a week ago Mr Benn had to get two of them away from her. I try not to think what could have happened to her if he had not heard her screaming.'

He did not want to think about it either. The whole time he was standing there, he had the feeling that Nina was somewhere listening to every word. 'It's dangerous for her, miss. I'll talk to her, she'll listen to me.' He had little faith in what he was saying, although Nina sometimes did take more notice of him than of the others. 'Would you call her for me, miss?'

'I'm afraid you'll have to wait. She got up before dawn to get her work done, and then took the short cut across the hills to Noetzie – we heard that a ship had run aground there.'

'I'll wait for her then.'

She did not invite him in but said he could wait on the bench under the oak trees beside the house. After a while she brought him some thin slices of bread and some coffee on a tray, and sat down with him. They talked about Nina again and it came out that she was getting seven shillings a week. If his pa were to find out, he thought, he would be sent to the village every month to collect it.

'I do not want to give the impression that I'm running Nina down, young man; if I did not see good in her, I would not have bothered. But she is too unruly.'

'It's because she keeps clinging to the Forest, Miss Weatherbury. She loves the Forest very much.'

'Why did she deny that she came from the Forest then? Why did she say she came from the Long Kloof, that she was a foundling? ... Why do you smile?'

'I'm smiling because she borrowed that story from someone else. Or half of it.'

'I will not know who or what to believe in the end.'

'Miss Weatherbury should believe me. I'll wait until Nina comes back and have a good talk with her. This is the best chance she's ever had – she can't come back to the Forest, she must try to do her work well and stay here.'

'Do you think you have any influence over her?'

'Perhaps. And in future I'll come to fetch her money at the end of the month myself and speak to her if necessary.'

'Why do you want to fetch her money?' The old lady was suspicious again.

'Well – actually it's my pa that sends for the money.' He felt like a thief. 'I just thought it might be better if I came to fetch it in future; Nina listens to me more than to my two brothers.'

'I don't understand why you want to take her money. If there is illness or real need at home and she feels she should make a voluntary contribution, that is fine. But you cannot just come and collect her money every month. I will not allow it.'

'You don't understand, Miss Weatherbury. Forest people are different. Everything is thrown in together.'

'Nina is no longer part of the Forest, so I do not see why you still want her money.'

'Neither do I, really.' He could not tell her it was because his pa had to buy a bloody gun. Miss Weatherbury was right, why did they have to take her money? But Miss Weatherbury did not have to go and say so at Barnard's Island.

By midday he was tired of waiting. He went to the kitchen door and told Miss Weatherbury that he would walk in the direction of the lagoon for a while. He wanted to see the place where the ships came in between the hills from the sea to get to the harbour at the village.

A footpath led past some marshy ground to the hills ahead. Yellow weaverbirds were calling in the reeds; they reminded him that he had last seen them at Wolwekraal! Other strange-looking, long-legged birds were standing on one leg in the water and little waterhens were swimming to and fro. They were different from the birds in the Forest, but he could still hear the call of a bush lourie far off in the wooded hills between him and the sea. In his heart he said: Miss Weatherbury, I'm afraid you'll have a hard time keeping Nina in the house.

The footpath turned towards the lagoon. Everywhere were the candelabra flowers, like big red balls with arms. At the foot of the first hill two wood and corrugated-iron houses sheltered close together in the bushes; two children waved at him; a cat was lying asleep in the sun.

The further he walked, the less space there was for the footpath between the hill and the lagoon. The water seemed to get deeper – he could not see yet where sea and lagoon met, for some huge rocks stuck out into the lagoon ahead of him. He came to another house, where there were children and chickens and a nanny goat by the house, and lots of washing drying over the bushes. Where the footpath started climbing towards the rocks, he looked down and saw a large rowing boat lying at anchor in a cove. Four men were sitting on the rocks, looking in the direction of the footpath as if they were watching out for someone.

'Hey! You up there!' One of them looked up. 'Have you seen a man with sacks and planks on his back?'

It was a beautiful boat. Large and solid looking. He supposed that they were going to row out on to the lagoon and were waiting for a mate as there were four oars in the boat. Otherwise they would be short of either an oarsman or a helmsman.

He felt restless. He could not understand it. He was no longer worried about Nina. Nina was safe. All he had to do before he could go home was to get her to listen to Miss Weatherbury, and then go and persuade his pa to leave her alone. No, the restlessness had to do with the boat; it was the useless rebellion of a child wanting the impossible.

He turned away and climbed the footpath leading to the top of the headland. In places it was slippery, then rocky again. Below him, to the right, the water of the lagoon grew deeper and greener, and to the left the hills came down almost to the water. The wooded hills on the other side of the lagoon seemed nearer.

When he came to the top of the headland he saw a dramatic gap between the hills in front of him. Where sea and lagoon met, the water whirled and foamed between the rocks as if it could not get through. On his side of the gap the cliffs soared up from the rocky shore and on the other side they rose straight up from the grey, whirling water. At the entrance from the sea, the waves were curling and foaming as if a stretch of rocks lay just below the surface of the water; a little further in, they seemed to reach a second bar. It was all – the foaming, whirling water, the cliffs, the hills and the rocks – breathtakingly beautiful, but he could not conceive how a ship could ever get through. The gap was wide enough, but everywhere rocks stuck up out of the water; against the cliffs on the other side there seemed to be deep water, but he could not believe that anyone would dare take a ship that close to the rocks.

He crossed the rocks and started to climb higher. In places he had to plan every step ahead so as not to find his way blocked by a sheer rockface. It was a dangerous climb; on some of the rock ledges the foaming water was right beneath him, only the slip of a foot away. The air was filled with fine drops of salty spray that blew against his face and were drawn into his body with every breath he took. Two men were fishing from the rocks with hand lines. A little further on he saw a man standing on a rocky ledge, peering out to the sea. When the man looked round, he seemed startled.

'You there, turn back!' he shouted. 'You can't go any further. Mr Benn gets very angry if you people try to climb round the point there! Do you hear me?' The roar of the sea was all around; he did not want to turn back. 'I say!' the man called out to him again, 'they never found Andries Prens that fell down there the year before last! Turn back!'

He stopped and stood with his back to the cold, wet cliffs – it was like standing in the jaws of a mythical beast. When he looked up the world seemed to tumble forward, confusing him for a moment until he realized that it was the clouds drifting by above the looming cliffs that created the illusion.

He walked back to where the boat was anchored. A fifth man was now sitting with the others but they still seemed to be waiting for someone.

Above the cove another footpath led up the wooded hill. A well-used footpath. There was only one place it could lead to and that was to the top of the hills. The sun was still high up in the sky, Nina would not get home early, he thought, and he started climbing the footpath. If he left it too late to get to Barnard's Island, he would find somewhere to sleep when it got dark and get home the next day.

The higher he climbed up the hill, the more he realized he had forgotten how big the world could be, how open, how vast. How blue the sky could be, how blinding the sun. A bush-buck track stayed with the path for a while and then swerved away again.

The bushes on the ridge were flatter: slanting to one side as if the wind had blown them over and they could not get up again. The sand got into his shoes and made his feet heavy as they had been the night before. The sand was darkish brown. The wind got cooler and the smell of the sea was in it.

The footpath followed the ridge towards another hill and started climbing again until it came to a place where the bushes had been cut back and there was a tall, firmly anchored flag-pole with a red flag flying from it.

A little way from the flag-pole a man was sitting on a bench. Motionless. Like a watchman. He was holding a long instrument to one eye and looking out to sea. To the right of the man the water lay far below at the foot of the cliffs in the gap. Every wave rolling in from the sea rose up at the entrance and broke with a distant thud.

But most wonderful of all was the ship out at sea, riding the waves, its white sails swelling in the wind. A living ship, not like the one at Noetzie. But, as at Noetzie, he was overcome by a feeling of mingled pain and joy and bewilderment. He looked down into the gap, at the waves rolling in, and he knew there would be little mercy for a man down there. In the Forest you could get yourself a gun against the biggest elephant, sharpen your axes against the highest tree, but against the power of the waves man would be helpless.

Out at sea the ship had suddenly shaken the wind from its sails and they were flapping – but only for a moment. Then they filled again and the ship swung round on a new course: straight for the gap between the hills.

He walked up to the man. There were grey streaks in his black beard and hair. His black coat was grey on the shoulders as if many a salt breeze had been embedded in the cloth. He was a big man. His face was deeply lined, strong and weathered by the sun and the wind. A solitary man. He could have been sitting up there for a hundred years. And if he was aware that someone was standing right behind him, he did not heed it – not even when he closed the instrument he had been looking through with a snap and got up. He walked to the edge of the cliffs and stood looking down at the water, then up at the sky, out over the lagoon and out to sea again.

He walked back to the flag-pole, brought down the red flag, took three other flags from a stone box with a wooden lid under the pole and hoisted them. When they shook out into the wind there was a white and blue one, a white and red one and a narrow blue one with a point and a white cross on it. The ship was coming closer to the shore and was hoisting flags too. Four of them. The man peered at the ship through the instrument, brought down the flags on the pole and hoisted four himself: a white and red one and a blue one with a yellow square in the middle as well as blue and white and the blue pointed one he had up already. The ship hoisted four new ones.

The man and the ship had communicated with one another by means of the flags. Without a word. He wanted to ask the man what the flags meant but the man had turned round and was hurrying towards the footpath. Half-way down he cupped his hands over his mouth and called ahead: 'Ahoy! Ahoy!' His words rolled down the hill and echoed back from the cliffs on the other side. Almost immediately another 'Ahoy!' came from the water's edge.

Four of the men down there were already in the boat: three at the oars and one at the helm. The fifth waited until the man was in the boat before he pushed them deeper into the water. Then he got in himself and took the oar at the back.

Four oars dipped together. Again and again, as if someone were beating time. They rowed out into the lagoon, their wake lengthening behind them. Gradually the sound of the oars in the rowlocks faded away.

Did the man live somewhere in the hills on the other side? Were they taking him there? No – once past the rock point the bows of the boat started turning towards the gap.

He ran along the footpath to the top of the rocks. When he got there, the boat had left the quiet water of the lagoon and was pitching over the rough water between the cliffs; the oars were cleaving the water powerfully and evenly. Further and further down the passage and nearer the reddish-brown cliffs on the other side, the boat kept on towards the open sea and the waves breaking and foaming in the gap. Half-way through, they were only an oar's length from the opposite cliffs and seemed to cling to the water with every pull of the oars to keep the boat from being flung against the rocks.

Two seabirds came hovering high above the cliffs, looking down at the boat in the gap.

Then the sailing ship, with only two sails unfurled, came in from the sea and drifted up to the entrance, where it lay rolling gently. The boat rowed away from rocks, passed the ship, made a wide turn and then came back to lie with its head alongside the ship like a calf against a cow, heaving in the swell. The man stood up in the boat, waited, and then, with the next wave, stepped nimbly over to the rope ladder against the side of the ship and climbed to the top.

The rowers pulled away and waited a little way off. Seamen clambered up the ship's masts like cats. Three, four, five, six sails were unfurled and filled with wind. The ship started moving slowly up the narrow passage, following the trail of the boat until it got to the calm water of the lagoon. It waited there for the boat to come through after it and pick up the man again. The boat then rowed back to the cove and the ship sailed up the lagoon to the harbour in the village.

The sun was low on the horizon when Miss Weatherbury opened the door to him.

'I thought you were not coming back.' She sounded relieved.

'A ship came in.'

'We saw it, yes.'

Nina appeared behind her in the door. Distrustful.

'Hallo, Nina.'

'How did you know where to find me?'

'Someone in the village told me.'

'Do pa and the others know?'

'Not yet.'

She pushed past Miss Weatherbury and came to stand in front of him like a vixen. 'Don't go and tell them where I am! Keep your bloody mouth shut!'

'Christina!' Miss Weatherbury scolded. 'Speak decently!' She might just as well have spoken to the door frame.

'Don't tell them you have found me! I am not handing my money over to anyone. Pa can get up from his arse and work for himself!'

'I came to ask you a favour.' She must have realized that he was not taking any notice of what she was saying for she suddenly became quiet and looked at him anxiously.

'Are you all right, Lukas?'

'Yes. But I'm asking you one favour in return for all the times I stood up for you, for all the times I didn't tell on you, for all the bark I helped you hack off your logs.'

'What?'

'Go home and tell pa I'm not coming back. I'm finished with the Forest.'

23

He found himself shelter for the night in the bushes above the lagoon and rose at daybreak in order to be at the flag-pole before the man. He had to find work.

Kristoffel could go on the beams. The devil could go on the beams for all he cared. What they would do about Nina's money was no longer his concern, and who was to keep her at Miss Weatherbury's even less so. He had squared his conscience about that early in the night.

Half-way up the hill he stopped to look round him. The sun was about to come out and the hills on the other side of the lagoon lay mirrored upside down in the water. Way back on the northern shore of the lagoon the little village sloped down to the water. On the rocks above the cove where the boat lay dry and tilted on its side, four pitch-black birds sat with their wings spread out waiting for the sun. Around him in the bushes the turtledoves joined in the dawn chorus one by one and a stray bat swooped past low in front of him.

He felt laughter welling up in him. He was hungry and cold but the feeling of release was far above food and warmth. It gave him courage. He would go straight to the man and offer to hoist the flags, wash them and iron them and mend them if necessary, keep the footpath clear, anything. He would work for a small wage, and food and shelter, as long as he did not have to go back to the Forest. He had done with the Forest. It was like an old coat which you took off and threw away. All night long he had been thinking it out, sorting things out for himself. When he had stood on the headland overlooking the entrance to the lagoon something had happened to him; he did not even try to understand it.

It seemed as if he suddenly had different eyes in his head, suddenly saw things differently. It was more than rebellion that had come over him. He was reaching out at something that was passing him by and he knew that if he did not grab hold of it, if he missed the opportunity, he would have to turn back home. Then he really would rebel.

He had to get work with the man on the hill. How he would get round him, he did not know yet; something warned him that the man was made of the same rocks as the cliffs round the gap.

When he got to the top, the man was sitting on the bench already. A white flag was flying from the pole. The sun was coming up, making a dazzling streak of light across the water; the only sign of life on the sea was a gull flying slowly towards the sun.

He walked up to the man.

'Good morning, sir.' The wind stirred in the man's beard and hair. 'Good morning, sir!' It was like calling out to a deaf man. 'Excuse me . . .'

'What do you want?' The voice growled deep within him; he spoke without taking his eyes off the sea.

'I'm looking for work.'

'There is no work around here.'

'I'm prepared to do anything.'

'I have no work for you.'

'I could look after the boat.'

The man turned round and looked him over carefully. 'Can you row?' he asked.

'No. But I can learn.'

He turned away abruptly and looked out over the sea again. 'This is no place for learners – nor for vagrants.'

'I'm not a vagrant, I'm looking for work. I only want a little money, and food and a place to live.' It was like talking to the rocks but he would not be driven away! 'I can clear the footpath. I can wash and iron the flags – I'll do anything.' The man's foot tapped the ground impatiently. The flag flapped in the breeze; a gull landed on top of the pole.

There was no work. He went back down the hill to where the boat lay and walked along the shore. A stiff breeze came in from the sea, making ripples on the water.

How long could he live on five shillings? How long would he be able to sleep in the bushes before the winter came? Did that mean he had to turn back home? No. The man would have taken him if he could row. He had to learn to row. He had to find someone who would teach him to row; he would offer to pay him the five shillings. What would he eat? Fish. He would have to catch fish. Where would he sleep? In the bushes.

A crab scuttled away sideways to a rock-pool and kicked up a little cloud of sand and shells beneath the water. A small black fish came out from under a rock and swam away over the crab.

Row. He had to learn to row.

Had Nina gone to the Forest as he had asked her to? He had better not depend on it too much. Perhaps he should go to the village and find a forest wagon and send a message with it. No. He had to go back to the boat and ask one of the rowers to teach him to row.

There was no one at the boat, however. The wind was rising; it came in through the Heads in gusts and whipped up the water until the waves were lapping higher and higher against the rocks round the cove. He sat down and waited. By midday the boat was floating at anchor and the water was high up the rocks.

The boatman who eventually came down the hill was the one the others had been waiting for the day before. He had a sack and planks on his back.

'Good afternoon!' He waited for him at the bottom of the path. 'Do you know anyone who could teach me to row?' The man did not show much interest. His eyes were green and looked in different directions; it was hard to say which one was looking at you. 'I'm looking for someone to teach me to row.'

'Have you got a boat?'

'No. I thought – the one over there perhaps.' He pointed at the boat in the water.

'Forget about that one,' the man with the squint said. 'That's not just any boat, that's the pilot-boat. If you touch it, John Benn will brain us both with one oar.'

'Is John Benn the man on the hill?'

'Yes. I saw you up there with him this morning.' He let the dripping sack slide off his back and put the planks down as well. 'I saw you talking to him?' He sounded suspicious.

'I was asking for work.'

'Then you went to the wrong man at the wrong time; when the south-easter blows up like this, John Benn is a difficult man to deal with.'

'If I had been able to row, he would have taken me on.'

'Oh, really?' he said, rather maliciously. 'I suppose he told you he was looking for someone to take Kaliel September's oar!'

'Who's Kaliel September?'

The sergeant had mentioned the name too.

'I am.'

It was a warning as well as a challenge.

'Why would he be looking for someone to take your place?' One eye turned to the outer corner and the other to the middle. 'Are you going away?'

'Yes!' It was a threat. 'I'm just waiting for the right ship to come in, then I'm off and they won't see me again. And don't think I need a place in John Benn's boat, it's him that needs me. Go and tell him I said so and see what he says.'

So there was discord between the man on the hill and Kaliel September. That was good. It gave him hope. 'When are you expecting the ship you're talking about?'

'Maybe next year, maybe next week, maybe tomorrow. The moment the ship comes in, I shall get on it and you can have my oar. Then John Benn can see how he gets on.'

'I don't want another man's work, I want my own,' he said, to calm the squint-eye. It would do him no good to upset him.

'Go and look for work in the village then; they hoist a white pendant at Thesen's when they need labourers. They'll take you.'

'What kind of work?'

'They've started carting stones for the approach to the new jetty. They'll take you there.'

'I don't want to load stones. I'm looking for work around here at the water and the boat.'

The man laughed, mockingly. 'Judging by your clothes, you've crawled out of the Forest.'

'I have come from the Forest, yes. But I'm finished with the Forest. I'll work for a low wage so long as I get food and shelter, and I'll work hard.'

It seemed as if both his eyes were trying to look straight at him. 'Listen, I can't pay you money, but I can give you food and shelter. You can come and work for me if you want to.'

'What kind of work?' he asked eagerly.

'Catching oysters, fishing, cleaning fish and drying it. More and more ships are coming here shipping wood, and the seamen are keen to buy anything that hasn't been salted. I also supply Mr Horn's hotel in the village with oysters and fish – my mother's the cook there.'

'I thought you were an oarsman.'

'I'm an oarsman too. But I can't live on what John Benn's paying. I make a bit of extra on my own. I had to get rid of some of my customers because I only have two hands. When John Benn shouts, you drop everything and run for your oar. He's been waiting up there for years now for the day when I don't get to my oar fast enough so that he can find someone else instead.'

'I'll work for you on condition that you teach me to row.'

'Stay away from the water, woodcutter. You've got ordinary blood in your veins; you have to have salt blood to work on the water. I should know.' Kaliel September stooped down to get his things together. 'My mother may be Coloured, but my father was a full-blooded Norwegian, a seaman on the teaships going to

Foochow.' He said it with pride. 'He was a seaman on the clipper ships. The sails were never furled at night and there was no room for a man with no guts when they sailed into a storm. That's the kind of blood that flows in my veins. Forest blood does not agree with seawater.'

'Where's your father now?'

'How should I know? Dead I suppose. Are you coming?'

'Yes.' It was better than nothing. He started following Kaliel up the hill. He knew what he was doing, he knew that he was changing course with every step he took, in an unknown direction. But he had no doubts.

The higher they climbed, the harder the wind tugged at their bodies, and the more it flattened the bushes around them. Kaliel kept on bragging about his blood.

'My father was on a ship that came in to mend its sails after a storm one day. My mother was a young girl then; seamen are funny, when their feet touch ground, they want to touch women as well – what's your name?'

'Lukas van Rooyen.' A dikkop bird rose up with a startled cry ahead of them and flew off noisily. 'Have you heard about the ghost ship at Noetzie?'

'I'm carrying some of her planks on my back.' They had to shout to make themselves heard above the wind.

'Have they found out anything about the ship yet?'

'Yes. She's from France, the *Phoenix*, a hundred and forty tons. All they found on her was a piece of paper with a date, with no month or year, and a few rotten corpses. Funny business. They say she had another name earlier. It's no use changing your name when ill-luck is upon you already.' He said it with a strange vehemence, stripping a handful of leaves from a tickberry bush as he walked.

Before dark he realized that he had underestimated Kaliel September: it was not blood that flowed through his veins, it was seawater.

They kept to the first footpath until they got to the crest of the hill, then they took a narrower path down a gorge in the direction of the gap. It led to a small rocky bay that looked as if it had been sliced out of the hills at the entrance to the passage.

'This is Coney Glen and here Kaliel September and the sea are boss!' It was a warning. A tiger marking out its territory.

On both sides of the gorge the cliffs went straight up from the water's edge; here and there a green shrub had rooted high up in a crevice and clung to the rockface where no man would ever get to it.

The gorge between the cliffs was lush and green, the undergrowth beneath the dark green milkwood trees dense and tangled: tickberries, yellow Cape weeds, pig lilies, aloes and creepers he did not know.

The house was at the foot of the further cliff and the undergrowth between the milkwoods had been cut away. Kaliel's house. Two wooden rooms and a third half-finished one. A motley dwelling. No two planks in the walls were the same, no two windows or doors. It was a sandmartin's nest and every beakful of mud had been fetched from a different pool. The roof was of rusty corrugated iron held down with stones from the sea. Above the front door the figure of a child, cut from wood, the paint blistered, stuck out like a giant horn. In the half-finished part a plank with the name *Midge* on it had been nailed in upside down.

'I see you're looking at my house,' Kaliel laughed behind him. 'Wait till this south-easter gets going tonight, and then you'll see how strong it is!'

'Do you live here?'

'I would not swop it for a palace.'

Selling had always said that all the stars, from horizon to horizon, tell stories; it was just a matter of knowing them. Kaliel's house was like that. Every wall, every plank had its own story:

stories of ships that had crossed the oceans of the world to be nailed into his house.

'The front door comes from the *Helen*,' he was saying. 'Years ago she was battered to pieces on the rocks right behind us – there was no pilot here then. They say all went well when she came in and she was moored up at the village for weeks, loading wood. The trouble came when she wanted to sail out again. Her captain took her out on the ebb-tide at night and he had her almost through when the tide suddenly got too strong and the wind too weak and the sea just took her. They say that in less than an hour the ship and her cargo were strewn all over the rocks for anyone to pick up. Joop Stoep gave me some of her planks. The next year it was the *Magnolia*'s turn.' Kaliel put out his hand and touched a broad, dark plank in the side wall. 'Jackson was the pilot here then – or rather the so-called pilot. He and the captain of the *Magnolia* each blamed the other for the disaster – she was wrecked over there at Black Point.'

'And the figure above the front door?' he prompted.

'I carried and dragged it from Plettenberg Bay on my own. I had always wanted to have a figurehead above my front door. I struggled for two days to get it here. It is the only piece of wreckage I've brought that far; the rest are all from ships that have perished around these Heads.'

He walked round the house with Kaliel, listening to his stories, seeing a strange world taking shape before his eyes. The *Harmony*: mad captain had tried to come in at low tide with an offshore wind. The *Luna*. A schooner, *Sovereign*. A ketch, *Musquash*. A brig, *Adolphus*: someone had hoisted the wrong flag. The *Julia Maria*.

'I didn't want to nail her planks to my walls at first, but John Benn said the curse had been broken the moment she had hit the rocks.'

'What curse?'

'She was a killer-ship, the *Julia Maria*. A hoodoo. She shook more than one seaman from her masts and broke their necks down on the deck or threw them into the water to drown. No seaman stayed on her very long. Then they changed her name to the *Munster Lass*, thinking they could cheat the devil that way but they didn't. When a curse is on you, it stays on you.' Again, the same vehemence that he had betrayed earlier that afternoon.

Inside the house there were more stories to be told. The floors were yellowwood sleepers packed closely together, also from a wreck. He had to stoop under three brass ship's bells and four hurricane-lamps to follow Kaliel through to the room at the back, and he stumbled over some cannonballs. In the back room rows of gutted fish were hanging up to dry.

Kaliel made the fire, peeled potatoes and put them in a pot with a huge chunk of freshly caught fish.

By the time it was dark, the wind was raging round the house of ship's skeletons so fiercely that it felt at times as if wind and sea had come to claim back every plank and the two of them with it.

'You're scared, eh?' Kaliel laughed as he dished up cold pumpkin with the fish on the plates. Porcelain plates, from different wrecks. 'Eat up. The house is strong. It's been through worse storms than this. Storms bring me luck – that's when I make my bonuses. On a night like this chickens drown in their coops on the decks; when the storm is over and the ships come into harbour, the cooks will pay two shillings a chicken without haggling. I haven't been able to keep chickens lately, I couldn't manage everything. If you want to work for food and shelter, you can start tomorrow. We'll raise a pig or two as well. They pay a good price for pork, they chew strips of fat against sea-sickness – it keeps the stomach quiet. Where's your stuff?'

'What stuff?'

'Your clothes and things.'

'I don't have much more than what I have with me.'

Kaliel shook his head. 'You bloody woodcutters, you're always miserably poor. You bring out more and more wood but you stay as backward as ever.'

'My people aren't woodcutters, we make beams.'

'Same thing. Forest is forest.'

'I'll work for you, but you must teach me to row as well.'

'Stay away from the water, it's not your place.'

Kaliel rolled out a straw mattress for him and gave him two blankets.

'If we come to an agreement you can finish off the third room and have it for yourself. Have you had enough to eat?'

'Yes, thank you.'

He slept little. Before dawn Kaliel was up brewing coffee and making more plans.

'This wind will take three days to blow itself out. It would be best if I showed you where the oyster-beds are; they're almost a day's walk from here if you don't have a tickey for a short cut across the lagoon with Stefaans Kuiper's boat. I walk. I don't pay a tickey. You walk as well. And remember, Kaliel September's oysters are known and his price is two shillings a hundred because they are carried in sacks; the others carry them on the back of a donkey and they taste of donkey sweat. Don't forget. Tomorrow I'll teach you to cut bait and bait the hooks, and I'll show you the sloops where you catch the fish. You get five pennies for a dried fish and you can never have too much. Can you lay a decent bush-buck trap?'

'Yes.'

'The ships pay well for dried meat. Can you set a blue-buck trap?'

'Are there blue bucks around here then?'

'There are a few left, yes.'

'I don't lay blue-buck traps.'

That annoyed Kaliel. 'You haven't even started working yet and already you are picking and choosing what you want to do?'

'I'm not laying blue-buck traps. I'll do the other work.'

'The captain of the *Lord of the Isles* paid me six shillings for a blue buck last time!'

'Where do all the ships come from?' He changed the subject.

'Some come from afar, others hug the coast going from harbour to harbour, trading. Most of those that come in through the Heads, come to get wood; a little butter and hides and eggs sometimes, but mostly wood. And food and fresh water of course. At the moment there are rumours of smallpox at the Cape and that's good for us as the ships on their way to the east prefer to come here for food and water now. You must fix the hen-coop and build a pigsty.'

'Where's the east?'

'Really, woodcutter, you people are dumb.' Kaliel got up and took an old map from a shelf and opened it out on the floor between them. 'Now you'll tell me you can't read, I suppose.'

'Yes I can.'

'That's a bloody wonder.'

The map was a strange new world on paper; it was yellow with age and tattered round the edges, but it showed him an unknown world. Kaliel had to light a lantern so that he could see the marvel better.

'What happens if a ship wants to come through in a storm like this?'

'Not even a coal-eater would dare to go past John Benn's red flag today,' Kaliel assured him.

'What's a coal-eater?'

'Steamship. No sails.' His contempt was undisguised; he turned aside and spat. 'Dirty things.'

With the wind burning his face and pushing his body, he followed Kaliel around for three days, learning where the best fishing places were and the oyster-beds, where to get tools, where to pick sour figs in December, how to clean and gut a fish.

'And remember, not an oyster of mine goes on a donkey!'

The wind whipped up the water between the Heads to a raging fury; when the tide went out the water raced through to the sea, and when the tide came in it swept through to the lagoon again.

'Woodcutter,' Kaliel said, 'you can say you've seen the gateway to hell now. I've seen it swallow men alive.'

'What do you mean?'

'We were clearing the footpath one day, fine day it was, the day after a full moon. I was going to go to the oyster-beds. Not a sail was in sight. Then John Benn suddenly shouted from the top to alert us. We ran for the pilot boat but there was nothing we could do. Two bloody fools – strangers it turned out later – came rowing down the lagoon on the outgoing tide. They were almost in the tidal stream when we got down there. We shouted at them from the rocks to turn back – they were too far in for us to reach them without getting into difficulties ourselves. Had they backed with their oars in time, they could have saved themselves, but they must have thought we were waving them on or something. When the current took them, the boat started whirling round like a mad thing. When they were swept through to the sea, they screamed like cattle having their throats cut with blunt knives. You hear that screaming for the rest of your life.'

'What happened to them?'

'They were swept right out to sea, woodcutter. No one ever saw them again. Not even a splinter of their boat.'

'That's terrible.'

'That's why I say, stay away from the water when you have ordinary blood in you.'

'Tell me about John Benn.'

'There's nothing John Benn knows that Kaliel September does not know too,' he said bitterly. 'But he sits up on the hill at twelve pounds a month plus four shillings and a sixpence for every foot of draught of every ship he pilots through and his oarsmen sit down at the water's edge at ten shillings a month and have to catch fish around the Heads where he can keep an eye on them all the time. If you don't do that, he looks around for another man to take your oar. He knows I know as much as he does, but who was appointed helmsman? Not Kaliel September. Donald Benn. John's brother.'

'Why weren't you chosen?'

'You have to have a ticket. I would have had ten tickets before Donald had one but I have the curse on me. He doesn't.'

'What curse?'

'Forget it.' Kaliel got up and dished up their food.

It was the third time he had flared up against his misfortune. Outside the wind was still raging and moaning in the rusty roof above their heads. The waves were breaking against the Coney Glen rocks with the sound of thunder.

'Tell me more about the man on the hill.'

'You have him on your brain! I tell you, John Benn is not the only one that understands the water's talk or the wind's whims, he's not the only one that sees the current's tricks far ahead. Kaliel sees it too. If the wind were to blow John Benn down those cliffs tomorrow morning, there is only one man around here that could bring in a ship and that's me. Not even old Sewell at Plettenberg Bay would be able to do it. I know which flags to hoist, I can read the flags, I know where the channels lie, I know where the reefs lie, but I don't sit like a god up on the hill; I sit down below.'

'You said you're waiting for a ship.'

'Yes, I did.' They were lying down, and the lamp had been turned down but he could hear the bitterness in Kaliel's voice again. 'I've been waiting for years.'

'You say many ships come here. Is it a particular ship you're waiting for?' He could not tell Kaliel that he was hoping the ship would come soon.

'You don't understand, woodcutter, you know nothing.'

'You talk under the blanket, Kaliel. Perhaps I'll understand better than you think.'

'Turn over and go to sleep.'

He did not sleep. He waited until Kaliel was snoring before he got up and went outside into the storm. There were things about Kaliel he did not understand, there were things about himself he did not understand – it made him restless. Was Kaliel a short cut to John Benn's pilot-boat or was he the long way round? Was there a choice between a long or a short way for him? Sometimes guilt caught up with him and he saw a beam half-finished on a scaffold or his ma's unshod feet; then he felt like clutching on to the cliffs so that the storm would hold him there and he would not be able to turn back. If he worked hard for Kaliel, he could sometimes ask a share and send it out to the Forest with a wagon fetching wood. Fish or a piece of meat. In the meanwhile he could look after Nina and try to keep her at Miss Weatherbury's...

He was groping for something to soothe his conscience, he realized.

The wind blew the spray from the breaking waves against him and made his eyes burn. Perhaps he could work for Kaliel until he found someone else to teach him to row and cut his own path to John Benn and the pilot-boat. Perhaps Kaliel's ship would come sooner than he hoped.

At sunrise he had to lay two bush-buck traps to the north of the flag-pole. Kaliel went with him but did not talk much, for he was in a sullen mood that morning.

'Kaliel...' he ventured, as he laid the first trap under Kaliel's watchful eyes. 'Say the wind did blow John Benn down the cliffs and you had to pilot a ship through, who would row in your place then?'

'Stop looking for a place in that boat, woodcutter! If there's an oarsman short we go to Joop Stoep who lives beside the lagoon. They've never had to call him to take my oar yet. And even if the wind did blow John Benn down there, they would never let me pilot a ship through. They would not even let me climb over a ship's rail!'

'Why not?'

'It's no business of yours.'

'Of course it's my business. Why wouldn't they allow you over a ship's rail? Have you committed some crime?'

Kaliel turned away and looked out over the sea. 'You're ignorant, woodcutter, you know nothing about the sea or its people or its rules. The sea has its own ways; only those with the sea in their blood understand it.'

'What ways?'

'Seems to me I'll have to tell you. A ship that sails on a Friday is an unlucky ship; the men will mutiny if they can.' There was a sadness in Kaliel. 'A seaman that whistles on deck is no seaman – he calls up a storm because he knows no better. A seaman is tough, woodcutter, tougher even than you forest people; they'll climb the highest masts in the fiercest gale on the darkest night; if there is no wind and the ship is drifting in the middle of the ocean and the food gives out, they'll eat the rats to survive. But at the same time a seaman's a coward too. When the ship's cat gets off, he wants to get off too for he knows that the ship will never reach port again. When he hears a ghost wailing in the hold, he gets off the moment they anchor again and if one with the evil eye gets on board, they throw him off.' Kaliel kept quiet.

'What evil eye?'

'They say you have the evil eye if your eyes are crossed – one looks at the devil and the other at the grave. No captain will take you on. They say you bring bad luck. Now you know, wood-cutter, now others won't have to warn you.'

'Where does John Benn live?'

'Down at the lagoon. The first house you come to.'

Towards the evening he walked over the hills to Miss Weatherbury's house. Kaliel did not believe him when he said that he only wanted to go and see how his sister was.

'You're scared! You're running back to the Forest!'

'I'll be back before dark, you'll see.'

But Kaliel kept on grumbling. 'You're lying. You're afraid of the evil eye; you're afraid, like the others on the boat! But without Kaliel they won't get over the bar and without Kaliel there's no meat in their pots because Kaliel sets the traps and shares out the meat to keep them quiet!'

'I'm going to see my sister, whether you believe me or not.'

'Who's your sister?' Kaliel asked.

'Nina van Rooyen. She works for Miss Weatherbury.'

Kaliel was shocked. 'Is she your sister?'

'Yes.'

'Well, you better tell her she's letting herself in for trouble. She must stay away from the hills. The captains are always on the lookout for white girls. Or perhaps she wants them to get her – they say the captains pay better than the seamen.'

He did not answer Kaliel, he just walked away. He did not want to start a fight over Nina, for there was little he could say in her defence. What Kaliel had said made him uneasy. He was powerless though. He has as much say over her as over the wind that blew without ceasing. But somehow he could not cut his ties with her as he had with the rest of the family, and that was why he had to go and see how she was. He had to tell her where he was, and that he had decided to work for Kaliel until he could find his own way to the pilot-boat.

Miss Weatherbury's house was bolted against the wind too; he had to knock loudly before she heard him.

She was surprised to see him. Almost glad. She thought he might have news of Nina. News? Yes. Nina had left three days ago; she had just taken her things and left.

24

There was only one way Elias van Rooyen could vent his anger –
on the scaffold, where he could chop at the beams with all his
might and fury. Then Barta came and reminded him of Saag
Barkhuizen, who had got a paralytic stroke after the wood buyer
had given him only a tickey's worth of coffee and a tickey's worth
of brown sugar for a full load of yellowwood.

It frightened him. Barta was right, when anger stayed inside,
it could finish a man. It was best to get rid of it.

'Kristoffel, you're not hitting in to fell a bloody tree! You're
making a beam!' He had been forced to take Kristoffel out of
Soois Cronje's team and put him at the beams for the time being.
He did not think it would be for long. Elias van Rooyen had a
plan. Just wait, he said to himself.

If someone had told him Lukas would go like that, he would
have told that person to his face that he was a liar. Not Lukas. He
might have believed it of Kristoffel even, but not of Lukas. Not
even a wretched dog just walked off like that.

The second day after Lukas had left to go and look for Nina,
Barta kept on saying she had a queer feeling. He told her it was
indigestion. Kristoffel had come home the day before with a nice
fat bush-buck ewe and Barta had eaten no less than three
helpings that evening. But on the third day he himself had
started to wonder what was keeping Lukas. Perhaps he could not
find Nina, he said to himself. Perhaps he had tried to take a short
cut through the Forest and had got lost. Or perhaps the elephants had chased him and he was up a tree somewhere.

The following afternoon Nina had come round the corner of

the shed unexpectedly. Just like that. But she would not come nearer.

'Pa,' she called, 'Lukas is not coming back!'

'What?' If only she would come closer so that he could lay his hands on her. 'What did you say?'

'He's not coming back to the Forest, Pa!'

'Where did you hear that?' He was shocked.

'He asked me to come and tell you.'

The little rotter, every time he tried to catch her, she ran off into the Forest. She would not even allow Barta near her. And the only time Kristoffel managed to catch her, she scratched him so hard that he had to let go of her again. They tried to lure her with food, but she snatched it so fast, they just could not grab her.

Where she slept that night, she alone knew. The next morning she was back, wanting Barta to give her Lukas's other pair of trousers and shirt, but he stopped Barta. Lukas could come and fetch them himself, he said.

'He's not coming back, Pa. He's going to find work in the village. He worked hard for pa, pa must give him his things.'

'I'm telling you, he can come and get them himself!'

Barta got it out of the brat that she no longer worked for the schoolmaster, that she was not working at all. The next day Martiens's team came across her at Iron's Neck on the gravel road. She was talking to a Coloured man they had never seen before. Willem drove him away. He said, if he had known what had happened he would have caught her and dragged her home. Willem said Lukas had always had it in him to run away. And Nina had always had the devil in her. It was true. Only God in heaven knew what she would bring upon them next.

But neither Lukas, nor Nina, had reckoned on Elias van Rooyen. They thought he was trapped on the Island, that his hands were tied and that they could mess around with him as they pleased. They thought he would take it lying down, the scoundrels, but they had forgotten that Elias van Rooyen was a man with a head for making plans. All right, it had taken him three months to get over the shock and disappointment of Lukas's leaving, but he had got over it. Lukas would come home, take up his axe and make beams until the world had had enough of beams. And seeing that Nina was not working she could come home and get on to the third scaffold. His plan was not to send Willem or Kristoffel for them, but that he, Elias van Rooyen, would take the ox reins and fetch them himself. For he no longer feared the bloody elephants, he was no longer trapped on Barnard's Island.

The plan had come to him one night as he lay thinking about his terrible lot. It came back to him suddenly that his grandfather had told them about the days when there were still a few of the Outeniqua tribe left, living wild in the Forest. How they had known every elephant path, how they used the paths to move through the Forest to hunt but that no elephant ever hindered an Outeniqua. The very next day he sent Kristoffel to fetch Hans Oukas at Deep Walls. Hans was no longer a wild Outeniqua but Hans would know the lore of his forefathers. They were attached to the old lore; Hans would know.

And Hans did know. 'If Master Elias had used Master Elias's head, Master Elias would have thought it out for himself and it would not have been necessary to call me away from my work. I am gardener to the forester and I wanted to finish my digging before dark.'

If he had not been so much in need of the man he would have brained him there and then. 'Seems to me you're forgetting the days when we were children together at Big Island, and how we started cutting together.'

'You were always lazy.'

'That's a bloody lie! You talk to the woodcutters, and they're bloody liars too! I'm working at the beams with hardly any help. Look at my hands. Do they look like a lazy man's hands?'

'I believe your Lukas just walked off, master Elias?'

If he hadn't needed the man so much ...

'A man can't keep his business to himself in the Forest. You'll see how well Elias van Rooyen will do once all this nonsense is behind him. Before the moon is full, Lukas will be back and I have a good mind to keep Kristoffel at the beams as well. I'm not in debt at the wood-buyer's shops in the village as the others are.' But that was not why he had sent for Hans. 'I'm planning to buy myself a heavy gun; while my sons are making beams, I want to shoot bigfeet but the buggers have been so bold here in Kom's Bush these past few years that I'm quite scared of them. That's why I thought about what my grandfather used to say about you Outeniquas walking the Forest with no fear of the bigfeet.'

'I know what you want to know, but it will cost you six sweet potatoes, Master Elias. Yellow ones.'

'Very well.' It was worth six sweet potatoes.

'It's not that we Outeniquas walk the Forest without fear of the bigfeet; the bigfeet are the old people of the Forest, you walk their paths with respect and stand aside when they want to come past. I believe they've marked you, Master Elias. Why? What have you done to them?'

'That's another bloody lie that's going round in this Forest!'

'I'm just saying what I've heard.'

'Tell me what I've asked you to tell me and forget the rest!'

'Give me a chance, I'm getting there. It's no use you being afraid of the bigfeet seeing you; by the time you're close enough for them to see you, it's too late. It's when you walk through the Forest and you don't know which side of the wind they are on, that's when the trouble starts. They get your smell long before you even know they are there.'

'How do you stop them from smelling you?'

'Ten sweet potatoes.'

'Ten sweet potatoes.' He had no choice.

'First pick yourself a nice bunch of buchu, bruise the leaves, take off all your clothes and rub it well in to your skin. That's the first thing. Then take the dung of a bigfoot and mix it with a little mud – more dung than mud – and rub yourself with that till only your eyes show, then you can put on your clothes again and you can walk right past them with the wind in the wrong direction and they will not smell you.'

It had cost him ten sweet potatoes. And dirty as it sounded, it was deliverance. It would let him leave the Island for the first time in years, he would have legs again, it would take him to the village again. He was free. He would go after Lukas and Nina and bring the blighters back.

That Saturday he sent Barta to pick the buchu and on the Sunday he sent Kristoffel to look for the dung.

'What are you going to do with it, Pa?' Kristoffel did not want to go.

'I need it urgently for a remedy someone gave me for my rheumatism.'

'What if the bigfeet trample me, Pa?'

'I didn't tell you to go and hold the bucket under their bloody arses! Look in Kom's sled-path, I believe there was a herd there all last week; they will have dropped dung somewhere.'

That night Kristoffel came back without the dung and then it started to rain which meant that he had to wait.

2 5

Lukas worked for Kaliel from dawn to dusk. He would have worked through the night as well if it could get him to the pilot-boat. But Kaliel was like a rock in his path.

'Stay away from Signal Hill and from John Benn, woodcutter. He doesn't like strangers around here!'

In the week after the storm they had to row John Benn through four times to pilot ships in.

Kaliel rebuked him the second time: 'Don't stand like a thief up there on the cliffs, Lukas van Rooi, watching the oars dipping in the water. You won't steal the knack of rowing by looking.'

Kaliel did not keep him away, though. Every time he stood up there it was like looking down on a dream. Every time the pilot-boat neared the foaming bar, he felt his body stiffening; when the helmsman's voice carried up through the cliffs together with the creaking of the rowlocks, he would estimate the distance between boat and ship. He clenched his fists when the boat came alongside the ship and the painter snaked through the air to be caught by waiting hands on the ship and John Benn stepped over on to the rope ladder. His body climbed up it together with the pilot's. Every time the ship rolled to starboard and the ladder swung out over the water, his hands also clung to the rope rungs.

He saw the sailors waiting on the swaying yards to unfurl the sails; when the canvas bellied out in the wind and the ship silently gathered speed up the passage, he knew John Benn's was the guiding hand bringing her safely through.

But the pilot-boat was still behind the bar then.

'It's when you're coming back that it's most dangerous,' Kaliel had assured him. 'You can't just row back. You wait and count whether the waves are coming in fours or sixes or fives, or whatever. I've seen them go in sevens. You wait until you know the pattern and know where the gaps are. If it's going in fours, the gap will be between the fourth and the fifth wave; if it's going in sixes, the gap will be between the sixth and the seventh wave. Now you wait for your chance – don't forget you're lying in rough water all the time, woodcutter, you must see that the current doesn't take you on to the rocks and make matchwood of you and at the same time you must look out towards Coney Glen because it's from there that the cross-currents come and pull the boat from under you!'

'It's a wonder you ever get back,' he said to Kaliel.

'You don't seem to believe me.' Kaliel regularly got annoyed with his ignorance. 'Ask any seaman that knows the waters of the world where he gets shit-scared and they'll tell you it's here, between the Heads where the Knysna goes through to the sea. That's what they'll tell you!'

He stood up there remembering Kaliel's words while the pilot-boat rowed round and round below like a beast waiting its chance to leap. He counted the swells, he saw the gaps, his body wanted to turn with the boat to get to the crest of the wave that ran before the gap in time. Together with the helmsman he kept his eyes on the swell coming up from behind because Kaliel had said that if it caught up with the boat, they were in dire trouble.

He saw them coming through, little more than a piece of driftwood beneath the towering cliffs, and it felt as if he was keeping them on the wave by his own will power – over the first bar and then the second, until the waves became smoother under them and they were safely back in Featherbed Bay. Calm water. Only then did his body relax and his hands unclench. He watched until they were back at the ship picking up John Benn and rowing back to the cove.

Sometimes he stayed up there watching the current foaming round the rocky point on the other side of the entrance or the porpoises playing down below in the water.

Every time he turned back to his work for Kaliel, his spirit rebelled in him because he had to stand on the side watching.

He pulled out his first big fish, he dragged and carried the first sack of oysters over the hills and swore to catch the first donkey he came across. He built a pigsty with rocks he carried from the sea. When the ships lay at anchor in the harbour, he packed the sacks with goods for Kaliel to go and sell.

At the same time, he was learning the name of every rock and cove around the Heads: Emu Rock, the rock that waited like a death-trap in the middle of the passage; Fountain Point, the rock mass behind the cove where the pilot-boat was anchored; Mewstone Rock, which rose from the sea like a little mountain at the entrance to the passage; Black Point at the other side of the lagoon and Black Rocks at the other side of the straits; Green Point; Monkey Point. Kaliel showed him where the bone caves were. He learned to know the directions of the wind and its whims. The phases of the moon. He got to know every fishing-boat that rowed out in the mornings to come back in the afternoon with shiny kob, yellowtails and steenbras, whatever had taken the bait that day, lying at the oarsmen's feet. John Benn had little mercy on a fishing-boat that did not immediately weigh anchor out at sea when he felt the weather change and hoisted the big white flag to call them back. Nor on those who tried to get away with a wet sack round the waist instead of a cork belt when the flag for belts was hoisted.

He got to know the other oarsmen of the pilot-boat: Book Platsie, James Nelson and Loef Bank. The helmsman, Donald Benn.

He got to know the ships and learned to understand Kaliel's love for those with sails and his hatred of the coal-eaters.

'Bloody stinking things. Cockroach holes. Chimneys instead of masts and smoke trails instead of sail. Look there, woodcutter, see for yourself!' It was the day after the storm had blown itself out.

Early that morning a storm-tired, three-masted schooner had

come from the south and started sailing up and down before the entrance. Slowly.

There was a red flag on the pole together with three others. 'Why doesn't John Benn let him through?' he had asked Kaliel. 'The storm's past.'

'The tide's not right.'

The next morning the schooner was still there, forlornly waiting to be let through, but the red flag was still on the pole.

'Why doesn't he let her through now? The tide's turning, isn't it?'

'The wind's not right.'

That same afternoon a steamship came. John Benn went and piloted it through with no trouble.

'At least a steamship does not have to wait for the wind, Kaliel,' he said when they had got back.

'You call that a ship?' Kaliel spat three times. 'You don't know what you're saying, woodcutter! Wait until you've seen where they make the fire that turns the propeller; the noise that drives away the fish and the funnels that cough up soot! Wait till you've seen the seaman that comes from that hole. Not even the devil's own stokers can be blacker with smoke and coal than they are. You better tell your sister to stay in the house.'

'My sister does not live here any more, she's gone away.'

'You should be glad.'

On the third day after the storm the schooner was still out there waiting.

'Why doesn't John Benn let her in?'

'As soon as the wind veers; it should be this afternoon. You'll see.'

They brought her through late that afternoon.

And every ship that came to be let into the harbour was different. Each had a character of its own. Old ships. Neat ships. Two-masted. Three-masted. Square-rigged. Longship-rigged. White sails. Dirty sails. Funnels. Careful ships, frightened ships.

Some seemed stubborn and impatient when the red flag would not go down. The coal-eaters were mostly arrogant as if they knew they had the advantage. But he should never have mentioned it to Kaliel.

'*What?* Give me a Yankee clipper with tough seamen for crew and I'll sail the shit out of a coal-eater!'

Every ship that came into the harbour, sailed out again heavily loaded with wood. Every time Kaliel was angry. Sometimes the anger became fury and then he would come back from the pilot-boat, climb the highest rock in front of his house and gaze out after the ship until the sails disappeared over the horizon. Sometimes he picked up stones and threw them after it as if he wanted to exorcise his Cain's mark that way. Sometimes he came and took it out on him, Lukas:

'You think you'll get my place in the pilot-boat, don't you? You think I don't know it. You think you can make John Benn soft by taking bush-buck meat down to his wife at the house, hey? You thought I didn't know. You think because *your* eyes are straight in your head, you're without a mark, but I'm telling you, you're as marked as I am! You're a woodcutter and the Forest will cling to you for the rest of your life! And just let me see you talking to the other oarsmen again – I'll throw you out and you can go and crawl into the bone caves!'

'I'll talk to anyone I want to.'

'Not while you're working for Kaliel September!'

'You don't own my tongue, I'll talk to anyone I want to.' He got up and walked away into the hills. It was better to stay out of Kaliel's way when he was like that.

April went by. On Steenbok Island and along the footpath to the village the stems of the candelabra flowers lost their bright red colour and turned brown and dry. The hot mountain winds of May came and tore them up, tumbling them along and throwing them against the bushes. June came. Time for galjoen fish.

Kaliel sent him out one morning to prepare bait and to go and see if the galjoen were biting yet. When he got back that afternoon, Kaliel was waiting for him.

'Didn't you tell me your sister had left?'

'I did.'

'Then it must have been her ghost I saw on the rocks above the cove. She's looking for trouble, there are a lot of seamen around.'

He wanted to tell Kaliel that he was mistaken. Or lying. That it could not have been Nina he had seen. He did not want it to be her. After she had left Miss Weatherbury's, he would have wrung her neck if he had got hold of her, because she had thrown away the best chance she ever had. But she was too stubborn and wayward to have realized it.

Afterwards he was glad that she had gone. There were too many canvas-trousered, limp-legged seamen rolling out of the ships at night looking for anything wearing a skirt. Neither he nor Miss Weatherbury could guard her all the time. He knew she would have gone back to the Forest, home, and it made his own guilt lighter. Her going back would have compensated for his staying away, and this eased his mind. He would never go back, even if his pa sent Willem and Kristoffel with the oxen to fetch him. He was not in the Long Kloof this time, where they could send a horse-cart to fetch him.

Was Selling still alive?

He turned to Kaliel and asked him when he had seen her at the rocks.

'About an hour ago. We were bringing in *The Lord of the Isles*, I think she thought you might be in the boat. You're worried – I would be too if she were my sister.'

He could think of no way out, he would have to go and find her and either get her back to the Forest or go on his knees before Miss Weatherbury to take her back. Why could his ma and pa not look after her? Why couldn't they see that she should never have been sent to the village!

*

She was not down at the cove or between the Heads. Only Book Platsie and Loef Bank were there, fishing from the rocks.

'Kaliel's giving you a hard time, isn't he?' Loef Bank said, laughing.

'Yes. Have you seen a skinny girl around here?'

'She was at the boat a while ago – Kaliel says it's your sister?' Book said.

'Yes.'

'Did the galjoen bite where you were fishing?'

'Yes. I caught five.'

It was getting late. A bank of fog was coming in from the southwest and it was already pushing in over the hills on the other side of the lagoon. He turned round and walked back the way he had come, thinking to himself: Nina van Rooyen, if I had an ox rein today, I would tether you to a milkwood tree! I cannot come looking for you every day and I can't look after you either.

He searched until the sun was down. He considered walking to the village a few times but didn't bother in the end. One moment he was angry because he had to walk around looking for her and the next moment his pity for her made him walk over the hills again. No matter how cross he got with her, he never stayed cross with her for long. But he did not want to have to look after her; the pilot-boat was what he was concerned about, not Nina! Book Platsie had said something about a boat he sometimes borrowed from a Mr Goldsbury to go fishing on the lagoon; you just had to hand over part of your catch as payment. Goldsbury. Why did the name ring a bell?

He searched for her until the fog was lying over Signal Hill and John Benn, and pushing in over the village. Then he gave up and went down Coney Glen to Kaliel's house, still anxious about her.

It was strangely quiet and everything had a dreamlike beauty in the fog. It was as if the sea and the lagoon knew they could relax their grip on the straits for a while because no man or ship or boat would dare attempt the passage while the fog stayed as thick as it was.

He was quite a way down the gorge when he looked up and stopped short in his tracks. Through the fog, less than a mile from the shore, he had clearly seen the shape of a three-master with every bit of sail crowded on to catch the almost non-existent breeze. A ghost of a ship, for when he looked again, there was nothing. Only the fog. But there was something strange about it.

Perhaps Kaliel would know something about the ship. He quickly followed the path down the gorge but when he got to the bottom he stopped in his tracks for the second time: Nina was there on the tiny stretch of sand between the rocks of Coney Glen. The breeze pressed her dress against her thin body, her hair was neatly cut and curled closely round her head. The dress and jacket she had on were of good quality. New. Where had she got them from?

Suspicion filled him and with it jealousy. He suddenly realized how different her beauty was from that of the pale, refined girls that sometimes came from the village with their gentlemen walking along the lagoon or riding their horses over the hills. Nina's beauty was untamed. Hidden, like the beauty of the Forest. No – she was like the ship somewhere in the fog: you knew she was there but you dared not put out your hand to touch her. She was Nina.

He was shocked and guilt-ridden. For a moment his body had forgotten that she was his sister.

When she looked up and saw him standing there, her pleasure shone in her face and she came to meet him. 'Lukas! I was looking for you!' She ran barefoot over the sand and threw her arms around his neck playfully as she always did. 'I was waiting for you! The cross-eyed man over there at the shack said you'd be back before dark.'

Her body was against him and he felt his own stirring. *Was he out of his mind?* He pushed her away from him but she took his hands and played with his fingers like a child.

'Where the devil have you been?' he scolded, trying to hide his confusion.

'I've been looking for you for days. I'd just about decided that you must have gone. Don't give me one of your angry looks, I didn't make a mess of it – not much.'

'The last I'd heard of you was from Miss Weatherbury. She said you'd just walked off again. Why did you have to do that?'

'But *you* sent me to tell Pa you weren't coming back!' she said. 'You asked me to do it. Then I stayed in the Forest a while. That's all.'

'Where in the Forest?'

'At the old place.' She stopped playing with his fingers. 'It's not the same any more, Lukas. The mouth-organ is rusty and out of tune, the bottles are dirty and beetles are living in them. I buried them – I don't think I'll be going back either.'

It alarmed him. 'But you must go back!'

'I told pa I would come instead of you but he's more difficult than ever. He does not want me at home, he wants you there. Ma just does and says everything pa wants her to now . . . The Forest is lovely after the rains, Lukas. The stinkwood flowers, the louries are greener than ever.' She suddenly became still and there was sadness in her. For the first time he realized that somewhere inside her there was pain that no one had ever known or cared about. The naughtiest child of Barnard's Island – but she was no longer a child and she could no longer go and find comfort in her strange love for the Forest or her mouth-organ and bottles. He wanted to put his arm round her shoulder and comfort her but he could not. Through all the years there had been a bond between her and him that had never existed between her and Willem or Kristoffel. Even on the days he could have murdered her, there had always been something between them that made him yield again. Nina was to him the sister that not even Emma or Kittie had been when he was a child. That was why he could not understand what had come over him, why he was so intensely aware of her. It filled him with guilt and shame. *She was his sister.*

'Nina ...' He could not take his eyes from her. 'Nina, you could not have been in the Forest all that time. Where were you?'

'I worked in the village. At the shop where I stole the mouth-organ,' she said, laughing guiltily. 'But I'm no longer working there, I walked out because the seamen who came in there could not keep their hands to themselves.'

'You must go home. I'll go and talk to pa, explain things to him. I'll talk to ma.'

'It won't change things, you know that as well as I do.'

'Let me go and try at least! Where are you going to stay? Where will you find work?' He remembered about the clothes. 'Where did you get the clothes you have on, Nina?'

'It sounds as if you're asking where I stole them, Lukas,' she said, in dismay.

'I didn't mean it like that.'

'I'm back with Miss Weatherbury.' It was like admitting defeat. 'I'm a *companion* now, a servant that's allowed to eat at the same table and take part in the conversation.'

It was a relief. The fact that she was back with Miss Weatherbury took away more than half his responsibility for her; it would give him time to be alone and get the devil out of his body.

'You're safe with Miss Weatherbury, Nina. Stay with her. If you've ever done the right thing in your life it was to go back to her.'

She stood boring her toes into the sand and did not look up. The fog made tiny drops in her hair and it curled even more. When she looked up, it was to challenge him with a question:

'Where else could I have gone?'

'I don't know. I only know that it's not right that there should be no place for you to go.'

'Ma did at least ask whether you had a place to sleep. The squint-eye says you're working and living with him.'

'Yes. I suppose I could ask the same as you did: Where else could I go?'

'You better pray that pa does not find out.'

'Whether he finds out or not, I'm not going back – come on, I'll walk you to Miss Weatherbury's gate.'

The next morning the fog was lying even thicker over the hills. Kaliel was not sure about the ship he told him he had seen in the fog. A ship in *that* fog? *That* close? Fog's a deceptive thing, woodcutter, especially to an untrained eye. Perhaps it's the *Blue Star*; her captain's usually drunk.

Kaliel sent him out early to check the bush-buck traps and urged him to come back quickly and work on the third room, as it was too cramped in the house as it was. And as soon as the fog started to clear, he was to set out for the oyster-beds; the next day was springtide, he had to start getting the oysters out early.

On coming back from the traps, however, he took the footpath going to Signal Hill. The sound of the sea was far off down below the cliffs in the fog; not a dove cooed, not a gull cried. Where the sun should be, was only a brighter spot in the fog – where John Benn should be, there was only an empty bench and on the pole the red flag was drooping.

Was the pilot sick? Signal Hill looked forlorn without its watcher. Or perhaps the fog had given John Benn a day of rest as well. Only he, Lukas van Rooyen, was too restless to relax. He did not feel like going back to Kaliel's place either; the work and Kaliel could wait for a day.

The fog was a thick grey-white cloud around him. He walked carefully down the slope below the bench; the bushes were wet and somewhere ahead of him the cliffs went straight down to the water. If his foot should slip, there would be no time to grab hold of anything.

It had been a night of confusion; questions came and pestered him like old bones from a grave. In the end Kaliel had got cross and told him to stop tossing and turning or go outside.

Questions. Anguish. Guilt. Why did he feel different about Nina? The question he kept pushing away caught up with him at daybreak: Was he Nina's brother? No! his body shouted, bombarding him with a thousand other questions. If he was not her brother, then who was he? Fiela Komoetie's child?

John Benn loomed up before him in the fog, standing near the cliff edge as if he was trying to peer into the fog.

'Good morning, Mr Benn.'

'Good morning, Van Rooyen.'

'I could swear I saw a ship in the fog yesterday.'

'You did. It's still there.'

He squatted down a little way from the worried pilot, and the fog and the eerie silence came and lay between them.

Just as there had always been a bond between Nina and him, there had been enmity between John Benn and him from the very first day. Enmity was not quite the right word perhaps; more like a barrier between them, like the bar across the entrance to the lagoon. There were days when it seemed as if the bar between the pilot and him was getting calmer, as on the day when John Benn had asked him about where he lived.

'I see you've moved in with Kaliel September.'

'Yes.'

'Do you work for him?'

'Yes. For food and shelter.'

'You're not the first woodcutter I've come across without sense, but you're the first one I've met who's without pride.'

'We're beam-makers, not woodcutters.'

'Is there a difference?'

He did not answer.

The fog made his clothes and his hair wet, and the questions went on tormenting him. If Nina was not his sister, he wanted to know the truth. How? Where did you find the truth if it had been buried for so long that it might be lost altogether?

'Are you deaf, Van Rooyen?' It was John Benn.

'Sorry.'

'Where's Kaliel?'

'He's gone to the village to get meal and rice and to see his mother. It's her birthday.'

'Go to Book and tell him to fetch Joop Stoep. The wind's freshening and the fog's clearing; they'll have to row me through. When Kaliel comes back from the village, tell him that the rules of the pilot-boat say that if an oarsman goes off without permission, he will be dismissed.'

The words jerked him to life. He looked past John Benn, at the ship lying at anchor in the clearing fog. It was at the mouth of the passage and dangerously close to the Black Rocks; not a flag or a pendant to ask for a pilot or to inquire whether there was timber to ship.

'Look where that ship's lying, Mr Benn!'

'I know. Tell Book to hurry!'

He started running towards the footpath with John Benn's words ringing through his head: *If an oarsman goes off without permission, he will be dismissed!* It was hope from an unexpected quarter. Early that morning Kaliel had said that nothing apart from a fish would come through the Heads that day, and he was going to the village. But for once Kaliel had been too clever. And he, Lukas van Rooyen, could not row! The road to the pilot-boat was open and he could not row.

He had always thought his chance would come when Kaliel somehow managed to find a ship – or when Book Platsie or James left. Book had said something about joining a fishing-boat one day and James often complained about his poverty:

'It's only Kaliel September that can make extra around here, only he can be at the oyster-beds and smell when a ship wants to come through.'

'Don't worry,' Book had predicted. 'Kaliel's turn will come. Dolf Blou also thought he could go fishing when he liked, and that John Benn and the boat would wait for him, but they didn't.'

Kaliel had got his chance the day that Dolf Blou had not been within hail of the pilot and a ship with a sick captain had to be brought through. But Kaliel could row. The road to the pilot-boat was now open again, but Lukas van Rooyen could not row!

'When John Benn told me to get in and take the oar that day,' Kaliel had told him one night, 'Book Platsie shouted, "Not him, not the squinter! He'll get us all drowned!" But the ship had to get through, the wind and the tide were right and they had to take me. I was in.'

His conscience pricked him for a while: Kaliel clung to his place in the boat as to his life. If he had to lose that place because of one slip, hell would break loose on Coney Glen and the Heads.

The fog was still thick on the lagoon – perhaps John Benn was mistaken; the tide was right but the wind was not enough to fill a headcloth with, let alone a ship's sails.

He would ask Book Platsie to teach him to row. Immediately. Tomorrow. He would pay him with the five shillings and Joop Stoep could stand in for him until he was ready to take over Kaliel's oar. He would have to find somewhere else to stay until Kaliel had calmed down.

When he came to the cove, there was only one oarsman at the boat: Kaliel.

The moment of hope was gone; his chance to get on the pilot-boat was gone.

'I thought you'd gone to the village?'

'I turned back. You were right, there is a ship out there in the fog. I don't trust it.'

'Why not?' Kaliel was suspicious, just as John Benn had been.

'If I was the pilot, I would have rowed over and asked the captain what his business was at the Black Rocks.'

'I thought you had gone to the village.'

'And I thought you had gone to the oyster-beds and were half-way there already!' Kaliel said angrily. 'The fog's clearing. You'd better get going if you want to get there before dark!'

'Where's Book and the others?'

'How would I know? And why do you keep staring at me as if I'm some kind of ghost?'

'How did you know about the ship?'

'I smelt it.'

John Benn's first 'Ahoy!' sounded from the hill. Book came from the bushes on the left, James from a little further off to the left. Loef came from Fountain Point and at the second 'Ahoy!', Donald stood in the footpath and called back up the hill: the signal that all the oarsmen were there.

He fetched the sacks and set out for the oyster-beds.

He met Nina just before he got to the milkwood tree.

'How many times must I tell you not to roam around on your own like this!'

'But I was on my way to see you,' she protested. 'With a message.'

She was wearing a blue dress with tiny flowers on it, and round her shoulders a thick black shawl.

'What's the message?' She was beautiful.

'Somebody from the Long Kloof was looking for you.' She watched him closely, as if she wanted to know what his reaction would be. 'I came across him on the gravel road at Iron's Neck.'

'Who?'

'He said his name was Latjie, from Master Petrus.'

Latjie, from Master Petrus. Latjie. He remembered the name but not his face.

'What did he want?' he asked. Her eyes remained on his and there was a little scornful smile round her mouth. 'What did he want, Nina?'

'He was looking for Benjamin Komoetie who used to live in the Long Kloof. He said they had sent him to tell Benjamin Komoetie of his brother's death. His brother Dawid.'

Dawid was dead. His brother Dawid had died. It was like an echo that rolled back through time dragging him with it.

26

Three days later, as the sun was going down and the full moon rose from the sea, he started walking. To the Long Kloof. Why, he did not exactly know, he only knew he had to go.

Behind him the ship that had come out of the fog was still lying at the entrance to the passage but he could not wait to see what it planned to do. In the sack over his shoulder was the fish he had caught between the Heads that afternoon; two and a half days he had been trying to catch that fish so that he would not go back with empty hands.

The first day Kaliel had kept on about the oysters he had not fetched, about the pig that was not tethered in the Cape Weed to eat, about all the other work that had come to a standstill.

'We've got a mad ship on our hands that thinks we don't know what it's planning to do! You know I have to keep my eyes on her all the time and here you are trying to catch a bloody fish!'

'What *is* that ship planning to do?'

'The ship is none of your business! You have to see that the work gets done!'

He let Kaliel talk until he dried up. Later that afternoon Book Platsie came and fished from the same rock.

'What's that ship doing there, Book?' he asked him.

'Praying for a gale, she is. We had one last year too. Comes here to commit suicide.'

'What?'

'Yes. John Benn was within hailing distance of her this morning. He told them to come away from the rocks but the captain said their steering gear's out of order, the shipwright's fixing it. He was obviously lying. And Kaliel of course wanted to get up

that ladder right there to beat the man up – you know how he
feels about anything under sail.'

'Why would a ship want to commit suicide?'

'She knows she can no longer win against the coal-eaters, not
even with ten more sails to her masts. The time for sails is past.
She sails from England, heavily insured, captain nicely bribed,
just enough seamen to get her here, and now the captain must do
something stupid that will look like the work of fate.'

'Why come this far to do it?'

'Where would he find a better place?'

It was dreadful to see the ship lying there. Nina came late that
afternoon and joined him on the rock, watching the ship.

'It's like an old elephant that knows his time has come and
goes to the deepest gorge to wait for the end,' she said. 'The
difference is, no one would be able to stand and watch the
elephant.' A fishing boat came through from the sea with dozens
of gulls wheeling and screeching above it. 'Shut up!' Nina
shouted at them.

'They won't hear you.'

'Stupid things, I hate them! Have you ever heard a seabird
sing, Lukas? They don't sing, they just make a noise as coarse and
hard as the things that grow along the shore. And they fight.
Especially the gulls. The forest birds *sing*. I don't understand how
you could prefer this rock perch to the Forest.' She was irritable.

'I'm going to the Long Kloof for a few days.'

She did not say anything, she just stood up and came to sit
close behind his back, away from the breeze that was cutting
through to the sea. He was tired of fighting against what he felt
for her; all he could do was to hide it from her so that she would
not become aware of it and shun him. Or be frightened by him.

'Are you coming back again?'

'Yes.'

'When?'

'I'll stay away for about a week.'

'When will you be going?'

'I want to catch a fish to take with me first.'

'Are they biting?'

'Only the small ones.'

He had hoped she would say he must not go, but she did not.

The ship was still there the next morning, safe and riding the swells. The sea was beautifully calm and there was only a gentle breeze; it was as if wind and sea had conspired not to help her destroy herself on the rocks.

From up on the hill John Benn watched her like a tiger; down on the rocks in Coney Glen Kaliel stood watching, sick for the three-masted barque at the rocks on the opposite side.

'Lukas van Rooi, I'm telling you, she won't let in a bucketful a day! That's good oak.' The night before Kaliel had been talking and making plans. 'All she needs are new sails and a little paint. I have enough rope for oakum for the seams and you could be beating it out in the meantime. I'll have the decks scrubbed and have her washed out with at least three barrels of vinegar; she'll be a crack ship by the time I've finished with her. She'll be queen of the sea and I'll name her *September* and you, woodcutter, you will not put your dirty feet on my ship. I hope you catch a bloody shark to take to the Long Kloof. What the hell have you lost in the Long Kloof?'

'I've got people there.'

Book Platsie came to fish again on the second day.

'I'm going to the Long Kloof for a few days, Book. When I get back, you must borrow Goldsbury's boat and teach me to row. I'll pay you.'

'You're going to the Long Kloof?' Book asked, surprised. 'Old pal, I'll teach you to row to England for a bunch of ostrich feathers. White ones. Wing feathers. Big ones. Joop Stoep promised me a feather for my hat but it's just talk, he's got no feathers.'

'If that's what you want a feather for, why do you want a whole bunch?' If he could, he would bring Book a blooming live ostrich in exchange for teaching him to row. The mere prospect was like a drop of new hope within his otherwise dazed mind.

'I want one for my hat and the rest I want to sell. The seamen who come from afar pay a shilling and more for a single feather. They don't know ostriches where they come from; they call them camelbirds, I'm told. They say the feathers bring you luck. I don't care so much about the luck, I just want to buy myself a donkey. Then I'll become a fish pedlar. They say you should go to the Forest and sell fish to the woodcutters – they're always hungry and stupid into the bargain. You can sell them anything.'

'They don't have money and they're not as stupid as you people think they are.'

'Then I'll barter the fish for honey and sweet potatoes and sell it to the ships.'

'I'll bring you the feathers.'

'And I'll borrow Goldsbury's boat.'

The name hit him again. 'This Goldsbury, has he been here long, Book?'

'Yes. For years. He used to be our magistrate but he's old now. The devil himself is magistrate at the village now: Jackson.'

Magistrate – magistrate – magistrate. Broad yellowwood floorboards, hard yellowwood benches. I'm Fiela Komoetie's child, your worshipful lord.

Jesus.

'Forget Goldsbury's boat, I won't set foot in any boat of his.'

'What's the matter with you now?'

'Forget it, I said!'

'What's wrong?'

'I'll see if I can get you the feathers.'

'Perhaps I can get hold of Mr Stewart's boat. It's just that the old thing leaks so much.'

'Ask for Stewart's boat – we can bail.'

He knew that walking to the Long Kloof meant walking right through the night and part of the next day. With every step he

gave, the fish lurched in the salt-sodden sack. Shortly before dark
he was on the other side of the village where the gravel road
turned off to Deep Walls. Soon the moon came out, lighting up
the path. In his shirt pocket he carried the five shilling coin.

There was little fear in him for the Forest that lay ahead like a
giant black mountain, but he was afraid of the questions that kept
tormenting him, the uncertainty of his situation. Who was he? If
he was not Nina's brother, who was he? Fiela Komoetie's foundling – no, she had had another word for him. Stray-lamb?
Hand-lamb? *Hand-child*. How old was he really? Lukas van
Rooyen was twenty. Benjamin Komoetie too. If Barta van
Rooyen had not given birth to him, who had? Did Fiela
Komoetie know but would not tell?

He moved the sack with the fish over to his other shoulder.
Questions were useless for every question destroyed itself against
the only fact in the mystery: Barta van Rooyen had recognized
him as Lukas without a moment's doubt, and that could only
mean that he had fallen in love with his own sister. Can I be that
rotten? I must eradicate it, get rid of it. But first I must free myself
from the uncertainty.

The moon was on his right when he walked into the Forest.
Kaliel's last word before he left was that he hoped the elephants
would trample him flat. The ship at the entrance to the passage
had torn Kaliel's nerves to shreds.

Shortly before he caught the fish, Nina had come again.

'Does Miss Weatherbury know where you are?'

'No. She's gone to Queen Victoria's birthday celebrations at
the McNicols'. I was not invited and neither was Queen
Victoria.'

'Does Queen Victoria have two birthdays then?' he asked. 'Mr
Benn hoisted the Union Jack for the Queen's birthday in May.'

'The McNicols weren't here then. They're having the party
this afternoon.' She was sitting next to him with her arms folded
round her legs. 'I am supposed to be with Matilda McNicol and

the new constable walking round Steenbok Island because it's not decent for them to go walking alone together. I just walked with them for a while because I'm not silly and I'm nobody's chaperone. I came to see whether you'd gone.'

'Promise me you'll stay away from the hills while I'm away.'

'I promise.'

He had still hoped she would show him that she was sorry he was going away, that she was afraid he might not come back. But she just sat there gazing out to the hills on the other side of the lagoon.

'What are you looking at, Nina?'

'Nothing. I'm listening.'

'What do you hear?'

'The water, the rock-pigeon back there somewhere, the way you breathe, that stupid gull – something creaks on that ship when the swell lifts it.'

'You've always heard things I don't hear.' She was quieter than usual; there was a stillness deep inside her.

'Lukas, if you could choose between being deaf or blind, which would you choose?'

'I'd choose to be deaf.'

'I'd choose to be blind.' She stuck her fingers in her ears and stayed sitting like that for a while. 'Now I can hear nothing, I can only see. The world's just a picture that moves. Dead.' Then she pressed her hands over her eyes. 'Now I don't see, I can only hear. If I were in the Forest now, I would hear many things . . . I wish a storm would come and throw that ship out there on to the rocks so that this waiting would come to an end!'

'Nina!'

She was still sitting with her hands over her eyes. 'I went with Miss Weatherbury to the village yesterday. I saw Willem. They've brought wood. He told me pa had left home the day before yesterday to come and find us. Well, you actually.'

He got up, pulled the line out and put fresh bait on the hook for he was suddenly in a hurry to get away. He decided to go on trying for a fish until dark and if he had not caught anything by then, he would just go.

'Did you tell Willem where I was?'

'No.' She opened her eyes and stretched her legs out in front of her. 'I told him you had left on a ship.'

'That was not necessary. Does he know where you are?'

'No. He says Kristoffel's with pa at the beams now and it's not going too badly at home. But pa's still angry about you.'

'I thought pa would have accepted things by now. I didn't expect him to come himself though.'

'Neither did I.'

When he threw in his line again, the fish bit almost immediately and pulled strongly at the hook. Hold on, he cried in his heart. Hold on!

When the fish was lying on the rocks and he was gutting it, the gulls came screaming around them.

'Go away! Go away!' Nina tried to drive them off, almost in panic. 'Lukas, make them go away!'

'They only want the offal, Nina.' He could not understand her fear of the gulls. She stood with her arms covering her head until he was finished and the birds had flown off with the last scraps.

'Perhaps the people in the Long Kloof won't even remember you,' she said, her eyes still filled with fear.

'If that were so, they would not have let me know about Dawid.'

'Perhaps they won't recognize you. Or you them.'

'I'll know them.'

'Perhaps they don't even live in the same place.'

'Then I'll go looking for them.'

'Where?'

'Till I find them.'

'Why?'

'Why are you asking, Nina?' His heart was beating faster and he got slowly to his feet.

'Just because. I'm afraid you might go there and ...' She

stopped, but she did not look away. 'You always wanted to go back, Lukas.' It was an open reproach. 'If I had not given you away years ago, after I showed you the way to the gravel road, you would have been there long ago.'

'Why did you give me away that day?'

'I don't know. Perhaps that is why I'm in a hurry for you to get away now, before pa gets here.'

'I'll be off before dark.'

'Be careful of the elephants. Especially at Jim Reid's Crossing just before you get to Kom's sled-path. It's one of their paths going into Kom's Bush.'

'I'll listen for them.'

'If they chase you, don't try to climb a tree in the dark; take off your coat, throw it down and run the way the wind's blowing. You'll have time to get away while they're trampling your coat.'

'I know. You're not the only one that knows their ways.'

'I know more about their dangers, Lukas. I've been in the Forest longer than you.'

'You must stay with Miss Weatherbury.'

'Where else?'

His hands were stained with the blood of the fish and his body was full of pain for her. He knew he had to turn away but he could not. The breeze lightly touched her hair, the tip of her collar blew against her face and there was something bewildering in her.

'I'll miss you, Nina.'

'I don't think you'll be coming back, Lukas.' It sounded as if she had already accepted the possibility.

'Why do you say that?' he asked her, uneasy.

'I don't know, it's as if you're gone already.'

'You sound like Kaliel, but you're both wrong. I'll be coming back. Like you want to hear the Forest, I want to hear the sea. I want to feel it on my tongue, in my nose, I want to see it change colour and mood every day. And the first opening in the pilot-boat is mine!'

'Why are you going back to the Long Kloof then?'

'Dawid was my brother long before Willem and Kristoffel were.'

'How could he have been your brother? He was brown.'

'He was my brother.'

'And you always loved them more than you loved us!' she cried out sharply.

The distance between them widened suddenly. 'I did not determine my fate, Nina. It's a mystery that's destroying me.'

'What do you mean?'

'Never mind. It's getting late and I must go.'

The moon was overhead when he sat down to rest for the first time. He had passed the sled-path and turned off into Kom's Bush and Barnard's Island way back. On the other side of Deep Walls he had almost walked right into a herd of oxen grazing along the road; not far from there he came upon the heavily loaded wagon that had been unyoked for the night. A heap of bodies were lying under the wagon, sound asleep; not one of them even stirred as he had walked past.

He had not gone far, when a branch suddenly snapped close by him in the Forest. He stopped dead, felt the direction of the wind and waited. There was something in the thickets but he could not make out if it was a buck or an elephant. He tried to breathe more quietly but found it difficult; the road was uphill most of the time and he was tired. When the second branch snapped, there was no doubt left in him – there was an elephant somewhere in the moonlit thickets east of the road, and he could not make out whether it was coming nearer him or going away. The croaking of the frogs had stopped around him and behind him, deep in the Forest, an owl hooted. When the next branch broke, it was further away from him and his body relaxed.

He waited for a while before walking on slowly. But he did not get far before he stopped again – the moonlight was shining on a huge cluster of ferns along the road. Nina never passed a cluster

of ferns on a windless day without waiting to see a single fern leaf
stir amongst the others.

'It means there's a fairy there, Lukas.'

He could never argue away the fairies in the ferns with her
when she was a child. Aunt Gertie's grandmother had come
upon a little man-fairy in the Forest one day and Aunt Gertie's
grandmother had got a great fright. Neither Aunt Gertie nor
Aunt Gertie's grandmother would have lied about it. So that
was that. Where a fern leaf stirred without reason, a fairy was
riding on it. He caught himself smiling and waiting like a fool
for a leaf to stir. It didn't. The moonlight fell upon the ferns and
he longed for Nina.

When the sun came up, he was on top of the mountain at
Avontuur, looking down on the Kloof stretching far below him.
In the sack the smell of the sea still clung to the fish; around him
the smell of dew-wet mountain herbs hung in the air and he
remembered it from long ago.

27

'Come on, Selling, walk!'

'I've walked enough now, Fiela.'

'No you haven't. You've only been to the dam once and you must do it three times.'

The doctor had told her to see to it that Selling exercised his legs every day. He had not wanted to get up again after Dawid's death, and the doctor said his legs would grow weaker if he didn't. And if she did not sit watching him from the house to make sure that he walked three times to the dam and back, as she had laid down that he should, he just took a few steps and declared he had had enough exercise.

It was only she, Fiela Komoetie, that could not rest, no matter how torn she was with grief.

God had hit them hard. In her sinfulness she often wondered if he had not been aiming elsewhere and hit them by accident when he had taken Dawid. Why Dawid, that had been so good of soul? What about all the goings-on in the Kloof since everybody had started selling ostrich feathers? When the money started rolling in at one end, morals rolled out at the other and the brandy bottle stood in the middle. Drinking and whoring. They had even started betting on which horse would win on Saturdays at Dugas and down in the Kloof.

'Fiela...' Selling was coming up from the dam the second time when he called out. 'There's someone coming up the road there. He's walked a long way, you can see.'

'Yes, Selling. Just see that *you* keep on walking.'

She had seen the figure too, but her eyes did not see as well as they used to any more. It was three months since Dawid's death and Selling still watched the road every day. Petrus had sent Latjie to tell Benjamin and then the poor creature had almost failed to find his way out of the Forest again. He had wandered around for more than a week and then he had met the girl that said she was the sister of Lukas van Rooyen who used to be Benjamin Komoetie. What was a girl doing alone in that Forest, she asked herself.

Lukas van Rooyen. It did not suit him.

Yes, God had hit them hard. Of her three sons she had nothing left. She still had Tollie, but Tollie was on his way to the devil with the rest of the Kloof. Drink. God knew, he had not learned to drink in her house. And he always ended up in fights. Petrus could not control Tollie either. Dr Avis, the church elder, from the village, had come and formed a temperance society amongst the Coloured people for what it was worth and at the first meeting Jan Julies had jumped up and shouted, 'To hell with temperance!' and walked out with ten people following him, Tollie among them.

It seemed to her that a temperance society was urgently needed for the whites as well. She had told Petrus so.

'You must turn back now, Selling!' He stood at the dam, watching intently the figure coming up the road in the Kloof. He still believed that Benjamin would come home after Dawid's death even if it was more than three months later. 'You must turn back now, Selling!' God knew, she used to watch the road herself till her eyes were sore, but not any more.

What was to become of Wolwekraal when she was no more, she did not know. Petrus had said, should things become too much for her, he would give her a good price for the land and the use of the house and the yard for life. Things would have to be very bad before she would sell. Every bit of land had already been bought from the Coloured people to make more room for the ostriches. From here to Haarlem, she was the only remaining Coloured landowner and they had been trying to push her out for a long time.

Selling was on his way back. Down at the boundary gate the man had stopped and stood peering up to the house.

No, she would not sell. With the help of God and the two men she had hired after Dawid's death, she managed to keep things going. Faas, the older of the two, was hard-working and took good care of the ostriches.

No, she would not sell. She would keep praying that Tollie would reform and would eventually come back and take over. But not to squander Wolwekraal on drink. She would fight that till her last breath.

Wolwekraal's ostriches were grazing west of her in the valley down the Kloof. Handsome birds. In a week's time she would start separating off the young birds, in twos. Not, as was now the fashion in the Long Kloof, giving every male bird two hens so as to double the number of chicks reared. Ostriches had to be promiscuous as well now. But not hers. An ostrich took a mate for life. It was their nature. Why try and mess up nature? Was the new prosperity not enough for them? All the boxes of clothes and stuff that were ordered from England and came by ship to Knysna and from there by ox-wagon to the Kloof were apparently no longer enough. Where would it end? Only a few still dug and planted; only here and there a piece of land was still tilled. Feathers were all that mattered. On the Sunday before last, Emma's preacher had come to hold a service down at Avontuur and according to him the signs of Revelation were upon them: the world would not last much longer, the end was in sight. And then he had become cross with her because she had asked him afterwards why he kept on getting Emma pregnant if the end of the world was in sight?

No, she saw the end coming in a different way. Rossinski said the price of feathers had to drop sooner or later and that when that happened many would fall with it.

'Fiela, why is that man standing down there looking up this way like that?'

'I don't know, Selling. Perhaps he's watching to see if we have any dogs. But don't stop walking.'

'I'm tired, Fiela.'

'Only once more, Selling. It's not for me you're doing it, it's for yourself.'

Poor Selling.

No, Kicker would not get a second hen. Pollie would drive it out of the enclosure in any case. She was still the most difficult hen ostrich on Wolwekraal and at nesting time only she and Kittie dared go into that enclosure. And Dawid when he was still alive.

'Lift your feet, Selling!'

First Benjamin, then Dawid. The week before Dawid's death she took the short whip and walked to Avontuur where she cornered Tollie right there in Petrus's stable and gave him the hiding of his life. But it made no difference, it had been too late.

'Kittie!' she called over her shoulder to the kitchen, 'see to the food; I can smell the pumpkin burning!'

The last of the aloe still had to be boiled out. Very few people still bothered to tap aloes – the feathers brought in enough. She had said to Dawid they were to keep on tapping, the price was good and they had to save for the day the price of feathers dropped.

God?

There was something strange about the way Selling was struggling to keep going and a shudder ran through her. Who was it? Why did Selling suddenly wave his arms like that?

God?

She got to her feet and started walking. Started stumbling. Started running. Selling was with the man, the man had thrown something down and had his arms round Selling to keep him up. God, it was a dream, she was going to fall over and wake up. It was not true. Please, God, don't let me be deceived!

But then he was standing there. A few steps away from her.

Benjamin. A tall, beautiful man in dirty, tattered clothes but with so much pride in his blue eyes. He was no longer Benjamin, her hand-child – he was a man. A white man. Her hands wanted to reach out to him but kept hanging at her sides. Never had she thought of him as white – as grown up, yes, but never as white.

'Aren't you going to welcome me, Ma?'

Ma. He had called her *ma.*

Praise the Lord, O my soul! It was a dream. Selling was crying and making the most awful sounds. No – it was her.

Please, God, give me strength and let me take it in. Her body was swaying forwards and backwards and her mouth could form no words.

'Stop crying, Ma. I've come back. There's a fish in the sack; I seem to remember that someone told me to bring back a fish. Don't cry. Look here, I've even brought the five shillings back.' He laughed and kissed her.

They had to give Selling sugar-water to bring him round and then get him to bed. He told Kittie to bring the Bible and read to him about the prodigal son. But Kittie kept on crying and Benjamin had to read it himself.

They did not kill a fatted calf, nor did they eat and be merry; they sat round Selling and talked about what had happened in the seven years that had passed. There were things Benjamin flinched away from, others he did not mind talking about. He spoke about the Forest and the elephants and the woodcutters and the place in the hills where the Knysna flowed through to the sea. But he did not talk about the Van Rooyens.

And little Fiela was afraid of him at first, but before long she was sitting on his lap. When it got dark, he lay down on Dawid's bed, too tired to wash, and fell asleep.

When the moon came out, she walked to the hills and thanked God on her knees until the stones cut into her flesh and she forgave the Laghaans as a thank-offering to God for Benjamin's return. There was no greater sacrifice she could think of.

The Kloof buzzed with talk. Petrus came, Miss Baby came,
Auntie Maria. Emma and her preacher came and he said a
prayer of thanksgiving, starting way back with Adam and going
on and on until Fiela had to say amen for him.

She took out Dawid's clothes and gave them to Benjamin and
threw his rags in the fire. A Komoetie didn't wear things like
that, she told him when he tried to refuse the clothes.

Then the rains came and the wild violets started blooming.
Colour flowed over the slopes: orange, pink and red. The first
bobbejaantjie flowers pushed through the soil and opened.

The ostriches started dancing; the shins and beaks of the males
turned red and they had to be separated off. Kicker was as
magnificent as ever and Pollie's feathers had a beautiful sheen on
them.

Benjamin worked as if he could not find enough to do. They
sowed the corn and when Rossinski came, he marvelled over her
hand-child that had come back.

'God is good, Fiela.'

'Yes, Mr Rossinski, God is good.'

A month after Benjamin had come back, she said to Selling:
'Selling, Benjamin's finished with the Forest, he won't go back.'

'There's a sadness in him, Fiela.'

'I know. It will pass.'

So many things of his childhood days still remained in him.
Where he used to play with his wooden boats on the stream then,
he now spent every Saturday afternoon knocking together a
boat-like thing from corrugated iron sheets until dark. When
that was finished, he made two oars.

'You're not going on to the pool in that thing!' she protested.
'The pool is three times as big and three times as deep now as
when you saw it last.'

But he still had his childhood obstinacy. And to cap it all,
Selling went and sat on the wall, encouraging him in his folly.

'Keep your legs straight, Benjamin, and your feet against the cross-plank! Your seat's not right, it must be raised.'

Then the boat was dragged back to the yard and rebuilt.

'Selling, you must stop encouraging Benjamin! What do you know about rowing?'

'About rowing?' Selling asked with indignation. 'What kind of talk is that, Fiela? I grew up along the Elephant River; you could say I grew up in a boat! When there was enough water in the river, we even had rowing competitions!'

She ran up and down on the pool wall like a hen ostrich, trying to stop them, while Selling sat like an admiral, giving the orders.

'Push the oars as far away from you as you can and keep your arms straight!' Selling called out to him.

'Stay away from the deep water, Benjamin!' she warned.

'Leave him, Fiela! He's not a child! Benjamin, twist your oars round a little, the blades must make less than a right angle to the water! Keep the blades just above the water and dip them in now! Together! Bring your body back smoothly and don't stick your elbows out.'

She could not stop him. However tired he was, Benjamin always had enough strength left in him to go rowing on the pool.

July went by. August. September. The ostrich chicks were thriving. Kittie brought the first evening flowers home and they spread their sweet smell through the house.

'He was a man when he came back, Fiela, but now he's a real man.'

'Yes, Selling,' she agreed. 'It's because he's no longer living on sweet potatoes. He's eating properly again.'

'It sounds as if he ate well while he worked for the half-caste.'

That was the one thing she did not like Selling or Benjamin to mention. It should not have been necessary for a Komoetie to work for a tramp.

As the months went by she discovered that there were subjects Benjamin continued to avoid. Like the Van Rooyens. But he loved to talk about the other people in the Forest. She did not pester him about it; there had always been an understanding between Benjamin and her. He would talk when he was ready. Not before.

The day he did, she suddenly wished she could have put it off. They plastered and whitewashed Dawid's grave that morning. When they were finished, she planted yellow agapanthus at the foot and Benjamin wrote the name at the top end.

'Ma ...'

She knew the time for talking had come and she felt her throat narrowing. Life had become whole again since Benjamin had come back; Selling would sing a psalm again while he was working; Kittie prepared the food without moaning; even the ostriches seemed a bit easier to handle when their feathers had to be cut.

He had made her burden lighter.

'Ma ...'

'Yes, Benjamin?'

'Years ago ma said that no child could have made it from the Forest to here. Does ma still believe that?'

Why was he bringing that up? 'Yes, I still believe it.' They said he had taken to the forest people immediately. 'Why are you asking about things that were over and done with so long ago? What difference can it make now?'

'I don't think this is over and done with, Ma. It has been worrying me more than ever lately; I feel I don't know who I am. I was hoping that I would forget it here in Wolwekraal, but I haven't. There are days when it's better than others but they're few, and then there are days that my common sense tells me I *am* that child and that the devil has taken possession of me.'

She put down the trowel with which she was making the hole for the plants and stood up: a wasp stirred from its nest.

'I told them to keep their hands off you but they would not listen to me! I had tried to fight for you, but they were too many and too strong for me! You were Fiela Komoetie's child and had

they left it at that, you would not be standing there muddle-
headed today!'

'Do you know who I am, Ma?'

He was so calm, like one in pain and hiding it. 'You're a lamb
that was deserted and put into Fiela Komoetie's care by God;
then others came and messed it up with a stupid story!'

'I didn't mean to upset you like this.'

'Don't turn away, Benjamin! We must talk this over properly.
Now. Right here over Dawid's grave so that he can hear, because
I'm going to ask you just one question before God: Who are you
to you yourself? Benjamin Komoetie or Lukas van Rooyen?
Which one are you in your soul? Answer me, Benjamin.'

He looked up to the hills and scanned them. His eyes came
to rest where the spring rose. 'The day I came back, when I
stood down there in the road, I knew I had come home again. At
last.'

At one stroke, his words swept away all the old bitterness she
still felt against the two peace-breakers that had started it all, the
bitterness against the magistrate and against the forest woman
and her husband. She felt elated and content. Benjamin was her
son and nothing would take him away from her again. She was
calm when she spoke:

'Let it rest at that, then. Don't try to find the ewe that walked
away from you; you won't find her. Fiela Komoetie picked you
up, you're her son. Forget about the Van Rooyens, you're
home.'

'That's not all, Ma.'

'I'm not stupid, Benjamin. I know your skin is white and ours
is brown. I know you can't stay in my house in this Kloof for the
rest of your life. I have provided for this, I've looked ahead. The
Laghaans' land is in my name with Mr Cairncross at the village.
I intended to put it in your name but I was stopped by those who
said you would never come back. I listened to them because my
faith was too weak, but tomorrow we're going to the village and

the Laghaans' land will be put in your name as it should have
been the day I bought it.'

'I cannot take the land, Ma. It's Tollie's and Emma's and
Kittie's land.'

'Benjamin,' she warned him, 'don't let us quarrel. You know
you're headstrong, and so am I, it must not cause trouble for us
now.'

'I have no right to ma's land.'

'Since when do you, or anybody else for that matter, decide
about Fiela Komoetie's property? When I took you, I took you as
my own. Dawid is dead and Tollie's drinking himself silly.
Emma and Kittie are girls, and I'm putting money aside for
them in the chest. If Tollie stops his drinking, the original part of
Wolwekraal is his. But the Laghaans' land is yours. In this Kloof
you will be known as Fiela Komoetie's foundling and I will see to
it that you will not be ashamed of it. The land I give you is only a
start; dig in while the feathers are selling well and buy more land
so that you will be strong when they say behind your back that a
coloured woman brought you up.'

'Don't talk like that, Ma.'

'I'm only telling you what you can expect. But I will see that
you're not shamed. We must build you a house so that you can
move next door.'

He bent down and started wiping away the splashes of white-
wash around the grave with his hands.

'It would be so easy if I could say thank you and we could do
just that; or if I could offer to buy the land from ma, but I can't.'

'I told you not to get stubborn!'

'Wait, Ma. You said we were going to discuss this fully today.
There is something ma does not know yet.'

'What?'

'I'm in love with my sister. With Nina.'

She suddenly felt cold. 'With your sister?'

'Yes.'

Then that was the sadness Selling had seen in him and that she had kept denying.

'How did that happen, Benjamin?'

'It just happened, Ma. I wasn't expecting it.'

'And she? What about her?'

'She does not know. I'm nothing but a brother to her.'

She walked past him to get to the hedge to find support for her body. Then that was what was in him when the mist came over the mountain from the sea. That was what was in his eyes when he sat staring into the candle at night. And she had told herself it was his longing for the sea. For if she did not stop them, he and Selling would sit down every night, talking about the ships sailing in and out of the harbour, about John Benn the pilot and his boat and all the things of the sea. At times she thought his sadness was caused by his years in the Forest. But now it turned out to be something she would never have expected.

The day after they had come to take him away, she wrote his name into the Bible: Benjamin Komoetie. With a pencil. Behind the mountain they had written his name into the book of the law: Lukas van Rooyen. With ink. And that was how his name stood under the law and ink did not rub out. She wanted to turn round and say to him: Get her out of your heart no matter how painful it is. Fight against it – it can never work. Stay on this side of the mountain and Wolwekraal will help to heal the pain, just stay here. There are girls in the Kloof that would wear out their shoes running after you.

But she did not say it. When she turned to him, her legs were weak under her because she knew there was only one way for him to go and that was back over the mountain. She would have to send him there this time.

She walked back to Dawid's grave and picked up the trowel. 'If she is your sister,' she said, 'blood would have stopped blood. The fact that you have fallen in love with her, is proof, once again, that I was right and they were wrong. But my being right cannot deliver you from Lukas van Rooyen; only one person can do that and you must go back to her.'

'Who?'

'Barta van Rooyen.'

Then she struck the trowel into the ground and dug and dug until she felt calmer.

28

In places the Forest was so wet that he had to take off his shoes and roll up his trouser legs to get through the mud. Everywhere water seeped through the spongy forest floor and drained away into the streams. Only by the birds could you hear that summer was already in the tree-tops; the wild chestnuts were blooming and he decided he would pick Nina a small branch on his way back.

In the footpath, just before Barnard's Island, he frightened three little blue bucks into the thickets and about twenty paces further on came upon a blue-buck trap. For a moment he played with the temptation to break the trap, but then walked past. Someone would only come and set another one.

In the sack over his shoulder was the wind-dried meat of half a sheep.

'Tell Barta van Rooyen, Fiela Komoetie has sent it.'

In the canvas bag were his clothes.

'Tell the Van Rooyens, the Komoeties know poverty, but we have never been in tatters.'

In his hand he carried Book a bunch of snow-white ostrich plumes. Kicker's.

He had left Wolwekraal late the previous afternoon. Somewhere in the night he had the most peculiar feeling that he was slowly walking out of Benjamin Komoetie and catching up with Lukas van Rooyen. He wanted to turn back and walk to the boundary between the two and just stand there until the conflict within him had subsided and peace was restored. But he did not turn back, he was in a hurry to get to Barnard's Island to ask what he had to ask, to discover the truth at all costs. Then he would take to the road again: to Knysna. To Nina. Coney Glen. Signal Hill.

It had not been easy to leave Wolwekraal. Only Fiela had understood. The only solace they had for Selling was that he would write regularly; there was a post-cart running between Knysna and the Kloof every week now. Still, their leave-taking had not been easy. On his way he had stopped at Avontuur to say goodbye to Tollie. Tollie had made it even harder for him to leave:

'I'm the only Coloured man in the Kloof with a white brother and now you're off again. Seems to me you've become too white for us,' he protested, drunkenly.

'If that were so, I would not have come back.'

'Why are you going away then?'

'Why don't you pull yourself together and help ma? She's not getting any younger. Stop drinking so heavily and go and take over Wolwekraal.'

'Ma does not want me there.'

'That's not true and you know it! It's your drinking ma does not want there.'

'I'm not drinking that much. Ma doesn't want my horse or my girl there either.'

It was useless. He said goodbye and left.

The sun was still high when he came to Barnard's Island. At the woodcutters' houses Aunt Malie and Aunt Sofie stood watching the children catching a squealing pig. Aunt Anna and old Aunt Gertie were hanging out washing.

Only round Elias van Rooyen's house was it quiet. About six beams were finished; a few freshly sawed yellowwood logs were lying at the scaffolds, but no one was at work. The only sign of life in the house was the smoke coming lazily from the dilapidated chimney.

The light was dim in the kitchen. Barta van Rooyen was at the hearth trying to get a fire going and she did not look round when he pushed the door open.

'Is it you, Kristoffel?' Something was different. She sounded old and tired and there was a strange smell in the house.

'It's not Kristoffel, it's me.'

'*Lukas?*' She spun round and stared at him as if at once frightened and relieved. 'I thought it was Kristoffel. Did he find you?'

'What do you mean, did he find me?'

'He went to the village to buy food and see if he couldn't find you. See if you'd come back. Nina said you had left on a ship.'

A smothered call came from the room at the back and he saw her hand go to her mouth.

'Who was that?' he asked.

'You haven't heard? About your pa?'

'No. What about him?'

He called again, more urgently.

'I'm coming, Elias! Lukas is back!' It sounded as if she thought he was their salvation.

Elias van Rooyen was lying in the other room, his mutilated body half-covered with snake leaves and kei bush leaves – that accounted for the reek of herbs hanging in the air.

He wanted to go outside and retch.

'See what's happened to your pa, Lukas. It's the bigfeet that did it. On the other side of Gouna River the cow picked him up with her trunk and threw him. He's been lying like this for months now. It took him two days to drag himself home; we didn't think we would pull him through. Black and blue he was from head to toe.'

The worst was the hatred and reproach in the two hollow eyes that watched him from the bed.

'Good day, Pa.'

'Skunk!' The word came from the mangled body as if it had been waiting there for a long time.

'Elias. Lukas didn't know that you had been hurt.'

'Skunk!'

Only the uninjured side of the body was covered with the rock-rabbit blanket. The leg that was not covered was bandaged to two yellowwood splints.

'We must borrow a wagon and get him to the doctor at the village,' he said.

'Skunk!'

'The forester said that too, but your pa would not let them touch him. Uncle Martiens fetched an old woman from Deep Walls to come and help, who knew what to do. She said he was lucky that only one leg was broken. Maybe the splints can come off now, I don't know. It's been four months – she reckons it will take a long time, but he'll be able to walk again.'

'Does Nina know about this? Has she been here?'

'Yes. Kristoffel found her. With an English woman. He would never have found her had it not been for the constable in the village who knew where she was working. Yes, she came, but she went back again. She was afraid you would come back and wouldn't know what was going on.'

'Skunk!'

'Stop it, Elias, he didn't know. He's only just come back. You'll see, everything will come right now.'

'Where's Willem?' he asked, bluntly, looking for escape.

'They're felling in White Place Bush.'

He walked back to the kitchen and felt an uncontrollable rage coming over him at the desperate situation he had walked into – it was like a trap. There were cold sweet potatoes and ash-bread in the house; sugar but no coffee, wood but no kindling. A dead beetle floated on the drinking-water with its wings spread open.

'When did one of you last take beams to Deep Walls?'

'Last week. Poor Kristoffel is alone on the scaffold now.'

'There's meat in the sack.'

'Meat?' She suddenly looked alive.

'Yes. Mutton.'

He fetched kindling from the shed and made a proper fire. He fetched drinking-water and tried to still his anger.

'When are you expecting Kristoffel back?' he asked. From the back room came a smothered cry.

'He should have been here already. I am worried about him.'

'When did he leave?'

'Four days ago. I see you have new clothes. Shoes too. Did you go far away with the ship? Did they pay you well?'

'I haven't been away with a ship, Ma, I've been to the Long Kloof.' She dropped the meat she was holding.

'To the Long Kloof?'

'Yes.' He waited for her to say something, to ask something, but she just looked away and then started packing hunks of meat into the pot.

That night a new devil came to torment him: What if Kristoffel did not come back? Who would make the beams then? Till Kristoffel got back, the snare was round his neck – he could not just leave them like that.

With the first light of day he sharpened the axes, rolled a log on to the scaffold and hacked at it uneasily, praying Kristoffel would turn up soon.

At midday Aunt Malie turned up with a bowl of lard. 'I see you're back – and back at work, too,' she said, somewhat unkindly.

'Yes, Aunt Malie.'

'I said to Willem, we'll never see Lukas again – shows you how mistaken one can be, eh?'

'Yes. When are you expecting Uncle Martiens and the others back, Aunt Malie?'

'In about a week. Bet's had her fourth baby; I'm sorry you didn't fancy her – they could have been your babies.'

'Ma's in the house, Aunt Malie. You can go inside.'

She seemed not to hear him.

'You pa's soul nearly left this earth, Lukas. He was badly hurt.'

'Yes.'

'You must get him out into the sun. It's too cold and damp in the house. I've told your ma but she's too soft to overcome his stubbornness.'

'I'll see that he gets into the sun.'

At dusk Kristoffel turned up, like an angel of mercy.

'Tomorrow we will carry pa out in the sun and I'll help you out at the beams until there's a decent load ready. Then I'm off. I'm telling you in good time so that you know.'

The next morning they carried a vehemently protesting Elias out into the sun. Within minutes the flies descended upon the sores and Kristoffel wanted them to carry him back into the house there and then.

'No. Get one of the children over there to come and fan him. Tell them I'll pay them a penny a day.'

They came in swarms to do the fanning.

By the third day it was obvious that the devil in Elias van Rooyen was not overcome yet.

'You're not cutting straight! Mainly you, Lukas!'

'I'm only cutting until the load's full, then I'll be off again.'

'Skunk!'

'I can't see why Willem has to be in his father-in-law's team when they already have too many. Why can't he come in with Kristoffel at the beams? They can do better than any woodcutter if they want to; the Long Kloof is prospering, people are building all the time, they need beams and frames and flooring and they'll cart the wood from the Forest themselves. The woodcutters have their hands tied by the wood buyers, but you are free.'

'You left like a bad dog and like a bad dog you want to run off again!'

'Forget it, Pa. Save your strength for getting well again.'

'You must buy me a gun. It's the same cow that waits for me every time. I thought I'd trick her, but I couldn't. I've been ruined for life. The day I'm back on my feet I'm going to shoot her dead!'

'Forget that too, Pa. Send Willem or Kristoffel to fetch Fred Terblans to come and shoot the cow. It's cheaper than a gun and far more sure.'

'Terblans wants money.'

'I'll pay.'

'Your ma says there is thirty pounds in your clothes bag.'

He knew she had gone through his things but he had not said anything. There was a constant uneasiness in her. At first he thought it was on account of Kristoffel, but when Kristoffel came back she was still uneasy. She was like someone trying to get away from his own shadow; after a week he came to the conclusion that she was walking round him in ever-widening circles. She never asked a single question about the Long Kloof.

By the end of the second week a good load of beams was finished and he became even more anxious to get away. But first he had to question Barta van Rooyen; he would not leave without an answer.

The last two days, when they were getting the sled ready and loading the beams, were like the end of a prison sentence.

On the Sunday morning he waited for a chance to take her aside, and got her alone when she came round the back of the house unsuspectingly.

'Don't go, I want to talk to ma.'

'I can't talk now, Lukas, I must go and wash your pa, he says the leg won't take his weight – perhaps you took the splints off too soon, perhaps the sun is not good for him . . .' She was not stupid, he could see she knew she had been trapped and was trying to escape. 'Perhaps the leg is still broken, perhaps your pa's inside was damaged too and we did not realize it. I see the beams are finished and loaded. Kristoffel says you're helping him as far as the gravel road tomorrow . . .'

'Yes,' he stopped her, 'and from there I'm going to the village. Pa's leg is getting better; Ma must just see that he gets into the sun every day. Help Kristoffel to carry him out, even if it is only for a short time each day.'

'Yes. But now I must go and get the fire going and watch the water; he won't let me wash him with cold water.'

'I'll leave ma ten pounds under the lamp.' He had to calm her. 'Spend it carefully. Willem said he'd be back again tomorrow. Ma must talk to him about coming to work on the beams – he'll come if you put a little pressure on him.' He kept leading her away from the thin wooden walls because Kristoffel and his pa were there somewhere behind them. 'If things get worse, send Kristoffel with a message to Nina – she'll know where to find me.'

'Why don't you go today? Willem can come and help Kristoffel get the beams to the road.' She was asking him to go. 'You've done so much since you've come back, the clothes you gave your pa and now the money as well.'

'It makes no difference whether I go today or tomorrow, Ma. But before I go, there is something I must ask you.' She looked startled. Her eyes seemed to be looking for a way past him but he stepped in front of her. 'No, Ma, you're not going to get away.' He must have it out with her now. He knew that if he allowed her to get away, it would take him days to pin her down again and everything in him protested against that. Barta van Rooyen owed him an answer and she would not get away.

'Lukas, I think your pa's calling! Let go of my arm, what's the matter with you now?'

'Pa can wait. I've waited a long time for this moment. You're going to look me in the face today, Ma, and tell me whether I am your child or not.' Her eyes went wild with alarm. 'Answer me, Ma. Am I the child that got lost? *Am I Lukas?*'

She was fear-stricken, her lips started to tremble and she had difficulty in speaking. 'What is this? How can you talk to me like this?'

'You have to tell me the truth, Ma, even if it is the most difficult thing you have ever done! Am I Lukas or am I not?'

'Who else?' she cried out. 'Who else? You're Lukas. I swore it before the magistrate and I'll swear it again. You're Lukas.'

He took his things and walked into the Forest.

At Deep Walls he turned north, to the Long Kloof. He walked like one possessed until the worse of the shock and disappointment had subsided. Then he walked more slowly. At times he walked blindly until he walked off the road.

He was Lukas van Rooyen.

When it grew dark, he found himself a place to sleep. At daybreak he got up and turned back to Knysna. To Nina. Life with her as his sister would be more bearable than life without her. His tired mind was incapable of comprehending anything else.

29

Two days later John Benn appointed him to the crew of the pilot-boat.

Kaliel had gone.

A clipper ship had limped into the harbour after a storm with a hole in the hull and every hand at the pumps, and had just made it safely through the Heads – Book told him about the whole thing with one of Kicker's plumes in his hat. The ship moored at the jetty in the village and while they were repairing her the seamen discovered that the ballast on board consisted mostly of old gravestones. When the captain wanted to sail, more than half the men stayed ashore and no coaxing or bribery or threats could get them on board again. That had been Kaliel's chance. He bandaged up the eye which squinted most, saying there was a grain of sand in it. The last they saw of him was on the foredeck of the clipper when she sailed out.

'And he did not even look to wave at us, Van Rooyen.'

'I can imagine that. What happened to the suicide ship?'

'When we woke up one morning, she had gone. That same afternoon we heard she had run aground at Plettenberg Bay. Quite cleverly done – the water was only waist deep and the crew could walk out and reach the sand safely. I think they must have realized our pilot never sleeps.'

John Benn ordered Book and James to teach him to row properly.

'The day will come, Van Rooyen, when it won't be only your own life that is hanging by your oar. Remember that. You've changed. Have you been in trouble?'

'No.' He knew John Benn knew he was not telling the truth.

He stayed on in Kaliel's house; he set the bush-buck traps and shared out the meat he caught, he fished and shared out the fish. He only went to the oyster-beds when John Benn gave him permission.

One day Book turned up with a donkey. 'If you're too stupid to go hawking, Van Rooyen, give me the stuff and I'll go.'

'And then? Who rows in your place when you're out hawking?'

'I'll hawk when the tide's out or the weather's bad; if things go wrong, Joop Stoep will stand in for me. Just call him in time when you see trouble coming. John Benn's already seen my donkey, I don't think anything ever escapes him.'

He let Book share out the profits: a third to Book himself, a third to him, and a third to the donkey.

But he sent the best pieces of meat and the best of the fish to Miss Weatherbury via Nina. Few days passed without her coming to look for him and sit with him where he was fishing or to go round the traps with him.

Often, when they had to row John Benn through the Heads, she stood on the hill, watching, or waited for them at the cove when they came back. One Friday a cross-current got up while they were still behind the bar and preparing to row back. To keep the boat away from the rocks and disaster, Donald had to shout out orders to them all and take them out into deep water. After that it took them an hour to get back to the cove again.

An ashen Nina was waiting for them.

'You might have been drowned!' she cried.

'Tell that to the sea.'

'What's the good? The sea does not listen to me any more than you do, and it has no more common sense than you have, either!' She walked off and stayed away from him for two whole days.

At times, he no longer understood her. She had been very glad when he came back but still there were days when she was like a cat with its claws unsheathed, looking for a place to scratch him.

On those days she told him she wished he had stayed in the Long Kloof – but on the very next day she would come and follow him around, hanging round his neck until he had to fight with all his power to prevent the barriers he had put up between them from crumbling.

There were days when he reconciled himself to being Lukas van Rooyen. To be part of John Benn's crew was a new way of life, a compensation, an achievement. A friendship grew up between himself and John Benn although they did not speak to one another every day.

He wrote to Wolwekraal regularly, and got Book to post the letters and to collect his mail. The first letter, in Kittie's hand, was a mixture of news from Fiela and Selling and Kittie herself: admonishings, questions, concern. Tidings from home.

Towards the end of October the first days of summer arrived. The first flamingoes waded peacefully on the opposite shore of the lagoon in the little sandy bays, the first swallows appeared and groups of people from the village came walking along the lagoon.

Only in him did summer fail to burgeon. A feeling of desolation came over him and spread around him. It seemed to stretch ahead of him like the years he would have to live though – alone. There were days when he wondered if he should not go back to the Long Kloof, where he could return as Lukas van Rooyen and everyone would accept it.

Nina was the first to detect something wrong and confront him in her outspoken way.

'What's wrong with you, Lukas? Talk to me!'

'When have I stopped talking to you?'

'Since you've come back.'

'That's not true.'

'It is! You don't play with me any more. Why?'

She was watching him closely. They were sitting on the rocks in front of Kaliel's house, cleaning periwinkles.

'Aren't you a bit grown up for playing now, Nina?'

'No! But if you don't want me to bother you, just say so and I'll stay away.'

'Nina . . .' He knew he would regret what he was about to say, but he had to do it. He had to try and get free of her. 'Nina, I don't want you to stay away from me but . . . Please don't get me wrong, but perhaps you should not come so often.'

'Why not?' It was a challenge. She stood up and threw the half-cleaned periwinkle she had in her hand on to the rocks, the shell shattered in all directions. 'Why?'

He had never seen her so angry before. 'I don't want you to misunderstand me, Nina. I'm not driving you away. Maybe I just don't want you to wander about alone, looking for me.'

It only stirred up the vixen in her the more.

'Fine then, Lukas van Rooyen!' she said, bitingly. 'I won't run after you any longer. You can rot in that pilot-boat for all I care because that is all you care about!'

'You're wrong, Nina.'

'When we were small I used to think you were cleverer and better than Willem and Kristoffel, but now I know you're stupid and a coward at that. So go to hell!'

'Nina!'

'Don't talk to me!'

When she whipped round and stalked away it was torture to sit and watch her go, to force himself to let her go; to let her walk out of his body. When she disappeared up the footpath, he felt desolate – exhausted, drained. A feeling of lifelessness.

Two days later John Benn sent for him. But before that, a proud Book came to show him his second donkey.

'What happened to the other one?' he asked Book.

'If I had not paid six feathers for him, I would have pushed him off the cliff. As obstinate as a bloody mule, he was, and I had to carry half the stuff!'

'What do you want two donkeys for?'

'Extend my business. But don't let John Benn know about the

new donkey. The old one's down at Joop Stoep's. I'll sell him to you for five shillings.'

'No thanks.'

Then Loef Bank came and told him John Benn wanted to see him.

John Benn sat peering out over a calm sea. A gull came gliding low over their heads: first the gull, then its shadow.

'I see Book Platsie's bought a new donkey.' It was a statement.

'Yes.'

'Then he must decide whether he wants to be an oarsman or a hawker – and it's time you and I had a talk, Van Rooyen.'

His first thought was that John Benn must be dissatisfied with him.

'What about, Mr Benn?'

'I've been watching you for a long time now, Van Rooyen. I don't get involved with my oarsmen; every one has his place in the boat and it must stay like that. So I am making an exception when I ask you, what is it that is troubling you? You're young, but your eyes are old. You wanted a place in the pilot-boat and I gave you one, but your eyes grow older every day. I see you sitting down there, fishing, but you sit there as if you were weighed down by the cliffs around you. Why? You disappear one day and they say you've gone to the Long Kloof, to your people. What people – if you come from the Forest? At the same time you handle an oar like a man from the sea. Who are you?'

'Lukas van Rooyen.'

'Why do you sound bitter about it? I had hoped you would talk to me of your own accord. I have given you more than one opportunity. A man's pride can stand in his way too long, Van Rooyen. Pride can become bitterness and then life loses its zest.'

'I feel no pride or bitterness. I feel nothing.'

'Then you're dead, Van Rooyen!'

'Maybe I am.'

*

Early the next morning the ship came. It was approaching from the east as if it had set its course from far and stayed on it, with every bit of canvas set against the south-easter, making for the Heads. A two-masted brig, square-rigged and heeling in the wind, with the sea foaming white at its bows.

There was something about the ship, an air of confidence or determination, perhaps, that made him leave the bush-buck trap he was going to set and start walking across the hills to the pilot's bench. By the time the ship reached the entrance the tide should be just about right and if the wind kept steady, John Benn would go and bring her through.

The brig was about a mile out when he stood beside John Benn.

'Where's Book?' the pilot asked.

'I think he's fishing down below somewhere.'

'He'd better be. I want every hand within hailing distance immediately. See where Book is and tell the others.'

'Is there something wrong?' The red flag was flapping limply on the pole.

'Just do as I say. No man is to leave his post unless I tell him to.'

Loef and Donald were at the cove. James was fishing a little further up the Heads from Book.

'The pilot wants us all within hailing distance,' he told them, and went to sit with Book.

An hour later the brig was riding at anchor at the mouth of the passage, sails furled, gently swaying.

'Is this another suicide ship?' he asked Book.

'No. I don't think so, too freshly painted and too neat. She's not one of our regulars either, I've never seen her before – she's asking for a pilot and she's in a hurry,' Book read the flags she had hoisted and added: 'She can forget about it, John Benn won't bring her through in this wind. Perhaps tomorrow morning. Why the devil do we suddenly have to hang about the boat a day ahead of time!'

'I wouldn't know.'

'I'll tell you why. It's because Book Platsie wants to go to the oyster-beds and John Benn knows it. That's why. He doesn't like my donkeys.'

The brig hoisted four new flags: a blue one with a red cross, one with two white and blue squares, a red one with a yellow cross and a blue and red one.

'What are the flags saying now?' he asked Book.

'She says she's running out of fresh water. I think it's a trick to get the pilot out. A captain in a hurry runs out of water very easily. But John Benn won't bring her through on this wind it can't make up its mind whether to blow or not.'

It was a long day. They could hear the brig creaking softly as she rode the waves and at times the voices of the seamen on her deck were carried to them on the breeze.

'I wonder where Kaliel is now,' he remarked.

Book laughed. 'I hope it's on the other side of the sea; the hotel is buying from me now.'

At dusk the brig weighed anchor and sailed to about a mile off shore where she anchored for the night.

He helped Book to clean his catch and then they took the cliff path home.

It was the third day that he had not seen Nina.

At sunrise the brig was back at the entrance. The water was slack and the tide had not yet begun to come in. On Signal Hill the red flag was still flying from the pole.

'Will John Benn bring her through when the tide turns?' he asked Book, as they both sat fishing from the rocks.

'I hope so.'

The wind was from the south-east. A strong swell was running.

'What do her flags say?'

'She wants a pilot. Her water's finished. Perhaps it's true. We brought in a clipper once after she had been at sea for weeks

without a puff of wind in her sails and her drinking-water had
run out, too. The seamen would have murdered for water that
day, Van Rooyen.'

The tide started to turn. After about another hour the wind
was steadier, and they pulled up their lines and waited for
John Benn's call. But the call did not come.

'Perhaps it's this wind he doesn't trust,' Book suggested. 'If I
were him, I'd get them through, though; there's a storm coming.'

'How can you tell?' It was a beautiful day with not a cloud in
sight.

'The swallows are flying too low for my liking and the hills in
the distance are too clear. Don't think summer's really here yet,
Van Rooyen; I haven't heard the redbreasted cuckoo calling its
mate yet. They seldom do before November's full moon. Mark
my words, there's a storm coming. A spell of cold weather as well
– perhaps John Benn's worried about the wind.'

'I expect so.'

It was the fourth day that he had not seen Nina. Somewhere
beneath the feeling of lifelessness in him, his longing for her was
growing – he dared not stop fighting it if he was to win against the
madness of his body. Resignation was his only deliverance. He
had reached the conclusion that the natural brother-and-sister
bond between him and Nina had snapped somewhere in the
years he had been away in the Long Kloof. That was why he had
grown to love her more than he should have. Not because he was
rotten. And only when he had conquered his emotions would he
feel like a normal man and live a normal life. But should he stop
his struggle to overcome it, he would get up and walk over the
hills to Miss Weatherbury's house and then his love for her would
destroy him.

'Van Rooyen!' It was Book, slowly getting up and watching
the brig. 'She's hoisting new flags . . . I don't like this and neither
will John Benn.' The next moment Book swore and cried out:
'There's trouble coming, Van Rooyen! She's going to come
through without a pilot! Let's go!'

At almost the same time the pilot's voice roared from the hill. The brig was suddenly alive with activity and hauling up the anchor. When the first sail swelled at the mainmast and she came into the wind, her figurehead swung straight towards the passage.

'Come on!' Book shouted, starting to run.

'Can she make it?' he asked Book as they ran.

'Yes! But John Benn's going to show the captain who's boss over the water between the Heads! We'll have to take him as far as Featherbed Bay where he'll go on board. I'm glad I'm not that captain!'

But whoever was captain of the brig apparently knew exactly what he was doing. The tide was still in his favour, the swell from the sea was high, and curled and foamed as it broke over the bar, but with the right wind he would be able to bring the brig safely through.

Not one of them dared speak when John Benn climbed into the boat.

When they came rowing round Fountain Point, the brig was half-way through and safely over the outer bar. She carried a mainsail and a topsail on every mast with a jib on the bowsprit. As she neared the inner bar she seemed almost cocky.

'*Oars!*' It was John Benn himself that shouted the order for them to stop pulling. Not Donald. Apparently only John Benn's hawk-like eyes saw the enormous wave rising from the sea behind the brig. Apparently only John Benn knew what would happen if the wind suddenly slackened or veered and the grey-blue wall of water caught up with the brig from behind.

When it happened, it was Loef Bank in the pilot-boat who cried out.

One moment the wind was swelling in the brig's sails, keeping her safely ahead of the wave; the next moment the wind dropped and the sails sagged like rags on the masts while the wave caught up with her and started lifting the stern higher and higher, at the same time thrusting the brig forward at a speed nothing could check – nothing except Emu Rock, waiting in the water, menacing, evil.

The foaming, breaking wave swung the brig round and threw her broadside against the rock. Donald at the helm cried out in despair. Then the fearful sound of timber splintering on the rock. The force with which she hit the rock snapped her foremast off and it toppled over the side in a tangle of rigging while the second breaker hit her mercilessly on the beam.

Wave after wave broke over the brig's side, like a giant hand making sure of its prey. With every blow the sickening sound of timber tearing from the wooden hull went up again and again.

'Row!' John Benn ordered.

Hands strained at the oars, rowing into the tide and the wind to get to the wreck. At every downwards plunge, spray flew up high over the bows.

'*Row!*'

Harder and harder they pulled. Lukas felt the sweat under his shirt and the spray in his face. It was like rowing into a nightmare. Stroke by stroke he meted out his strength and prayed that he would have enough. They rowed in amongst the wreckage while the helmsman steered them closer to the dying brig. Then a seaman's trunk with a body clinging to it came alongside the boat.

'Oars!'

John Benn reached out and pulled him into the boat.

Oars strained against rowlocks. He tasted the salt of the spray in his throat for his breath was coming in gulps. They rowed past the wreck and back again – another seaman was retching and hanging on to a hatch and again John Benn's hands were there to bring him in. People were standing on the rocks at Coney Glen, hauling seamen out of the water.

Row, row, row. Round and round, through the wreckage that kept knocking against the sides of the boat like creatures in torment. Wave after wave broke over the remains of the brig, washing away more wreckage. A table. A chair. A barrel bobbing past. A kettle. All around them the tide was sweeping the wreckage up into the lagoon. Planks. Hatches. John Benn helped a third seaman, bleeding, into the boat and laid him with the other two on the bottom.

'Row!'

They were going round again when Donald cried out from the helm:

'Oars! On your side, Van Rooyen! Give him your oar!'

At first he did not see him. Then there was a head and an arm above the whirling water – the face of a young seaman, his eyes full of fear. And his fifteen-foot oar did not reach the reaching hand!

'Come closer!' he shouted to the face. 'Come closer!' But the head and the arm suddenly disappeared under the water. 'Come up!' he shouted to the water. 'Come back!' Then the head and the arm rose above the water again and grasped at the oar. 'Grab it!' The arm folded round the oar blade, the face rested against the wood and the eyes looked right into his.

'Bring him in slowly, Van Rooyen. Slowly,' John Benn said. Slowly. But there was no strength in the arm.

'Hold on, seaman!' he shouted. 'Hold on!'

But the seaman was no more. The head and the arm and eyes were there still, but life had departed. The eyes were looking still, but they no longer saw. The water lapped over the nostrils and the head and the arm slowly slipped into the water.

'Row, Van Rooyen.' John Benn's voice was far away and tired. 'Row.'

He could not. He wanted to search in the water with the oar to reach the man and bring him back. The man had been hanging on to the oar. Alive. How could he suddenly be dead?

'Row, Van Rooyen.'

He wanted to close his eyes and sit there in the boat, but the helmsman kept every oar pulling till there was nothing more to salvage.

There was no strength left in him for rowing back, but somehow he kept pulling with the others. A half-naked seaman was lying at his feet, his back covered with scars of old floggings. He was alive. He was breathing.

At the cove there were crowds, on foot and on horseback. Men up to their waists in the water helped the pilot-boat come in. Hands helped them from the boat. Hands carried the seamen away. Blankets. Women crying. Coffee. A bottle of Cape Smoke. People. Faces.

Somebody put a coat round his shoulders; a woman he had never seen before gave him a beaker of coffee but his hands were too cramped to hold it.

'There was nothing more you could have done, Van Rooyen.' John Benn's hand was on his shoulder, but somebody pushed him away. It was Nina. And she was crying.

He wanted to talk to her but could not, there was no strength left in him for talking. Book Platsie came past on his hands and knees and somebody helped him up.

There were too many people, too many hands, too many eyes. He had to get to Coney Glen and away from the seaman's face. His arms and legs were limp with exhaustion.

She helped him to the footpath. Half-way up the hill he collapsed.

'Lukas, get up! Please get up!' she pleaded with him. He could not. He struggled from the footpath into the patch of shade behind a tickberry bush.

'I saw a man die, Nina. I saw him die.'

She kneeled down by him and cradled his head against her soft warm breasts, rocking gently. He felt life slowly seeping back into him – intensely: the last of the sun's warmth was in the sand under him, a rock-pigeon called, the smell of the sea was in his clothes. He was breathing. He was alive. The seaman was dead but he was alive and Nina's dress was wet and underneath the dress was a woman's body that did not stop him when his arms went out and pulled her down with him to the sand. He stroked her hair. She stroked his face. Their bodies met, their faces met. They did not talk. Lukas van Rooyen stayed between them. That kept him from bursting through the last barriers.

They clung to each other until the sun started to go down and John Benn came slowly up the footpath.

When she got up, she shook the sand from her dress and looked at him with eyes filled with questions he could not answer. Then she walked away.

As Book had predicted, that night a storm came up from the south-east, raging as if bent on destruction. Twice he had to get up and go out into the wind and spray to put more rocks on the roof. After the second time he kept the lantern burning and lay listening to the storm. He no longer worried about perversion in himself for it was not there. He was not Lukas van Rooyen. He did not know where the knowledge had come from – it was just there. As the seaman had died on the oar, so Lukas van Rooyen had died on the footpath behind the tickberry bush. Deep inside him something stirred like a speck of light in the dark; it was too deep to reach, but it did not belong to Lukas van Rooyen, it belonged to the unknown in him. He had had the same feeling as a child when he had pushed his wooden boat out on to the stream, and again at Noetzie when he had seen the ship lying between the rocks. It was the feeling he had whenever his oars touched the water.

The lamp threw dark shadows against the walls. The darkness outside made the dirty windows black; in front of the cracked one a torn, dusty spider's web hung like a tattered sail. Outside, the tide would be bringing the wreckage back from the lagoon; the wind and the current would strew it on the rocks for the looters to pick up when the sun came out. Somewhere the body of the seaman would wash up too. But only the body, for it was only his body that had slipped in under the water. That was a comfort.

No, he was not Lukas van Rooyen. Did anybody know who he

was? Did anybody know something he did not know? Why had
Barta van Rooyen sworn before the magistrate that he was
Lukas? Did Fiela Komoetie know the truth and would not tell it?
Did Elias van Rooyen know? The truth was hidden inside him
and he could not dig into himself to find where his own beginnings lay. The only beginnings he could find were Fiela Komoetie
watching over him like a big brown angel – Dawid galloping
with him on his back until his teeth clattered – Selling carving
him a horse from a pumpkin skin. Moments breaking through a
bank of fog when he tried to think back as far as he could. Parts of
a dream of which the rest was lost. He could not discover within
himself how he had got to Fiela Komoetie's door.

But Barta van Rooyen had lied when she had sworn to the
magistrate. Blood would have stopped blood in the footpath that
afternoon, and Nina had not stopped him.

At daybreak he would go to John Benn and get his permission
to go to the Forest. For two days at the most. Barta van Rooyen
would have to swear once more. Before God.

The raging wind was tearing at a corner of the roof again; he
would have to go out and put more rocks on it. But before he had
his shoes on, he heard someone at the door. It was not the wind, it
sounded as if somebody was beating against the door with his
hand.

When he opened the door, Kaliel stumbled blindly in. He
looked battered and thin. He fell on the straw mattress in the
corner and slept.

He was up at the flag-pole by dawn. John Benn sat huddled in
his greatcoat against the wind.

'Kaliel's back!' He had to shout to make himself heard above
the storm. 'He's sick. They've thrown him off the ship at the
Cape and he came back on foot – it took him more than a month!'

The pilot showed no surprise. He shook his head and asked: 'Is
he down at the shack?'

'Yes. He can't get up and everything I give him to eat or drink, comes up again.'

'Go and tell my wife, she'll know what to do. You don't look too good yourself. Did you get any sleep?'

'No.'

'Go and tell my wife about Kaliel and see that you get some sleep. It's the shock.'

The wind was growing fiercer. A gull was trying to fly into the wind and was blown backwards.

'I have no time for sleeping, Mr Benn. I need your permission to go to the Forest, urgently. I'll ask Joop Stoep to take my place for a day or two.'

'Are you in trouble, Van Rooyen?' It was more than a question, it was a hand held out to him.

'No – not yet.'

'Sit down.'

'I can't. Kaliel is very sick and I must get to the Forest.'

'Sit down! Kaliel won't die. There is strife in you this morning; I want to know what you're fighting against.'

'Against my other self.'

John Benn looked at him for a long time and then turned and peered into the storm. 'See that you're back when this storm dies down.' That was all he said.

The storm was raging in the Forest too. In Longvlei Bush, not far from Deep Walls, a white pear was lying across the road. A little farther on, an uprooted candlewood was leaning on a kalander and a stinkwood tree.

It was like walking through a stormy sea of swaying, creaking trees and undergrowth; at times it felt as if the wind was matching its strength against every trunk and limb and root, and against him. Trunk rubbed against trunk and the Forest seemed to be fighting against the wind's onslaught.

When he got to Kom's Bush the first raindrops fell. By the time he crossed the Gouna Drift he was soaked to the skin, but he did not care. Barta van Rooyen was a beacon somewhere ahead that he had to reach before dark and that was all that mattered.

The door was bolted from the inside. Kristoffel came and opened up.

'Where have *you* come from?' he asked, surprised. 'Did the wind blow you here?'

'Good evening, Kristoffel.'

They were eating. A bed had been pulled up to the fire and Elias van Rooyen was sitting on it under the rock-rabbit blanket, fully dressed. One side of his face and neck looked like old dry leather and he held the spoon in his left hand.

'Good evening, Pa.'

Elias called out, 'I see the dog that runs away always runs back again!' The mocking words had a touch of gladness in them, though.

Barta van Rooyen was sitting on the other bed. She stopped chewing and stared at him.

'Good evening, Ma.'

She got up slowly; a buck surprised from its lair, knowing there was no time to flee. When she swallowed, the food seemed too large for her throat.

'Good evening, Lukas.'

She knows why I'm here, he thought. She knows.

Elias van Rooyen was obviously getting much better, he seemed to be master of the wooden house and everyone around him again.

'Come and sit down!' he said, genially. 'You're wet through. Barta, put some more wood on the fire and give him something to eat. Is the wind blowing in the village too?'

'Yes, it is.'

Kristoffel took a bundle of clothes from the foot of the bed to make room for him to sit down.

'I was lucky with a bush-buck yesterday,' Kristoffel said. 'Ma will dish you up some.'

Barta came past to the hearth timidly. She looked old and worn.

'How is everything going?' he asked, disguising the turmoil within him.

'If you're asking how Willem and Kristoffel are doing, I can tell you that they are doing very well,' Elias bragged. 'They're working together at the beams now and things are going splendidly.'

'I see you've dug a saw-pit.'

'Yes,' Elias said, 'they're felling heavy wood now; it's better that way. I told them, if you want to go in for floorboards, you have to fell the big ones. We had to buy more oxen and we could do with two more yet. The forester at Deep Walls says he has two he'll sell at a pound a piece. It's too much, I told him, they're old; I'll give him one pound five shillings for the two and not a penny more.'

Barta sat down on the other bed again, but she did not eat the rest of her food. She just sat staring at the floor, deeply troubled ... She knows, he said to himself, she knows.

The most difficult thing was to hide his impatience from them and talk as if he had come on an ordinary visit.

'Then Fred Terblans came and asked ten shillings to shoot the bloody cow. I gave it to him, the last penny I had, and told him explicitly that it was the cow with half an ear missing, and he went off and shot a confounded bull with half a tusk missing! Now he comes and tells me he has searched for more than two weeks and nobody has ever heard of a cow like that in the Forest.'

'Uncle Fred's lying to pa,' Kristoffel joined in. 'Uncle Martiens says he knows the cow, she's been around here for years and Uncle Dawid saw her with a herd in Lourie Bush once. I said to pa, Uncle Fred was too damn lazy to track her down, that's what it was.'

'How is pa's health now?' Outside it was barely dark yet, and it was a long time to bedtime and daybreak when he planned to corner Barta van Rooyen. 'How is the leg getting on?'

'Wretchedly. No one knows what I've been through and even less how it's getting on. I keep telling your ma, but your ma's not what she used to be either. I can hardly lift this right arm of mine, I swear it's broken too. And my leg is far from better yet.'

'Can pa walk on it?'

'If I don't take too big steps.'

'Then it can't still be broken. If it was, pa would not be able to walk on it at all.'

'I may be walking on it,' he countered indignantly, 'but I'm telling you, it's not gone back to its proper place yet and I'll never get on a scaffold again. My lot is to sit around for the rest of my life and I must take it as it is. What else can I do? If you come back now, all three of my sons will be in the team and we could make door frames as well. We could buy a heavy gun and shoot bigfeet and then we'd show them!'

'Elias . . .'

It was a whisper, like a call for help. She sat hunched, her hands lying limp in her lap, and for a moment he thought she was going to fall forward. Fear gripped him: she was ill! There was something wrong with her and he seemed to be the only one that had noticed it – Kristoffel was putting wood on the fire and Elias van Rooyen was talking about door frames and elephants and making wagons.

'Elias . . .' It was a call for help. Urgent. But Elias van Rooyen was felling wagon wood.

'Pa, ma's saying something!'

'What is it, Barta?' When she did not answer immediately, he went back to the wagons. 'I tell you, wagon building will pay in the Forest. I've thought it over well, I'm not lying awake in my wretchedness at night for nothing. I make plans.'

'Pa!' Oh God, there was something wrong with Barta van Rooyen. He wanted to jump up and take her by the shoulder and shout: Not now! Please, not now!

'I have my plans worked out before anyone else even starts to think about a problem.'

'Pa, there's something wrong with ma!'

'What is it, Barta?' he asked, a little impatient. 'Are you feeling ill? Is it the tightness in your chest again? Kristoffel, give your ma a dose of the herb brew there on the shelf – Lukas, can't you get her a bottle of something from the doctor at the village? Your ma's been sickly for quite some time now. Don't forget, your grandmother dropped dead just like that from her heart. Are you feeling ill, Barta?'

Her head was sagging lower. Kristoffel held out the beaker with the brew to her but she would not take it.

'What is it, Barta?'

'I took the wrong child, Elias.' The words were torn from her like pieces of her own flesh. 'I took somebody else's child.'

Neither Elias van Rooyen nor Kristoffel realized what she had said. Only he knew. She had spoken to Elias but she had told *him*. She had stripped Lukas van Rooyen from him when he had not been expecting it and the shock chilled him. Suddenly he was no one.

'What are you talking about, Barta?' Elias van Rooyen asked, sounding frightened. Kristoffel just stood there with the beaker in his hand, asking:

'Has ma got a pain?'

'It was not Lukas,' she said.

'Woman, what are you talking about?'

'I took somebody else's child that day. I only found out when it was too late, after we came home with him. Then I thought it was my imagination and I pushed it away but it would never stay away for long and now it never goes away. The last time he was home, he asked me about it, I told him I had sworn it before the magistrate, but I swore falsely. He is not Lukas.'

'My God, woman, you're delirious!'

'No, Elias, I'm not. I'll go to the magistrate and tell him because I can no longer bear it; the burden is too great. Our Lukas's bones were picked up along the Gouna River; he got lost and the angels took him.'

'Woman, you're delirious!' Elias persisted in his confusion. 'You picked him out right away from amongst four others!'

'No, I didn't. Just before I had to go into the room the man that brought his box, the tall one with the spectacles, came and stood just behind me and said, "The one wearing the blue shirt." I was so scared and confused, I could not think properly, but when they opened the door and pushed me into the room, there were five children standing there instead of one, and the one in the middle had a blue shirt on...'

He did not wait to hear the rest. He just got up and walked past a bewildered Elias and Kristoffel out into the storm. They did not try to stop him. They just sat staring at Barta, dumbfounded.

He found the footpath and kept on walking. The only reality was the wind and the rain and the noise of the Forest. The rest was anger and turmoil and fragments of memory coming back to him. One man, one bloody man on a horse-cart, had had the power to turn Benjamin Komoetie into the ghost of Lukas van Rooyen and he had had to walk the Forest for years. He had had no choice.

One single sentence: *The one wearing the blue shirt.*

He remembered the shirt so well. Dawid had had to go and buy it in the village. Willem had worn it to a rag. And one man had had the power. Not God. Not Fiela Komoetie. Not Goldsbury. The tall man. What right did he have? Hatred surged through him as he remembered every day he had had to stand on a scaffold, every beam he had had to make, every day that he had waited for his mother to come, the nights on the bed in the kitchen, the day he had tried to run away. How many years?

Nina was not his sister. The thought could not still the storm seething inside him; it brought him no gladness or relief.

One man's will. One man's power.

He would kill him with his bare hands.

As he stumbled through the storm-ridden Forest he was only faintly aware of his clothes and his skin being torn. While he was on the footpath, he had to aim for the sled-path; while he kept to the sled-path, he had to aim for the gravel road; the gravel would take him south to the village. He would remember the house where he had slept that night. He would remember the man.

Barta van Rooyen had known, she had known it all those years, but somewhere in the torment he found forgiveness for her; he would never forget her face when she told them.

At times it was difficult to know whether he was still on the footpath, but his direction was right. South. There was a taste of blood in his mouth, he must have bitten himself the last time he had stumbled and fallen over the branch in his way.

And from the chaos inside him came the insistent question: Who was he?

Don't try to find the ewe that deserted you, for you won't find her.

No, he was not looking for the ewe that had walked away from him, he was looking for the man that had acted god, the man that made him Lukas van Rooyen.

The one wearing the blue shirt.

One single sentence. One single sentence that had made Fiela Komoetie walk over the mountain so many times, that had made Selling sit and watch the road for so long.

By the time he reached Deep Walls, the storm had just about blown itself out. His chest was burning, his feet were aching inside his mud-filled shoes but once he was on the gravel road he felt better. The Forest was no longer so close to his body, the road was wider and he could walk faster.

Who was he? What was his name? He was gripped by a strange fear. Every ship that came in through the Heads had a name. Every tree in the Forest, every bird, every man he knew, every half-white seaman's child in the village. How long would he have to go on with the dead Lukas van Rooyen's name hanging round his neck?

He would walk until he found the man. The tall one. He would go and confront him with the guilt that would stay with him until the day he died.

At daybreak the storm was past. But not the storm inside him.

When the sun came out, he walked into the village and found the magistrate's office with little trouble. From there it was like returning by old tracks, that had been made years ago. The house was not in the first side street towards the lagoon, it was in the next one. The fourth house from the corner.

His body was tense. His mind was tense. A woman opened the door and when he spoke, even his voice was tense.

'I'm looking for a tall man with spectacles, one of the men that helped to count the people in the Long Kloof years ago.'

'What did you say?'

He repeated it, impatiently.

'I'll call him.' She closed the door and bolted it.

He did not think ahead of what he intended to say or do, he just stood there waiting. He had at last come to the end of the roundabout route that had been taking him in the wrong direction for years, just because someone had deliberately shown him the wrong way at the start.

In the distance the sun lay over the cliffs round the Heads. The water of the lagoon looked grey and cold, the wind had started to blow again, half-heartedly, driving the clouds in over the village.

Footsteps shuffled to the door, a hand fumbled to unfasten the bolt.

It was he. The man. Older, thinner, stooping. A cataract had formed in one watery blue eye and his moustache hung limp over his mouth.

'Yes?' the man warily, standing behind the lower half of the door.

For all his loathing, he could not find a single word to revenge himself on the man.

'What do you want?'

Nothing. He just stood there looking at the man, watching him becoming suspicious.

'Who are you?'

Perhaps he was beginning to recognize him; perhaps that was what was making him so nervous.

'Who *are* you?'

'Nobody.'

He turned round and walked away.

Not to Coney Glen. He took the short cut over the hills to the sea. He crawled in under the cliff into the bone caves and lay down like a sick dog.

He no longer tried to think coherently. He just lay there, listening to the sea as if looking for comfort in it. A hundred feet below the waves were beating against the rocks, sending the foam flying up into the air.

Far out to sea a large clipper, masts crowded with sail, leaned into the wind and ploughed through the waves to the north.

Slowly his body began to relax. The sun warmed the cave and dried his clothes. Merciful sleep came over him.

30

When it was time to write to Benjamin, they all sat down round the well-scrubbed kitchen table as they did for evening prayers.

'Have you sharpened the pencil, Kittie?'

'Yes, Ma.'

'Don't scrumple up the corner of the page with your arm like that, the letter must be neat. I don't want him to be ashamed of it.'

She saw Selling fold his hands on the table before him and wait for Kittie to start writing. Usually she allowed him to dictate to Kittie first, but today he would have to wait, for she was too worried to hold back any longer. Twice the post-cart had come without a letter from Benjamin.

'I'm ready, Pa,' Kittie said.

'Your father will not begin today, I will.'

'But Fiela!'

'Quiet! Kittie, tell him ma says there is a cloud over ma's heart with worry for him. We have had no news of him. If all is well with him, that's fine, but if things are going wrong for him, he must let us know what we can do to help, apart from praying. Tell him ma says...'

'Not so fast, Ma.'

God knew why she was so worried about him. She had been thinking about him all night. After he had left, he had written at the bottom of one of his letters that the woman had said he *was* the child. Nothing more. If something is weighing on your heart, it weighs down your tongue as well. She knew.

'Tell him, ma says to be down is one thing, and to get up again

342

is something different. It is easier to stay down, but once you're up, you find strength to stay up. Tell him ma says...'

'Not so fast, Ma, I'm only at the second *up* now.'

'Write neatly, Kittie, don't make your letters as big as a child's.'

She no longer took up a pencil herself, but that did not mean she no longer knew how it should be done. In her days they still used to write with a goose quill and ink her father had made from gunpowder and vinegar. They wrote neatly.

Selling started to fidget.

'Tell Benjamin ma says he must come home if things get too much for him. Tell him we've started on the house on the Laghaans' land.'

'Must I tell him about Tollie, Ma?'

'No.'

'We'll have to write and tell him sooner or later, Ma.'

'Not today.'

He had enough to worry him, without worrying about Tollie. It was bad enough that Wolwekraal had to bear the disgrace. Tollie was in jail and letting Benjamin know about it would not get him out. Petrus reckoned it might even be Tollie's salvation, because he would get at least five years and there was no brandy in jail. Drinking and knife stabbing. If it weren't that he could have got the rope, she would have wished that he had killed the dim-witted girl. She drank as much as he did and he wanted to bring her to Wolwekraal. They must have thought Fiela Komoetie would be too weak to stop them.

'What must I write now, Ma?'

'It's your father's turn now.'

Selling was full of the flock of ostriches which was on its way to Knysna; she knew he would not rest before he had told Benjamin about it. They had come and bought six year-old birds, Kicker's and Pollie's chicks. Whether the poor creatures would get to the other side of the ocean, she did not know. According to Petrus, they were to be shipped to Australia. The people there wanted to breed them for the feathers as well. But what would happen if the ostriches decided they had had enough and wanted to get off in the middle of the ocean? Especially Kicker's lot. Rossinski said the Government was very much against the whole business; another flock had been shipped from Mossel Bay a couple of months before but only three had made it across the sea. The Government wanted the feathers to be sold overseas, but not the ostriches.

'You've dictated almost a full page, Selling! You know old Miss Hettie at the post office moans when the letter is too thick.'

'She's not carrying it over the mountain herself, is she? I have to tell him to tell the captain to take sacks to pull over their heads if the water gets rough.'

'How many seamen will be kicked dead by the time the sacks are over their heads?'

'But I also want him to tell the captain to fasten catch-poles on the deck.'

'Say it then and get it done with, Selling. There's something else I want to add.'

God knew, she was desperately worried. Had something happened to him? Was he sick? If they did not hear from him she would have to take to the road again to go and see what had happened. Even if it took her a week to get there.

'Pa's finished, Ma.'

'First write your piece, Kittie. I only have a word or two to add.'

Kittie always told him the Kloof news and about little Fiela. Clever child, little Fiela. Wolwekraal would see to it that she got as much schooling as she could and learn about the Bible. Miss Baby herself had said that the child was clever.

'Ma may end off now, I'm finished.'

'Tell him ma sends greetings to Nina.'

31

To think that Barta could have brought it upon his family. The shock was too much for him. At dawn he limped outside on his broken leg to get to the shed where he could be alone. When Willem and Kristoffel came to start on the floorboards, he could not look them in the face. They were upset, too. Kristoffel must have told Willem.

To think that Barta had brought it upon his family. The wrong child. It was her luck that the child had been taken away from Coloured people otherwise it could have been nasty. At least the magistrate would be able to say that the child had been in the care of white people since then.

It would have been better if Barta had kept her mouth shut about it. After all those years she could have kept quiet about it and nobody would have known. But now she suddenly wanted to go to the magistrate and unburden her soul. He told her straight away that he would not be going with her; Willem or Kristoffel could go with her. In his condition he would not make it to the village in any case, and anyway the cow was still around somewhere and she was moving through the Forest like a thief in the night.

So it was the wrong child. Barta could have landed them in big trouble. It could have been an idiot child like the one Faas Struwel had at Veltmas Road, that went around slobbering and making funny noises. Or a deformed one. It was Barta's luck that he had been normal.

Yes, there had been days right at the beginning when he had looked at the child himself and wondered if it could really be Lukas, but that was only because he could not always understand how a child of three could have walked to the Long Kloof. He did not dwell on it too much – you should never fill your head with too many puzzles, your veins would swell up from it.

Now, Barta could have got them into a terrible mess. She should have kept quiet. For you could not help wondering whose child he was. Where had the Coloureds got him from? The child had always looked a bit tall for his age; in the end he had grown taller than either Willem or Kristoffel and Willem was tall, too.

For all he knew, it could have been a rich man's child. An illegitimate child that they had to get rid of. If you knew the details, you could turn it to your advantage. It costs money to bring up a child.

When Lukas had turned up so unexpectedly the night before, he had thought that he had come to take up his place on the scaffold again. When Barta had revealed the truth, he had just got up and walked out. Had not even said goodbye.

'Pa?'

'Yes, Willem?'

'It's not right.'

'No, it isn't.'

'He was always different from us.'

'Yes, that's true.'

'Kristoffel says he just got up and walked out.'

'Yes.'

'It's a shame. He wasn't bad.'

'No, he wasn't bad. Your ma should have kept quiet.'

Kristoffel came up and wiped the sweat from his face. 'Funny,' he said, 'Aunt Malie must have known. She and Nina had a tiff one day when Nina threw a stone and injured her hen. I heard her say to Nina if Lukas was Lukas she'd eat her headcloth.'

32

The sun was in the west when he woke up. The bank of clouds on the horizon was a brilliant red and the wind had veered to the south-west. There was not a sail or a trail of smoke on the foam-capped sea.

He tried not to think. He would think it all out when his courage had returned.

He put out his hand and picked up a small, sun-bleached bone from the cave floor. It might have been from a child's little finger.

None of the four bone caves in which he had been scratching around over the months was large or deep, but far back in time smallish people must have lived in them for a very long time. Bushmen perhaps. In every cave there was layer upon layer of bones of man and beast; also stone implements and tiny beads made of shell. He had once collected a handful of the tiny beads for Nina. She made a bracelet from them and wore them round her arm and said it felt creepy – they were dead men's beads.

One man. One man – no, he would think later when he felt better.

He looked out over the sea and thought to himself, the cave-men must have looked out and seen the world down below them. They too must have watched the unceasing waves come rolling in and seen the gulls and cormorants fly to their nests for the night. Whatever they wanted to depict, they painted on animals' shoulderblades or on stones, for the walls and the roofs of the caves were too rough to paint on. He had once found a stone with seabirds and an elephant painted faintly on it in reddish-brown. Kaliel found a piece of bone with a strange-looking sailing ship and a whale on it. The whale was not strange, the whales came to calve in the bay every year during July and August and September. It was the ship with the unusual sails they did not know. Kaliel had sent him to John Benn with it.

'Where did you get this?' the pilot had asked.

'In the bone caves.'

John Benn looked at the painting for a long time, closely, and then looked out to sea. 'It's an old Chinese junk. They could only have drawn it if they had seen it – if they had seen it, it can only mean that people sailed these waters much earlier than we thought. Go and put it back in the cave.'

Who had done the drawing? Who had made the little beads and the implements? All that was left of them was bones bleached white by the sun for others to sift through to try and find out who they were.

Who was Benjamin Komoetie? He tried to stop his thoughts but could not. Lukas van Rooyen was as dead as the bones he was sitting on but who was to take his place?

One man had done it. One man with power. No. There were many men involved. One man's seed in a moment of forgotten lust, and a child stood at Fiela Komoetie's door. One man's word, and the child was Lukas van Rooyen. One man's command, and a ship lay wrecked on Emu Rock and a seaman clung to an oar, too tired to live. There was power in man that was different from the power of the sea or the power in the elephant that kept Elias van Rooyen trapped on the island. In man it was hidden where no one could see it and no one would know when it would emerge and where it would strike. For only man apparently had the power to choose between destruction or preservation.

The one wearing the blue shirt.

Who was Benjamin Komoetie?

The cave was suddenly oppressive – he must get outside! He crawled out and stood on the ledge in front of the cave but there was no escape from the question that was troubling him. He climbed to the top of the hill and started walking.

Who was he? What was the good of asking? There was no answer . . . Still, he was someone. He was somewhere. Not in his legs, not in his arms, not in his body – wait! He walked slower. He *was* in his body. It was like a revelation. He was in his body – and bigger than his body too: he stretched as far as the horizon, to the blue of the sky. He was trapped within a body but at the same time he was free. Lukas van Rooyen and the seaman were dead, but he was alive and he could be whoever he wanted to be. From deep inside him surged a feeling of power that frightened him.

He saw the flag-pole in the distance and set out for it. Somehow, there was suddenly less confusion in him, less fear. Relief.

Nina was not his sister.

Gladness stirred in him. She was a woman . . . he suddenly wondered what strange power there was in her that touched him so deeply. It was the same power that had been in Fiela Komoetie when she ruled over Wolwekraal, when she ordered an ailing ostrich chick to lift its head, when she protected Selling. He had seen it in Barta van Rooyen only once: when she admitted to having taken the wrong child.

The power of a woman was different, he decided: sly, fearless, changeable as the moods of the sea, but he knew instinctively that that was the power against which his own would be measured.

John Benn was sitting on the stone box under the flag-pole, mending the white flag with a sailmaker's needle and thread.

'I just came to say that I'm back.'

The needle stuck in the cloth; John Benn looked up. 'You look a mess, but you sound better, Van Rooyen.'

'I am. And from now on I will be known as Benjamin Komoetie. It's not a new name, it's my old name. I will help out until Kaliel is well enough to take over again, and then I'll be going back to the Long Kloof. To my people.'

'You *are* better. You're still a riddle, but you have become the man I expected to find in you – Komoetie, you said?'

'Yes.'

'It's a good name, an old Hottentot name.'

'That's right.'

'Go and tell Joop Stoep you're back.'

'Joop Stoep will have to stand in for me today as well, Mr Benn.' He was suddenly in a hurry. 'With your permission I would like to go to Miss Weatherbury's house now.'

The pilot pulled the needle through the thick white cloth. Somewhere in his beard a smile seemed to be lingering. 'Of course,' he said.

A Note on the Type

This book was set via computer-driven cathode-ray tube, in a typeface called Baskerville. The face is a facsimile reproduction of types cast from molds made for John Baskerville (1706–1775) from his designs. The punches for the revived Linotype Baskerville were cut under the supervision of the English printer George W. Jones.

John Baskerville's original face was one of the forerunners of the type style known as "modern face" to printers—a "modern" of the period A.D. 1800.

Composed in Great Britain.